The Girl Behind the Gates

BRENDA DAVIES

The Girl Behind the Gates

HODDER

First published in Great Britain in 2020 by Hodder & Stoughton
An Hachette UK company

2

Copyright © Brenda Davies 2020

The right of Brenda Davies to be identified as the Author
of the Work has been asserted by her in accordance with
the Copyright, Designs and Patents Act 1988.

A CIP catalogue record for this title is available from the British Library

Paperback ISBN 978 1 529 37454 4

Typeset in Plantin Light by Hewer Text UK Ltd, Edinburgh
Printed and bound in Great Britain by Clays Ltd, Elcograf S.p.A.

Hodder & Stoughton policy is to use papers that are natural, renewable
and recyclable products and made from wood grown in sustainable
forests. The logging and manufacturing processes are expected to
conform to the environmental regulations of the country of origin.

Hodder & Stoughton Ltd
Carmelite House
50 Victoria Embankment
London EC4Y 0DZ

www.hodder.co.uk

To Nora and all the thousands of women who suffered similarly, some of whose stories will never be heard.

★★★

And to all the unseen angels working, often under difficult circumstances, in psychiatric hospitals and other mental healthcare facilities around the world, as well as for all those in their care. Never give up!

Author's Note

As a medical practitioner, I've always tried to be aware of and grateful for what I learn and benefit from on my journey alongside those people who trust me with their care. Nora is but one of the many who have taught me and helped me heal myself as I became a fellow traveller in their lives for a while. Their courage and effort in working on themselves, overcoming issues of the past and finding new paths forward have been a constant inspiration to me.

Over the years I tried to encourage Nora to tell her story, but she always backed away from doing so. However, several times she asked me if I would write it for her. I always refused. Then following her death in 1995, one of her friends sent me a note and included a letter from Nora reminding me of her request. So, at long last, this is a true yet fictionalised account of Nora's story – where all names and places have been changed to protect everyone. I've also added some characters who are simply a work of fiction.

Brenda Davies
January 2020

The Girl Behind the Gates

PART I

Chapter One

1939

With collars upturned, hats pulled down and coats firmly buttoned against the taunting November wind, the congregation of St Francis's Church trickles steadily into the pool gathering around Father Matthews who, in white cassock and green chasuble, provides an island of hope in the ocean of gloom. For England is at war.

Friends enquire solicitously about sons and husbands who have already been called up, unable to fully mask their relief that their own loved ones have, as yet, escaped the military's attention. Parents smile and joke with the priest, hiding their fear with the false bonhomie that will help their sons march out with courage, while those men old enough to remember Ypres and the Somme hurry by, avoiding the gaze of fresh-faced youths whose shining eyes speak of their naïve dreams of adventure and honour.

Nora Jennings hangs back a little, trailing behind her parents as she searches the crowd. Her often playful green eyes are uncharacteristically serious, her face pale and troubled. She tucks behind her ear a wayward strand of chestnut hair, usually so tidy but this morning done in a distracted hurry, then returns her hands to her chinchilla muff where they unconsciously fuss with the mantilla hurriedly stuffed there. She glances at the statue of Our Lady and begs for her intercession, making silent bargains she vows to keep. She'll work for the poor; sing like an angel; praise the Lord every day; live like a nun . . .

Mr and Mrs Jennings, unaware of Nora's anguish, wait plac-
idly for their turn for the final blessing from Father Matthews.
Nora looks on numbly, wishing she could disappear.

'Thank you, Father. Lovely sermon.' Her mother smiles,
touching her hair to ensure that none has strayed from the
chignon that supports her hat, resplendent with its curved
feather.

'Yes indeed,' her father intones, keen now to shepherd his
family home, away from the frosty morning.

'And beautiful singing,' says Father Matthews, enveloping
Nora in his beaming gaze. 'You have a daughter with an angel's
voice.'

Nora attempts a faltering smile and drops her eyes until her
mother's elbow reminds her of her manners. 'Thank you,
Father,' she manages, her eyes shying away from his, desperately
hoping that he hasn't seen the secret sin she's trying so hard to
hide.

Mrs Lampeter, the Jennings' housekeeper, holds Nora in her
gaze, all too aware of the reason that her smile and her eyes tell
different stories.

The next morning, the house wakes early but Nora has already
been up for hours, kneeling by her bed, head bowed, her face
testament to the earnestness of her prayer. Her trembling hands
finger rosary beads as she adds an extra paternoster to each
decade of Hail Marys.

She finally opens her eyes and stands. She rubs her knees,
stiff after kneeling for so long, and sweeps her eyes over her
room. They settle on the teddy bear and rag doll that share the
small wooden chair next to her chest of drawers, guarding over
her as she sleeps as they have done since she was a small child.
She walks over to the chest of drawers and looks at her most
prized possession, a musical box with a ballerina poised ready to
pirouette. She wants so much to turn the key, let the music
soothe her as it has done so many times before, and she reaches
out her hand.

A tap on the door startles her, and her hand halts in mid-air. Her heart races. She stuffs her rosary into her pocket and hurries over to her bed. She sits down, lifts her head and gulps down air as nausea threatens to overwhelm her. 'Yes?'

Mrs Lampeter peers in, duster in hand, and steps hesitantly into the room. 'Are you well, Miss Nora?' Her voice is unsteady and she clears her throat.

'I'm fine, thank you, Mrs Lampeter,' Nora lies, holding eye contact only long enough to be polite. A long silence somehow squeezes itself into the next tiny moment.

Mrs Lampeter stares at Nora. 'Miss, I brought you something.' From her apron pocket she pulls a small parcel and a note, and places them tentatively on the bed beside Nora. She turns and hurries from the room, closing the door behind her, before Nora can gather herself enough to say anything.

The moments tick by and Nora remains motionless. Then, almost involuntarily, her right hand unclasps from its partner and moves towards the little offering. She slowly unfolds the paper and reads.

Sorry, Miss. I'm ever so sorry if I'm wrong, but if you're in the family way, and you don't want to be, these might help. No more than three tablets.

Eyes wide with fear, Nora reads the note again, then fumbles to open the little packet. A small bottle falls into her hand. She turns it over and reads the label – quinine tablets. She stares, puzzled, then understanding rushes upon her.

Oh God.

She closes her hand tightly around the bottle while tears run down her cheeks. Tears of shame. Tears of hope. Tears of gratitude. And now, the nausea rises again and this time she can't quell it. Vomit surges into her mouth while she scrabbles for the chamber pot and retches. When it's finally over, she freezes, straining her ears, terrified that someone has heard. She knows that if she doesn't go downstairs soon she will arouse suspicion, but one look in the dressing-table mirror at her pale, tear-stained face frightens her. She licks the corner of a handkerchief and wipes her face, then nips her cheeks to pink them up a little. She feels unsteady on her feet and doesn't fancy getting down those stairs. *Come on, Nora, you have to do this*.

Holding tightly to the banister, she creeps down, then hovers outside the dining-room door where she won't be seen while she settles her breathing. She watches for a moment as her mother fusses over the crockery and checks everything on the sideboard – it must be perfect for Daddy, though he already has his head buried in his newspaper. Nora steps forward gingerly and, as her mother turns to greet her, Nora sees the anxiety and questions that leap into her eyes.

'Are you unwell, dear?'

'A little,' Nora murmurs, turning towards the sideboard, nausea rising as she looks at the huge breakfast laid out there. After a few painful mouthfuls, she mutters an excuse, grabs her schoolbag and hurries from the room. At least on the walk to school, she doesn't have to pretend.

Nora wishes the day would just pass. She manages to sit through mathematics, despite feeling as though everyone must be able to see her shame written across her face. The teacher drones on about revising for the end-of-term tests, but Nora barely registers any of it, focusing instead on the hope that came in the form of a little brown bottle.

At break time, she tries to avoid her friends, saying she feels unwell – which is about the only truthful thing she has said to anybody all day. By the afternoon, concentration is almost impossible and, at the sound of the final bell, she springs from her chair like a jumping cricket, grabbing her satchel and almost knocking over one of her friends in her dash to escape.

The smell of freshly baked teacakes tweaks at her nostrils, but rather than the usual sense of happy anticipation it brings, it makes her feel even worse. Just a few weeks ago, that smell would have meant some treasured time in the kitchen with her mother – just the two of them. But not today. Looking her mother in the eye is more than Nora can manage.

'Mummy, I'm still not feeling too well,' she says, registering the concern on her mother's face and hating herself for being the cause of it. 'I think I'll just go and lie down.'

Her mother reaches out and touches Nora's cheek. 'Yes, you're pale. Mmm . . . you just rest then. I won't disturb you, just come down to dinner if you feel better later.'

Hours later, Nora hears her mother approaching her bedroom door, tiptoeing so as not to disturb her. She turns her back to the door and huddles under the covers, feigning sleep. After a few seconds, she feels her mother retreat, leaving a trail of her sweet floral perfume behind her.

Nora listens as the house relaxes, preparing for sleep – odd clicks and cracks, the last crunchy nestling of the logs in the grate as they snuggle down behind the fire screen. She tiptoes across to her chest and turns the key of her music box. *Liebestraum* fills the air, calming and soothing as the little ballerina pirouettes. She eases open the middle drawer of her chest and searches among her underwear. Her fingers brush the little glass bottle and, heart drumming, she slides it from its hiding place. She hugs it to her chest, closing her eyes. 'Please forgive me for what I've done and for what I'm going to do,' she whispers. 'Please, please . . .'

She bows her head even lower and bites her bottom lip until both the pain and the metallic taste of blood become too much for her, then presses the nails of one hand into the palm of the other until it hurts. Perhaps this will somehow help persuade God of the urgency and sincerity of her prayer. 'I'll do anything, just please let it work. I promise, I'll never be wicked again.' She stands up, rubs her sore knees, then sits on her bed and once again reads the label on the bottle. She tips out three tablets into her hand. She replaces the cap, then hesitates. She opens it again and adds another tablet just to make sure.

Chapter Two

Nora begins to surface, as she often does, with music playing in her head. She's singing 'Ave Maria' with the choir and thrills as she feels herself reaching the highest notes, her heart full of gratitude for the gift of her voice.

Ave Maria, gratia plena
Maria, gratia plena—

And then, with a jolt, she's fully awake. The horror of her reality fills her with dread, all the more acute because forgotten in the moment of waking. She slips her hand down into her pyjama bottoms and fingers herself, then carefully withdraws it, pleading silently to see her fingers tipped with red. But her hand is clean.

It didn't work.

The nausea that is becoming all too familiar starts to rise again. She leaps out of bed, fumbling for the chamber pot, a rush of saliva dripping into it as her stomach contracts and the acrid taste of vomit fills her mouth. 'Oh, God.'

She closes her eyes but tears still escape down her face. What should she do? She tries to catch her breath, rests against the bed, but something doesn't feel right. She wrinkles her brow and cocks her head, listening. The world feels somehow distant. She shakes her head, taps her ears. Everything seems strange and far away. She can almost hear the sound of her brain working, like the irregular ticking of a broken clock. She closes her eyes and shakes her head again. Maybe it's a little better . . . But now there's a strange buzz . . . as though numbness had a sound.

She tries to concentrate but a wave of nausea floods through her and vomit fills her mouth once again.

In the next exhausted pause, she looks at the little bottle. What if someone should discover it? Her blood pounds. She pushes it under her pillow for now. Mrs Lampeter will help. *What day is it? Tuesday. She doesn't come on Tuesdays.* 'Please, please, God, help me. What can I do?' She feels ill. Her head aches, her vision is blurred and her hearing feels stranger than ever. *Please, God. Don't let me die.*

The door to her bedroom flies open and there is her mother, a look of horror on her face, her eyes darting from the chamber pot to Nora and back again. Nora looks up but doesn't bother to try to hide it; she is too exhausted to care any more.

'When did you last have your curse?'

'I can't remember,' Nora whispers.

'Nora. Could you be expecting?'

Nora looks at her mother, struggling to make out the hazy words. 'No,' she says with as much conviction as she can manage.

There's a yawning silence. Her mother looks unconvinced but finally leaves, closing the door behind her. Nora sinks to her knees, tears coursing down her cheeks. When she has cried so much that her face is sore and swollen and she has used up all her tears, she crawls back into bed and rests her head on the cool, soothing pillow. She reaches out for the only thing that will comfort her: her Bible.

Hours later, she is still trying to read the same passage, but the words just keep slipping through her mind like water through cupped hands. She finally gives it up as a bad job and puts the Bible back down on her bedside table, just as her mother enters her room without knocking. Nora's breath catches in her throat.

'Push over,' her mother says, in that way they always used to talk when they'd share cosy chats and little titbits of news about their days. But lately there's been a gulf between them, which Nora knows is of her own creation.

'Nora, you have to tell me the truth.' Her mother's tone is firm but gentle, but Nora still avoids her eyes.

'I'm just not feeling well. I have a headache and I can't hear properly,' she says, hoping desperately that her mother can't detect the shake in her voice.

There's a pause, then her mother places a hand on Nora's arm. 'Nora. I want the truth.'

'What about?'

Her mother withdraws her hand, suddenly impatient. 'Nora! This is the last time. Tell me the truth. Are you sure you can't be in a family way?'

Nora's breathing seems to have stopped and yet her heart is racing as her stomach clenches and sweat beads on her brow. For the first time in many weeks, she finally looks at her mother, whose eyes shift through anger to frustration to worry, before settling on fear. All at once, the true extent of the anguish Nora is causing to her loved ones hits her – made worse by the knowledge of more to come. Tears fill her eyes and her lip trembles and slowly, finally, she nods.

Time stalls, then fear, sadness and guilt tear at her heart as she watches her mother's mouth fall open in astonishment. She freezes as her mother's brow puckers, her eyes searching Nora's face as though looking for anything that might prove that this is still the daughter she thought she knew so well. Nora turns away, no longer able to bear the agony of her mother's disappointment.

'But Nora, you don't even have a boyfriend . . .' she whispers, then she blanches as the thought that has haunted Nora occurs to her for the first time. 'What will your father say? Oh, goodness.'

'Please don't tell him,' Nora begs, clutching at her mother's hands, but her mother moves them out of reach, her fingers flicking in a shooing motion, as though fending off contamination. A surge of confusion floods the gulf between them, love drowned in the whirlpools of fear spinning in Nora's belly as she flounders in the horror of the possibility that her mother might not love her any more. She'd expected this kind of reaction from her father, but never her mother.

'Mummy . . .'

Her mother's eyes finally meet Nora's once more, their usual fire extinguished. She seems to Nora to have aged a decade in the last ten seconds.

'Who is the father?' Her voice wavers, balanced on the brink of collapse. Strands of hair that have escaped from her mother's chignon hang untidily at her neck and down her jumper. Nora resists the urge to gather them up and tuck them back into their usual flawless arrangement.

Nora lowers her head. 'I can't,' she mutters.

'What do you mean, you can't? Tell me this minute. Who is the father?'

But Nora's jaw is set just like her father's when he is determined not to be moved, and this seems to infuriate her mother all the more. In a silence more sinister than rage, she stands and sweeps from the room.

Nora huddles on her bed. 'I'm sorry, I'm so sorry,' she gasps, the now all-too-familiar tears welling in her eyes once more.

After a few minutes that feel more like days to Nora, her father's voice bellows up from the hall below. 'Nora, get down these stairs. Now.'

She sits stock-still and huddles closer to herself. She looks down and sees as though from the outside that her hands, usually so steady, have begun to tremble.

'If you aren't down here in one minute, I shall come up there and get you.'

Nora shudders and stands, smoothing down her dress. She has never heard him so angry – and that is saying something. She picks her way down the stairs, clinging to the mahogany banister for support, faintness threatening to overcome her. She feels strangely separated from her body. Her father glowers up at her from the hallway, then, without a word, points to the parlour.

This room, which has held fun and laughter, bouncing children, afternoon teas and Christmas singing, feels foreign to Nora now. Her beloved piano stands quiet, withholding from her its music and its white-toothed smile.

'Who is the father?' he barks. A vague dismay settles over Nora – of course that's all he cares about – before she sweeps it away. Even with the fear of what might come threatening to choke her, Nora knows she cannot tell. She hangs her head, silent.

Her father advances on her and she flinches. He stops in front of her and brings his face ominously close to hers. 'I'm asking you – who is the father? You will tell me.' Even muffled by the effects of the quinine, the heat of his voice blasts into her, burning her cheek. She's been here before, many times. The only thing she can do is remain very small and very still, but after what feels like a century, she risks lifting her head, just in time for his hand to make contact with the side of her face with a sharp cracking sound. She reels sideways, stumbling to keep her balance, her hand cradling her cheek.

'Henry!' Alarm laces her mother's voice, but her father is already reaching for the leather belt that hangs from its hook by the fireplace – an ever-present reminder to the children of the consequences of misbehaviour. It's been some years since he has used it on her, but Nora remembers well not only its bite but also the degradation that far outweighs the pain.

'Henry, don't.' Nora's mother steps in front of her. 'No, Henry.'

Her father pushes her mother out of the way and grabs Nora's arm, ignoring the silent tears running down his daughter's face. The blows come in rapid succession, striking her back, her arms, her legs, her head – whichever part of her the belt can reach. Nora tries to block it all out, focusing instead on his heavy breathing that becomes almost a series of grunts as he tires. She learned long ago how to get out of her body and curl up in a safe corner by the ceiling until it's all over. She watches her poor body as it twitches and crumples until, exhausted and spent, her father finally pushes it to the floor.

'Do you know what we've sacrificed for you?' he bellows. 'Have you any idea? And this is how you repay us. Your life as it could have been is *gone*. Do you hear?' Nora looks up into her father's face. It is ugly in anger and his eyes hold no remorse, only fury. 'I'm finished with you,' he spits, and the break in his voice deepens the one in Nora's heart. He turns and storms out of the room, his belt discarded on the carpet beside Nora's beaten body. Nora lies still, unable to move or look away from the tears staining the carpet at her mother's feet.

The front door slams. The clock ticks off small portions of time and, somewhere inside her, Nora knows that her life will be similarly ticked off, bit by bit, by some unseen hand. She knows, somehow, that she will have ample time to regret how she has killed her parents' dreams, their pride in her and, seemingly, their love for her.

When Nora finally awakes to her surroundings once more, her mother is gone from the room. The clock strikes eight thirty. She pushes herself to her feet gingerly, the pain of the beating renewed with every movement. Slowly, she climbs the stairs to her room and collapses, finally tearless, onto her bed.

Chapter Three

Nora's eyes search the blackness for any clue as to the time. Everything feels arrested, its natural rhythm stilted by the horror of the last few hours. Untethered from the life she had blithely looked forward to, she is adrift, her bearings lost. There is no safe harbour in sight. She listens to the silence and it fills her with foreboding.

With careful fingers she examines the tender swelling on her cheek, then gingerly explores the welts on her arms and her back. She's aware of soft, cushioned sounds as she shifts in bed, and pauses. She shakes her head and hears the friction of her hair against the pillow. Closing her eyes, she listens to her own shallow, stuttering breaths and closes her eyes in gratitude at the return of her hearing.

The floor is cold as she tiptoes out to the bathroom, pausing on the landing to listen. Then alarm clutches her throat with icy fingers: she is alone. She feels her father's belt's work with every step down the stairs to the hallway, where again she stops to listen. The only sound is the comforting ticking of the grandfather clock. Hardly breathing, she edges over to the doorway of the parlour. Silence. Blackness.

A tiny sound emerges from the darkness and she stops still. As her eyes adjust, the figure of her mother emerges out of the darkness, sitting limp and motionless. And then there's light, her mother's hand withdrawing from the lamp she has just switched on.

Each of them freezes at the sight of the other. Nora can hardly bear to see the face she loves so pale and drawn, the narrow nose blue at the tip, the eyes that seem to have sunk into their sockets during the last few hours. Things have irrevocably changed, though a new order isn't yet established, and both Nora and her mother languish in the void – the no man's land of shock.

A familiar sound, usually joyful, now terrifying, startles them both. A key turns in the front door and Nora presses herself back into the wall. In the slice of hallway she can still see, her father leads a parade of men into the parlour. Fear grips her heart and roots her to the ground with the vain hope that she could become invisible.

'Mildred?' Her father's voice is cold, insistent. Nora aches, watching her mother's struggle as they seek out each other's eyes in the full knowledge that they can protect each other no longer. Nora shrinks, taking refuge in some inner corner of her being to which she still, mercifully, has access. 'Where is Nora?'

Her mother doesn't respond, but she cannot help the sharp dart of her eyes that reveals Nora's whereabouts. Her father spins round and stares at her, his eyes so cold they burn. Nora stands perfectly still. She yearns to help her mother, who makes one final plea to her husband with fearful eyes while hauling herself onto shaky legs. She pauses briefly, righting her balance, before leaden steps take her straight past the huddle of men and towards Nora.

'Good evening, Mildred.' Dr Rayne, their family practitioner, holds his trilby in front of his chest, as he might if he were offering condolences. Her mother looks around, her eyes wary. 'Father Matthews,' she rasps, lowering her eyes.

Dr Rayne steps aside and, using his hat as a pointer, introduces the other man – small, squat, and with a pompous air that swells him up like a turkey. 'This is Dr Mason from Hillinghurst Hospital.'

'Hillinghurst?' her mother gasps.

Nora has heard this dreadful word from time to time around the village, and has sensed the garland of shame and fear that always accompanies it. Her eyes bore into the man, who oozes a sense of power that is almost palpable – a power that could silence the clock from its ticking. Yet when he reaches out his hand towards her mother, she ignores it, leaving it to drift back and hang foolishly by his side. Even at this hour, he looks as though he's just arrived freshly bathed and groomed, his hair plastered to his head with a knife-edge parting – a Brylcreem advert for the older male. Nora watches her mother shrink as though she, too, were preparing for a beating, and her own blood runs cold. 'What are you doing here?' her mother demands of the man, a lioness defending her cub. Nora's eyes fill with silent tears: her mother must still love her, after all.

'I think you ought to speak with your husband, Mildred,' Dr Rayne says, his voice soothing. He holds a hand out in an attempt to support her, but she recoils from him as though he were a snake. Dr Rayne's eyes flit from her mother's face to that of Father Matthews, whose agonised expression speaks of the war between compassion and duty that rages inside him. Nora shifts, her movements stiff and painful, and the frozen tableau cracks.

'Henry,' Dr Rayne says hesitantly. 'Are you sure you want to do this? Surely there's another—'

'I'm quite sure. There's no choice.' He turns to Nora, not quite meeting her eye. 'Go upstairs and wait.'

Nora cowers on her bed fully clothed, her hands tucked under her armpits and her cheeks flushed with crying. Slowly, she rises and hobbles to the mirror. The swelling on the side of her face is red and angry, and her hair looks like the bird's nest she found in the garden last summer. As her trembling hands work to right it, her thoughts frantically search for an answer to the question that has plagued her now for weeks: what can she do to prevent herself from being the source of any further pain or shame for her parents and her family? Panic rises in her and she casts her eyes around the room. She bites her lip again until she can taste the blood, but even that might not be enough, then her eyes spring open. Her sewing kit! There are needles and pins and scissors ... She opens her chest of drawers, retrieves the box and scrabbles through its contents. She takes out the scissors and pushes up the sleeve of her jumper.

There's no pain. She's beyond that now. But as she pushes down harder, she's both curious and surprised that it's actually quite difficult to cut through skin. She changes hands and tries her other wrist, but all she manages are a few red marks and, here and there, a tiny, sprouting droplet of blood. She tries again with more urgency, more pressure, and finally manages to cut through, releasing a little more blood to the surface and, with it, a strange, welcome relief.

A sound just outside the door startles her. Her heart races and her breaths come in short gasps. The anaesthetic effect of shock lifts abruptly and her vision clears. She hurries to sit on the bed and hides the scissors under her thigh, wincing at the flare of pain in her wrists. Stupid girl for thinking it would help. She tugs her sleeves down to cover the evidence of her foolishness. Her fingers trace the swelling on her face – that's sore too. Her father and his belt did their work well.

All at once her mother is in the doorway, looking like a ghost version of herself. 'You'd better come downstairs,' she mutters, holding open the door, but Nora remains on the bed, her eyes downcast.

'I'm sorry,' Nora murmurs, blushing at the inadequacy of the word in the face of her parents' ruined lives.

'You must come down, Nora,' her mother urges. She begins to turn away, but stops suddenly, her eyes fixed on the counterpane. 'What have you done?' Her mother's whisper sounds like a scream in disguise.

Nora follows her mother's gaze and sees the smear of blood on her bedspread. Her heart sputters. 'Nothing,' she says, but her hand betrays her as it moves to cover her wrist.

'Let me see,' her mother commands, grabbing at Nora's arm. Her mouth falls open as she examines the cuts, then her eyes dart to Nora's. 'Nora . . . No . . .' As Nora shifts to hide her wrists, the quinine bottle is dislodged from under the pillow and she gasps. Her palpable fear alerts her mother. Time stops. They look at each other, then at this tiny bottle, which holds the power to blow their lives apart completely and possibly for ever. Nora moves quickly, trying to push it under the pillow again, but her mother grabs it and squints at the label. A groan escapes into the boundless space that now separates them.

'Where did you get these?'

Nora looks away, silent.

'Nora, where did you get them?' her mother demands.

'I bought them,' Nora mutters, steeling herself to maintain eye contact.

'When?'

'Yesterday.'

Her mother pauses, as though gearing herself up to ask the impossible. 'Have you taken them?'

Nora lowers her eyes.

'When?'

'Last night.' Tears begin to course down her cheeks again. 'I'm sorry,' she sobs.

'Nora,' her mother hisses, 'that is not only a sin against God, but it's a crime for which you could go to prison.'

Nora gasps, her eyes wide and her hands trembling. 'Oh, I didn't know . . .' But her mother is already leaving and Nora stares after her, desolate.

Nora stands stock-still, cut off from everything including her own thoughts, but aware that somewhere the world is continuing without her. She glances around the room, trying to make sense of this new reality in which there seems to be nothing she can depend upon any more. She reaches out her hand and clutches the chest of drawers to steady herself, her heart drumming a beat in her ears, the room swaying about her. *What have I done?*

Her body seems to move of its own volition. Her hands pull down her sleeves. Her legs walk to the door. Her eyes lead her to the top of the stairs, but her legs refuse to take her any further. Her lungs draw a painful breath. Her heart still pounds in her ears, and slowly she forces one foot to move onto the first of the stairs, her hand clutching the rail for support.

Father Matthews looks up and clears his throat, looking sick with shame. Nora's eyes are flat and dull but dry as, like many a martyr before her, she walks into a nest of vipers. *This is what it must feel like descending into hell.* Father Matthews looks at his fellow conspirators, his eyes darting from one to the other, seeming to search for something to break this impasse. 'Maybe this is for the best,' he offers weakly. 'You know what people are like in a small place – lots of rumours and . . . Well, there'll be no peace for you here now, Nora. It's better that you disappear for a while.' His voice quivers.

Nora looks at him blankly until he drops his eyes, self-disgust painted on his face like a mask. Her father stands in front of the ashes in the fireplace, while her mother, trembling, sinks onto the sofa and pulls her cardigan around her. The parlour is chilly, now that the fire has died. Nora moves to stand in the centre of the room at her father's silent command, her eyes cast down, feeling like a defendant in a murder trial. She eyes the fire screen that stands to one side. The usually bright, cheery roses her mother patiently embroidered are now open, screaming mouths. Dr Rayne clears his throat and steps forward. 'Nora, your father came to see us this evening and told us of the situation, which, you must be aware, is very serious.' Nora drags her eyes away from the accusing roses and focuses instead on her own clasped hands. She must trim her nails – it's irritating when they tap on the piano keys. 'First we need to be sure that there actually is a pregnancy, so I have to examine you.'

Nora flinches. She's known Dr Rayne all her life. He delivered her in her parents' bedroom upstairs. He examined her throat when she had tonsillitis. He listened to her chest that year when she had bronchitis that seemed to take for ever to go away. He stitched her leg when she fell on some glass. But he's never examined her intimately. She looks up at her mother, her eyes glassy with fear and shame.

'Your mother will be with us.' Dr Rayne's voice is strangely soft. Perhaps he does pity her, then. 'Mrs Jennings, where can I do the examination?'

'Maybe in Nora's bedroom,' she says, her voice low with defeat.

'Very well. After you.' He gestures towards the open door and Nora and her mother have no choice but to precede him through it and up the stairs.

Dr Rayne prepares to examine Nora, who lies on her bed, trying to cover herself with a towel. 'Nora, I have to examine you,' Dr Rayne says patiently. Nora lets go of the towel, turns her head and stares at the girl looking back at her from the wardrobe mirror. How sad and lost she looks. How hollow. Nothing like the lively, smiling girl who laughed and loved to sing and play the piano. Maybe that one is gone. She prays that, for the sake of this miserable girl in the mirror, this will soon be over.

'Probably three months,' Dr Rayne says gravely to her mother, who buries her head in her hands.

While Nora dresses, Dr Rayne washes his hands, then signals Nora to sit down. He looks resigned as he holds up the empty quinine bottle, wagging it back and forth like an accusing finger. 'We have to talk about this.' Nora's stomach swoops with a sudden nausea. How could her mother have betrayed her? 'Nora.' Dr Rayne's gentle voice calls her back and her eyes move reluctantly to his. 'Did you take quinine to try to get rid of the baby?'

The words echo in Nora's ears.

Get rid of the baby?

Her mouth opens but there are no words. Nothing she can say will make any of this right.

'Nora. Did you take quinine to try to abort this child?' His voice is louder and more insistent this time, and his eyes search her face, as though he'll find the answer written there. She holds his eyes for a long moment, then, finally defeated, she gives a tiny nod. He breathes out a long sigh. 'Where did you get them from?'

Nora's gaze remains on the floor. Her mother rallies. 'I think that is enough,' she says, her voice shot through with an unusual strength. She takes Nora by the wrist, and Nora winces and pulls away.

'What's wrong with your arm?' Dr Rayne reaches over and Nora tries again to resist. His brow furrows and Nora looks desperately at her mother. 'What are you hiding?' he asks, his eyes darting back and forth between the faces of mother and daughter. Slowly, he looks back at Nora's arm and pushes up her sleeve.

He takes a sharp breath and steps back, fixing Mildred with a steely gaze. 'You knew about this?'

Mildred's eyes plead for mercy as she puts an arm around Nora's shoulders. 'Please . . . just let me take care of her.'

Dr Rayne's scowl deepens. 'Mildred, you must know that this is a criminal matter and compounds an already difficult situation. Nora is unmarried and pregnant. Attempting to procure an abortion carries a term in prison, as does attempting suicide. As does aiding and abetting. You must know I cannot do that. The facts of this must be reported.' He gathers his jacket, looking older and more tired than ever.

'Please . . .' Mildred begs.

Dr Rayne turns away from her, shaking his head. 'Perhaps when you're both ready, you could come downstairs.'

Nora's mother puts her arms around her daughter, and they look into each other's red-rimmed eyes, both tearful now. Nora wishes she could crawl out of her skin and nestle within her mother's bosom where once, what feels like a very long time ago, she was safe. Her mother holds her in silence, her cheek resting on Nora's hair.

'We must go downstairs.' Mildred leans back and focuses on Nora's frightened eyes. 'Come. Wipe your face. Pinch your cheeks. Pull down your dress. Let me see your hands. Nora – no cream. You must remember to look after your hands. Come. We'll talk to these people. It'll be all right.'

Nora clasps her arms around her mother. Yes, now it will be all right. Her mother does still love her, even though she's been wicked. They trudge down the stairs hand in hand and Nora allows her mother to lead her back into the parlour where one glance at her father's face tells her that Dr Rayne has told him everything. The fire her mother's love rekindled within her sputters and dies.

Despite his diminutive stature, Dr Mason seems to fill the whole room. He gives a stiff little bow, clears his throat, stands with his feet apart and his arm held slightly in front of him, his chin raised a little. Nora can't help but think of the bad actor in the performance of *The Taming of the Shrew* she saw last summer and, despite the situation, feels a bizarre urge to laugh.

'Mr and Mrs Jennings, I offer you my sympathy in this matter. First, I should make you aware of the legal issues, then I will be willing to answer your questions and make provisions.'

Make provisions? Nora reaches for her mother's hand but is arrested by a single look from her father, and withdraws it. 'The Mental Deficiency Act of 1913 categorises four types of mentally disabled people. The only one I need bother you with here is that of the moral imbecile.'

Nora shrivels inside, sick with humiliation.

'Such people, since 1927 termed "moral defectives", include those such as criminals, alcoholics and prostitutes –and also unmarried mothers.'

Is that how she is to be known? An unmarried mother? A moral defective? What happened to just 'Nora'?

'Such people may be a moral threat to others and therefore they must be strictly controlled and segregated,' he continues. 'Other measures may also be necessary, but we don't need to bother ourselves with them for now.'

Nora's face burns and she wishes that she could just disappear, that the floor would open and swallow her whole.

'I don't understand. Nora's a good girl, really,' says Mildred.

'I have no doubt that she knows the difference between right and wrong, Mrs Jennings, and yet she has found it impossible to behave within the moral values of society. Tragically, there is yet a further complication, in that she admits to having attempted to procure an abortion. Heaven knows what damage she has caused to the unborn child. A suicide attempt also needs to be taken into consideration.'

Nora's mother gasps as the stark reality of the situation finally dawns on her. She shoots a pleading look in her husband's direction. Nora glances back and forth between them, struggling to understand the silent war playing out behind each of their eyes. Her mother steps forward. 'Henry, stop this. It can't happen—'

'Mrs Jennings,' snaps Dr Mason. 'If you would prefer, I can talk to your husband alone.'

She takes a deeper, more controlled breath and smooths down her dress with shaking hands. 'No. I'm fine.'

He coughs, then continues on as though uninterrupted. 'Provisions under the Act are that young women such as your daughter be committed to a mental hospital, or to some mental deficiency colony forthwith, where she will receive such treatment as is deemed necessary.'

Nora feels rooted to the spot, her face blank. She is vaguely aware of her mother sinking onto the settee, but she herself couldn't move if she tried.

'In this case, however, we must also consider the legal route, since we have here two criminal offences.' His eyes rest momentarily on Nora, as if waiting for her to deny her actions. When she says nothing, he presses on. 'Were she imprisoned, it would undoubtedly bring shame upon the whole family, and slurs and accusations against yourselves as parents. And of course, a prison sentence would no doubt be long. I doubt that your daughter is equipped for such a life. There would be prolonged suffering for everyone concerned. I would suggest that you think very carefully before pursuing the legal option.' He appraises Nora as though she were an animal at the market. 'You also need to bear in mind that, should your daughter make another suicide attempt and be successful, the two of you as parents could also be tried and imprisoned.'

'Stop,' sobs Mildred, her hands to her ears. 'Stop!'

'Mrs Jennings, please get a hold of yourself,' Dr Mason barks impatiently. 'These two options are both valid under the Act and, if I may say, many physicians would not be giving you a choice.' He tugs on his waistcoat and takes his pocket watch from its hiding place and snaps it open, looking wounded. He glances at the time and closes it again. 'Mr Jennings, do you have any questions?'

The whole room seems to collapse into a pit as the clock ticks away the moments and Henry makes no attempt to reply. 'Well then . . .'

Nora feels faint, as though her whole being is dissolving into nothingness and she'll disappear – which, though frightening, might be the best thing for everybody. Her only island of refuge might be her mother, but as she dares to let her eyes move to her, what she sees there is equally terrifying. Her mother is pale and trembling, just like Nora herself, her face like a puppet's mask. And as she opens her mouth, the voice that comes out sounds alien to Nora's ear. 'What will happen to the child?'

'Much will depend upon how much damage your daughter has already done to this unborn. It's impossible to be sure. The children of moral defectives are often themselves defective. Neither your daughter, nor the child, is capable of managing themselves and their affairs. Where there are also criminal propensities, as we see here,' he shoots a look of disdain at Nora, 'they require care, supervision and control for the protection of others. I assure you the child will be taken care of.'

During the interminable silence that follows, Nora watches from the safety of her corner of the ceiling while her body stands silent, focused on the silky fringe of the chenille cloth on the side table. Part of it is twisted out of line and unable to hang properly. Her mother would usually be so particular about such things. Dr Mason springs open his pocket watch a second time and his impatience with this dreadful family fills the room.

'Not prison,' Henry says quietly.

Suddenly Nora is back in her body. 'Help me, someone; please help me!' she screams – but there is no sound.

In a groggy haze, Nora drags herself up the stairs once more, her mother following behind her. Reproach snaps at her heels with every step. Judgement claws at her face and terror seeps through her skin so that she can almost smell it. She scans her bedroom. Her pretty dresses hang in the wardrobe and below stand matching shoes side by side, ready to walk, dance or run away. 'Mummy, what shall I take?'

'I don't know, darling.' Nora's heart soars with hope at this rare endearment, but as she reaches out, her mother shrinks away from her and Nora's hand is left hanging in mid-air. Somehow, a couple of skirts, jumpers, some underwear, a toothbrush and a nightdress are packed into a small leather case.

'Do you think I could take one more thing?' Nora asks. Without waiting for an answer, she grabs her music box and stuffs it into the corner of the case. She looks longingly around her cosy bedroom, and it only just occurs to her that it might be a good while before she sees it again.

Nora finds herself down in the hallway with no notion of how she got there. 'Daddy,' she calls from the parlour door in a voice that no longer feels like her own. He stares stonily ahead. Then, as a hand clasps Nora's elbow, he turns his back to her and instead faces the empty grate. He leans on the mantelpiece and rests his head on his arm, as though it has suddenly become too heavy for his neck to bear. The front door opens and the cold night air rushes in. 'Mummy,' Nora cries, but there's no reply. No kiss. No tearful embrace. Her mother sits in a state of shock, staring straight ahead. Nora could beg them not to send her away, promise them she'd never stray again, plead for mercy. But nothing makes sense any more. Nothing is as it was just a few hours ago. She bites her lip and holds back her tears: she dares not cry again in case she never stops.

Out on the driveway, a hand at her back bustles her into the rear seat of a black sedan. She will never forget her mother's heartbroken face framed by her white lace collar, nor her father's rage and, underneath it, the disgust in his eyes. But now she can only see these things in her mind's eye, for the door has already closed. Nora is dislocated, amputated, lost.

She stares out into the black night as the car speeds away, leaving her home and all she knows behind. She puts a hand to the cold window. Tomorrow the sun will come up. The postman will deliver letters. The village shop will open. Her family will have breakfast. But where will she be?

When Nora opens her eyes again, she sees for the first time the great, looming building ahead, silhouetted in the moonlight. Is this Hillinghurst? The hospital that people hardly even dare to mention in case it should somehow hear and touch them with its inherent malevolence. As terror laces its fingers round her throat, she glances back through the rear window as if she might escape from here. But, as she does, the tall gates close between their two huge stone pillars, separating her from all she has ever known. She clasps the back of the seat in front of her and shudders.

Chapter Four

Nora awakes suddenly, her mouth bitter with the unfamiliar taste that she takes a minute to identify as loneliness. Not aloneness. Not solitude. Utter isolation. A pit of nothingness.

Her full bladder brings her crashing back to reality. She opens her eyes, and the terror that engulfs her contracts into a cold, hard mass that stifles her breath. She wants to scream, but she is paralysed. She glances around the stark room. Paint that may once have been cream clads the cold, bare walls. She raises a hand and pushes against the wall. It doesn't give. It's real. The blanket is coarse, prickly fibres interwoven with the rough wool. She nips it, rolls it between her fingers and pulls it up into little hillocks. She raises her head from the lumpy pillow and stares at this space enclosed by walls and a door, with its single bulb hanging from the high ceiling. No wonder it's so cold down here.

She puts her hand back under the blanket and touches her arm, her chest, her breast, her gently swelling belly, feeling the softness and the warmth of her skin. She's here in this cold foreign place, but she's alive.

Suddenly, a face cut into tiny squares appears behind the wire mesh in the minuscule window of the door. A handle turns.

'Get up, Jennings.'

'I need the toilet.' Her voice sounds strange and husky to her own ears.

'Come with me.' The nurse leads her barefoot into a corridor with a cold black marble floor and points to a large open door. 'In there.'

In trying to pull it down, she realises that she isn't wearing any underwear. She sits on an icy seat and relieves herself. Her feet are blue. And why is her back cold? She looks around and realises that the hospital nightgown is split down the back. She blushes at the thought that she's walked all the way down the corridor with it gaping open. She wipes herself with shiny Izal toilet paper, but makes no move to get up until nausea rises and she springs up to vomit in the toilet.

She wipes her mouth and sits down again. With a burgeoning sense of dread, she allows herself to remember more of yesterday's events. There are still gaps, but . . . She brings her hands to her face, trembling. Her father and his anger. Her mother and her drawn, dry-eyed face. No goodbyes. Her musical box. Father Matthews, Dr Rayne. Strangers. A car. Cold. A woman . . . who? Then nothing. She tries to push her mind into the hole in time but it refuses, a pony shying at the first fence.

'What are you doing in there?'

The harsh voice startles Nora. With neither question nor complaint, she follows the owner of the voice back down the corridor, trying to hold together the back of the split gown. She focuses only on what is directly in front of her. White mid-calf dress, black cardigan, thick lisle stockings; stocky calves, solid ankles; black shoes with low heel. The right foot throws itself slightly sideways before it makes contact with the floor. A sort of cap over dark hair tethered in a bun. The cold jangle of keys. The nurse opens the door and Nora shuffles inside. She turns to ask her a question, but the door has already been closed and locked behind her.

She turns back to the room, wondering what she's supposed to do now, and she sees that someone has put some things on the foot of the bed. She examines the pile, turning each object over in her hands before moving on to the next one. There is a bundle of folded clothes, an enamel bowl with an inch of cold water, some carbolic soap, a scratchy towel, a toothbrush, a tin of dentifrice, a comb, some hair clips, a bowl of grey porridge, a spoon and a tin mug of tea. A pair of black lace-up boots are by the bed. All of Nora's worldly possessions now fit in one pile. She stands still. Then something inside her stirs and she starts to move slowly, a silent litany keeping her on track.

Nora wash.

Nora dress.

Nora eat.

Nora drink tea.

Nora brush teeth.

Nora sit on bed.

Nora wait.

She closes her eyes and listens. The choir is singing in St Francis's Church, her own clear soprano taking the solo.

Ave Maria ...

The door opens and the music stops. A youngish man in a starched white coat enters the room, his left leg dragging slightly as he walks. His face is broad, his eyes hazel and fringed with blond lashes and his fair hair, though slicked back, seems to Nora to be in danger of toppling into his eyes at any minute. His lips are generous and his nose a little flattened. Maybe he's a boxer. He wears a gold signet ring with a seal on the little finger of his right hand.

'Miss Jennings, I'm Dr Stilworth. May I sit down?' Without waiting for an answer, he pulls the single chair from the corner and lowers himself onto it. 'I wanted to introduce myself. I will be taking care of you.' His accent is pure upper class, and Nora relaxes a little. Surely this man of good breeding will understand that she shouldn't be in this place. 'You'll have a meeting with Dr Mason soon, and you'll be very busy today.'

Will I? What will I be doing? How can I be busy?

'So, I'll come and see you again tomorrow. If there is anything you'd like to ask me, please do. We're all here to help you get well.' She tries to say thank you – thank you for coming, thank you for helping me. But there's no sound. She stares at him and he eventually looks away and raises himself from the chair. He places it back in the corner where it belongs. He stands in front of her, his feet together, and makes a little bow. 'Miss Jennings.' And he is gone.

Minutes pass and Nora waits, wondering vaguely what happens next, but she can't find it in her to care much. Everything is numb.

Eventually, the door opens again. 'Nora, I'm Nurse Hatton. You're to see Dr Mason. Come.' This softer voice gives Nora courage to look into the accompanying eyes. Something in their depths moves her in the middle of her chest. Tears fill her eyes and, though she wants to blink them away or dry them with her hand, her body seems unwilling to move and she feels their warmth coursing down her cheeks. She cannot take her eyes from those opposite her that seem to say they care that she is lost. 'Nora.' The woman reaches out and places a gentle hand on her shoulder. 'Nora, it's all right. You need to come with me.'

She stands obediently and hobbles towards the door, trying as she does to rearrange her toes in the stiff leather boots. Already, her heels are sore. The loose green smock hangs off her body, hiding its gentle curves. Despite its excessive roominess, the black cardigan feels a bit of a comfort against the cold. But the thick stockings are uncomfortable and, even though she's tied knots at the top to try to keep them from falling down, she has to hold them up as she walks.

'Walk up straight, Nora,' says Nurse Hatton. Though it's a command, it seems to have some music to it and Nora plays it again and again in her head as she follows along the corridor like an imprinted duckling. The nurse finally stops outside a tall, ornate door, taps upon it and listens. She gives Nora a reassuring smile, opens the door and gestures to Nora to go ahead into the room. 'Nora Jennings, Dr Mason.'

The door closes behind Nora and she stops still in a room that feels like a different world. It has a window through which she can see a slice of garden. She gobbles up the feast of sensation to savour later. There's a graceful silver birch and some willows, and though they're bare, they look beautiful swaying in the November wind. She imagines the sound of the twigs tapping each other gently as the wind passes through them. She can almost feel the carpety softness of the grass under her feet.

The world is still as it was yesterday, but between her and that world stand those dreadful gates.

She moves her gaze to Dr Mason and it strikes her that the formality of the room, with its books in glass-fronted cases, reflects the man himself. He stands behind a large mahogany desk with its brown leather blotter, a beautiful gold-capped pen and some folders and papers and photograph frames pointed away from her, painfully reminding her of her parents' turned-away faces. And there, in the middle of all of this, her musical box, the ballerina perfectly poised, waiting patiently for the music to commence. Nora's eyes smart and she blinks at the sight of this treasure that doesn't belong here.

'Sit down, Miss Jennings,' Dr Mason commands, and Nora does as she is told. Dr Mason clears his throat. 'Now that you are here, I want you to know precisely where we stand.' His voice is clear, controlled, deliberate. She thinks he's probably a tenor and wonders if he sings. 'You know what you have done and why you're here. This will be your home now.'

She blinks. That word could never be applied to this place. She stops the words and reframes them in her mind: 'This will be where you will live.' *Live? Will I live?* 'This is where you will be . . .' *What, exactly?* She forces herself back to the moment and tries to listen.

'It will be best for everyone if you consider your family dead.'

Her heart feels as though it has stopped beating altogether. *What? How could that be best? Did they die in the night? Did my mother's heart break? Am I still alive or am I dead?*

'Miss Jennings! Please pay attention. Everyone adjusts and forgets in time. You've been a wicked, cunning girl, and here you'll learn to live a better life with the values that I'm sure your highly respected father has tried to instil in you.'

She twitches in her chair as a jolt of shame runs through her, then spreads and burns like pepper under her skin. But it's soon followed by hopelessness – what Father Matthews has always called the last trench before the mortal sin of despair. She cannot allow herself to succumb to yet another mortal sin, so she refocuses her eyes on the musical box, wondering if the ballerina will still be able to dance when the music starts again.

'I know it may be hard, but these are the just deserts for your behaviour.'

Was I so wicked? Yes, I suppose so. I'm a sinner. Fire. Brimstone. Just rewards for sin.

In slow motion, Dr Mason lifts his watch from his waistcoat pocket. His thumb flicks the catch and the little gold cover springs open, catching the weak sunlight from the window. Something in Nora smiles at the beauty of the sun on the gold – but then it's gone. Just a flash. He checks the time. 'Nurse will take you back to the ward.'

'But I have to—'

'Yes?'

But the little spurt of energy that broke through the cotton wool in her head is already spent and she can't remember what she was going to say.

'Tomorrow.' The one word is a door shut. She is dismissed. His hand reaches forward and alights smartly on a little brass bell, whose cheerful sound jars with its surroundings.

The door opens and Nurse Hatton enters. 'Come, Nora,' she says, but Nora can no longer hear any music in the voice.

The clock says ten past six. Nora sits in a large, foreign room crammed with women who look as lost as she feels. There's a strange smell and a lot of noise, and she can't make sense of any of it. The light has gone from outside and someone is pulling heavy curtains across the tall windows.

Despite being surrounded, there's an emptiness around Nora that is so dense and heavy that it somehow supports her body in its position on the chair. Loneliness and fear threaten to engulf her once more. There's no way out.

'Nora. Nora!' A cold, toneless voice. 'Dinner is at half past six. Get ready.'

Did I have lunch? And tea? Was there cake? Toasted teacake would be lovely. We could toast it on the fire on the long toasting fork and then eat it dripping with butter. 'Don't make a mess now. Would you like strawberry jam?'

'Go and wash your hands for dinner.'

She feels her body lift off the chair and wonders at the mechanics of that. How did her legs know what to do? And now she's walking, following everybody else. How strange. She sits on the hard bench and more people join her. Others are already there. They're all wearing similar clothes – drab green and black – but some of them move differently and can't seem to sit still. The woman opposite constantly moves her head and opens and closes her mouth and Nora finds it oddly fascinating. And that girl, why is she staring like that? Then Nurse Hatton wheels someone in and sits her at the end of the table. Her twisted hands make clawing movements and she's chewing even though no food has been served yet. Nora looks away.

Nora's hand moves involuntarily to her head and she fingers her scalp. It's sore and sticky in places. *Did someone really put a cloth around my shoulders and cut off my hair?* Hair that had only been cut maybe three times in her life, and at each, her mother had tried to hide her tears as the curls fell? *Then was I really made to sweep up that last reminder of who I used to be into a newspaper?* This must be some sort of nightmare. She'll wake up soon. Her parents will come and take her home, having made their point that she's a bad girl. They'll be furious about her hair.

Another nurse with heavy-set legs, a weightlifter's shoulders and hairs growing from her chin stands a way off, staring at the table and the people sitting around it. Those ruddy cheeks must bury her eyes when she smiles. The clang of a bell reverberates through the hall and, in unison, spoons clatter against metal bowls in a deafening din. Nora looks from one drooling face to another, and yet another chattering aimlessly to no one in particular. It's bewildering. Not one person is as young as she is and it seems that every head bent over the soup is grey. *Where did all of these people come from? Why are they here?*

She lowers her gaze to the soup in front of her and is surprised to see that her hand is holding a spoon filled with thin brown liquid and is raising it to her mouth. She swallows and savours the spread of warmth as the soup makes its way to her stomach. Someone puts a piece of bread in her hand and her mouth opens, teeth bite, jaws move and part of the bread is gone.

She tries, but she cannot find the music. She searches in her head where she usually hears it, but it's gone. Grief pours into her chest. Despite all these people around her, now she really is alone.

Chapter Five

Three weeks

So as not to offend the sensibilities of the local populace, Hillinghurst Hospital hides itself behind screens of trees that serve as protection or imprisonment, depending upon the viewer. The building has an architectural grandeur that has always seemed – to Nora – incongruous with its function, with wide sweeping steps protruding like a tongue ready to snatch up and devour unsuspecting visitors. Gothic arches simultaneously beckon and warn. The pain of hundreds of souls that Nora has always sensed hanging like a shroud over the building is, she is discovering, all too real.

Nora kneels on the marble floor, a bucket of soapy water at her side as she scrubs. Her cardigan sleeves, even though rolled up to her elbows, are wet, and the cold wool makes her shiver. She wrings out a grey cloth and mops up the dirty bubbles, then shifts her bucket and shuffles on her knees to the next patch of dirty floor. She tenses as she hears footfall, but quickly resumes her scrubbing. Three weeks here have taught her to keep her eyes down and get on with her work. Shoes and stockinged legs come into view and stop. Nora freezes, the sudden taste of fear metallic in her mouth.

'Nora.' She exhales. It's Nurse Hatton. Thank God. 'Leave your things here and come with me.' Nora clambers to her feet and follows the nurse obediently. Nurse Hatton leads the way to the dormitory and Nora trails behind, trying to ignore her sore knees and the backache that now plagues her every minute of the day.

'Sit down.' Nurse Hatton indicates Nora's bed and pulls up the one metal chair for herself. 'Nora, it's your birthday! A lady brought you this.' With a smile and a flourish, she produces a little package wrapped in yellow crepe paper and tied with string. She places it on Nora's lap. Nora holds the little parcel in both hands then hugs it tight to her breast. 'My mother?' she asks, and her mouth cracks into a smile. The movement feels foreign.

'No ...' Nurse Hatton says hesitantly. 'I'm sorry, I should have thought ... No, the gift is from a Mrs Lampeter.'

'Mrs Lampeter?' The disappointment threatens to overwhelm her. 'Oh ...' She tries her hardest to feel grateful, but her eyes brim with tears.

'I'm sorry, Nora. She said she was your friend.'

'Yes. She is,' Nora says, feeling even guiltier for her reaction. She brushes her tears away and lowers her eyes to the parcel.

'Are you going to open it?' Nurse Hatton encourages.

Nora holds the featherweight package in her sore, chapped hands and her fingers tremble as she tugs at the bow. The sunshine-yellow crepe paper brings memories of past birthdays crashing over her. Tea and jelly and custard. Friends with party dresses. Playing pass-the-parcel, postman's knock, musical chairs. How the girls all fawned over Robert, her cousin who, in the early years, was the only boy. Mummy's cakes, with icing and sugar hundreds-and-thousands sprinkled on top. She and Auntie Isabel with their frilly aprons and big smiles. Rubber balloons and presents. Then, when she was fifteen, Mummy and Daddy gave her the musical box, and she danced to *Liebestraum* along with the ballerina. And last year, Robert gave her a silver chain.

She unfolds the paper carefully and slowly, eking out the experience of a few seconds to last as long as possible. Inside the first fold is a piece of paper with laborious handwriting. The pen has smudged and scratched here and there.

Dear Miss Nora,
Many happy returns of your birthday.
I'm sorry for what happened.
Your friend,
Eileen Lampeter

'What was it that happened, Nora?' asks Nurse Hatton, her voice gentle.

'I got pregnant and now I'm here,' Nora says mechanically.

'I'm sorry,' Nurse Hatton says. 'Truly sorry. And you should be proud of yourself, still trying to smile when I know you're disappointed. I'm very sad that this has happened to you.'

Nora cannot speak, but tries her hardest to communicate her gratitude with her eyes. Nurse Hatton places the note gently on the bed beside her as Nora lifts the last veil of paper. A tiny hand-knitted matinee jacket, smocked and exquisitely edged in crochet, lies with its matching bonnet and mitts on their yellow bed. The soft white mitts appear to be holding a little rose-scented soap. Nora can feel Nurse Hatton watching her as she fingers the mother-of-pearl buttons with their pink, blue and green lustre, her eyes shining; her skin suddenly takes on the glow of pregnancy. She looks up just in time to see the nurse brush away a silent tear.

'How are you feeling about being pregnant?' Nurse Hatton finally ventures.

Nora places her hand on her belly. 'I hated it at first and I just wanted it to go away, but now I feel little flutters and know that the baby's safe, and I'm happy that it didn't die. I'm ashamed that I did . . . you know.'

Nurse Hatton leans forward and gently touches Nora's arm, but Nora tenses and the nurse withdraws it and lowers her head, focusing instead on the gift. 'It's beautiful,' she says. 'I should put it somewhere safe if I were you. Don't let Sister see it or we'll both be in trouble.' She gives a conspiratorial wink as she slides her hand between the bed frame and the mattress. 'Don't be long,' she says with a smile that doesn't quite match her pale face and damp eyes. 'Make sure you get back before anyone notices you're gone.' She briefly touches Nora's shoulder, then leaves her with her thoughts.

Nora holds the tiny garments up to her cheek and strokes them across her face. Their softness feels impossible. She arranges them tenderly on the wrapping paper. She kisses the parcel, silently thanks Mrs Lampeter, then carefully and reverently hides it.

Later, when Nora is in the kitchen peeling vegetables, and still feeding off the pleasure of Mrs Lampeter's thoughtfulness, not only in bringing the gift but also in spending hours making it, an aide comes thundering towards her.

'Jennings! Dormitory. Sister Cummings wants to have a word with you.'

This is enough to put the fear of God into Nora, because from the day she arrived at Hillinghurst, Sister Cummings has seemed to delight in humiliating her at every opportunity. Even the mention of her name makes Nora tremble. She dries her hands and is almost pushed along the corridor by the aide.

Just looking at Sister Cummings's face blotched with rage is enough to tell her that she is about to be made to pay dearly for something.

'Get over here,' Sister Cummings yells, her arms crossed and her eyes flashing. As Nora approaches, her eyes are drawn to her bed, which she had left perfectly made but is now in complete disarray. The mattress is on the other side of the room, and on the bed frame lies the little jacket on its yellow crepe-paper bed, and the bonnet beside it. As Nora glances around, trying to get her fuzzy mind to understand, she sees the mitts and the other bootee on the floor.

'Where did these come from?' Sister Cummings bellows, but before Nora can say anything, Nurse Hatton's voice comes from behind her.

'I put them there. Somebody brought them as a gift for her birthday and I hid them for when the baby comes.'

Nora opens her mouth. 'No, I—'

But Nurse Hatton shoots her a silencing look. 'I put them there,' she says again.

Sister Cummings's hand comes like lightning and the slap sends Nora sideways, almost knocking her off her feet.

'Leave her alone,' shouts Nurse Hatton, rushing to Nora's side and taking her arm. 'Look at her. She's pregnant and she's got nothing and nobody. What's this little gift to you?'

'How dare you? Remember your place,' Sister Cummings hisses, her eyes steel and her face menacing. 'You're finished here, Hatton.' Her voice is low but more threatening than the loudest of shouts.

Nurse Hatton yanks off her cap, releasing a shock of red-blonde hair that tumbles uncontrolled over her shoulders. 'That's fine by me. I don't want to be part of this sadistic circus any more. But you leave her alone. This is not her fault.'

'Jennings, get back to work. Hatton, I'll see you in Matron's office.'

Nora stands rooted to the spot, shaking, feeling the colour draining from every bit of her face except where the slap landed.

'Wake yourself, Jennings. Now!' and a finger points to the doors of the ward.

Nora totters away, hardly knowing where she is going.

The next day Nora watches through the window, tears running down her cheeks and over the angry red welt on her face, as Nurse Hatton walks away. She looks strange in normal clothes, out of uniform. Then, as though she feels Nora's eyes on her, Nurse Hatton turns and gives a little wave, accompanied by a lovely smile and that same conspiratorial wink that warms Nora's heart, even though it does little for her grief. The punishment of four days with just water and a bowl of porridge each day seems nothing compared with the loss of the one person in this place who seemed to care.

Chapter Six

Seven weeks

Nora cannot quite believe that it's Christmas morning and she won't be with her family. Her heart aches with memories of evenings of cutting strips of paper and gluing them together to make streamers, and her mother bringing them cups of cocoa with the warning not to drink it while it's too hot. Carols around the piano; the nativity play in church. The excitement of her father bringing home the Christmas tree. Her mother would put newspapers on the floor to stop the needles getting on the carpet, then she'd hold the tree up straight until her father managed to secure it. Meanwhile Nora would wait, hardly able to contain herself until the box of decorations was opened . . . As she stares out of the window of this soulless room onto the frosty morning below, she can hardly bear the pain. Tears stream down her cheeks. No sound, no real awareness that she is crying; just liquid grief pouring from her eyes.

From here she can see the southern English countryside, its patchwork of fields separated by hedges that have withstood storms and gales over aeons of time. Sturdy oaks are gathered in intimate groups, while sycamores, their sticky buds still under wraps, guard the land even as the north wind punishes them. Soon snow will soften the contours, then finally forsythia will splash the spring with yellow blossom and snowdrops will nod at fairy rings of crocus. *And maybe I'll be home walking with Robert among the bluebells . . .*

A flash of movement draws her eye. Someone is coming up the drive on a motorbike. She blinks. Can it be? Surely not . . . Her heart feels as though it will either stop or burst out of her chest altogether. She blinks again, her hands now flat on the window and her mouth open ready to laugh or scream, she doesn't know which.

Robert parks his bike and alights, unfastening his leather helmet and finger-brushing that wonderful blond hair. He unbuttons his jacket and – *oh my goodness* – he's in army uniform. Her right hand curls itself into a fist. He's going to war, then . . . She can hardly breathe, cannot take her eyes off him as he bends down to take something from the pannier.

Oh, it's a present! He's brought me a present. He's come to take me home. We can be married. It will all be all right . . . Her tears of sadness become liquid joy as her forehead touches the window and she gulps long breaths of relief.

He moves towards the building and out of sight – he'll be coming up the steps. Now he'll be talking to them downstairs. They'll come and get her. She'll be home for Christmas lunch and Mummy will hug her and Daddy will say he's sorry and so will she and they can sort out about the baby and what they're all going to do. Nora feels so weak with happiness and relief that she has to lean against the window for support, hardly aware of the iciness of the glass or her aching back.

But a movement on the path below catches her eye, and Nora turns to look out again. It's Robert and he's running. He jumps back on his bike and roars off. He reaches the gates and is through them in a moment. He is gone. And she is again left behind.

Her heart clenches. What's happening?

As the truth dawns on her, her hands curl into fists and start hammering on the window. 'No! Robert! Come back! Robert!' she cries, but he neither hears nor sees her and she slumps down to her knees, her face squashed up against the glass. She weeps with a heart-wrenching sound that is more animal than human, and eventually subsides into a whimper. 'Robert . . .'

The fresh young face of the new probationer nurse, Jamison, bends over her. 'What's wrong?' she asks urgently, and Nora clutches at her hand.

'Robert . . . he was here, I saw him. What happened? Why did he leave?' She looks back at the window, keening that inhuman sound again, her hands trailing on the glass as if to try to catch him and bring him back.

'You're not allowed visitors,' Nurse Jamison says with a gentle voice, glancing around as if hoping that someone will tell her what to do.

Nora slumps to the floor, desolate, tears still pouring from her closed eyes. She is back to that night – that one and only night that she could have conceived. It was such a brief but wonderful encounter, when a kiss led them so rapidly from adolescent dreaming to adult desire. Neither of them had thought beyond that one delicious snatched hour. Would she change it if she could? Deny herself the joy of having been kissed, held, touched? And that painful but wondrous moment when he became part of her? No.

'Jennings, get up!' someone barks, then turns to Nurse Jamison, who is crying softly. 'And you – go and sort yourself out.'

Nora doesn't move, even though she's already learned to jump when anyone shouts. They can do what they like to her now. Nothing matters any more. A strong hand grips her wrist then her arm is yanked and she is on her knees. 'Get up!' Too exhausted to even be afraid, Nora allows herself to be dragged towards a chair where the hand lets go of her arm and a foot pushes against her knee. She slumps like a rag doll. Nothing really matters now.

Minutes pass, with Nora immobile in some far-off place where there is neither pain nor thought nor time – just a state of nothingness. And when she eventually opens her eyes, it's to face a horrible new reality. He isn't coming for her. She lets out a howl of anger. But Nurse Jamison's words – 'You're not allowed visitors' – ring in her mind, and the fury dissipates as quickly as it arrived. It wasn't his fault. He would have come to see her if he could. So, when eventually she is allowed visitors, he'll come . . . and so will her mother . . .

Then she sees him again in her mind's eye, leaving, only now realising that he wasn't carrying the present.

Chapter Seven

Five months

Nora shuffles towards Dr Mason's office, her footsteps faithfully following those of the aide, with her odd posture and her arms swinging at a strange angle. Nora, too, has acquired a gait that she'd never quite understood in pregnant women before she was one herself – inclined slightly backwards, supporting her aching lower back with her hands and allowing her swollen belly to lead the way. She allows herself a glance out of the windows. The short, dark days have given way to lighter evenings, and April showers are the order of the day. She hopes her mother will be enjoying the spring spectacle – the magnolia tree from the kitchen window and the camellias, browning now as the morning sun warms them too quickly.

As the months have passed, a sense of acceptance has settled within Nora, alongside the endless grief. Her main concern is that her baby must be coming soon, though no one will answer her questions. Nurse Hatton would have done.

Just as she approaches Dr Mason's door, the baby kicks and she holds her hand lovingly to the tiny knee that protrudes. Her mind returns yet again to the fact that she has no idea what preparations should be made for the arrival of a baby. She often thinks of the family joy around the birth of her cousin's first child a couple of years ago – the tiny pink newborn, her little body dressed in clothes that had been so lovingly made for her – and, whenever she does, waves of sadness threaten to engulf her. She'll be the only one truly welcoming this baby. But that means that she must make it as special as she can. She'd have liked to knit some things, but she's not allowed to use knitting needles any more. Never mind. At least there'll be Mrs Lampeter's matinee jacket. She frowns. Surely they'll give it back to her when the baby comes.

Dr Mason's door opens into the familiar office and, as always, her eyes go first to her ballerina still standing there awaiting the music. Her heart yearns to run to the desk and turn the key and make her dance one more time. *One day ...*

Dr Mason sits behind his desk and, unusually, one of the chairs at this side of the desk is occupied. Nora draws a breath as she recognises the reed straightness of the back, the tilt of the head, the hair tucked under the maroon felt hat. She feels a surge of disappointment. Why is she here? Something must be wrong. Has someone died? Nora swallows loudly. She makes a quick tour through shock, dread, hope and fear, then she pauses, collecting herself and trying to settle her racing heart, whose frantic beating feels as though it should be visible through her smock. *Show no emotion, Nora.*

'Come in, Nora.' Dr Mason gestures towards the empty chair. 'You have a visitor. Come. Sit.'

Mrs Lampeter turns slightly and Nora hopes that her eyes don't betray her lingering sadness that her visitor is not her mother. If Mrs Lampeter does see it, she's kind enough not to show it, though her eyes are uncertain and sad. Nora's few steps to the chair feel as though she's wading through a swamp. *Am I allowed to speak?* She's learned to check out everything for permission; anything spontaneous can have painful repercussions. She looks at Dr Mason, hoping to find an answer.

'Hello, Miss Nora.' Mrs Lampeter's attempt at a smile is only partially successful, but Nora finds herself smiling in a way she hasn't for months.

'Hello, Mrs Lampeter.' She can hear her voice an octave lower than it used to be, but still soft and warm, and allows herself a second of something akin to pride that she hasn't lost her manners. The look and the moment linger between them, and Nora mentally hugs this woman with all her might, though her hands remain securely clasped in her lap. She can feel Mrs Lampeter leaning towards her even though she hasn't moved, and between them the love flows as it always did. For the first time in what seems like years, Nora feels whole.

Dr Mason clears his throat, almost as though he's aware that he's witnessing something deeply intimate that part of him at least doesn't want to interrupt. But he does so regardless. 'It is our usual policy to allow no visits until people are settled, and then only from family members. However, since there has been no attempt by any family member to see you—' words uttered so carelessly that Nora gasps and feels her heart will stop beating from the pain – 'and since Mrs Lampeter assures me that she's a good friend of the family, I've decided to grant her visiting rights.'

'Thank you,' Nora whispers.

'Mrs Lampeter has visited several times,' Dr Mason says, 'and she has written letter after letter asking to see you. I hope you will be very grateful for her persistence.' Nora hears him talking but nothing he's saying seems important right now. Mrs Lampeter is here and that's all that matters. But still he drones on. 'And for her friendship, which, in the circumstances, you are lucky not to have lost.' He fixes Nora with a stern frown.

Nora lowers her eyes. He cannot possibly know how she feels about this woman, who has been a fact of her life throughout all her life. She has protected and cherished her, noted her joys and her ills; prompted her to put away her toys; changed her bed when she wet it without betraying her to her father and his belt. How this woman has loved her like a mother, yet never dropped the respectful 'Miss' from her name. He cannot know how Nora's heart aches that she has betrayed this woman just as much as she has betrayed her parents and Robert, and how moved she is that, despite all of this, she is here.

'Thank you, Dr Mason,' she whispers again, and though Mrs Lampeter doesn't move a muscle, Nora can feel her hand gripping her own in reassurance, just as it has done in the past on the mornings of exams, on the days after Nora had been disciplined by her father, as it probably would have loved to do on the morning she brought the quinine.

'Yes, well . . . You can use the family room,' says Dr Mason, springing open his pocket watch. 'Half an hour. My secretary will show you the way.' He raises his hand and Nora flinches, but it merely lands sharply on the little brass bell. They are dismissed.

Nora's heart accompanies the little ballerina in a joyful pirouette, and a smile that she dares not reveal glows within her. 'Thank you,' she and Mrs Lampeter say in unison, neither daring to look at the other yet. They follow the middle-aged secretary to the room and Nora, excited at the prospect of half an hour of freedom, lets her hand gently brush Mrs Lampeter's coat for an instant.

The family room is surprisingly pleasant. At the centre of the mantel stands a photograph of King George VI in splendid Garter robes, and a tall window looks out onto the garden, where the trees are waving proudly in their pale and youthful foliage. The sight of the vase of forsythia resting on the black marble hearth makes tears well up in Nora's eyes – such beauty doesn't belong in this godforsaken place. The door closes behind them. She stands like a child in the middle of the room and puts out her arms to Mrs Lampeter, who softly, tenderly, encloses Nora in a motherly hug. She hasn't felt this well for what seems like a lifetime.

'Miss Nora—'

'Mrs Lampeter—' they begin simultaneously, then smile, pause and wait. Mrs Lampeter sits on one of the chairs by the fireside and Nora follows to sit on the other, though she wishes there was not such a distance between them. She sinks down into the overstuffed leather armchair and has to hold in a groan of pleasure. Only now does she realise how uncomfortable the stiff, wooden chairs she has become used to are.

'How are you, Miss Nora?'

Nora can see Mrs Lampeter's gaze taking in her short, uneven, lifeless hair that once was a cascade of shining chestnut curls. As well as the dark shadows under her eyes. Nora pictures the sore place on her cheek where she feels she has a bruise. But since she has no access to a mirror, she has no idea really what she looks like now – not that she would be able to do anything about it anyway. She also knows that apart from her huge baby bump, she's much thinner, and of course her hands are cracked and red and bleeding. Though she knows it is vanity, she blushes, ashamed that Mrs Lampeter is seeing her like this.

'I'm all right . . . Don't worry about me,' Nora says, but she knows she will. 'More importantly, how are you? How is my mother? And my father? And Robert?' The questions tumble out all at once.

'They're all fine.' Mrs Lampeter hesitates. 'They all miss you, I'm sure.'

'Do they know you're here?'

'No, Miss Nora. I thought it best not to say.' Nora's eyes fall to her lap as she struggles to hold back her tears. Mrs Lampeter breaks the silence with a quavering voice. 'I'm so sorry about the tablets, Miss Nora.'

'No, Mrs Lampeter,' Nora says, reaching across to touch her friend's sleeve. 'You were so kind. Please don't be sorry. And thank you for the beautiful matinee coat and the bonnet and bootees.' She could never tell her that they, too, became an instrument of deprivation and loss.

'Miss Nora, there's something I want to tell you.' Mrs Lampeter sits upright and takes a deep breath, preparing herself as she meets Nora's questioning face. 'Me and my Pat was pregnant when we got married. It was early, and everyone thought our Jess must be a honeymoon baby, but she wasn't. It doesn't mean you're wicked, Miss Nora. You have to forget that. I wouldn't want it to happen to my girls, and I'm sad that it happened to you. But all this . . .' She looks around and waves a hand to indicate everything. 'This is terrible. I don't think God wanted any of this to happen just because you made a slip.'

Nora's eyes remain in her lap, and the tears spill over.

'Might it help if you told them who the father is?' Mrs Lampeter suggests tentatively. 'He could marry you and it would be all right.'

Nora shakes her head firmly. 'I can't do that, Mrs Lampeter.' Her voice cracks and she turns away.

'Don't fret, Miss Nora. When is the baby ... ?' but Mrs Lampeter's voice trails away as Nora looks down in embarrassment and confusion and sees the liquid forming a pool around her feet. 'Oh, I'm sorry,' she says. 'I'm so sorry.'

Mrs Lampeter reaches out to grip Nora's hand. 'Nora, it's all right. Your waters have broken, that's all. Let me get somebody.' And she's out of her chair and calls from the doorway. 'Please, someone help.' Then she's back at Nora's side, holding her hand, smoothing her brow. 'Your baby's coming soon, that's all. It's going to be fine.' Her voice is soothing and, though Nora continues to clutch the arm of the chair, she hasn't missed the dropping of the formal 'Miss' and a flood of gratitude almost drowns out the pain.

The burly aide arrives at the door and takes in the scene. 'Come with me,' she barks at Nora. 'And you – you'd better go.' Mrs Lampeter takes Nora's arm and helps her up. 'Didn't you hear me?' The aide's voice is rough.

'Please, let me stay,' Mrs Lampeter begs.

'Absolutely not. You need to leave now.'

Nora's hand clutches at Mrs Lampeter. 'Please don't go.'

'Now!' The aide's face is like thunder. 'Or you'll have your visiting rights withdrawn.'

'But I want to—'

'Now!'

Mrs Lampeter watches helplessly as the nurse bustles Nora out of the door. 'I'll come back as soon as I can,' she calls, her voice thick with tears.

Nora looks back and, despite the encroaching fear of what is to come, all she can think is: when will she see her friend again?

Chapter Eight

A searing pain takes Nora's breath away and she gasps for air. 'What's happening to me?' she says, her voice strangled.

'You're having a baby, that's all,' the aide says dismissively. 'Stop making such a fuss.'

Another pain assaults Nora and a sound emerges from her throat that she hardly recognises as her own. She wants her mother, Mrs Lampeter, anyone. But the aide looks ahead while Nora's eyes fix on the dreaded stark white sign jutting into the corridor: TREATMENT ROOM. She shivers. Though she's never been to this room, she hasn't escaped the stories and screams that come from within, nor the sight of people being wheeled out after shock treatment with red marks on their foreheads and rubber gags still between their teeth. Her heart fills with terror as she is pushed over the threshold. No natural light and a four-lamped contraption that is a perverse caricature of a chandelier. Brown leather straps, complete with buckles, emerge from the sides and corners at the foot of the iron-framed bed. A wheeled trolley holds an array of instruments and bottles. Two shiny kidney bowls. A metal pail on the floor at the foot of the bed.

Sister Beatrice Cummings is checking a pile of towels and sheets. She glances at Nora, who shivers at the idea that this woman – who, ever since the incident with Nurse Hatton and the baby clothes, has gone out of her way to make her life miserable – will be presiding over the birth of her child.

'Let's have a look at you and see what's happening,' says Sister Cummings, not bothering to meet Nora's eyes. She motions to the young probationer, Nurse Jamison, to help get Nora onto the bed. 'Get her a gown. This baby might not be far away.' She turns her back and puts on a face mask and then dons surgical gloves.

Nurse Donaldson does likewise. 'Take off your knickers and open your legs.' Nora's eyes move from one to the other of these three women, mortified by her sodden underwear, but she does as she's told. Hands move roughly about her belly and then grip above her pelvis. 'Head's engaged,' Sister Cummings announces to no one in particular. Rough fingers enter Nora and move quickly. She gulps and grasps handfuls of the sheet, but fights against herself to hold still and feels immeasurably relieved as the hand is removed. Sister Cummings takes off her gloves. 'Shave and OBE and be quick about it.'

Another spike of pain wracks Nora's body. Her eyes search the room for any relief but there is none to be had. Sister Cummings places her hand on Nora's belly and checks her watch. The women are busy around her and Nora looks on, watching as much as she can from her disadvantaged position. She daren't ask questions, having learned by now to say no more than absolutely necessary.

Her body is moved, her knees bent and a razor pulls at her pubic hair. It scratches her delicate skin, the numerous nicks leaving her stinging and making her wince. Fingers open her, stretch her and scrape away at places that have only twice before been touched by hands other than hers – once with loving tenderness and once in mortifying examination. Embarrassment seems as pointless as complaint and Nora lies there, numb. A small glass of warm castor oil is shoved towards her and a hand helps lift her shoulder so she can manage a drink. The smell of the oil immediately raises bile in her throat and Nora turns her head away.

'Take it all in one gulp,' says Nurse Jamison gently, with a surreptitious glance at Sister Cummings's back. 'That's the best way.' Nora complies but retches, her eyes streaming. 'Well done,' whispers the nurse, though her eyes shift immediately to Sister Cummings, who thankfully seems occupied with Nora's notes and has neither seen nor heard this lapse of protocol.

Another contraction wracks Nora's body and she whimpers, clutching the sides of the bed. Sister Cummings, her hand again on Nora's swollen abdomen, checks her watch. A flurry of activity involving a metal basin, a funnel, a large jug and red rubber tubing comes to a sudden halt and a wobbly trolley arrives at the bottom of the bed. Nurse Jamison squeezes Nora's arm.

'Nora, this won't hurt, I promise,' she says, and a second later Nora gasps as something is pushed into her anus. One of the nurses holds the funnel on high and starts to pour in warm, soapy water. The following minutes fill her with more disgust and embarrassment than she thought possible. As the smell of faeces fills the air, she wishes for the first time that she were dead.

'I'm so sorry,' she says and closes her eyes, just as the next contraction starts its swell to an inconceivable climax of pain. She screams and places her hand on her belly, urging her baby to be patient, to be healthy and whole. She tries to think of her mother but memories of that beloved face refuse to surface. She closes her eyes, turns her head and prays to become invisible.

Someone lifts her to the sitting position as another contraction comes, and Sister Cummings issues abrupt instructions to her team to let her examine Nora again before they move her to the bath.

'I need to go to the toilet,' Nora pants.

'No, you don't.'

'I do,' says Nora, squirming on the bed. 'Please let me go to the toilet.'

'Lie down.' Sister Cummings's hand presses Nora back down onto the bed and once again forces her legs open to examine her. 'Get her next door to the bath, quickly,' she says, 'or this baby will be born there.'

Though there's comfort in the warm, soapy water, Nora's nails cut into Nurse Jamison's arm as she grabs for support, while the next contraction appears to change direction and grasp the top of her womb, then drag its way down her belly. She screams. Nurse Jamison hands her a towel. 'Let's get you out quickly, Nora.' She helps Nora dry herself and gives her a clean gown.

'Now you'll regret what you did,' a voice whispers in her ear. 'Was it worth it, you little slut?' Nora starts and looks around to see Sister Cummings staring down at her with loathing on her face. Even through the pain, a shiver of horror makes its way down her spine at the cruelty of this so-called nurse. *Why does she hate me so?*

Sister Cummings pulls Nora's hands down to her sides and forces her wrists into the leather restraints. She straps her ankles with her feet up on plates on metal rods that have been screwed to the bed. Nora's back arches in frenzied frustration.

'I need to move,' she gasps.

'Well, you can't.' Sister Cummings is between her legs again. 'Lie still.' But the next pain is too much to bear and Nora screams and lifts her buttocks off the bed, bucking away from Sister Cummings's hands. The slap on her inner thigh is swift and hard but is lost in the next scream, charged and looped, careening into the walls, slicing the air. Then breathless moments, before the next seismic crescendo of pain, her whole being trembling, the visceral torture exacerbated by being tethered to the bed. She suddenly feels a white-hot wave of rage towards Robert. *Why didn't you tell them? Why didn't you come for us? Why? You said you loved me. You should be here.* She will use this surge of energy to birth this baby that will be hers and hers alone, no matter how they were abandoned.

'Lie still,' someone snaps. But the next pain is already coming and Nora screams out again, pulling on the restraints and shaking her head from side to side. Nurse Jamison clutches Nora's hand in warning, but not quickly enough, and another blow from Sister Cummings fills Nora with fury.

'Get off me,' she screams, and the next slap strikes across her face and makes her freeze.

'Control yourself.' Cummings's voice is cold and harsh. 'You got yourself into this situation and now you have to deal with it. Shut up and do as you're told.' Tears of impotent rage stream down from Nora's eyes and pool in her ears as she clenches her teeth and the urge to push comes with the next contraction.

'Don't push yet!'

Nora imagines her baby making its way out into the world and wonders whether it's a boy or a girl, though what does it matter as long as it gets here safely? She mustn't do anything that will impede its progress. She must do as she's told and so, with the next contraction, she steels herself to be still and quiet and to breathe rather than push.

Oh, my goodness. How can I not push? And right on cue comes the command and the permission. 'Push!' She bears down, a groan escaping through her clenched teeth. 'Now, one more big one.'

'You can do it, Nora,' Nurse Jamison urges, seemingly having forgotten Sister Cummings's presence. And, as the next wave of pain comes, Nora pushes with all her might. She feels herself rip, but she no longer matters. *Just let my baby be safe.*

'The head's out.' Someone thrusts a cloth into Sister Cummings's bloody glove. She places her hand on Nora's belly and waits a second or two and, feeling the next contraction start to gather, she says, 'Last push, Jennings. Now!' There's a squelching sound and a sudden rush and then silence. No one seems to be breathing. No one says a word and the seconds tick by. Nora's eyes dart around, her neck aching as she cranes to see.

'Is my baby all right?' she gasps.

'Yes,' Sister Cummings says tersely and, after what seems an age, the baby's cries fill the room. Nora breathes and tries to lift her arms, but they are still restrained. 'Can I hold it? Is it a boy or a girl?' There's no response and anxiety rises in her throat. She pulls again against the restraints. 'Is something the matter?' she whimpers, but again no one answers. She cranes her neck and sees Nurse Jamison carrying a bundle towards the door. 'Can I hold my baby? Please let me hold my baby?' She pulls against the restraints, but is distracted by another hand on her belly and a softness emerging between her legs as the placenta delivers. *Ah, that's what they were waiting for.* She sighs with relief. *Now they'll let me have my baby.* She breathes and waits. 'Please, someone, give me my baby.'

*　　*　　*

Two hours later, Nora sleeps fitfully in the dormitory, exhausted both from the birth and begging to see her child.

Nurse Jamison slips quietly into the sluice. How cold it feels. The baby lies uncovered on the cold slab. Nurse Jamison tiptoes towards her. She knows she'll be in big trouble if anyone sees her here. She can hardly breathe with the horror of it. The baby is perfect, beautiful, but, as her thin little chest rises and falls, her abdomen sucks in. She is in respiratory distress. Tears spout from Nurse Jamison's eyes and she puts a hand to her mouth, then reaches out to touch the baby. What can she do? Who should she tell? Is it a mistake that it is here, cold and alone? But she knows absolutely that it is not. The child has been left here to die.

'Nurse. What are you doing there?' Sister Cummings's harsh voice comes from the doorway.

'I-I thought it would be adopted,' she stammers.

'The children of moral defectives are likely to be defective themselves,' Sister Cummings says coldly. 'This is none of your business. I'll see you in my office in fifteen minutes.'

'But, the mother—'

'The mother has no rights here. I will see you in my office in fifteen minutes. Now go.'

'But—'

'Jamison! Go and blow your nose and pull yourself together. Fifteen minutes.' She holds the door open pointedly.

Nurse Jamison stares into Cummings's eyes and for just a moment imagines standing up to this monster. But the chill of the cruelty she sees there kills this fantasy, just as surely as Sister Cummings is killing Nora's baby. Nurse Jamison lowers her eyes and, ashamed, walks away. Sister Cummings follows, closing the door behind her.

Chapter Nine

The sharpness of the knock on the door surprises Dr Mason. Only one person would dare to knock like that. This young doctor is hard work. He sighs. 'Come in,' he calls, his exasperation at yet another interruption creeping into his voice, while his attention remains with the piles of patient notes, overdue reports and letters to colleagues scattered on his desk.

'Dr Mason.' Dr Stilworth's tone is urgent, his breathing rasping with anger as he limps in and supports himself by resting his hands on the desk.

'Yes, Dr Stilworth. What is it? It had better be worth interrupting me for.' Dr Mason's mouth is set and he deliberately focuses his attention on screwing the cap on his fountain pen, though he cannot ignore his junior's distress or the effort it appears to be taking to control his anger.

'Dr Mason, I need to talk to you about Miss Jennings's baby.'

'What about it?' He watches the heat rise up Dr Stilworth's neck, leaving a tell-tale sheen of sweat. 'Sit down, man.'

But Dr Stilworth remains standing, clinging not only to the desk but also to his anger and his dignity. 'I understand that, at Sister Cummings's order, the child was left uncovered on the slab in the sluice and died there. I've heard of such things happening, of course, but for it to be one of my patients . . . It amounts to infanticide.'

Dr Mason lifts his eyes. 'That's a harsh term, doctor. Please, sit down. You have much to learn.'

Dr Stilworth trembles with fury. 'Is there another term that could be used for this barbaric act?'

'Doctor, sit down,' Dr Mason repeats, shaking out a

handkerchief and beginning to clean his spectacles with slow, circular movements, still avoiding his junior's gaze. He places them on his nose and finally looks directly at Dr Stilworth. 'I'm sure you've read Mr Darwin, and also Mr Churchill, D.H. Lawrence and the many other eminent scholars who have written on the subject of the hereditability of the gene that causes morally defective behaviour?'

Dr Stilworth bristles but says nothing.

'I am in agreement with Mr Churchill and his goal to improve the British race, and prevent delinquent behaviour from affecting society at large. And though indeed it's very sad, we must do our best to contain the situation. Those who may already be infected – like this child – well, for the sake of her, who may have suffered dreadfully in life, for the mother and for all of us, this is the best route.'

Unable to hold himself back any longer, Dr Stilworth explodes. 'To be murdered?'

'Dr Stilworth! Take control of yourself. What would have been gained by allowing this creature to live?'

Dr Stilworth stares, incredulous. 'A creature?' His voice descends to a whisper and he swallows loudly. 'It was a perfectly formed little—'

'Doctor!' The imperious voice stops Dr Stilworth in his tracks. 'Remember your position and maintain some decorum. The child was not murdered. Nature was simply allowed to take its course.'

'The baby died of neglect – and hypothermia,' Dr Stilworth storms, then pauses to collect himself. 'This tiny newborn . . . on a cold marble slab in an unheated sluice on a cold spring evening, gasping until it could gasp no more. You surely cannot condone that?'

Dr Mason, his face now almost puce, hammers his fist on the desk. 'Doctor, let us not forget that the mother had already attempted to abort this child – that is, to kill it! Who knows what serious damage such a large dose of quinine may have caused to the foetus?'

Dr Stilworth's mouth is dry and his heart pounds in his chest. 'That's right. We don't know, but we seem to have assumed—'

'Doctor!' Dr Mason thunders. This young man's behaviour is insupportable, and Dr Mason is shocked that even now he will not be silenced.

'We made an oath – to do no harm,' Dr Stilworth continues relentlessly. 'How can this ever be acceptable? She was only hours old but she still had rights, for God's sake. I really must protest in the strongest terms.'

Dr Stilworth finally stops, breathing hard. Dr Mason watches as the fight slowly drains out of his opponent, and he feels a flash of compassion. He remembers that kind of passion from his own youth. However, he must win this battle or else risk anarchy. 'Dr Stilworth, protest away to your heart's content. But close the door as you leave.' He retrieves his pen, briskly unscrews the gold cap and begins to write.

Chapter Ten

In the Hillinghurst grounds, blossoms nod prettily and birds share their song beneath a bright clear sky, but Rowan ward reflects none of the beauty of May. Nora sits amidst the moans and mutterings, outbursts and blasphemies, and the smell of urine that permeates everything, weeping as she has these last three weeks since she gave birth. She has shrunk into herself, her neck buried between her shoulders that hunch forward to form a cocoon of protection for her broken heart. Her head droops to her chest, her hair matted with fragments of her last meal – and maybe also the one before that – and food spatters her green smock. Tight binding flattens her breasts, smothering their natural desire to produce milk for the baby who no longer requires it. Her knees are spread, her feet folding inward until her toes touch as if she, herself, were a foetus.

In the beginning her wailing would be tolerated for a short while before she was yelled at or slapped into silence. Now she's quiet much of the time, though now and then heart-rending grief bursts into the ward, disturbing patients and staff alike. 'It's like the racket on the night they take calves away from their mothers,' someone grumbles.

Peggy Hart watches from her seat by the window, her saggy face sad, her mouth set in a down-turned line that extends into the jowls hanging from her jaw. Her eyes are fogged with cataracts and her mind clouded by age, but Nora's pain takes her back to her own monumental struggle just to breathe after her own baby was taken. Day after day trying merely to survive so that some day she'd find him. Of course, she never did. And now, most of the time, she manages to cope by being numb. But this girl . . . this poor girl . . .

Peggy has looked on as various members of staff have demanded that Nora shut up, get up, clean up, wash up. At first the girl's food was taken away untouched, but now they're forcing her and Peggy can't stand having to see it – to have to watch this girl being humiliated and abused. She wishes she could help.

So, just as she did yesterday, and may well do again tomorrow, and the next day and the next, Peggy levers herself out of the chair and pauses, a comma of humanity. She yanks up her lisle stockings, keeping her eyes on the girl. She shuffles across the ward until she stands directly in front of the unseeing Nora, and watches, occasionally shifting her weight from one leg to the other. After fifteen minutes or so, she shuffles back to her usual place by the window and eases herself back into her chair.

Today Peggy has been watching since breakfast time and Nora hasn't moved a muscle for over an hour. Peggy limps painfully across to stand before her. She's breathing – that's good. Maybe she's asleep. Peggy holds out a hand to check, but then withdraws it. If she's asleep, she doesn't want to wake her. At least she's not making any fuss today, so she'll likely be safe.

'Are you asleep?' Peggy whispers, but there's no response and, after a few minutes of shuffling foot to foot, she makes her way back to her chair.

Next day, Peggy once again stands before Nora, shuffling her feet, pulling at her hair, her mouth chewing. 'Nora . . . ?' Peggy has found out her name from Mr Warwick. 'I'm Peggy.' The silence hangs between them for a moment, then, furtively looking around in case anyone is listening in, Peggy asks, 'What happened to your baby?'

Nora flinches and Peggy waits. A slick of saliva makes its way from the corner of her mouth, down her chin and finally onto her smock. 'Where's your baby?'

Nothing.

Nora's body remains very still, then, just as Peggy starts to turn away, Nora opens her eyes though her head remains sagged between her shoulders. 'They took it away,' she whispers, and a tear rolls down her cheek and drips off her chin.

'Where did they take it?'

'I don't know,' Nora rasps, and tears now run silently down her face to pool on the floor between her feet.

Peggy sways back and forth then shuffles away, leaving Nora to her grief.

It's almost lunchtime the next day when Peggy makes it across to Nora, who weeps silently in her chair. She stands for a while just watching, head cocked on one side and her brow furrowed.

'Do you want to play draughts?' Peggy whispers. 'Or dominoes?'

But Nora isn't up to playing games.

By the next morning, Peggy is more agitated than ever. She sits in her chair, rocking back and forth, then hauls herself up. One of her slippers doesn't seem to want to stay put so she shuffles along, sliding her right foot to keep the offending slipper on. After a few steps she lets it go and proceeds with one foot bare. She pulls at Nora's sleeve.

'Nora, you have to eat. You have to look OK. If you don't, they'll say you're really sick and then bad things happen.' She pauses and watches, then pulls on Nora's sleeve again. 'Nora, you have to be all right.'

'I'm not all right,' Nora moans.

Peggy bends closer. 'I know. But if you tell them you're all right and let them see you're all right they'll leave you alone.' Nora's neck remains bent, like the stalk of a dying flower. 'Nora, you have to. You don't want them to give you treatment.'

'Go away.' Nora slips into disconsolate sobbing, while Peggy, unsure of what to do, wrings her hands until, after a while, she trudges back to her window.

Suddenly, there's a flurry of activity as two nursing aides march down the ward. Peggy, standing by her window, starts to panic, and she grabs at her chest, pain etched on her face. Her knees wobble and she clings to the window frame, a low moaning sound escaping on her breath. *Please don't let them hurt her.* She steadies herself, her back against the cool glass, and takes long breaths. Dry sobs wrack her body and her shoulders tremble. *Nora, they'll hurt you. Sit up. Be all right.*

Without a word, the two burley aides, one male and one female, tie Nora's hands to the chair with old bandages. She pulls against the restraints, a futile act that the staff completely ignore. A piece of mutton cloth is tied around her neck to act as a bib. And then it begins. Peggy lowers her head, tears trickling down her cheeks. She can't bear to watch.

Nora thrashes around, desperate to avoid the spoon. Food splatters everywhere. The two aides continue until one of them, now with a glob of food on her cheek, snaps. At some silent signal, they move in unison. The man clamps one hand to each side of Nora's head to hold it straight while the woman prepares a spoon of mashed-up food. Then she holds Nora's nose until she has no choice but to open her mouth to breathe. She forces the spoon home and dumps the contents into Nora's mouth. Nora gags and dollops of mush erupt from her mouth. A hand clamps over it until she has no choice but to swallow, and now coughing erupts, spraying spit and porridge everywhere. Her wrists, red and sore from previous similar episodes, jerk on the restraints, and she squirms in the chair, inadvertently kicking the female aide who stiffens and looks intently at the man.

'Warwick,' she yells, and Stan comes hurrying down the ward. Everyone feels the shift in pace and urgency. Patients start to mutter, moan, wail and stamp their feet. Some of the women shield their faces, while others just look away. One of them prays out loud. Those tied to their chairs twist and turn, wrenching on restraints, rattling buckles, rocking back and forth, beating a loud tattoo on the wooden floorboards. Those with unrestrained feet kick. One straitjacketed woman starts to scream. Peggy pulls her hair, shifting her weight from one foot to the other. It sounds like Bedlam.

Before Stan can reach the harassed group, Nora kicks out again. Peggy wants to scream. *Nora, for God's sake, just eat.*

'Can I try?' he asks. But the aides are not about to relinquish their authority now.

'Just hold her feet,' the man barks. Stan goes reluctantly down on his knees in front of Nora and holds her ankles.

'Nora,' he croons. 'Come on, Nora. You have to eat something.'

'Look, you little bitch,' spits the woman. 'You're going to eat this, no matter how long it takes us.'

And with Stan gripping her feet, someone steadying her head, and her eyes as tightly shut as she would like her mouth to remain, the battle continues. She hardly has time to swallow before they stuff her mouth full again, and from time to time it looks as though she'll choke. She writhes about and bites down on the spoon. Then, as it's forced from between her teeth and back again, she accidently sinks her teeth into the finger of the hand torturing her. A vicious slap across her head makes her neck snap backwards, and the half-empty bowl of slop falls to the floor, splattering Nora's smock, her hair, her face and also the staff.

A rough hand pulls on the knot of the bib and wipes Nora's face with it, smearing food and saliva everywhere. Then the restraints are untied and they haul Nora out of the chair. She slips in the mess on the floor, stumbles and falls, crying out in pain. The male aide grabs a handful of the back of her smock, and with it some of her hair, and drags her along the floor towards the isolation room. Stan looks on in dismay and some-one appears with a bucket and mop.

Peggy pulls her hair as a hissing sound emerges from between her clenched teeth.

The next morning, Nora is not in her usual place. It's almost eight o'clock and Peggy is frantic, tugging at her hair with her dirty nails, plucking at her smock, picking off imaginary fluff. She drops her head into her hands and starts to scratch her scalp until it bleeds.

Stan watches from the nurses' station and elbows his old friend, Gladys, who is busy beside him. These two have nursed together for almost ten years and they've seen some dreadful things, but it never gets any easier to witness. 'Gladys. Have you seen Peggy?' They both look across at Peggy, who has been here since before they came as probationers all those years ago. Without a word, Gladys puts down the laundry she's holding and makes her way to Peggy's side.

'Peggy,' the voice is kind and motherly even though Peggy is twenty years her senior. Peggy stops scratching her scalp and sits perfectly still, her hands, bloody now, still in her hair.

Gladys, round and homely, bends down until her head is level with Peggy's and gently lifts her hands out of the tangled mass of her hair and places them in her lap. 'Peggy, what's the matter?'

'What have they done with Nora?'

'Now Peggy, don't get in such a state,' Gladys cajoles. 'She needed some time alone. She's fine. Don't worry. She'll be back on the ward soon.'

'Is she having shocks?' Peggy whispers tremulously.

'No, Peggy. She isn't,' says Gladys, but Peggy continues to peer at her suspiciously. 'She'll be back, Peggy,' Gladys reassures her again. 'Don't worry. Will I bring you a cup of tea?'

Peggy doesn't answer but Gladys waddles off to make some tea anyway.

The smell of urine is unmistakable when Dr Stilworth enters the isolation room. He surveys the scene in dismay and anger rises within him like fire. The only item in this padded, windowless cell is a stained mattress lying diagonally across the floor of the room. Nora lies prostrate upon it. She's naked – God forbid that she should eat her clothing or strangle herself with a sheet! But at least she isn't straitjacketed, he thinks.

Nora's hair is matted and her face caked with yesterday's slop, and a wave of shame washes over Dr Stilworth. This woman is hardly recognisable as the beautiful girl he met that first morning just a few months ago. *What have we done?* He wants to scream and shout and bang his fists, rip away the brass observation peephole with its welded peg on the inside of the door that prevents the cover from being removed. No wonder those who are trapped in here behave as they do, regardless of the threat of further punishment. How can they win?

He struggles down on his knees beside Nora, trying to somehow screen her nakedness with his body, and his fury synthesises into two words that now roar out from him. 'Sister Cummings!'

Sister Cummings arrives and stands in the doorway, seemingly unruffled by the angry summons. Dr Stilworth wonders which is the greater assault on his senses: the smell of urine, or the floral perfume the sister is wearing in the presence of this poor wretch of a human being for whom she is supposed to care.

'Yes, Dr Stilworth?' Her beautiful face with its sharp blue eyes has a spiteful, haughty air that makes Tom shiver. *And I'm a doctor. What about the patients?*

'Why is Miss Jennings here?' he demands.

'Miss Jennings,' says Sister Cummings, pausing to allow her sarcastic tone to register with this young pup who hardly knows his way around the institution and dares to question her authority, 'Miss Jennings violently assaulted one of my staff.'

'How did she do that, Sister?' he asks.

'She bit her.'

Dr Stilworth pauses, sure he can't have heard correctly. 'Bit her?'

'Yes, Miss Jennings here was resisting being fed and bit one of my aides.'

'Why was she being fed?'

'She's refused food almost every day since . . . these last three weeks or so, and she's lost weight, so now she has no choice in the matter. She will be fed.'

'And how was she being fed, Sister Cummings?'

'As we always feed people, Dr Stilworth,' she retorts, her eyes holding his with a taunting glimmer.

'Yes, I've seen that a couple of times. If you were to try to feed me like that, I would bite too,' says Dr Stilworth, struggling to remain professional. 'Sister, I want her bathed and dressed – *gently*,' he orders, 'and please wash her hair and then return her to her own bed in the dormitory.' He stands up. 'Then please call me and bring her some tea and toast with butter. Her lack of appetite is caused by grief, not defiance, and she should not be treated in this way.' His eyes are cold but their depths hold fury longing to erupt, and this is enough, at last, to silence Sister Cummings, who watches him as he limps out of the room without a backward glance, anger punctuating every painful step.

But it's not over. Sister Cummings is furious, too. There's a hierarchy to be respected and she will make sure he learns that. As she moves back into the ward, her lips thin and tight, with a snarl ready to erupt at a moment's notice, the staff are prepared. When she's in this most implacable of moods, anything could happen. Someone will have to pay for this humiliation – and it won't just be Tom Stilworth.

Dr Stilworth limps along the corridor towards Dr Mason's office, cursing the disability that prevents him from marching in with his head held high. He knew it wouldn't be long until news of yesterday's debacle reached his boss, and sure enough the summons came as soon as he got in this morning. He knocks at the door ready for a showdown, whatever that might mean.

'Ah, come in, Tom.'

Tom? He never calls me Tom.

'Come, sit down.' Dr Mason waves Dr Stilworth to the fireside chair and takes up the one opposite. 'I've been wanting to have a chat with you.' Dr Stilworth takes the chair offered him, puzzled and wary of this odd change in Dr Mason's attitude. 'Tom, you've been here about a year now, I think?'

'Almost.'

'Yes . . .' Dr Mason pauses and pulls at his waistcoat. 'Tom, you've had a very privileged upbringing – Eton and Oxford, I understand – and I must say that we are very happy to have you here with us.' *Ah. So that's it. He's been doing some homework.* 'You could have a great career in psychiatry. But I do think we need to talk about the hierarchy here,' the older man continues, 'the cogs that keep the wheels of the hospital turning, as it were. A couple of reports from the nursing staff make me question whether you've quite understood the dynamics, Tom.'

'Maybe I haven't, though the disagreements I've had here – if I can call them that – have been about philosophy, not dynamics.'

'Quite so. I believe you studied philosophy before turning to medicine?' Dr Stilworth nods. 'As you know, we have around six hundred patients here, some with serious mental illness and others with issues of dependency and institutionalisation. If we're to accommodate all their needs, we must run a tight ship and respect the chain of command. We cannot stand on each other's toes and cause ripples.'

Dr Stilworth thinks how important it is to have ripples and challenge to the command, but says nothing.

'I advise Matron Endsleigh of what I expect and she passes those expectations on to the nursing sisters, who then hand them on to the nurses and eventually to the nursing assistants and so on. Of course, as a doctor, you report directly to me.'

'I understand. But where is my place in that hierarchy? It would seem that I have no place – or power – whatsoever.'

'Ah, come, Tom. It's not about power.'

But Tom is in no mood to be placated. 'Isn't it? I don't actually want power, but I do expect that some daily decisions about patient care could be mine, and I see it as my duty to comment when I think that what happens is not about care at all.'

'And do you think you have witnessed such instances?'

Tom stares. *Is the man blind?* 'Indeed, I have. And often several times a day.' Dr Mason looks genuinely shocked. 'May I speak freely?' Tom asks.

'You may.'

'With respect, sir, I don't think you see what happens on the wards. I don't think that anyone dares to tell you. And so, I'm afraid that it appears that you collude with decisions that are punitive rather than healing.'

'Collude? Punitive?'

'Yes, punitive. I thought of mental institutions as places of refuge. I hoped that this hospital would give people shelter from the storms of life, with an atmosphere that would encourage and nurture their growth and help them return to the world as useful human beings. Instead we appear to demand that they're obedient, grateful dogs, despite their suffering. Surely that just demeans them and prevents them from ever becoming responsible human beings.'

Dr Mason leans back in his chair, a surprisingly genuine look of interest on his face. 'Go on.'

'The patients who make no fuss and obey the rules are regarded as "good". But often they behave that way only because they're cowed into being passive and dependent. I'm glad to see that we haven't yet damaged Miss Jennings to that point.' He shakes his head, sadly. 'If someone tried to force food into my mouth, I would kick and resist. Wouldn't you? And if I were locked in that dreadful airless room with my anger and pain, I'd scream and hammer on the door to get out.' He pauses as his voice dies a little, smothered by the emotion he's been trying to hold back. 'The patient in question today is that same young lady whose child was . . .' His voice breaks a little and he pauses again and breathes until he regains control. 'Whose child died not a month ago. She has been abandoned by her family. She is desolate, grieving, possibly with postpartum depression to boot, and probably the last thing she wants to do is eat. She was being quite brutally force-fed when she rebelled. Actually, I'm delighted that she objected. It means there's still hope.'

'You're sounding rather messianic, Tom. That young woman may well have been in prison had she not been admitted here. And her family have made a sensible choice to get on with their lives and let their daughter settle.'

'I'm sorry, sir. I've read the file and I understand that the diagnosis, in the eyes of the law, would lead to her being here for many years, if not for the rest of her life. But can that be right?' He stares into the empty grate, shrinking low in his chair. 'Are we just seeing the diagnosis rather than the person? I just wonder who Nora Jennings really was before she made the mistake – or series of mistakes – that led her here.'

Neither speaks for a long moment, and it is Tom who breaks the silence. 'I have a painful moral dilemma, you see. As I see it, there are two options. If I do what I believe to be the right thing, which is to prompt them to grow and get well, I know they'll need to go through a phase of being even more angry and frustrated about being here. That will get them into trouble, and they will be punished. The second option is to stand by silently and watch as they collapse in on themselves and become empty shells that no longer resist being here at all, but that means sacrificing all hope of them ever being well again. But, as doctors, aren't we supposed to be helping them get well?'

'Do you think that those are the only two options?'

Tom looks sideways at his boss, who he really does try to respect. 'I'm still trying to find another,' he says with a faint smile. 'At present I'm forced to conclude that I cannot in my integrity – nor do I have the moral right to – do less than be faithful to my Hippocratic oath and try to prompt their recovery, whatever their fate. Otherwise I am no longer the doctor I aspired to be.'

A trace of sadness crosses Dr Mason's face and a pained silence descends between them.

'Sometimes, I think we cater more for the needs of the institution than the needs of the patients,' sighs Dr Stilworth. 'If we have quiet, tidy wards, we look no further. Many of the patients who have been here a long time have become almost invisible – examined maybe once a year unless there's a problem, and simply maintained in their sad state with no attempt to do more than keep them alive.'

'Tom, these people are here to be cured if possible, but there are some cases that are beyond hope of cure. Miss Jennings is one of them. The moral defective is genetically programmed to behave that way.'

Dr Stilworth searches the older man's eyes sadly, looking for something – anything – on which he can pin his hopes. 'What if we're wrong about that? What if there is no such gene?'

Dr Mason starts tugging on his waistcoat, a tic that Dr Stilworth knows signifies his discomfort. Next, he'll be checking the time. And, yes, the pocket watch flips open right on cue. Dismissal is imminent. 'Tom, great minds are still working on these things. But I agree, we must try to strike a balance. Let's see if we can do that, shall we?'

Dr Stilworth nods. 'Yes, sir.'

'When you have any further observations or complaints, would you be kind enough to bring them directly to me? I won't have Matron undermined, nor the nurses humiliated. But I'm impressed by your passion.'

'Thank you, sir. I will.'

Dr Mason's eyes are wistful. 'You remind me in some ways of my younger self,' he says. 'It came to me as a sad shock that no one really gets well. Yes, they quieten over time, but maybe you're right. Perhaps it would be a healthy sign if they protested more – and if we let them do so.'

They both stand. Dr Stilworth feels a sudden, unprecedented desire to shake Dr Mason's hand, but he stifles the impulse. He turns to leave, but Dr Mason's voice arrests him. 'How is Sir Peter?'

'My father is well, thank you.'

Dr Mason nods. Dr Stilworth hopes that the exchange between them was prompted by something other than the older man having discovered his aristocratic ancestry. His hand is on the door handle when Dr Mason speaks once more. 'Tom . . . Did Miss Jennings eat, once she was allowed back to her room?'

'Yes, sir. She managed almost a slice of buttered toast and two cups of sweet tea.'

Dr Stilworth allows himself a triumphant smile as he limps back down the corridor to make his last check on Nora for the day. He pauses on the threshold of the day room and scans the patients for Nora. He sees her and is about to approach her when he notices Peggy walking over to her from across the room. He leans against the door frame to watch.

As Peggy shuffles closer to Nora, her face contorts occasionally, thick saliva trailing down her chin and finally dripping in a slimy glob on the floor. As usual, her stockings are slipping down her legs and the faint smell of soiled underwear follows her. Her smock is caught under her belly and pulled up at the back to reveal more leg than is appropriate. In her hand, she holds a biscuit. When she reaches Nora, she bends forward slowly and places the biscuit on the arm of Nora's chair, then hobbles away.

Tom looks on, transfixed, barely daring to hope.

Nora sits perfectly still, though her eyes come to rest on the biscuit. She stares at it for a long time. Then a sudden, heaving sob forces itself to the surface and exits her mouth like projectile vomit. Nora's body folds forward until her head is between her knees as she wails, fighting to draw breath between the spasms of her escaping pain and sorrow.

Tom's breath catches and his eyes moisten.

Without a word, Stan exits the nurses' station and makes his way towards Nora. Gladys leaves the ward and returns with a cup of tea, then stands beside Stan. They take up their places as silent witnesses, forming a protective tableau around the grieving mother. Neither of them touches her nor attempts to stem this torrent of grief as Nora bathes both her soul and her broken heart with her tears.

When the waves of grief finally abate, Gladys touches Nora's arm, soft as a butterfly. She picks up the now cool cup of tea and hands it to Nora. 'Nora,' she whispers. 'You can start to get better now.'

The cup of tea remains untouched. Every now and then a new wave of grief emerges and finds its way to the shore of Nora's consciousness as, at last, her soul expunges the pain. Sister Cummings watches from afar, her face an unreadable mask.

When Nora finally raises her gaze, her eyes are swollen and red, but clearer. She looks at Gladys for a long moment. 'Thank you,' she whispers. Finally, Nora searches for Peggy, who is rocking back and forth in her chair by the window, weeping silently. Slowly, Nora lifts herself from her chair, picks up the biscuit and hobbles towards Peggy, who watches her in confusion until Nora breaks the biscuit in half and puts one piece on Peggy's smock, keeping the other in her hand. They look at each other and, without a word, a friendship is forged that will last for the rest of Peggy's life and, for Nora, much longer.

Tom turns and leaves. He's superfluous here, for now.

Chapter Eleven

1942
Three years

With a rushing sensation in her ears, her head swimming and her heart pounding, Nora hovers with her foot in mid-air, on the threshold, hardly daring to move. She steadies herself with her hand on the door jamb, a sense of unreality numbing her as she stares beyond the doorway into a world that's been out of her reach for so long. Beyond those dreadful gates, she can see the countryside landscape that lies beyond, proud and beautiful: copse and woodland, garden and grove clothed in clusters of blossoms. Time and loss have taken their toll and the Nora who now prepares to step out is not the same person who was brought here against her will that long time ago.

Descending this small step into the black-tarred yard feels like a great leap, and once again she withdraws her foot into the comparative safety of this building which, like it or not, has become the only reality she now knows.

The soft summer air stirs and gently caresses her face, cajoling her, teasing her, daring her to come out. She closes her tired eyes and inhales the warm, sweet air, drinking it in as though it were wine – honeysuckle with rose undertones, and a hint of lavender not quite fully in flower. The scent enters every cell and stirs buried memories, hauling them into unwilling focus. Roses, chosen for their perfume, in the back garden of her home in Fenshaw. Lavender in their untidy spriggy clumps with their deep purple spikes. Her mother, trug over one arm, cutting flowers on her weekly redecoration of every table, windowsill and level surface that could hold a vase. Robert and herself playing in the garden in bathing costumes while her mother, laughing, sprays them with the garden hose; making daisy chains, searching for ladybirds; jars of honeysuckle by her bed, sometimes with a sweet little note from her mother . . .

She looks down at the drab uniform of anonymous shared clothing that is dumped on her bed each morning, and remembers swirly floral skirts. Her heart clenches. No, she mustn't go there – too painful. She opens her eyes and blinks at the bright sunlight. Nora doesn't want to ruin today with sad memories, for today is special. For the first time since arriving at Hillinghurst, Nora is to be allowed to walk outside with Gladys.

'Go on, then,' Gladys chivvies from behind her. 'Look lively or your time will be up before you get started.' And Nora responds to the motherly hand in the middle of her back, almost tripping into the yard.

She closes her eyes, her face raised to the heavens, and thanks whoever might be up there for allowing her this bit of freedom. With just a few more steps, she is beyond the shadow cast by the building, standing on the lawn, wishing she had sandals instead of her heavy clogs. How she longs to feel the grass between her toes! She stares in wonder at the earth around her as though she has never seen it before, then up through the gently waving trees to the jacaranda sky. Unconsciously, her head mirrors the movement of a sparrow as it picks its way from yard to grass, and she turns to see Gladys watching her with a smile growing on her lips. 'Which way can I go?' Nora asks, trying to keep any eagerness out of her voice, just in case.

'Which way do you want to go?'

She glances around and sees a series of arches covered with pink roses that tumble over each other as they vie for the best view from the top of the trellis. 'That way?' Nora queries, still unsure about whether she really does have a choice in the matter.

'OK.' Gladys smiles. 'Come on then.'

The walk that begins with Nora's hands buried into her pockets in an attempt to restrain herself, soon finds her trailing them over tendrils of sweet peas and pricking her fingers on a briar sucker she clutches as she passes. Now she's twelve and walking with her grandfather as he prods here and there with his walking stick, clapping with glee as a tiny green frog hops away. She's there again, walking in patches of wild garlic, kicking up its pungent odour with her wellington boots.

'Nora.' Gladys's soft voice interrupts her reverie. 'Let me show you something.'

She points at a little wooden peg by the side of the path. 'This is a marker. When you're allowed to walk by yourself, you'll be able to walk to one of these markers then turn and walk back. The nurses will be able to see you, so don't go past it or you'll be stopped from coming out on your own again. The next time we come out I'll show you the next one, though you might only be able to come to this one for a while.' Nora peers intently at this little piece of wood that curtails the freedom she's so recently been granted. 'So, for today, it's time to walk back.'

Nora stands still for a moment, and then, much to Gladys's astonishment, kicks off her clogs, spreads her arms and spins round and round, twirling like a little girl. She can almost feel herself at eight with her white ballet dress fluttering out around her.

Gladys watches, mesmerised. But she is not the only one.

Joe McConachie is also having his 'walk', though from the direction of the men's block and from the confines of his wheel-chair. He watches, charmed and amused, but then Gladys notices him and he cringes with embarrassment that he, ugly and disabled, should be caught admiring the pretty girl. He wishes he had never ventured out. 'Hello, Joe.' Gladys's voice is familiar and kind.

Nora stiffens as her eyes follow Gladys's gaze. The man parked in the middle of the path is dishevelled, his shabby tweed jacket covering a blue plaid shirt minus its collar button. Over his lap is a khaki blanket that hangs down a way and is then tucked up under him. The footrests are vacant. Nora quickly drops her head and steps behind Gladys, hiding like a shy child behind her mother, though she wonders who he is and what happened to his legs. Then she feels guilty when, as if he heard her thoughts, he looks down at his lap and sadly turns his head away.

The atmosphere is suddenly charged and the first flutters of alarm begin to stir in Gladys's mind. She knows that this will all have been observed and interpreted and she has a sick feeling in the pit of her stomach that there will be consequences for Nora.

'Carry on, Joe,' she says. 'Nora, it's time for us to get back.'

Chapter Twelve

The following morning, Sister Cummings sits at her desk ready for handover, crisp from head to foot in her blue starched uniform, white stockings, perfectly pressed cap and burnished shoes. Her belt buckle is buffed to a fine patina. She's already checked the bath book, bowel book, teeth book and medication charts to acquaint herself with details of every patient on her ward. The night shift is ending and the day staff should be arriving any minute now. Already, the patients line the walls, bent and cramped into closely packed chairs. The usual suspects are straitjacketed to prevent them hurting themselves or others. Some wear helmets to protect them from harm; others are bibbed to catch the steady stream of spittle that will soak their clothing within half an hour. Most are fairly quiet. It is 6.59 precisely.

The ward – down which her staff will walk any second now – is broad, with a dark, shining oak floor that is polished every morning and mopped with a soft cloth several times a day. Woe betide any dust that dares to settle upon it. The high, vaulted ceiling with iron arches betrays both the age and expectations for the hospital. Built to house two hundred patients, it is now severely overcrowded with about six hundred, and more are still being admitted while staff numbers remain static. The only choice, as far as Sister Cummings sees it, is to run it like a military operation, and the staff need to either respect that, or leave. In her opinion, these patients need to be controlled and treated like the badly behaved children they are, by giving them the discipline they should have had when they were younger. She has no truck with namby-pamby therapies. A good slap is what they understand, and if that's not enough to get the results she expects, then the punishment obviously needs to be more severe. It's very simple and she wishes that people would just get out of her way and let her get on with her work.

She knows what it's like to suffer, having looked after her much-loved mother whose screams of pain while she dressed the open, stinking, cancerous crater where her breast used to be could only be quelled with opium. Many a night she could hardly sleep because of the fear that would rise up at the thought of having to do the dressings again the next day. The only thing she could do to survive was to harden herself to other people's pain. Eventually she cut her own feelings off so that she could bear to do what needed to be done and, by default, she became an untrained, unpaid, excellent, if granite-hearted nurse. In Sister Cummings's opinion, the patients here have nothing to complain about and should feel lucky that they're looked after at all. Life isn't fair and that's all there is to it. You just have to get on with it.

She pulls herself out of her reverie and looks at her watch again: 7.01. The day staff are late. They'll get the sharp edge of her tongue when they do arrive. And, as if they'd heard her thoughts, Gladys and Stan enter through the tall, ornately carved door, chatting happily, until Stan sees that Sister Cummings is on deck. His expression changes and he nudges Gladys, who is oblivious and carries on talking animatedly. Sister Cummings's face is blotchy with rage, her hands clenched by her sides.

'How dare you wander in as though tomorrow would do?' she booms. 'You're late. Let's get the handover done and you'll all stay over at the end of your shift.'

Fifteen excruciating minutes later, and the handover is complete. The night staff are off to their beds and the day staff now scuttle to their posts so as not to ruffle Sister any further. But Gladys is not off the hook yet.

'I want to talk to you about Jennings,' says Sister Cummings.

Gladys pales. She's been dreading this since yesterday. She knows that whatever she says can and will be twisted in order to support whatever decision Sister Cummings has already made.

'What's been happening out there?'

'Sorry, Sister?' Gladys says, trying to inject her voice with confusion, her heart sinking all the while.

'Feigning stupidity doesn't suit you,' Sister Cummings snarls. 'With Jennings and McConachie.'

'Nothing's been happening, Sister.'

'Don't give me that. She's been lazing around like a dying wallflower for months and now, one walk out and she's pirouetting about and fawning over a man.'

'I think she was just thrilled to be out in the fresh air and Joe was out and stopped, that's all.'

'I'm watching her. If I see any evidence that she's returning to her old behaviour, I'll have her for breakfast.'

Gladys sets her chin and gathers her courage. 'What old behaviour?'

'Don't pull that with me. You know exactly what I mean. She got herself pregnant and it's our job to make sure it doesn't happen again. Yet I give her one bit of freedom and what does she do with it? She's flirting.'

Gladys feels warmth creeping up her neck. She should just let go, back off and say nothing, but she just can't. 'There's been no flirting, Sister. They met briefly by chance and Nora actually seemed frightened and shy.'

Cummings narrows her eyes, surprised that this nurse, who has never once contradicted her, is choosing this moment to fight back. 'I don't think so. It's all a ruse. She knows the moves. She's done it before.'

'Maybe she just had a little slip,' Gladys says, her voice firm.

'A slip? And do you think she was that lucky? To get pregnant on one slip?'

'Some do,' Gladys retorts, shrugging. But something in Sister Cummings's eyes tells her that there's a painful story there.

'Well, I don't believe it. Any more of that and you know what I'll be recommending.'

Gladys's blood runs cold and her breath hitches in her throat. She knows how Sister Cummings works. It would give her great pleasure to set Nora up as the example to remind Dr Stilworth to mind his own business. 'Would you prefer we suspend her walks?' Gladys offers, hoping to avoid future issues. She knows how the trap is set.

'Not on your life. Give her plenty of rope.'

Gladys shudders. There's something new afoot and a gust of icy wind seems to follow Sister Cummings as she moves. No one is sure about what's going on, though there has been plenty of gossip. Whatever it is, it isn't pretty. This has been building for years, and everyone has heard her say she'd make Tom Stilworth pay for humiliating her. That was even before last week, when he shouted at her after finding her towering over Nora who was sprawled face down on the floor in a pool of Lysol. It's been war since then – silent and cold as ice, but always lurking in the background. What he wrote in Nora's notes for everyone to see didn't help, either. That was tantamount to a declaration of war, probably with Nora Jennings being the main casualty.

Fall at entrance to sluice. Circumstances of fall unknown. Fully conscious. No apparent injuries. Reports having slipped on wet floor. Witnessed by Sister Cummings. Observe. Tom Stilworth.

'What was that Tom Stilworth was preaching about?' Sister Cummings mocks, and Gladys forces herself to concentrate. '"Give them freedom, dignity and responsibility?" Fine – let's do that.'

'Maybe she's not ready for that,' Gladys counters carefully, desperately trying to damp down the storm Cummings is whipping up.

'But didn't he say we should unlock the doors and give them the key to health and freedom?' Her voice drips with sarcasm and her cruel mouth forms a hard, ugly line.

'I think it's confusing for them to go from one extreme to the other. I can take it more slowly with her if you wish, Sister. Maybe I didn't set the boundaries clearly enough. I could—'

'Stop drivelling. Get her ready for her walk and show her the grounds. From today, she'll go alone.'

Chapter Thirteen

1943
Four years

Nora sits by the window, staring out at the sixteenth season she's observed at Hillinghurst. She can hardly believe she's been here for so long. The cold, grey winters, snow scattered on distant hills and drifted into hedgerows. Beauteous yellow springs with daffodils and primroses and a plethora of wild flowers. Fruit-filled summers when she longed for the beach and her mother's laughter and playfulness.

In the autumn she was allowed to walk prescribed distances alone, yet always under the watchful eyes of the staff. During these all-too-short outings, she often felt giddy with a long-forgotten sense of freedom. The reds and golds of the leaves swirling like flamenco dancers delighted her, and she searched for acorns and pine cones as she'd done as a girl, remembering how she would collect things for the harvest festival and practise new hymns with the choir. And now another winter is approaching and the leaves have lost their crispness and are becoming a squelching mulch, and the grass has already started to lift up its coat. Nora wonders what the next year has in store for her.

Whether working in the laundry, having a precious walk or lying on her bed exhausted but unable to sleep, Nora is haunted by thoughts of her baby. Grief can still overwhelm her. She replays the memory of that slushy rush when, after all the labouring and tearing of flesh, her child just slid out. It's all she has. She longs to be able to say 'him' or 'her', but no one will give her even that much information and she tortures herself with questions. Where is he or she? Does he know there's a mother who loves him? Does she have new parents who love her? Is he strong and sturdy? If only she could have held her, mapped her face with her finger, she'd have a picture she could hold in her heart.

So, whether scrubbing the floor or washing the clothes, she attacks her work with gusto, wishing she were just as able to remove the stain of illegitimacy from both the child and herself, while the pain in her sore, chapped hands at least distracts her from her constant inner turbulence. It's her penance for the sin of unmarried motherhood and the shame that she tried to abort her child – she knows that. The wounds will never heal. And on top of all that, she also grieves that her own selfishness caused her mother also to lose *her* only child, and for this, she can't forgive herself.

At least she has found a friend in Peggy, though. Sometimes it frightens her to think that, at sixty-five, Peggy has been here for forty years. She had her baby in the poorhouse, then when her baby was taken for adoption, she tried to commit suicide and was sent here. Without family or anyone to support her, she's never been able to leave. *I don't want ever to accept that this place is my home. I can't stay here all my life.*

Thoughts of suicide wax and wane, and in the last few months Nora has made plans. Loosely – but plans nevertheless. She could hang herself in the woods. She could steal someone's tablets – lots of people seem to hoard their medicine rather than taking it. She could maybe poison herself. When she was a little girl her grandmother used to teach her about the poisonous berries in the forest in case she'd pick them by mistake. Deadly nightshade or foxglove would work. These thoughts of suicide soothe her because no one can take them away from her, and if she really wants to do it no one could stop her either. But then she thinks of her child and knows she must stay alive to find it.

Nora often ponders on what it is to love and whether or not love really exists. The quivering strand of love that she'd perceived as strong seems to have been easy for Robert to break.

Does he still love me? Will he come for me? Why hasn't he already?
And did her parents ever really love her? If they did, how could
they abandon her like this?

Then, one day, it occurs to her to ask. She can't believe she's
never thought of that before. She waits until she and Gladys are
walking outside together, then asks baldly, 'Gladys, who adopted
my baby?' Gladys looks away. 'I won't tell anyone you told me. I
promise.'

'I can't.'

Nora feels a prick of guilt for placing Gladys in this position,
but not enough to stop her now. 'Can you at least tell me if it was
a boy or a girl?'

There's a silent moment, and when Gladys returns eye
contact, Nora sees the compassion and sorrow written on her
face. She holds her breath.

'A girl,' she says simply.

Nora sighs, a rare smile suffusing her face. 'I knew,' she whispers, nodding, and she reaches out to touch the older woman's
arm with her fingertips. 'Thank you, Gladys.'

Gladys opens her mouth as if to say more, then quickly turns
away.

One day Nora will find her daughter. This is the only thing
that keeps her alive.

The next day, out for her walk alone, Nora kicks a stack of
leaves that lies on the path and, lost in her thoughts, realises just
in time that she's almost at the little peg that indicates this is as
far as she's allowed to walk. She pauses, then defiantly steps one
foot past it before she turns back. Eyes to the ground, she hears
a familiar sound and glances up. Coming along the path towards
her is Joe in his squeaky chair. She no longer puts her head
down to avoid him, though Gladys has urged her to be very
careful. She said there'd be hell to pay should Sister Cummings
catch wind of any developing friendship.

Nora's thoughts flick to Sister Cummings. She who deliberately walks across the bit of clean floor that Nora has just
scrubbed, then shouts at her to start all over and 'wash it

properly this time'. Who screams her name from the ablution block, where she has 'accidentally' spilled the contents of a bedpan and then wants Nora to clean it up, and who hits and pulls hair in the privacy of the sluice, knowing that Nora has no means of redress.

'Hello,' Joe says, pulling on his lap blanket nervously. 'By yourself today.'

Nora smiles shyly and stops, gazing at the ground, but then her eyes creep up towards his face almost of their own accord, though they stop short of meeting his eyes. He must be mid-twenties and is quite handsome, really. She's aware that she's crushing the campion she picked a little while ago, and with an embarrassed flick of her fingers she lets it fall to the ground.

'I've heard the nurse call you Nora, so I know your name. I'm Joe. How long have you been here?' Joe asks, his hands balanced on the rims of his wheels.

'Four years. You?'

'Nine,' he says.

Nora's eyes widen and her heart feels as though it might stop. *Nine years. Could they make me stay that long?* 'Why?' The question slips out of her mouth before she can stop it.

'I tried to kill myself,' he says without emotion. 'As you see, I botched it. I fell when I was trying to get onto the railway line and the train came and all it did was cut off my right leg and my left foot.'

'Oh, I'm so sorry,' Nora says, shocked and flustered.

'Don't be. My own fault.' Then, to Nora's astonishment, he laughs. 'When I came round two days later, it was almost dark, and I thought I'd made it and was in heaven because there was an angel in my room.'

Nora's eyes widen. 'An angel?'

'It turned out to be a nurse in one of those fancy contraptions they wear on their heads.' He chortles, but then his face changes again and he gives the blanket another nervous tug. 'It's a crime to try to kill yourself so I could have gone to prison, but they wouldn't have been able to look after my legs so they sent me here instead. To be "cared for". Can you imagine? I'd have been out by now if I'd gone inside.'

Me too, Nora thinks.

'What about your family?' Nora asks, painfully aware of how hers simply abandoned her.

'They never really wanted me anyway. I was only a last-ditch attempt to save their marriage and I couldn't even do that properly. My father eventually left with some blonde and my mother ended up here a couple of years after I did. She's buried in the cemetery.'

'Oh . . .' Nora wrings her hands and feels the urge to escape.

'Look at me, talking about myself. Tell me about you?' Joe asks. But Nora freezes. She has not been asked to talk about herself in such a long time. And she doesn't want this man, who has suffered so much, to be burdened with her problems. A blush edges its way up her neck. 'I-I have to go,' she stutters.

'Wait! We could just . . . chat?' Joe says in a pleading voice and Nora's eyes finally meet his. He's lonely, she realises with a lurch. But then her attention darts back to the main hospital building as she remembers Gladys's warnings. Sure enough, there, in one of the windows, is a shadow. Her heart races. 'I have to go,' she says and turns away. Then, feeling Joe's crushed gaze on her back, she turns back again. 'I'm sorry,' she mumbles.

'Don't worry. It was nice to meet you,' he says, smiling bravely. 'Go on. It's OK.' And he makes a little shooing gesture with his hand.

Nora pauses. 'Maybe next time, we can talk more. I don't have any real friends here . . .' They share a small smile, and she hurries off down the path.

Back on the ward, the nurses have been summoned and Sister Cummings looks around, daring anyone to speak.

'Enough evidence for everyone now, is there?' She pauses for effect, a prosecutor delivering her closing speech. 'Is everyone satisfied that the course is clear? Or are there even now some among you so soft-headed that you still quibble about what needs to be done?' She glances around, ready to crush any dissent. 'Not that it matters, really, what you think,' she adds, shrugging. Let them not have any illusion that they have any real power in the matter – nor even an opinion that's of any consequence. Any such idea needs to be squashed like a bug. She closes the file and stands up, scraping her chair on the polished floor.

Stan gathers together the notes and squares the pile, packing them down with a sharp bang on the desk. He turns them ninety degrees and does the same thing again, all the while avoiding Sister Cummings's eyes, though he knows that she'll be watching him. This is the biggest protest he dares to make without risking the loss of his job. It's silent insolence and he knows it, but someone has to register something.

'Did you have something to say, Stan?'

He continues to fidget with the notes. He looks up directly into her eyes, wondering who he hates most in this moment: her or himself. 'No, Sister. Nothing at all.' He lowers his eyes again in shame.

Matron straightens her pristine headdress and pushes her hair securely under it. Her uniform is perfectly pressed, the newly starched collar and cuffs striking a sharp contrast to the maroon serge. Her years in this work have taken their toll, and it's a relief to think that retirement isn't far away. A whole life given to the service of the insane, from probationer nurse to the highest rank. And for what? A life deprived of marriage and children, and with a social life as barren as her womb within her. She sighs.

'Sister Cummings.' She lifts her face and looks at the woman standing in her doorway, who she knows is just waiting for the opportunity to depose her. But if she has her way, this woman will never have the ultimate power over her nurses. Cummings makes her uneasy. Yes, she's clever, cunning enough not to get caught so far, but Miss Endsleigh's antennae twitch whenever she appears. Were she not protected by the medical director,

Matron would have disposed of her long ago. But, instead, she smiles. 'Please sit down. What can I do for you?'

'I'd like to talk about Nora Jennings, Matron,' Sister Cummings says with a sweet smile.

The discussion is not altogether unexpected. People may think that she's in her ivory tower and not paying much attention to daily life on the ward, but she has her ear to the ground and she's also picked up concern about Nora Jennings from other quarters. That young man, Dr Stilworth, hasn't helped as much as he might have, either. There's no smoke without fire, and his concern for this young woman hasn't gone unnoticed. Those who step across the very narrow border between what's considered proper and what is not in the doctor–patient relationship are not easily forgiven. She's not saying that there is anything untoward, but she knows there's been talk.

'There's gathering evidence that the moral defective gene is beginning to show itself in her behaviour, particularly around one of the patients from Elder – Joe McConachie.'

Now, that does surprise her. Miss Endsleigh was the sister on the ward when Joe was admitted all those years ago, and his plight as a double amputee taxed even her own hardened sympathies at the time. A handsome, bright, young man in his prime ... She pulls her wandering thoughts back to Sister Cummings. 'Tell me more.' She listens and, as Cummings outlines her argument, Matron realises she has no option but to acknowledge that Cummings has made sure all the criteria are met.

'This is a very serious step, Sister. You're sure of your information?'

'Yes, Matron. We feel that, for her own sake and also for that of Joe and any of the other men in the hospital, this really is the only course of action.'

Matron wonders who the 'we' is in that sentence, but lets it pass. She suddenly feels weary. All these young women. How many more? And she's grateful that the final decision will not be hers.

'Leave it with me,' she says, hoping that the dismissal implied in her tone is not lost. And it isn't. Sister Cummings is already on her feet.

'Thank you, Matron, for your time and trouble.'

As she closes the door, Matron reflects on those words – time and trouble – and she gives an involuntary shudder.

In the next few days, plans are underway before Dr Stilworth is made aware of them. When he finally overhears a conversation between Stan and Gladys – one that in retrospect he feels was contrived to let him know – his mind reels. He pulls at his collar, his tie suddenly tight and suffocating. With his lab coat flapping behind him, he hurries as best he can, cursing his leg. *This cannot be allowed to happen.*

The invitation to enter can't come fast enough and Dr Stilworth is through the door as soon as courtesy will allow, his anger spilling over into his balled-up fists, which he swiftly stuffs into his pockets. Dr Mason betrays no surprise, and it's clear he's been expecting this visit.

'Tom, I think you'd better sit down. And tidy yourself up a bit, man, you look a state.'

'I'd rather stand, thank you,' says Tom, smoothing his hair and straightening his tie.

The older man puts down his pen. 'Doctor, sit down, for heaven's sake!' Tom reluctantly does so, perching on the edge of the chair. Only then does he become aware that Matron is also in the room. Ah, they were expecting him. Matron looks serene, her headdress a beacon of white in this dingy room. Her knees are pinched together, her shining, laced shoes exactly parallel to each other.

'Good morning, Matron,' he manages stiffly. 'I apologise, I didn't see you there.'

She bows her head slightly. 'Good morning, Dr Stilworth.' But Tom's eyes are already on his boss.

'I imagine this is about Miss Jennings,' says Dr Mason.

'I cannot believe that you would sanction this barbarous act,' Tom explodes, then immediately regrets his tone. This attitude will get him nowhere and he knows it. He draws in a deep, calming breath. 'Sir, though this may have been allowed under the 1913 Mental Deficiency Act, there is nothing in the 1930 Mental Treatment Act that would indicate that this could still be condoned. Nor is there anything in Miss Jennings's behaviour that would indicate that this is a necessary course of action.' He's trying his best to be professional and make a good case rather than doing what he wants to do, which is scream and shout against the injustice of the plan.

'It may not be compulsory, but it is a matter of clinical judgement. *My* clinical judgement.' Dr Mason's voice is so calm and reasonable that Tom has to fight the urge to reach across and shake the man.

'She's so young – just twenty-one.' Even he can feel the frailty of this pathetic plea.

'Dr Stilworth – Tom – Miss Jennings will soon come into her sexual prime. And we know that she already disregarded the teaching of the Church and her parents and got herself into this situation. Our job now is to ensure that this will not happen again and that the gene for moral defectiveness is not spread further. In any case, the decision is made.' He pulls at his waistcoat and then snaps the pocket watch open.

'Might you consider that a few years from now she will have matured and this will not be an issue?'

'Dr Stilworth, I will not allow her to transmit the defective gene to another generation.'

'But this is abhorrent. It's eugenics. And nothing has been proven about a defective gene.' Tom's voice has risen despite his desperate attempt to keep calm.

'Greater minds than ours have thrashed this out. Winston Churchill stated, in its favour, that his aim in life was to improve the British breed and protect British society from the threat of the feeble-minded and insane. Nora Jennings is a moral defective and it's our duty to do what is best for her – and for society at large.'

Tom is incensed. 'And you truly believe that this is what is best for her?' He shakes his head. 'I cannot agree. I'm appalled at the senselessness and horror of this. Dr Mason—'

'Dr Stilworth! I don't need you to agree. Please remember who you are and where you are. You will respect me in this matter.' Dr Mason's face is a blotchy puce. 'You have tested my patience for too long, and I have borne with it. But now you have gone too far.'

'I apologise if I appear disrespectful, Dr Mason. I do know that you are acting with your highest integrity in this matter. But the history of eugenics is not pretty, and we are seeing the dreadful, far-reaching consequences of this abomination of a philosophy worldwide. Look what has just happened in Nazi Germany. Unless we stand against such beliefs, we'll find ourselves in the gutter of humanity.'

Matron's hand trembles as she mops her forehead with her handkerchief. 'Dr Stilworth,' Dr Mason says stoutly. 'Let us try to remain professional.' Tom bristles at the patronising tone. 'Look at this logically. If she were not in our care and protection, we have no idea what she would be doing.'

'Probably what she was on course to spend her life doing before – going to church, singing, meeting boys, falling in love, getting married, having children.'

'Yes,' Dr Mason exclaims, 'that would be fine if it were in that order, but Miss Jennings has already shown that she has disregarded such a moral path. That is the whole point! And we've been over it countless times.' He takes a shaky breath. 'The Royal Commission recommended this course of action with regards to the "unfit" so that it would be impossible for them to have children and thus perpetuate their unfortunate inherited characteristics. And controlling them by detention for life is the price they felt we must pay for the health and well-being of our wider society.'

Tom gives a snort of exasperation and disgust, then lets out a long breath and lowers his eyes for a moment in an effort to control himself. To accuse his superior of believing such poppycock would not go down well.

'Tom, it might be beneficial for you to study the scholarly papers on the subject.'

Unable to contain himself any longer, Tom's frustration bursts forth. 'I'm well acquainted with the work on sterilisation of degenerates. I know that the state of Indiana, from whence one of those authors comes, has supported the eugenicist's theory and made sterilisation mandatory, and also made it illegal for mental patients to marry. But surely, we must think for ourselves. I apologise, sir, but I feel that any honourable human being must see that we cannot do this. We have no moral right.' He takes a breath. *In for a penny . . .* 'In fact, I don't think we have the moral right to segregate them from society or from the opposite sex, either. Thirty years ago, Mr Churchill's ideas were refuted as being uncivilised. One wonders just how he could make such ludicrous judgements. Labour camps; mass sterilisation. He even suggested that anyone convicted of a second petty criminal offence must be feeble-minded and therefore detained in a labour colony for an indeterminate period.' He shakes his head in despair. 'Surely we cannot agree with such sweeping generalities?'

'Tom, I—'

'Sir, the Feeble-Minded Control Bill rejected mandatory sterilisation, even though it still made it an offence to marry or even attempt to marry a mental defective. So, if Nora Jennings were to be thought of in such terms, then how could we complain that she remained unmarried? I think it's shocking that we still uphold registration and segregation. Josiah Wedgwood was right when he denounced it as a violation of human rights. Surely, we have done with this. Enough young women have been forcibly sterilised. Please let us not be led down this path of pious savagery.'

'Tom, the decision—'

'Britain never legislated for sterilisation. Detention in institutions was the chosen path. And has Nora Jennings not already suffered enough by being detained and robbed of so many of her human rights? Please do not take this one from her.'

Dr Mason springs to his feet and slams his fist down on the desk. His neck is flushed with rage and his pulse beats visibly in his temples. 'The decision is made,' he bellows. 'The procedure will take place tomorrow morning. You will not be required in attendance, so you can protect your precious conscience. Now, kindly leave my office and close the door behind you.'

'Dr Mason—'

'Get out of my office this instant.' He sinks to his chair, leaving Tom staring. 'Now!'

Tom turns to Matron. 'I apologise, madam,' he says curtly. 'Good day.'

Dr Mason looks up. 'Nine o'clock tomorrow, Matron. This matter is closed. Shut the door after you, doctor.'

Chapter Fourteen

1943
Four years

Nora is out on one of her walks, carefully navigating the narrow path. Briars clutch at her shoes, tangling in her socks, drawing blood from tiny, stinging scratches. And then she sees the men. Old men in well-mended jackets, young men in dungarees, men with wheelbarrows; all of them slow and ponderous, but working there in the magical, fertile outdoors. Each team has a healthy-looking younger man in a green coat, giving orders and inspecting work. There are rows of Victorian glasshouses, filled with pots of seedlings, then beyond, a wild woodland with silver birch, elm and willow. She longs to keep walking, but she's been told she's not to go beyond here.

Nora watches in amazement and the closest thing to delight she has felt for a long time, but hot on the heels of that joy comes a pang of jealousy at the fact that only the men are allowed to work out here. It strikes her that the only men she has encountered since being brought here are Dr Mason, Dr Stilworth, Stan, and that awful aide who threw her in the isolation room. And Joe, of course. Otherwise it's become a woman's world. But that doesn't seem to have rendered it any gentler. Gladys is motherly, yes, and Nurse Jamison seems sensitive, but the others seem devoid of any human feeling whatsoever. Her thoughts turn to Peggy and how their lives have somehow become wound together through pain and loss, each helping the other to survive in this world that doesn't seem to care.

There's a sudden scuffling sound and Stan appears, accompanied by one of the nursing assistants. Even through the fog of her musings, Nora can't help but notice that he seems distant and distracted. 'Nora, I want you to go back to the ward and sit by your bed, and have your coat ready.'

She stares at him, her brow furrowed in confusion.

'Come on,' Stan chivvies her. 'Don't argue, I want you back on the ward now.'

But Nora's feet won't move. 'Why?' she says in a voice that sounds, even to her own ears, unusually whiny. Why does she have to lose the one tiny freedom she is ever allowed, just to sit in her room?

'Nora, now.' Stan's eyes hold hers and she knows she has no choice but to comply.

She comes back feeling sulky, and waits for what seems like hours, watching out of the window as the sky has become grey and sullen, a bit like her mood. She hates to have nothing to do – too much space for too much thought. Although the work is hard, in many ways it's a blessing. She quite likes working in the laundry. All the hospital clothing is laundered together, sorted for mending, gathered into piles and distributed daily in those anonymous bails. Doctors' white coats are washed separately and starched and pressed so that medical staff can draw a pristine uniform each day. Nora takes pride in repairing them with neat stitches, turning collars by hand, sewing on buttons. And day by day, life has somehow become more bearable.

The clouds that were silent grey ghosts are suddenly swollen and angry, arguing with each other, their occasional explosions of temper lighting the sky with silver flashes. Here and there the rain falls in thick, slate-grey curtains. Then there's a respite, but clouds continue to gather, their anvil tops predicting further clashes. Nora waits, craning her head to watch the battle in the sky through the window.

Stan's voice startles her. 'Nora, are you ready? Transport's here.'

'Where are you taking me?'

Stan gathers up her coat and hands it to her. 'Nora, put your coat on.'

Nora remains rooted to the spot. Cold fear licks at her chest. Something's going on but she has no idea what. Stan is avoiding her eyes and though he's always kind, she can't deny that, at the moment, she feels she cannot trust him.

'Nothing to worry about,' he says, though he himself looks decidedly worried.

'But where am I going?'

He hesitates slightly, then mumbles, 'You're going out for a ride . . . to have your appendix out.'

Her brow crinkles in a frown, the green eyes below questioning. 'Why?'

Stan looks away, colour creeping up his neck. 'It's just a precaution,' he says.

'But I don't need my appendix out.'

'Nora, best not make a fuss. Come on now.'

Stan ushers her out of the building and into the waiting hospital van. She feels a mixture of excitement and anxiety as she is driven out of the hospital grounds for the first time in four years. She turns and looks back at those tall gates, thinking of all the times she's wondered if she was ever going to see them from the outside again. They look very much the same.

The van has turned to the left, away from Fenshaw. Tears prick her eyes as she wonders how she would feel if the journey had taken them the other way. She might have seen her mother at the shops, or some of her friends, or even Robert . . . But she knows she must be very strict with herself. She can't afford an emotional excursion into the past. It hurts too much to think of how they've all abandoned her. Dr Mason was right. It was easier when she started to consider herself an orphan, completely alone in the world. She looks out of the van windows at old familiar landmarks, drinking them in. How strange! Some things have changed, but others are just as she remembers. But then she looks straight ahead. This is not the world she belongs in any more.

★   ★   ★

The next day, Nora wakes up in the strange hospital bed. Even before she has the chance to get her bearings, she's aware of the pain in her lower abdomen and the concerned, angelic face of a young nurse hovering over her. 'Can I get you anything?' she says, her brown eyes smiling kindly into Nora's. Nora blinks but says nothing. 'Some water? Anything?' the nurse asks as her hand reaches out to straighten a wrinkle in the sheet.

'I'm fine, thank you,' Nora finally croaks.

Days pass and Nora becomes familiar with the strange routine – woken very early to wash and have her bed made with her still in it. Very odd! Compulsory bedpan. Bed bath. The nurses' round with Sister and the same questions each day about how often she's opened her bowels and how much she's had to drink. Visiting times are the loneliest times of the day, when everyone but her seems to have someone at their bedside with flowers and grapes – always grapes, it seems – and happy faces. She wishes she could disappear, then. She tries to hide herself under the sheet or play a game with herself, trying to guess who is visiting whom.

Then one morning, Sister – nothing like Sister Cummings, thankfully – appears with a special tray and, without explanation or ceremony, pokes around at the still tender wound then proceeds to cut the tiny, neat knots and tweezer out the catgut stitches. She stands admiring the scar with satisfaction, and only then addresses Nora.

'Now you've had your stitches out, you'll be discharged back to your own hospital. Your escort will be back in a moment. She just slipped out for a short break.'

'Oh . . .' Nora has so much she wants to ask, yet she's learned that it's always best to say nothing. Everything can be twisted, misinterpreted and come back to bite her – perhaps even here. But one burning question spills out of her. 'Why did I have to have my appendix out?'

A cloud ripples the surface of the sister's brown eyes. 'Your appendix?' There's a beat of silence.

'My appendix. I had my appendix out.'

The sister's shining eyes become dull and she looks away, flushing, as some fleeting clarity flashes across her face. 'I think you'll have to ask the doctor,' she says and smiles, but the smile does not reach her eyes.

Nora feels a pang of sadness. Something's going on, though she doesn't know what.

As she waits for her transport back to Hillinghurst to arrive, Nora sits quietly, thinking. She would never have thought she'd be relieved to be going back there, but she is. Things might be difficult there – the food less plentiful and poorer in quality, the nurses handy at giving the odd slap to keep people in line, and of course having to deal with Sister Cummings – but at least it's familiar, known.

She wonders whether Joe knows where she is. There was no time to tell him, she was just whisked to the hospital van and found herself here. Not that she had anything to pack or anyone else to tell, except Peggy.

The van arrives and Nora gets up to meet it. Just as she is about to get in, she sees something that makes her stop still. A little girl is running around the hospital grounds. She has a bright green balloon, and is patting it along then chasing it as her mother watches, smiling. The child's father walks along behind her, no doubt knowing that the balloon will burst soon enough, but enjoying this simple, shared pleasure in the moment. Is that how it is in normal families? Before she can ponder further, her escort shoves her impatiently in the back, and Nora looks away and climbs into the van.

As they near Hillinghurst Hospital, the inevitable water tower and chimney loom in the distance, as forbidding now as they were to her when she was a child, when the 'madhouse' of Hillinghurst was whispered about as if even its name might bring a curse upon someone. It could never have dawned upon any of Nora's family that one of their number would ever bring shame upon them by being committed here.

Today, however, Nora tries to see it differently as she catches the first glimpse of the gates and the gardens stretching out like a cat in the sunshine, as flowers and vegetables hum and chatter their messages to each other, carried by armies of bees and butterflies.

Once on the ward, Nora is told she must stay in the day room today. No work. No walk. She sees that there's a new admission who sits in restraints. There's an awful smell. She must have done something in her knickers. She struggles against the leather straps, then her face contorts into what could have become a yawn, then her head falls forward and she's asleep. Medication.

Despite herself, Nora has a glancing thought that it's good to be home.

Chapter Fifteen

1944
Five years

Nora taps her foot nervously, the only outward sign of her growing excitement and agitation. Her regular visits from Mrs Lampeter suddenly stopped five months ago, and when Nora built up the courage to ask about it, Dr Stilworth said that she was very ill and in hospital herself. However, today Nora is to have a visit. She longs to see her dearest friend – indeed her only friend, apart from Peggy and Joe. She arrives in the family room with five minutes to spare, having brushed her hair several times and pinched her cheeks to make them look rosy. She has polished her clogs on the back of her stockings then smoothed out any wrinkles. And now she waits.

When Mrs Lampeter enters, Nora feels a jolt of shock deep in her belly. Her friend is bird-thin and her tweed suit hangs around her like a tent. A rather spectacular green felt hat clings precariously to the back of her head, threatening to fall off at any moment. Leather, stocky-heeled lace-ups appear to be weighting her in place, lest she be blown away by a capricious wind. Her face, always round and cheery, is now drawn and thin; her skin, once ruddy, is now putty grey and she has composed her features so as not to betray what is in any case so obvious. But behind it all, love still beams from her eyes. She constantly shifts her gaze away from Nora's searching eyes, as though this will help protect their secret. But too late. Nora has already seen it. It is the same look that a neighbour had before she died of consumption.

Nora's wide smile freezes. She takes the older woman's arm and smiles valiantly through her fear. 'Mrs Lampeter, it's wonderful to see you. I'm sorry you've been so ill. I hope you're feeling better?'

Mrs Lampeter smiles weakly, but a fit of coughing interrupts and she has to pause, holding a handkerchief to her mouth. 'I'm all right, Miss Nora. And what about you?'

'I'm fine,' she lies.

'I brought you some scones. I hope they'll let you have them.' She holds out a paper bag.

Nora smiles. 'Ooh, thank you, Mrs Lampeter. How lovely,' she enthuses, bubbling with a mischief that she hasn't felt these last five years. 'Maybe we should have one now, just in case.' Mrs Lampeter's eyes fill with pleasure. But still a gap opens between them – a hammock of time cradling an uneasy silence. They look into each other's eyes, each aware the other is lying. 'Mrs Lampeter, is something else wrong? Apart from . . . your cough, I mean.'

Mrs Lampeter reaches out and takes her hand. 'I have news about Robert.'

Nora's heart flips. 'Robert?' A long list of possibilities parades through Nora's mind, accompanied by both excitement and fear.

'Yes,' and Mrs Lampeter pauses. 'There's no easy way to say this. Nora, I'm afraid he was badly wounded in Italy.'

Nora clasps her hand to her mouth. 'What happened?' she whispers.

'It's difficult to know – that's what war does. He had a head injury.' Nora clasps her hand to her mouth. 'He's been in Stoke Mandeville Hospital since March and is getting better. I hear they can do amazing things nowadays.'

'Oh.' Nora is distraught, her thoughts reeling. A longing to see him. Sadness that she won't be able to go. And, undeniable, residual anger at his abandonment, all those years ago . . .

Mrs Lampeter takes her hand. 'I'm sure he'll be all right, Miss Nora. He was unconscious when he got to the hospital, but he's awake now and being cared for very well, I'm sure. But I thought you'd want to know. Maybe you'd like to remember him in your prayers.'

Nora feels a wave of guilt. She hasn't prayed for a very long time. She avoids Father Matthews when he comes to take confession and to bring Holy Communion, unable to forget that he was there that night and said and did nothing to help her. And she feels abandoned by God as well as everyone else – apart from Mrs Lampeter, of course.

Another bout of Mrs Lampeter's coughing intrudes into Nora's thoughts. 'I can't even go to see him,' Nora whimpers.

'I'm so sorry, Miss Nora. I don't know what to say.'

'Do my mother and father know?'

'Yes. They've been there with him.'

Nora's face falls. 'They've never been here with me,' and tears fill her eyes.

Mrs Lampeter's eyes widen and she looks trapped. Nora hastily wipes her tears away and gives a watery smile. 'No, please don't worry, Mrs Lampeter. I'm glad he has them to visit.'

Mrs Lampeter sighs. 'I'm sorry for all this trouble, Miss Nora.' She pauses, looking deep into Nora's eyes. 'Do you not want to tell them about Robert? I could even tell them for you. It might make things . . .' but Nora's colour drains and Mrs Lampeter's voice fades away.

'You knew?' Nora whispers.

'Your love for each other was written all over your face.'

Nora's eyes brim with tears. 'I couldn't do that. There'd be even more shame because we're cousins. Best nobody knows.'

'But you're here –' Mrs Lampeter glances around – 'in this awful place. On your own . . .'

'Dr Mason said it was already a disgrace for all the family, and that's even without them knowing about Robert. I've done enough damage as it is. I can't . . .' Her voice wobbles and she blinks quickly, then takes a deep breath and tries to smile. Mrs Lampeter's eyes fill and furrows pucker her brow. Nora reaches out to touch her arm. 'Mrs Lampeter, what about you? Have you been very ill?'

'Yes, I have, Miss Nora. I shouldn't really be here. I wouldn't like to give you or anyone else an infection.'

'You have an infection?'

'I do.'

'Is it a very bad infection?' Her voice trembles.

Mrs Lampeter looks steadily at her. 'Yes, Miss Nora, I'm afraid it is.'

'Oh, I'm so sorry.'

Mrs Lampeter squeezes Nora's hand. 'I might not be able to come again,' she says steadily.

'Please don't say that.' Nora's voice is just a whisper.

'I'd rather say it than have you wonder. I would never stop coming if I was able to come. I hope you know that.'

'Yes, I do. Is there anything I can do to help?'

'You could remember me and my Pat and the kids in your prayers too.'

'I will, Mrs Lampeter, I will, I promise.' And she promises right now, to the God she has not spoken to for years, that she'll start to pray again.

'Miss Nora, I have to go. I'm sorry, but it's best I don't stay too long.' She coughs again and Nora stiffens as she sees the flecks of blood staining her friend's handkerchief.

'I want to hug you, Mrs Lampeter.'

'That might not be—' but already Nora's arms are around her and she plants a kiss on Mrs Lampeter's cheek.

'You are my best friend, and I love you.' Nora stands back and takes a long look at Mrs Lampeter. 'Please take care of yourself, and I'll pray for you all. I'll see you when you're better and, in the meantime, don't worry about me.' She stands back and smiles bravely, though her heart is breaking and she knows that, in all probability, she will not see Mrs Lampeter again.

'Thank you, Miss Nora – Nora.' The little intimacy touches Nora just as much as it did on the day of her baby's birth, and she smiles. Mrs Lampeter clutches the arm of her chair to steady herself and stands still for a moment until she has her balance. With a long look she takes in Nora's green eyes, her porcelain skin and the dark hair struggling into a slight wave, despite the rough and untidy cut. She brushes down her coat with her hand and squeezes Nora's fingers. 'I'm proud of you, Nora. Any mother would be proud to have you as a daughter.'

Nora blinks back tears. 'You've been like a mother to me – a best friend and a mother.' She takes a step back, no longer able to bear it. 'Thank you for my scones,' she offers limply, hugging the little package to her as Mrs Lampeter walks away.

Though she holds herself together as long as she can, as soon as Mrs Lampeter is out of sight, Nora crumples. Wrapping her arms around herself, she sobs. Suddenly she feels a presence beside her, and a hand is thrust towards her.

'Give!' the aide demands. When Nora holds the packet even closer, the aide's voice goes up several decibels. 'Give! That woman's dying of consumption. We don't want her infected things here. She should never have been allowed in here.'

'She's not dying. Don't you say that,' Nora rasps, pushing her away. 'Don't you say that!' she wails again, but already a whistle has blown and staff descend on Nora from all sides.

'She's violent and out of control. She hit me!' the aide shrieks as Sister Cummings appears.

'Violent, eh? Well, that'll be the last visit for you, young lady.' There's a sneer of satisfaction on her face as she snaps her fingers. 'Wet pack,' she shouts. 'Now!'

Nora cowers but still holds on to the packet. There'll be no mercy now. Hands drag her by the arms until she loses her balance and stumbles and she is pulled along the floor, someone holding a handful of hair, another her smock, and the little bag tears and the scones roll onto the floor and are crushed to crumbs under countless feet. 'No,' she wails. 'It's not fair. I hate you all!'

They tear her clothes roughly from her body and force her down onto a trolley where she continues to shout and struggle, pulling on the leather restraints until her wrists and ankles are red with blood. They steep sheets in icy water and lay one after the other after the other on the metal bed, while Nora can do nothing more than watch and wait in fear. Finally, she's untied, and four male nurses, who seem oblivious to her screams, her pleas and her nakedness, descend upon her and lift her up, one holding her head tightly, another her shoulders, another her body with her arms pinned to her sides, and the fourth her feet, and for a moment she's suspended over the pile of soaking, freezing sheets onto which they finally lower her. They hold her still by whatever means and with whatever force it takes, Nora fighting and crying out every bit of the way. One after another, they wrap the sheets very tightly around her, mummifying her from neck to toe, until she's a stiff, shapeless parcel, shivering uncontrollably and totally helpless. They place a cold compress over her eyes and she's imprisoned, the frustration of injustice and grief boiling over inside her. The only thing she can do is scream; each time she does, they slap her viciously.

'One more outburst, Jennings, and I'll tape your mouth,' Sister Cummings shouts. But Nora isn't spent yet and screams again. 'Tape her mouth!' cries Sister Cummings and, finally beaten, Nora slumps, though the panic continues within. The only thing that can still move is her mind. The only place where there's any warmth is between her legs, where she's wet herself in fear.

Breathe. Be calm. It has to end sometime.

Someone lifts the cloth from Nora's eyes and Sister Cummings fixes her gaze from only a few inches away. 'You won't win, you little bitch. I can play this game just as well as you can – and for even longer. You can never win. No point in trying. And no more brats like the last either. Thought you'd had your appendix out, didn't you? Sterilisation, my dear. What do you think of that then?'

Nora feels as though she will burst with rage and grief, but the only things she can move are her eyes, which dart about trying to escape this horror. But there is no way out. She cannot move. There is no other place to go. *Sterilisation! How dare they?* She thrashes her head from side to side and screams with fury, but there is no sound, no relief, since she cannot open her mouth. She scrunches her eyes shut. *If there is a God, help me!*

And suddenly she feels a release as she bursts out from the top of her head. Out of her poor, bound body, now lying there below her in its white shroud. Now they cannot reach her. She is free and she feels grateful to her father for all the practice he and his belt gave her when she was a child. She watches as her body relaxes, and feels a rare swell of triumph.

Chapter Sixteen

1946
Seven years

Dr Stilworth's face is increasingly lined, years of fatigue and irritation marking him permanently. Sometimes, during his morning ablutions, he cannot meet his own eyes in the mirror. He's sick of being the futile thorn in the flesh of the establishment, though hope occasionally sparks that his efforts might one day prompt radical change. Of course, he has a choice. He can stay and try to make a difference, or abandon ship – and he'd be lying to himself if he pretended he hadn't given the idea a good deal of thought. But despite it all, he can't let go. And in any case, there are new needs here now since the war. There are many men with shell-shocked minds, missing limbs, lost identities, who nevertheless seem to have lots of visitors, which is strange since the so-called 'mental' patients get very few.

Nora Jennings concerns him still as he watches her steady deterioration. Though the war is over, battle obviously still rages within her, to the point that she seems not to have noticed the blooming of spring. This used to be one of the few things that could tease a rare smile from her, despite the humiliation, degradation, assaults and punishments she is forced to deal with on an almost daily basis. There seems to be little he can do to protect her. She was not allowed to attend the funeral of the only visitor she ever had – a Mrs Lampeter – and she registered her objection by refusing to work, something that didn't go down well with Sister Cummings. There'll still be some revenge for that to come, somewhere along the line. He is distracted from these dark thoughts by the sight of Nora herself, who is walking badly and appears to be wincing with every step. He glances around at the nurses, busy with their endless cleaning and administration, none of which appears patient-related. Hasn't anyone noticed that something's wrong? 'Sister Cummings, do you know why Nora is walking badly today?'

She glances at Nora, her face blank. 'Apart from her usual attention-seeking, you mean?' she says dismissively.

Dr Stilworth frowns. 'I don't think this is attention-seeking behaviour. She appears to be in pain.' Sister Cummings rolls her eyes heavenward and returns to her ledger. Dr Stilworth balls his fists but says nothing, watching Nora struggle as she makes for her chair. He walks over to her.

'Pandering to her will only encourage her,' Sister Cummings calls after him, not looking up from her paperwork.

He ignores her studiously. 'Nora, come and sit down. What's happened here?' He guides her to a chair and beckons to an aide to come over. 'Nora, I need to take your shoe off.' As he lifts her slender leg onto his knee and starts to ease off the shoe, she flinches, and his nose wrinkles as the smell of infection assaults him. Nora grasps the arm of the chair and tries to withdraw her foot. 'I'm sorry, Nora, but I need to see your foot.'

Slowly, he eases her foot from the shoe and stops still, aghast. 'My God,' he gasps. The stocking is stuck to her toes with blood and pus – no wonder it smells so foul. He looks up at Nora, whose eyes are scrunched shut and whose mouth is puckered in pain. 'Nora, I shall be as gentle as I can, but we have to get this stocking off.' He raises his eyes to the aide who stands by, looking surly. 'Bring a bowl of warm water with some antiseptic and some clean towels, please. I'll be back shortly.'

But as he starts to get up, Nora grabs at the sleeve of his white lab coat. She mutters a pathetic 'Thank you', and lifts her other foot a few centimetres from the floor. She sits white-knuckled in the chair as he unties the lace of her other shoe and removes it as carefully as he can. Shock and anger suffuse him as he finds a similar stinking mess of pus and blood seeping through the fabric of her stocking.

The aide kneels down with the bowl of water and starts to remove the stockings. 'No,' Dr Stilworth says sharply. 'Leave the stockings and soak her feet in the water for ten minutes. I will come back and remove them myself. Add a little antiseptic.' He approaches Sister Cummings's desk as quickly as his damaged leg will allow. He knows he cuts a ridiculous figure when trying to hurry, but fury burns away any trace of self-consciousness. 'Have you seen Nora's feet, Sister?'

'No,' she says, not looking up from her work.

'Why not?'

She sighs impatiently and slams her pen down. 'No one reported anything wrong.'

'Can't you see that she can hardly walk?' Dr Stilworth is incensed. 'The days of harsh, unsophisticated methods – in other words, of cruelty – are coming to an end, Sister. This is reprehensible and I will be reporting it to both Matron and Dr Mason.'

'You must do as you see fit, doctor.' Her insolent eyes dare him to do so.

'Be sure that I will. And should anything befall Nora or any of the other patients in the meantime, I will investigate with all powers available to me. Do you understand?' She holds his gaze with arrogant silence, narrowing her eyes. 'This is the end of this battle of wills between us, Sister. I give you notice that I will fight you openly now – and I will win.'

He goes back to Nora and tells the aide to get out of his sight. He kneels back down on the floor, lifts Nora's foot onto a towel on his thigh and very gently separates the fabric of the stocking from the suppurating wounds beneath. He still can't comprehend what he is seeing. Every nail has been cut so low and so roughly that each toe bears a raw, oozing sore where the vulnerable nail bed is not only exposed but traumatised. He notes with astonishment that these wounds are several days old. How could they have been missed? He relieves the other foot of its stocking to find similar wounds. He looks up into her grateful eyes, questioning, but she blinks and looks away.

'What happened, Nora?' he asks, lips tight and face pale with shock and rage.

'Nothing,' she whispers.

'Who did this?' But she's silent. He prays that this is the result of rough, clumsy and careless work rather than a calculated punishment. Probably he'll never know.

'Sister!' he thunders, his voice carrying along the ward and causing every head except hers to turn. He stands and calls even more loudly. 'Sister, I can stand here and call you for the rest of the day if you wish, or you could come now and look at these wounds.' She looks up and makes not a move. Tom raises his voice further. 'If I have to shout so loudly that Dr Mason and Matron hear me in their offices, I will. I do not accept your disrespect of me or of the people you have been honoured to have in your care. You are a nurse, and I want—' He breaks off as she finally stands and stamps her way down the ward. Tom waits until she is standing beside him, glowering up at him.

'I want Nora's feet gently but thoroughly cleaned, then dressed daily until they are completely healed. Please have one of your nurses apply paraffin jelly and have them dressed with the utmost care. All dressings must be soaked off in warm water for thirty minutes prior to any attempt at removal. No shoes. I'm sure we can improvise some footwear that spares her toes until they are completely well. Do I make myself clear?'

She nods, but there's no trace of remorse. The fury that surrounds her is palpable, but for once Dr Stilworth is above it. 'Let me say again: if anything should befall Nora or any other patient – or indeed any member of staff – I will take that very seriously indeed.' He turns to Nora. 'I'm so sorry, Nora,' he says. 'I know you dare not tell me who did this, and you don't need to. Please don't worry. We will get these dressed for you and, in the meantime, I want you to keep off your feet for a few days. You will have a wheelchair and the staff will help you in and out of it.'

Nora gazes at him with fearful eyes.

'Don't worry, Nora. We'll get it all sorted out for you.' He fixes Sister Cummings with a stare and his voice becomes steely. 'Won't we, Sister?' He turns to leave then halts, as though something has just occurred to him. 'Sister.' He turns to look her in the eye. 'Bearing in mind the seriousness of the condition of Nora's feet, it might be an idea if you were to dress them yourself, since you are the most experienced member of staff here. And, of course, I'd like to examine them, so please do send for me when you've taken the bandages off and I'll come immediately before you dress them again.'

He looks back at Nora. 'Nora, I'm putting you in very good hands now. Your feet are going to be fine. I don't want you to worry about anything.'

He straightens up, his face almost unreadable. 'Sister, please may I see you in your office?'

An air of repressed rage like the vibration of an impending storm floats around Sister Cummings, who stays rooted to the spot.

'We can do this here, Sister, or we can do it in the privacy of your office. Personally, I don't mind which.' He turns once again and limps up the ward, where the staff seem to be holding their breath. Sister Cummings scowls but then falls in behind him, her face like thunder.

Dr Stilworth holds the door open until she follows him inside, then he closes it quietly behind her and remains standing while she takes her seat at the desk. He regards her for a long, silent moment, allowing himself the relief of finally being at the point of speaking his truth regardless of consequence. And when he opens his mouth, the voice that emerges is clear, controlled and powerful. 'I have no idea why you hate this woman so much. I can only assume that something in your own past makes you behave as you do. I pity you in carrying such a burden that must contaminate every area of your life. However, you cannot be allowed to continue to mistreat Nora Jennings – or anyone else for that matter – any longer. You are not fit to hold a position that allows you to harm people.' He takes a breath, watching Sister Cummings, whose eyes remain focused on the desk in front of her. 'I shall report this to Dr Mason and Matron and demand an enquiry. I will not rest until you are dismissed from this hospital. Do you understand?'

Sister Cummings makes no move, and Dr Stilworth quietly leaves the room.

The next morning Sister Cummings is in her office as normal, but is unusually quiet. The staff mill about, wondering what to do, since there has been no morning handover and no list of demands from the sister. Shortly after eight thirty, Dr Mason and Miss Endsleigh enter the ward and proceed directly to the office.

Stan looks at Gladys who raises her brows, shrugs her shoulders and looks mystified. Then she turns to the younger staff. 'Come on now, you know your routine. There's lots to be done. Let's have this floor mopped and make sure that everything is as Sister would want it. Come on. Look sharp.'

In Sister Cummings's office, the voices are strained and hushed.

'Why?' Dr Mason asks. 'You are a bright, efficient woman and have been with us for some years now. This is not the first time that there has been concern about your treatment of the patients, and I regret that I have not taken those complaints more seriously in the past.'

But Sister Cummings is not fully there. She is Beatrice Cummings, seventeen and deliriously happy; in love for the one and only time. She sees her life laid out in front of her, married with happy children playing at her feet. Then everything changes. Memories flash through her mind – her mother becoming sick and unable to manage the house; she herself having to leave school before her final exams in order to care for her; discovering her beloved boyfriend hand in hand with another girl. Her mother bedbound, her breast rotting with putrid, cancerous sores that only she is allowed to see. Hearing the banns read in church for the marriage of her love to another girl. Beatrice ripping up a beautiful dress and stuffing the fabric in her mouth so she cannot scream out loud.

'Do you have anything to say?' Dr Mason's voice cuts through the mist of years and finally Sister Cummings looks up at him.

'No.'

'Then I have to tell you that you will be leaving the hospital this morning. At least that will relieve you of the embarrassment of having to appear at an investigation of your abuse of some of our patients.' He turns to Matron. 'Matron, is there anything you wish to add?'

Miss Endsleigh shakes her head. 'Perhaps you could gather your personal belongings now.'

Sister Cummings, pale but dry-eyed, opens her desk drawer without a word, takes her pen and a comb, closes the drawer carefully and stands. Dr Mason opens the door and stands back. Sister Cummings steps out and, without even a final look at the ward, walks away with Dr Mason and Matron at her heels.

The ward is deathly quiet, as if even the patients know that something momentous is happening. The eyes of all the staff follow the procession out of the ward. Gladys looks at Stan and they hold each other's eyes for a moment, then Stan claps his hands. 'So what are you all staring at? Come on, there's work to do.'

Chapter Seventeen

1956
Seventeen years

Ever since the dismissal of Sister Cummings, years ago, there have been changes on an almost weekly basis. Sure, the odd slap still happens – the older staff are too set in their ways to change everything. And people sometimes 'fall out of bed' after a confrontation. Occasionally there are still shouts and screams from the sluice or the treatment room, but, on the whole, things are better. There's also a new drug – chlorpromazine – that has quietened a lot of patients, although the side effects aren't pretty. And it's by no means the most effective change to have come to Rowan.

In 1953, a television was installed so that patients and staff alike could watch the coronation of Queen Elizabeth II. It was a public holiday, so there was only a small crew of nurses, but they sat together with the patients to watch the black-and-white images and listen to the choir of Westminster Abbey and the cheers of the crowds. Tea and plates of cake and biscuits were passed around. There were the usual moans and groans with the odd scream for good measure, but what dominated were animated conversation and sighs of wonder, with just the odd yell telling someone to quieten down. A party followed, the trees and bushes decorated with red, white and blue bunting, a Union Jack flying high. The Salvation Army band was a hit, getting hands clapping, toes tapping. Both staff and patients danced. Nora wore a pale green flowery frock with a nipped-in waist and a narrow tan belt. She even had beige sandals. Joe looked smart in his navy jacket and a red tie that looked striking against his white shirt. He smiled at Nora and she at him, though they kept their distance. Dr Stilworth, in a grey suit rather than his white coat, didn't dance because of his leg, but smiled encouragingly at the patients who did, while Dr Mason was seen fleetingly, wandering about smiling at people and exchanging a few words here and there before making a smart though dignified getaway within the hour, allowing the staff to relax again.

The effects of the television on staff and patients were remarkable, and so, music followed. Alma Cogan and Matt Monro, Bing Crosby and Petula Clark have an effect on morale that's nothing short of miraculous.

But some things don't change. On winter mornings, cold fog rises up from the earth and clings to the trees, while the souls of the departed creep around, just as they did when clothed in their tortured bodies. Nurses emerge from the knee-deep mist, torches in hands, awaiting a dawn that will bring relief from the deep gloom of grumbling skies. Though the patients are alive, many are quiescent, their spirit extinguished. Stilled and silenced for so long, they sit tethered, eyes vacant as they wait for a final release.

A change in Nora has been noted. Quizzical eyes follow her and questions form in the minds of her keepers. Relieved of daily bullying and punishment, she can breathe, and even though life may still be hard and empty, Nora, at thirty-four, is alive once more.

But today, she hasn't felt warm since she awoke in the middle of the night, her toes frozen, chilblains itching and sore. The bitter wind blows under her dress and sneaks up past her knees to the chafed inside of her thighs. Her one regulation sanitary towel is sodden and uncomfortable, and it's not yet lunchtime. She carries her basket of peelings and scraps and inches out of the door, bracing herself. Her hands smart at the new assault on her broken skin, and newly closed cuts spring open again, oozing blood. She hardly feels it any longer.

At the back door of the kitchen, old men – coughing and wheezing, heads bowed and eyes screwed – suck the last life out of second-hand tobacco they've scavenged. Feet stamping, gnarled knuckles made purple by the cold, they pull their old, threadbare jackets around their even older bony bodies. There's neither conversation nor eye contact, no social smiles. Just hacking coughs and furtive glances. The men shuffle out of Nora's way as she hoists the pail to the high lip of the bin, tips it and waits till all the cold, wet scraps slide into the open mouth. Then, returning to the kitchen, she takes up her place in the corner.

Nurse Jenny Turret is in the kitchen collecting tea and coffee for the staffroom. She pauses and puts both hands flat on the countertop, leaning forward with her weight on her hands. Pristine in starched white collar and cuffs and high cap, she hunches her shoulders, her head hanging forward. Nora watches surreptitiously from where she stands peeling yet more potatoes, concern clouding her face. The presence of Nurse Turret disturbs her. She puts her head down and concentrates on her own work, hardly feeling her cold, chapped hands as she drops one potato after the other into icy water. Her hands anaesthetised by the cold, more than once she cuts herself. She glances over at Nurse Turret every few seconds.

'What are you gawping at?' Nurse Turret snaps, drawing the back of her hand across her nose, embarrassed at her own distress. Nora quickly tries to reassemble her face, deconstructing the concern written upon it. 'I asked you what you're gawping at.'

Nora drops her head again and starts to quiver all over. She knows there's no appropriate answer. Really, none is required. She tries her hardest to disappear, but her heart is thumping in her chest. She suddenly remembers Peggy – beautiful Peggy – and the day of the biscuit. Marshalling all her courage, she puts down the knife and dries her hands on her apron. Shaking with fear, but her face set in determination, she makes her quiet way to Nurse Turret's side and takes a deep breath. 'Are you unwell?' she asks in a tremulous voice. 'Can I get you some water?'

The nurse lifts her tear-stained face and looks at Nora with incredulity. None of the patients has ever asked after the staff.

She doesn't say anything and, after a few moments, Nora turns to go back to her corner. That's it now; she must be in real trouble. But then Nurse Turret starts to sob and Nora turns, confused and a bit frightened. Nurse Turret looks at her through her tears, and the words just tumble out. 'I was pregnant. I lost my baby.' A spasm shakes the nurse and her head drops lower until she rests her forehead on her hands and weeps.

Nora looks on helplessly. She has no idea what to do, though her heart breaks for this poor woman. Then words form, and almost involuntarily pop out. 'I'm so sorry,' she murmurs. 'I lost mine too. I know how you feel.' She has an urge to touch the nurse, offer her some physical comfort, but dare not.

Nurse Turret raises her head and looks at Nora, her eyes wide. This is the most eye contact she's had with a patient in years. Then, in a low voice, as though she too is afraid, she says, 'How can *you* feel sorry for *me*?'

'I'm sorry,' Nora mutters, retreating a few steps.

'Don't be. Even though it was before my time, I know you lost your baby, and I know you've had a very hard time here over many years. I'm like one of your jailers. How can you find it in your heart to be sorry for me?'

'I don't know,' Nora stammers. 'I just know how awful it felt. I'm sorry.'

Nurse Turret sighs and runs her fingers through her hair. 'No, Nora. It's me who should be sorry. I don't think any of us have thought too much about your grief and pain – any of you. I think we thought you didn't have feelings like us.'

'Why not?'

'Because you're . . . well, you're . . .'

'Defective?'

The nurse blushes. 'How did you have the courage to offer me comfort?'

'I'm sorry – I don't know.'

Nurse Turret just looks at her. 'You don't need to be sorry. It was very kind of you.' Nora's confusion is clear on her face, and the nurse continues. 'We're not allowed to express our feelings here. Whether we might feel fond of someone, or dislike them, it doesn't matter; we're not allowed to say anything.'

'Oh. I didn't know that.' Nora thinks for a moment. 'But you ask me how I feel and expect me to tell you . . .'

'It's different.'

'Why?'

'Because I'm staff and you're a patient.'

'Oh.' Nora pauses, taking a few moments to process this. 'But we're both women?'

'Yes, we are.'

'But not equal women?'

Nurse Turret looks embarrassed again, then the mask is back. 'I don't have time for all this chatter,' she blusters, and Nora, admonished, retreats back to her corner, and back into herself.

The following day, when Nurse Turret comes into the kitchen, Nora keeps her head down.

'Nora, how are you today?' Nurse Turret calls over to her.

Nora's knife hovers over the potato she's peeling. *Is she really talking to me?*

'Nora? How are you today?'

Without moving her head, Nora steals a glance along to where Nurse Turret is standing. 'I feel sad,' she says, her voice barely audible.

'I'm sorry.'

Nora freezes, astonished. None of the nurses has ever instigated a conversation with her, let alone expressed sympathy with her. Well, Gladys does sometimes when they're out on one of their walks, and Kumar sometimes jokes a bit at night, but that's all. Nora's body tingles. Something amazing has just happened. She wonders if she dares continue the conversation.

'And how are you?' she asks shyly.

'I feel a little better today, thank you,' says Nurse Turret, with a weak but definite smile.

'That's good,' whispers Nora. She lifts her head a little and smiles, too.

Chapter Eighteen

1961
Twenty-two years

Gladys enters the day room with her usual cheery smile. 'Are you ready?' she says. Nora, who has been ready and waiting for the last couple of hours, smiles. She enjoys her walks with Gladys, who is kind and yet keeps her in line if necessary – like the day when Nora and Joe were chatting and she was quite impatient with them both. But in the main, she behaves rather like a benevolent grandmother. 'Come on, then,' says Gladys. 'Are you going to be warm enough without your cardigan?' Nora loves it when Gladys says things like that. It's so long since anyone seemed to care one jot about how she is or who she is, but she knows Gladys does.

They walk together, chatting with ease about how Nora feels and about this new television programme, *Coronation Street*. Lost in conversation, Gladys takes them on a different route. The dog violets and wild honeysuckle are just starting to share their scent and Nora, as always, touches the flowers as they stroll along, remembering walks with her grandfather.

They come to a place where the branches are low, tenderly reaching out to each other until they almost touch. Some of the new leaves are starting to adopt a livelier spring green; the light filtering through them has a soft, golden glow. Nora pauses to take in the beauty of it, her mother's voice in her head – *Fill your memory banks . . .*

But the afternoon sun glints on something in the sparse undergrowth. She shifts her gaze and sees that there are dozens of small objects in the grass. She stares, transfixed. 'What are all those little things?' she asks, glancing at Gladys.

Gladys's face changes instantly. Her smile disappears and she looks distinctly uncomfortable. 'Come away, Nora,' Gladys says, pulling on Nora's sleeve. 'This isn't a nice place to walk.'

She attempts to steer Nora away with an urgency that only serves to increase Nora's curiosity. 'But what are they?' she persists. 'There's so many of them.'

'They're nothing. Now, come away or we'll be late back.'

But Nora stubbornly hangs back. She's not so easily put off at thirty-nine as she was at seventeen. 'They can't be nothing,' she scoffs.

For the first time in all Nora's years of knowing her, Gladys looks irritated. 'For goodness' sake, Nora. If you must know, they're grave markers. This is the cemetery. It's where people who once lived here are buried.'

'Here in the institution?'

'Yes.'

'Oh, yes. Joe said his mother was buried here in the cemetery.' Nora's eyes linger a few moments longer, then wander to an area where the little markers are huddled together as though for comfort. Then, a tug on her sleeve brings her back to herself. 'Nora, come away.'

For once, Nora disobeys, staying rooted to the spot. 'Why are those ones over there different?' she asks, pointing.

Gladys doesn't meet her eye. 'Nora. We have to go. I shouldn't have brought you here. It's an awful place. We'll be late and there'll be hell to pay.'

Though she finally walks after Gladys and away from the graves, Nora can't help but look back at them. 'But Gladys, why are they here?'

There's a long pause and then, her voice heavy with reluctance, Gladys responds. 'They're children's graves. Now, do as you're told. Hurry up.'

Nora stops still, her brow puckering in confusion. 'But there aren't any children here.'

Gladys looks flustered, something else Nora hasn't seen before, which only makes her even more curious. 'Nora, we're going right now,' she snaps. 'If we're not back before the bell sounds for supper, we'll both be for it.' She walks on and Nora finally does as she's bidden, allowing herself to be guided along the path. But part of her still lingers in that place with its shifting light. Suddenly, a cold shiver creeps up her spine, enveloping her neck and causing beads of cold sweat to form on her brow. She stops abruptly and is left behind until Gladys realises she's not following.

As Gladys turns, Nora finds her voice again, tremulous and breathy. 'Gladys, who adopted my little girl?' she demands. She watches as Gladys blanches then blushes, avoiding Nora's eyes.

'I don't know,' she manages as she turns and walks ahead, her shoulders looking more hunched, as though her neck is trying to disappear between them. Nora watches as if from down a long tunnel, and eventually trudges in Gladys's footsteps.

Sitting in the day room, questions assault Nora's mind, tapping their impatient toes, begging answers, seeking resolution. The little metal markers have resurrected a long-forgotten memory of the time when her grandmother died. She was only six or seven at the time but, as if it were only yesterday, she can see her mother lifting the black net veil over her face to mop away the tears while her father's hand cups her elbow in support. She pictured that evidence of his love for her mother for years afterwards, remembering it every Sunday when the family visited the grave after mass.

The speckled grey granite headstone said so much in just a few words.

In loving memory of Beth Anderson.
Faithful wife, beloved mother and grandmother.
6 June 1868–27 November 1927
Rest in peace in the loving arms of the Lord.

Her grandmother was loved and remembered. She was an early summer baby who had an early winter passing and had lived for fifty-nine years. She was faithful to her husband and had raised her children to bear their own. She was wished rest and peace now that she had completed her task, and was with Jesus, who loved her and would hold her for ever.

Nora can't stop thinking about the difference between her grandmother's beautiful, well-tended grave and those tiny afterthoughts in the dirt outside. Does anyone come here and cry about these people? Will anyone come and cry over her when she dies? She wonders if the amount that people cry is dependent upon how much they loved the person who died. How can Nora have cried so long and so much – and still – for the baby she never met, even though she's alive but living somewhere else? She wonders if she's still with her adoptive mother, or if maybe she's a mother now in her own right. 'I might be a grandmother,' she whispers to herself.

But as she sees again the afternoon sun slanting through the trees and the light dancing on the grave markers, her heart clenches and her blood seems to freeze in her veins. She looks straight ahead with a strange mixture of confusion and clarity. *Surely not* … But the graveyard reels her in as if she's been harpooned. Her heart starts to race and her hands claw at the arms of her chair. No … it can't be …

She has to know. She glances around furtively, then stands up. Most people are watching television. She is almost at the door when Gladys's voice surprises her, making her jump. 'Where are you going, Nora?'

Nora turns and manages to look directly at Gladys. 'I'm going to the toilet,' she mutters, and turns away before Gladys can question her further. She waits for a few seconds outside the day room, gathering all her courage, then sets off as casually as she can. Out in the corridor, she ignores the left turn that would take her towards the toilets.

She keeps close to the wall, trembling but resolute, never looking back. She can hardly breathe. The back door is in sight. Quietly, she opens it and exits into the yard.

Then she breaks into a run.

The trees are silhouetted eerily against the dying sun. It's so cold, and she realises too late that she isn't dressed for the weather, but her body surges forward, spurred on by a will and urgency of its own. Branches clatter together as the wind gathers, making a noise like toothless, chattering old women. She presses on through the wooden gate, then hurries along the path. An owl, disturbed by her passing, screeches as it flaps out of its resting place on silent wings.

Under the trees the light is dim, and she shivers as the damp air enshrouds her. She stumbles along between silver birch and elm and willowy saplings that grab at her as she rushes past them. Then, all of a sudden, she is in the clearing, where she can see the first of the markers claimed by ivy creepers and the remains of last summer's periwinkle and bluebells. As her eyes adjust to the falling dusk, she can see, stretching out into the distance, within the wood and beyond, hundreds of them, some in rows and some haphazardly placed, soldiers fallen in battle. She stands stock-still, her frozen hand gripping her throat, her other arm across her chest, clutching her side, as if to prevent herself from falling apart.

Something half remembered from all those years ago rushes unbidden into her mind, and her hand covers her mouth as a yelp escapes. She can see Nurse Jamison dashing from the sluice at the back of the treatment room, avoiding Nora still lying on the bed, her birth wounds being stitched. The fear and shock on the nurse's face as she ran out, her hand half covering her tears.

Nora starts to run again. Gone is her concern about the noise she is making or who might catch her. Twigs catch in her hair, scratch at her face and tear holes in her stockings. She realises that she has lost the path, but something instinctual pulls her forward. Her foot catches in a tree root, sending her sprawling in the dirt as her hand jars against one of the markers, its little central spike puncturing her palm. Instantly she is on her feet again, unaware of the bleeding from her hand or the blood mingled with tears that streaks her face. Her chest burns as her breath comes in jagged gasps. And suddenly she is there. She stops, gulping deep breaths. It's been years since she has run like that.

The markers are huddled together, defending the tiny corpses they guard. She falls to her knees. Could it be? *Please God, not . . .* She can't even bear to finish the thought. She claws away rotting vegetation, searching, brushing her hair off her face with her sleeve; creeping forward, her knees bleeding as she frantically examines every marker, clearing them of their layers of grime.

Each bears a series of numbers.

1939 8.7.1922

1910 6.4.1918

Did these babies die in 1939 and 1910 respectively?

2038 23.9.1937

2249 11.12.1942

Or are the last numbers the date?

2197 18.6.1939

And the first a hospital number?

2361 16.1.1940

2410 19.3.1940

Hospital numbers and dates, then. Nothing to say who had lived and who had died or anything about the life that had passed between.

And then she freezes.

She stares, hardly daring to move. Her heart races and her breath comes in painful rasps. She has found a cluster of graves of babies who died in 1940. Her hands tremble as she slows down, hardly daring to look, yet knowing she would search for ever if need be. One by one, peering through the falling twilight, she examines every date and number, feeling a stab of guilt every time she passes over one, glad that it is not the one she is so desperate and terrified to find.

Her breathing ceases as she sees 1529 – her own patient number. She closes her eyes, staving off the moment of truth.

For what seems like an eternity she hangs suspended out of her body in a safe, numb place far above. She sees her body resting back on its heels, motionless, its eyes staring. Then its hand reaches out, clearing dirt from the numbers.

1529 30.4.1940

It must be some cruel joke. A nightmare? *Please.* Her bleeding hands trace the contours of the earth slowly, lovingly – not even a swelling, a ridge, a hint of a disturbance. She caresses it. But then she digs, forcing her nails into the hardened soil, skinning her knuckles, filling her recent wounds with filth, glorying in the pain. Mixing her blood with this earth that has contained her flesh without her knowledge for all these years.

She is not aware of her wailing, nor of the sudden commotion around her. Or the arms that lift her, dragging her away. Neither Stan's tenderness nor Gladys's motherly tones can reach her.

'Come, Nora,' Gladys coaxes. 'It's all right. Come.'

But nothing is all right, nor will it ever be again.

'Poor little bugger,' Stan mutters, his voice thick with anger and sadness.

They carry her screaming, struggling body back to Rowan, where Gladys undresses her and gently lowers her into a warm bath where, after a while, her body seems to almost melt into the warmth, limp and silent as the light fades out of her eyes. Gladys bathes Nora's cuts, cleans her nails, washes her hair and finally wraps her in a blanket and demands a wheelchair to take her to the dormitory. Stan pushes the chair in silence, and the grim cloud of purpose emanating from both him and Gladys demands a clear way, and respect for this grieving mother.

Chapter Nineteen

Weeks later, Nora lies motionless and unseeing, hiding in a protective cocoon of her own making. A silent, detached world for one, with neither borders nor end. Here, nothing exists any longer – not even Nora herself. 'Nora,' Gladys coaxes every now and again, but Nora is unreachable, confined to her own private theatre where, while she's awake, the film of her life rolls inter-mittently before she sinks once more into the oblivion that is her one answered prayer.

The soapy sponge is gentle on her face. From a far-off, misty place she can perceive the sadness in the hand that guides it as it cleans her skin. She hears the tinkling splashes of water as the sponge is rinsed and wrung out over the enamel bowl. But she feels nothing. No movement. Nothing matters. They can do with her whatever they wish.

As though someone has heard her, Nora's arm is lifted and the sponge sweeps around her armpit before her hand is placed back on the sheet. Towels are moved. Her torso is raised to a sitting position and bent forward, a position she'll hold all day if some-one doesn't move her again. Something is pulled over her head. Her arms are guided into sleeves and for a moment stick out like a scarecrow's until someone guides them back to rest beside her body. Her body is lowered backwards onto the bed, her head onto the thin pillow. A sheet is pulled up, a blanket placed over it. Her body moves involuntarily as someone lifts the corners of the mattress to tuck in the corners of the sheet. And then, she is still. A hand settles momentarily on her brow. A kindly gesture no doubt, but too late for Nora. She is no longer there.

$$\star \qquad \star \qquad \star$$

The weeks become months. The routine continues. Discussions take place. No one really addresses Nora – there'd be no point, anyway. The tube by which they feed her is changed. Her personal hygiene is catered for. Her catheter removed and replaced. Her period is stemmed with a rough sanitary towel. Dr Stilworth does his daily rounds and hopes for change. Each day he raises her arm or leg and releases it, and each day the limb stays where he's put it until he applies pressure to replace it on the bed. He raises her head and removes his hand, and her neck remains rigid until he presses down on her forehead to settle it back on the pillow. He shakes his head sadly. This strangest of all signs – waxy flexibility – is still present and doesn't bode well. He scribbles in her file.

   No change. Catatonic stupor.

Summer is long gone and autumn will soon give way to winter and still there is no change apart from Nora's wasting muscles and stark pallor. Having completed his examination, Dr Stilworth places a gentle hand on her brow then walks away, his shoulders hunched with the weight of the responsibility he feels for this woman's state. He finally approaches Dr Mason's office, his steps as heavy as his heart. He's grateful that the old man hasn't hassled him. Now that he is Dr Mason's second in command, Dr Stilworth pretty much runs the ward. But he's tired. His leg aches and his walking is deteriorating. Sometimes, as he looks at himself in the mirror as he shaves, he observes his greying hair and wonders where his life has gone. He knocks on Dr Mason's door with trepidation. 'Dr Mason.' He dispenses with the usual small talk. 'May I discuss Nora Jennings's case with you?'

He has long resisted what his clinical judgement knows needs to happen next, but now he sits with the proverbial cap in hand at the feet of the master in whom he has had little faith and not much more respect. For some years he has avoided getting caught in a one-to-one situation in this room, where Dr Mason's authority surrounds and almost suffocates him. Better when there's a dilution forced by the presence of others. Of course, he knows that Dr Mason must be aware of his disrespect, but neither of them has had the courage to confront it. Now he looks at his chief – old, a little bent, and looking even more tired than he himself feels – and for the first time in a very long while, he feels pity for the man.

Dr Mason's waistcoat is, as always, buttoned except for the last, but no watch chain hangs there now; a gold watch weighs down his left wrist instead. His coat is still starched and pristine and his pinstriped jacket hangs on its hanger on the hat rack. 'Come. Sit,' Dr Mason says, gesturing to a chair with his well-manicured hand. Tom resists the urge to rebel by choosing a different one, as he usually does, and hopes his boss registers this token of Tom's change of heart. He places Nora's notes on the desk between them.

'As you know, she has been in a catatonic state for many months. There's no change apart from the usual muscle wasting. My concern is that she could now continue to a permanent vegetative state unless we attempt to interrupt it.' He's surprised that he's managed this well-prepared statement coherently and without letting out the emotion he feels bubbling up within him.

'And what do you propose?' There's no hint of satisfaction or gloating in Dr Mason's tone. A simple clinical question. Tom is grateful.

'Though it's possible that recovery may be taking place on some level while she's closed in and protecting herself from the outside world, we're at the point where further delay becomes risky.'

'Indeed. So?'

'Sadly, I think we have little choice but to use electroshock.' Even as he says this, he remembers the promise – one he should never have made – all those years ago: 'I promise you I will never endorse this treatment for you.'

Dr Mason strokes his chin. 'I think, in the circumstances, this is the most acceptable path,' he says gravely and with none of the relish and fire there used to be. 'So, yes, go ahead.'

Tom exhales. Much as he hates this treatment, he has seen its life-saving benefits from time to time, and certainly nothing else he has tried has made any difference whatsoever to Nora. He fears it could be her last chance. 'I'll set it up.' He stands and gathers the notes in front of him. 'Thank you, sir.' He looks sadly at his old adversary for the first time in some years, a reluctant respect growing between them.

'Shall I say daily?'

He holds his breath. Painful memories surface of a former patient who received electroconvulsive therapy several times a day for many weeks, hardly recovering from one shock before the next was given. Though he was certainly less disturbed at the end of perhaps a hundred treatments, his memory was wiped clean and his entire past was lost. And he was one of the lucky ones. For every memory Tom has of this treatment working, he can recall a dozen cases where the patient did not recover but suffered serious fractures during the uncontrolled seizures. And, of course, there were those who died. He didn't want any of this for Nora. She'd been lucky to have escaped such horror before and, apart from being institutionalised, she'd remained pretty well intact – until she found out the truth.

'Yes, let's try once daily and review her progress.'

Tom walks down through the ward to the nurses' station. Stan and Gladys are chatting, both of them also showing signs of age and of the harrowing life lived along with their charges. They have become Nora's guardians. Tom puts down Nora's notes on the desk. 'Electroshock once daily, starting tomorrow,' he says, and turns without a word. He walks, and keeps on walking out into the grounds. Sometimes he loathes his job.

Chapter Twenty

Tom hates the smell of this room. He hates its atmosphere. Yet, like a surgeon who spends all his time immersed in blood and guts and pain, he's accustomed to his professional milieu. One day, he knows, he might even miss it. He trails his hand along the rail of the trolley, his eyes intent on Nora's closed eyes. Her mouth is distorted – the lips dry and misshapen, not yet having fully recovered from the mouth gag. Her skin: how it has aged. The translucent, honey glow of only a few years ago has faded. Her eyes appear lost, fallen into the depths of their sockets. Tom prickles with guilt and shame for his part in what's befallen this once beautiful woman. What a tragedy. He tightens his grip on the rail, superfluous as he is. Only there because, if there were no one by her side in recovery, she'd have to be strapped down.

An hour ago, he had walked alongside her as she was wheeled catatonic into the treatment room for her eighteenth ECT. He was there as she was prepared, her motionless body in its split gown, the grotesque napkin in case she should soil herself. Her neck had been extended until straight. The nurses had lined up at each side of the bed. One would hold her head, another her shoulders, another her feet and another her body, immobilising her to minimise injury. He had prepared the ECT machine. Sister had prised Nora's mouth open and inserted a rubber gag. He had finally prepared the electrodes and, having switched on the machine, applied them, one to each temple. He had watched as her body jerked and bucked, the nurses utilising all their strength to hold her safe, even though her hands and feet were restrained.

Some never lose consciousness and are terrified, and later confused and somnolent; most struggle and fight. Nora does neither. Until now, there's been no change and he knows that there must be a point at which they stop subjecting her body to this dreadful invasion. But the likelihood of her recovery then will be slim, and she could stay like this indefinitely. Catatonia can be like that. He wonders about how many more her brain can stand, and also how many more his heart can bear.

A nurse bustles into the treatment room to take Nora's obs, and Dr Stilworth pulls himself away, busying himself with the notes, flicking back to recap on Nora's history, but really only playing for more time before he'll have to leave. The nurses can deal perfectly adequately with recovery. He knows that they know that too. Eyebrows will be raised as to why on earth he hangs around for so long, but he no longer cares.

Behind him there's a murmur, or maybe a soft groan, but certainly a sound. He pauses, frozen, and only turns when he hears it again. No sound of any kind has issued from Nora these months – not after previous ECTs, not with any kind of treatment or any examination designed to elicit a response to pain.

But there it is – and now her eyes flick open for a moment. Her breathing remains deep and regular.

He prays.

Meanwhile, Nora watches the images dancing on the backs of her eyelids, trying to decipher the chaotic thoughts tumbling and turning in her mind. She opens her eyes again, bewildered, tries to focus. Spinning, tilting, trying to regain balance then shifting again. *Find something to focus on.* A spot on the ceiling. There. But then it starts to move and roll and spin. She presses her head into the pillow. *Stop. Please stop.* But no. She clutches handfuls of the sheet to steady herself. *Yes. The treatment room. Yes.* And, again, she blinks.

Tom clears his throat and, elated, he turns away and blinks the tears from his eyes. Then he gathers his notes, gently taps on the rail of Nora's trolley and walks away. 'Call me if there's any change,' he says, as he limps out into the corridor. He walks as quickly as he can, not yet ready for the brouhaha of Rowan. He needs to think. He must be very clear in his clinical judgement.

He can't help but agree with Dr Mason that to stop ECT abruptly would be unwise. Though Nora is now awake, she may still be deeply depressed. And while ECT has done its work to break the catatonia, and prevented Nora from remaining in a vegetable-like existence possibly for the rest of her life, she will now return to the grief and harsh reality from which she managed to escape for a while. The situation is complex, to say the least.

The next morning, Nora is fully awake and she complains lustily as they wheel her into the treatment room – she remembers what this means and shouts and pulls against her restraints. Once inside, she looks up at the smiling aide who forces the mouth gag between her clenched teeth with a mixture of rage and fear in her eyes. Her body remembers this, too. Holding her terrified eyes with his, he slowly draws a finger up her chest, between her breasts and then around each nipple.

Bile rises in her throat and she thrashes about, arching her back. He continues to smile as he lazily massages first one breast, then both. She watches his gloating eyes with horror as he becomes more aroused and his hands move more roughly. Nora screams silently with frustration and rage, bucking and thrashing. He bends his face closer, his mocking eyes boring into hers. 'I don't know what gives you the gall to have such airs, after what you've done, you little whore,' he hisses, his face so close now that Nora can smell his vile breath. 'Look at me. Open your eyes and look at me!' He moves his hand lower and fumbles with her gown. He pushes his fingers between her legs. 'And don't forget,' he rasps, 'it'll be worse later if you ever say anything.'

Nora's ability to remove herself from her own body fails her, as fear and fury vie for supremacy. Her eyes bulge wide with fury as she tries with all her might to squirm away from the invading hand. She longs to spit out the mouth gag and spit out her anger right in his face, and her impotence enrages her all the more. But there's nothing she can do.

From the corner of her eye she sees a movement the aide has not. Dr Stilworth is in the doorway, a look of horror spreading across his face. 'Get off her,' he bellows and the aide leaps back. 'You bastard! Leave her alone!' Nora's eyes dart back and forth as she tries to communicate with Dr Stilworth, the mouth gag still firmly in place.

'I was just completing her prep for the ECT,' the aide says, raising his hands defensively.

Dr Stilworth pushes past him and removes the mouth gag. Nora coughs and gasps for air. 'You, you …' she screams, unable to find the right words to describe this monster. Dr Stilworth releases her restraints and gently slides his arm under Nora's back while using the other to pull the sheet up over her, giving her back what is left of her dignity.

The aide just stands there, watching.

'Nora, I am so sorry this happened to you,' says Dr Stilworth, and Nora feels his rage in his shaking hands as they envelop hers. 'Gladys!' he shouts. 'Come here and look after Nora.' He turns to the aide. 'And you. Get out of here and wait for me in the ward. The police will be called. Do not try to run. You're not fit to wipe her shoes, you swine.' Tom is white with rage, but as he turns back to Nora, who is being tended to by Gladys, his face is the picture of shock and concern. 'This should never have happened, Nora. Nothing I can say could possibly make up for this. I am deeply ashamed and profoundly sorry.' And he limps out.

Days later, Nora awakes from a disturbed sleep, blinking as she adjusts to the light. The first thing she sees is Dr Stilworth's face, tense with sorrow, peering at her with something in his eyes that, at first, she cannot place, but then recognises as a depth of loving care that she used to see sometimes in the eyes of her mother when she was ill as a child.

'There you are,' he says, his voice gentle and tender. 'Welcome back.'

She feels a light pressure on her arm and tests her muscles against it as she usually does with restraints. But the pressure falls away immediately as Dr Stilworth withdraws his hand.

Nora holds his gaze as she searches his face. His hazel eyes are clear and bright and his too-wide lips move into a slow smile. 'It's all right,' he says. 'You're back. You've been very sick, but you're safe now.'

Nora shakes her head. She still feels as though she is clambering out of a murky hole, her brain slowly responding as though it had been steeped in tar. She blinks again and shakes her head, but she can't quite remember where she is. She pulls her eyes away from his and looks around the room, trying to orientate herself, but it is all just so confusing and she returns her gaze to his face almost immediately.

'It's all right, Nora,' he repeats gently. 'Just take your time.'

Bewilderment surrounds her like a veil. What day is it? She can't remember yesterday. What is she doing lying down when it's daytime? Anxiety wells up within her and she attempts to sit up, but immediately the world spins. She feels so weak. A hand moves behind her neck to support her head and she finally manages to sit up.

The room is frighteningly familiar, but she still can't quite place it. She holds onto the bed, grasping the sheet in her hands, and looks around with wide eyes.

'Nora, you've been very ill and you're still very weak, but you're getting better. Nurse will take you back to your own bed soon.'

Why is he being so kind? But then he has always been kind. But why? She closes her eyes again and almost falls back onto the bed. Why did she have to wake up? She was so calm and tranquil in her cocoon. She feels a surge of frustration that this man, who clearly cares so much about her, has forced her back into such a cruel existence. She is standing in a garden trying to peg together scraps of memory on a washing line, but the wind snatches them away, scattering them out of her reach. A walk with Gladys . . . some markers in the ground . . . a horrible, animal screaming . . . She presses her head back into the pillow to escape the recollections that begin to settle into a crazy mosaic, dovetailing to form a picture of pain and suffering. No, she doesn't want to remember.

The pain raises its head and lunges at her like a striking snake. The world that has consisted of a narrow tunnel down which she peered through a black mist begins to come back into focus. She lifts a hand and brings it into view, moving it cautiously, examining her fingers, the clean nails and unusually smooth skin. Its pale softness seems foreign. She lifts the other and stares at it. Strange. Where has she been? What's happened?

There have been times in her inert state that she imagined herself walking, dancing, playing the piano, singing. She searches her mind as though it's an old, derelict house, looking in every room to see what's there, but then retreats from the fragmented memories that threaten to engulf and choke her. The horror of all that's happened these last years. Poignant, excruciating. But proof that she's still alive. Events from years ago beside those from yesterday, the stark contrast searingly painful; snatches from her teens interspersed with snippets from six months ago, interspersed with barren silences. The timeline of her life starts to flow, viscous as lava at first but slowly speeding up to match reality. And suddenly, relief that she can still think and remember floods through her. Even though the memories are painful, they are hers, and one of the few things that belong only to her. Tears well up and slide down her face.

Dr Stilworth draws closer, and she starts. She'd forgotten he was there. She stares at him, a little puzzled, then looks away. When she brings her eyes back to his, accusation burns within them and Tom starts back. He hasn't seen this much fire in Nora's eyes in years.

Her eyes fill with tears, which quench the flames and turn them into pools of sadness and despair. 'You knew about my baby,' she whispers. It is a statement, not a question, and she finally turns her back to him.

Chapter Twenty-One

The days pass slowly as Nora starts the uphill journey to recovery, her grief as raw now as if she'd lost her baby yesterday. At the approach of the day things seem just a little better, even if only for fleeting moments. But Nora is lonely, imprisoned, and with all that time to think, a new fear emerges that soon eclipses all others: bit by bit, she is sure she is losing herself. Whenever she feels she might pass out from the terror of this, she forces herself to recall memories from her childhood, so as to preserve those parts of herself that are irrevocably bound within them. The look of loving pride on her mother's face when Nora sang. The delicious secret sense of mischief as she prepared a surprise concert for her parents. Robert in his silk cravat and the tender touch of his hand on hers long before they dared kiss.

The knowledge that her child is dead leaves her with a haunting, enduring grief and has killed the hope that sustained her for so long. The hope that somewhere her child was growing, healthy and thriving with a family who loved her. And more – the hope that, one day, Nora would find her. Whenever she finds herself replaying that fantasy of finally meeting her daughter in her head, she feels ridiculous and stupid. How could she have fooled herself for so long? She knows the answer, though: because otherwise, what was there to live for? Just more of this. She draws the thin sheet over her face and prays for oblivion.

'Nora.' Dr Stilworth's voice pierces the mist and reels her back into the present. 'Nora. Sit up. Nurse has brought you some tea.' She hauls herself up and attempts to orientate herself. She feels her face, soft and sagging; runs fingers through her greasy hair. Tears slide down her sunken cheeks. Layers of dreams, fragments of conversation, half-forgotten encounters – the dust motes of her life – hang in the air, then ignite torrents of emotion long buried but never extinguished. Whips of pain, shards of sadness, wisps of joy, snatches of delight, recollected passion. All arise and fade, bruising her painful mind, denuded of its defences.

'Am I ever going to get out of here?' she whispers.

'One day, I'm sure,' says Dr Stilworth, though she can tell that he doesn't really believe it.

She sits in the day room surrounded by chaos and despair. Though the aide who assaulted her is gone, she can still feel his hands imprinted indelibly upon her skin. She can smell them even though she has scrubbed her body until it is red raw. And every time she thinks of him, she feels a murderous rage flare deep within her.

She notices how respectfully Dr Stilworth approaches her during his rounds. She has erected the barrier between them – she knows that. He was part of the deception, part of the reason why she will never be happy again, so she has no choice. If he tries to get closer, she scowls at him from under hunched eyebrows – something she's never done before – and shows him her defiance rather than despair. He deserves her anger. They all do. She's glad when he says nothing and eventually moves away.

She turns back the covers and puts her feet over the side of the bed, using her anger as her strength. She can feel him and Stan turning to watch her, but she doesn't care. Let them watch.

Nora stands up on shaky legs, holding onto the bed for support, then lets go and tests out her balance. She's thin and feels somehow taller and much older than she did those few months ago. She pauses to steady herself then, slowly at first and in a very straight line, she starts to walk, her head held high. Dr Stilworth steps back out of her way and she ignores him and keeps on going. The other nurses move aside to make way for her, and she feels as powerful as Moses parting the Red Sea. The ward is deathly silent. She heads straight for the doors and out into the corridor, slowly but with a mounting sense of purpose. She can feel dozens of eyes watching her, but she pays them no heed. She gathers confidence and speed and strides towards the outside door, sensing Dr Stilworth and Stan following a good way behind her, but still she refuses to acknowledge them. She opens the door and steps out into the pouring rain, still in her nightdress. Soaking wet, she holds her head erect, paying no mind to the fact that she is now wet through. She pushes forward into the strong wind.

'Shall I bring her in?' Stan asks, his voice hushed, as though afraid to break Nora's trance.

'Leave her,' she hears Dr Stilworth say. 'She'll come back when she's ready. Just keep a careful eye.' And she feels them keeping a respectful distance as they follow her along the muddy path towards where Dr Stilworth knew she was heading the moment she took her first step: her baby's grave.

Back in the dormitory, after supper and a warm bath, Nora looks out at the night sky, watching, just as she did as a little girl, star after crystalline star switching on to light up the heavens. The sliver of new moon climbs to meet them. It seems to her that the heavens are preparing to welcome her home. A sky full of freedom to explore, yet Nora is withering day by day in this glorified prison. In all these years she's rarely contemplated the ultimate escape. But now . . . Enough. She has been here twenty-two years. Eighty-eight seasons. Enough shame, enough humiliation, enough ridicule. Enough of this life. She does not want to grieve through even one more of her child's birthdays. Not one more Christmas morning remembering Robert's receding back as she banged on the window and was dragged away. Not one more.

Her muscles relax and her shoulders fall as a wave of power flows through her body. For the first time she realises that she can be the architect of her own fate, can take command of her life – or death. And with that realisation comes a sense of freedom and hope.

She tiptoes back to her bed. Since long ago, a pressed blue cornflower and a pink campion that Robert picked for her one early summer have kept each other company in marking a passage in her Bible that has kept her sane in the face of all the humiliation and abuse she has endured. It's too dark to see, but her fingers trace the outlines of the precious flowers. They have always sustained her with their fragile beauty, oases in her emotional desert.

She doesn't need to read the lines. She knows them by heart.

Chapter Twenty-Two

1966
Twenty-seven years

Dr Mason is weary. The years of being alone, making the hospital his home, the staff his family and the patients his children – naughty and in need of discipline, but still his – have taken their toll. He has made several attempts at the obligatory speech, but each has ended its life in the waste-paper basket. In the end, there's little to say, since there's little of which he feels proud. This is not what he hoped for when he became a doctor, nor when his heart led him to specialise in the care of the mentally ill.

He takes a long breath as he surveys the gathered throng of staff looking up at him. *How can it be that I know so few of them? Where have I been?* He may have one last chance to make some small reparation for what he has been part of. Suddenly, he knows what he wants to say – and it's not written on the pages he's holding in his hands right now. He folds them carefully and slips them back into his inside jacket pocket. He takes a long breath to steady himself, clears his throat, then opens his mouth. There is not so much to say, after all.

'Tomorrow I will be departing with a heavy heart with regard to the legacy I leave behind, but hopefully future generations will think before they demonise us dinosaurs of psychiatry too much. We can do that well for ourselves.' He pauses and looks at the few faces he does know well – Tom Stilworth, Matron, Stan, Gladys . . .

'Some may have thought that I was not in possession of a heart, let alone love and empathy, but I assure you today that

I have all three. I will think of you all, as well as those who have been and still are in our care – *your* care. Go well. Thank you.'

And with a simple bow, he turns to leave. Dr Stilworth stands and applauds and others follow until all are on their feet. Dr Mason glances back over his shoulder and registers with surprise the applause he feels he doesn't deserve. He holds Dr Stilworth's eyes for a moment and then continues off the stage. He walks, for the very last time, the familiar route back to his consulting room, where he has one last task to complete.

Nora has been sitting waiting on a chair outside Dr Mason's room for some time when he finally arrives, his head bent, looking thoughtful. He looks at her as though he's never seen her before.

'Nora, please come and sit down.' His voice is kind, but she hesitates, not quite daring to trust him after all this time. After a few moments, she perches on the edge of her usual chair.

'Nora, I'm sure you have heard that I'm about to retire. I have some things for you. In fact, I really should have given you these things a long time ago, and for that I beg your forgiveness.' She keeps her head down, though her eyes lift just enough to see that her ballerina is still, after all these years, poised mid-pirouette, just waiting for the music. She is confused. Is this a trap? A game? Is she supposed to respond? She settles for a cautious silence and watches as Dr Mason's hand moves towards the music box and grasps it and moves it forward. He lifts it and with two hands holds it out to her. 'I want to return this to you. It's yours, and always has been.'

She makes no move to take it.

'Nora, it's yours,' he insists, but she continues to look on silently. 'Nora.' He holds it out further towards her so that it is mere inches from her clasped hands, and his voice cracks. 'Please take it.' She lifts her head a little. 'I have had this here on my desk since the evening you arrived many years ago. It has never been played. I have never taken possession of it. It has just been here and I want you to have it back now. I am very sorry that I deprived you of it for so long.'

She raises her eyes to his tired face. When did he get to look so old? But then she looks old too, she supposes. The only features she now recognises when she looks in the mirror are her mother's eyes. She pauses, then lifts her hands and holds them open like a child. Gently, he places the precious weight of the music box into her hands and her fingers close around it, slowly and in a kind of ecstasy. He withdraws his hands, but she still doesn't move.

'Take it, Nora. Please. It's yours,' he says again. Another catch in his voice. Slowly, she draws it towards her chest, holding her breath until she feels her lungs will burst. Then she snatches it, speeding it through the last few inches in case he should change his mind. Now she has it in her hands, she feels unable to be parted from it for another second – wonders how she's managed without it for all these years. She wants to thank him, but she cannot speak; she simply curls her body round this one last bit of the life she used to know, and hugs it just as she wishes she could have hugged her baby.

Dr Mason coughs, clearing his throat. 'There is something else, too.' He twists around a little to reach for something behind him while remaining perched on the edge of his desk. He produces a sizable packet, sealed but bulging. 'These are yours also. They are letters. I am deeply sorry, Nora.' But she hardly hears him as she involuntarily gasps and stretches out her hand to take the packet, hugging it up alongside her other treasure. But still he continues, the slight tremor that appears in his voice finally prompting her to dare to look at him.

'I ignored your grief and used it to try to subdue your natural resistance.' His eyes are moist as he looks away into the distance, summoning the courage to proceed. 'I should never have deprived you of communication with your family.'

Now she stares at him, seeing him as a frail old man, but she hardens her gaze as she thinks of her baby. She can never forgive him for that, no matter what apology he brings today.

'There's nothing I can say other than that I'm sorry. I ask for your forgiveness, but know I don't deserve it.' He pauses, perhaps trying to find more words; perhaps hoping for an absolution she cannot give.

He bows his head. 'Thank you, Nora.'

She knows she is dismissed, and slowly she rises, then turns to leave, carrying her treasure with her. But something moves in her heart – a tiny fluttering she hasn't felt for a very long time. She pauses and faces him.

'Thank you,' she mutters, her voice barely audible. Dr Mason lifts his head and his eyes find hers. He will hold onto those two words until the day he dies.

Chapter Twenty-Three

Nora opens the packet and turns out its contents onto her bed, her eyes wide, her heart racing. Dozens of envelopes addressed in her mother's hand. Tears sting her eyes as she fingers each one lovingly, making the experience last as long as possible. She closes her eyes and allows the memory of her mother's smile to envelop her. She inhales a half-remembered scent. She can feel on her fingertips the softness of her mother's skin and hear her gentle voice singing a lullaby. She can feel the pride as she stands upon a stool as her mother arranges the folds of her white taffeta dress and then places the veil ready for her first communion, then lifts it and kisses her cheek. 'You look beautiful,' she says, and bends to adjust the hem. Nora looks down on her mother's hair from her unusually elevated position. She can see how the long hair is wound around a doughnut fashioned out of old stockings. There are tiny patches of pinkish-beige peeping through the strands of dark chestnut hair – the colour almost identical to her own before grey threaded through it.

And now she can see her mother standing in the kitchen, her belly huge. She whispers, 'Quick, Nora, come and feel,' and she places Nora's little hand on her belly to feel the sweet, gentle kick of her unborn sister. A sister who sadly was not destined to live for more than days. And up beyond her mother's wrists there's flour from kneading the bread. Then the moment she longs for when they sit together at the kitchen table with one of the little buns straight from the oven and all dripping with butter, Nora with a glass of milk and her mother with a cup of tea. Just the two of them before her father comes home.

She gathers the letters in handfuls and holds them to her

chest and silently weeps. One by one she looks at the envelopes and arranges them by date. November 1939. An unsealed one – a card – for her birthday, November 1939. Then another, probably a Christmas card, 22 December 1939. And so on until her bed is covered with her past, these envelopes probing her memory, prodding her emotions – emotions she has not allowed herself to feel for many years. Letters and cards, year after year until 1958 and then . . . nothing.

Hands trembling, she opens the first letter. The paper is yellowed by time, but the script is unmistakable. Perfectly formed and slanting – her grandfather had been a schoolmaster after all. Her mother must have had to practise very hard to produce this perfection. Nora closes her eyes, hardly daring to read, so afraid of being reminded of her guilt and shame now tidily stored in some distant part of her mind, but how easily it could be opened, unleashing a Pandora's box of pain. She takes a breath and starts to read.

My darling Nora,

She blinks and stops, looks out of the window. She takes a deep breath, her heart beating as fast as a hummingbird's wings. This is enough, that she is greeted in this way. These three words say all she needs to know. Might it be best not to read more, just in case? She could hold the magic of these three words for the rest of her life and be comforted by them and never need more. She sobs, knowing that she cannot stop now.

Please forgive us for this terrible thing we have allowed to happen to you. I cannot bear it that you are just there, yet out of reach, and that I cannot touch you, or see you or talk to you at this time when you have never needed me so much. I am so sorry that we could not have talked about what has happened and maybe we could have found a better solution. I have failed you as your mother and I will make it up to you, my dearest Nora. I promise.

We are not allowed to visit you yet. The legal situation seems very complicated and controlling in a way we could not have imagined. It seems like there's a whole huge system to overcome, but we will. I assure you we will.

I will visit you when I can. Please forgive your father too. His pride is hurt and he is not himself. I'm sure that all of this will be ironed out and very soon you will be home. I hope they are taking care of you and that you got the warm clothes I sent you on Monday.

It may comfort you to know that we all miss you. There is a hole in our lives. But we are all as well as we can be, so please don't worry about us. Just stay strong and well and we will all be together very soon.

Your ever-loving
Mother

Nora smooths out the single sheet of paper, which immediately springs back to the position that has been enforced upon it for the last twenty-seven years. She wonders how long it might take her to smooth out her own creases if ever she's released from here.

She stares at the letter and then reads it again and again. When she has read it so many times she can recall every word, she opens the next – a birthday card bearing a painting of a ballerina.

Happy 18th birthday.
We hope you are well and look forward
to you being home by Christmas.
Your ever-loving Mother and Father

Letter after letter, card after card, mapping out the days, the weeks, the months, the years – her lifetime, witnessing her mother's descent into hopelessness and despair and eventually an early death. Nora remembers her own similar journey, though the death was not corporeal. The theft of her identity as a girl, a woman, a daughter, a mother, even a human being, was paralleled by her mother's loss of identity in relation to Nora. But for her mother was added the guilt that she had, in part, been instigator of this tragedy – though this could never equal Nora's regret that she, herself, *was* the tragedy.

The last letter is one that Nora has been consciously avoiding. It looks official and has clearly been opened and read, then taped shut. The envelope is addressed to Miss N. Jennings, Hillinghurst Hospital. She rips it open.

> *Stoke Mandeville Hospital*
> *Mandeville Road*
> *Aylesbury*
>
> *4 August 1944*
>
> *Dear Miss Jennings,*
> *This letter, addressed to you, was in the pocket of Sergeant Robert Harcourt when he was rescued at Monte Cassino, unconscious and with a serious head injury. He remains critically ill yet we are hopeful that he will make a good recovery.*
>
> *As soon as he regained consciousness, he was insistent that his letter be posted to you.*
>
> *If you wish to visit him, please contact the hospital. I know he would be happy to see you.*
>
> *Yours sincerely,*
> *Cornelia Robinson*
> *Matron*

Nora can hardly breathe as, with trembling fingers, she unfolds the yellowing pages that are smeared with dirt and what looks like blood. Though so many years have passed, she recognises it instantly as Robert's handwriting. Her mouth feels suddenly very dry and, clutching the letter tightly, she looks out of her window, her vision blurred by tears. *How can a broken heart keep on breaking?* She brings up an angry hand and dashes away the tears, takes a long breath as everything around her seems to disappear, leaving her in an island of silence. Just her and Robert.

> *15 May 1943*
>
> *My dearest Nora,*

She refolds it quickly, her hands shaking. Can she bear to read this? She blinks and takes deep, gulping breaths and then she unfolds it again.

I've written and rewritten this letter so many times. I find it easier to help others to write theirs – something that has helped preserve my sanity. People's lives here can be completely changed by the mail, and maybe that goes for the people at home too. (This isn't said to try to manipulate you into writing to me.)

I've wanted to talk to you so badly for so long. I heard from Uncle Henry that our baby had died and

Nora crumples the letter. *You knew? All this time, you knew? Even when I didn't? Even my father knew? And my mother? And they never came?* She closes her eyes as an inner scream rises and she wants to tear at her skin, pull at her hair, run amok. But her body remains perfectly still as icy fingers of fury clutch her throat. Should she move a muscle, she will never be able to stop. She hardly dare even breathe.

What seems like hours later, though in fact maybe only minutes, she smooths out the letter with trembling hands and continues to read, her eyes blurred by tears, her heart feeling like a cold stone in her chest.

I am so sorry that I couldn't have been there to share that with you, to hold your hand so that we might comfort each other.

Nora looks away into the distance, breathing through her anger, then once again comes back to the words on the yellowing page.

I don't know where you are, how you are, or what has happened these last four years, but I'll send this to the last address I have for you – that awful place – and hopefully they can forward it to you. I miss you still but don't want to disturb your life.

Nora, I'm such a huge disappointment to myself and not at all what either of us thought I was. I haven't forgotten and am ashamed that I haven't been in touch, or around to help you.

But first of all, my dear Nora, don't worry about me. I'm managing fine. The separation from home, family – and you, of course – is much more painful than the war, and homesickness is crippling. So much feels like a nightmare, with patches I don't remember at all, and many that I'll never be able to forget. Sometimes something simple changes everything. The other day I saw a little rabbit. I could hardly believe it – it was so normal in a place where nothing is normal. Then I thought of the rabbits in the fields around Fenshaw and was reduced to tears in ten seconds flat. I wanted so much to be home. Sometimes I can hear you singing in church and my heart aches to actually be there listening to you. I hope you're still singing, in spite of everything.

Life here alternates between drama and tedium with little middle ground. Though we're at war, battle is less frequent than you'd think. Often, I find myself wondering why we're here; what it's all about that we've been forced to leave home and all that we love, to fight a war about human rights, when, in conscription, our rights were taken away. It makes no sense at all.

Nora, I wish I could say that I'd enlisted out of a sense of duty and honour, but in fact I did so out of cowardice. It seemed less frightening to be at war than to face you and your family and to have to deal with things. It also gave me an opportunity to be tested and find out whether I was really a man. And the men with whom I've shared the awfulness of war have become like family and I found I could fight with them rather than against the enemy, standing together in some small way protecting those at home. It gave me a cause. In respecting them I found again some of the self-respect I lost in abandoning you. I've done my best not to let anyone else down as I let you down and that has sustained me.

I've spent many an hour with an inner argument about armed conflict, trying to distinguish the act of killing from the act of murder – the one apparently being worthy of honour and praise and the other of punishment and disgrace. I'm still working on it, but I know that if I make it home, I want to work for a better way of defending human rights than killing people over them. I've often tried to imagine the men we kill as they were before someone decided we were enemies. Devils, as *propaganda would have us believe, or men just like me, who long for peace and to go home, who miss touch, and love, and cosy fires to sit round and talk, laugh, sing. What makes one of us the hero and the other worthy only of being killed? They carry photos of their loved ones in their tunic pockets just like we do. (I wish I had a photograph of you.) We're all men, just of different cultures, wearing different uniforms, having different-coloured skins perhaps, but simply men nevertheless. I am the enemy to him just as he is to me. There's no morality here. But battle would be impossible to sustain if we started to think of our common humanity. Sometimes I feel such respect for these men who are trained to kill me just as much as I'm trained to kill them.*

I've been shocked at the things we've done here and the senselessness of it. Though we try to think that someone has a bigger map and can see more of what's really going on. I wish it were all at an end. It's just stupidity. Please, God, this will be the last war.

Most of the men have some kind of memento and – please don't think me stupid – I brought your handkerchief with me. I fancy I can still smell you and your perfume on it and it makes me feel less lonely. I miss our talks, our laughter together, our singing and all the other things we shared. Please forgive me for unburdening myself like this. When I come home, I want to

And there it stops. She turns the page over. Nothing. She clenches her fists and hammers on her bed, then drops her head into her hands and weeps. All this wasted time. All this wasted sorrow. All this wasted life.

She clutches her arms around her knees and rocks, tears coursing down her cheeks. Finally, she picks up her music box and turns the key. The ballerina springs to life – so easily, even after so many years of waiting. How she wishes that she could do the same. She looks out of the window and in the distance sees those tall, iron gates. But the yearning to finally walk out through them withers. She turns her gaze once more to the ballerina. Round and round . . . round and round. She closes her eyes, and finds herself humming along to the familiar, forgotten melody.

PART II

Hospital is packed full of patients, some of whom need a great
deal of attention

Chapter One

Janet sits, mug in hand, opposite Dale, his beautiful brown eyes regarding her with sympathy. The acute ward of Hillinghurst Hospital is packed full of patients, some of whom need a great deal of attention. She's just had to retrieve a knife from a distressed ex-husband. 'Heavy morning?' he asks her.

'You could say that. And it's not over yet—'

'Uh-oh! Here's trouble . . .' Dale interrupts, looking past her out of his office and into the ward.

Janet puts down her mug and turns just as the door opens and Dr Derek Pauling, Janet's supervising consultant, leans in through it. Even in this serious moment she can't help but think of Robert Redford: with that shock of thick hair, tanned complexion and amazing blue eyes, Dr Pauling is handsome enough to be auditioning for any leading role. His usual air of supreme authority is intensified by the thunder on his face. 'Dr Humphreys, my office in five minutes – if you're not too busy, that is.' And with that he leaves, his sarcasm still hanging in the air like a noxious smell.

Janet turns back and catches Dale's eye. 'Oh God. Now what?' She sighs heavily and gets to her feet. She's only been here a couple of weeks, but already she knows that look.

Five minutes later she stands outside Dr Pauling's office, hair brushed and lipstick reapplied. She smooths down the skirt of her suit and takes a deep breath before she taps on her boss's door. As she opens it and steps over the threshold, it occurs to her that she has never actually been into the inner sanctum. She steps inside and glances around surreptitiously.

Dr Pauling's office is as immaculate as the man himself. His desk bears a brass plate showing not only his name but a string of impressive qualifications. Photographs of a pretty woman and two young blond-haired boys are framed in silver, and a black Anglepoise lamp gazes down at the burnished wood. Apart from the desk chair, there are two more at the opposite side of the desk, and against the wall a small sofa decked with tastefully matching cushions is perfectly placed – of course.

He waves Janet to one of the chairs on the other side of his desk, while reaching for the phone. 'Phyllis, could you please let Dr Sheridan know I'll be another couple of minutes? Something's come up.' As he puts the phone down, his eyes fall on Janet appraisingly. After a moment or two of uncomfortable silence, he speaks. 'We need to get things straight, Dr Humphreys. We can't expect the staff to excel if we doctors don't. Sitting around drinking coffee gives the wrong impression.'

Janet stares. This is ridiculous. Does he think she can't discuss the patients and manage a cup of tea at the same time? Despite her best intentions, she rises to the bait. 'I drink *tea*, actually, and I don't just sit around. I'd had—'

'I don't intend to argue the point. In any event, you seem to have time on your hands—'

'That's unfair,' she says, trying to make her voice as assertive as possible. How she wishes that at times like this she didn't feel like the little girl with the regional accent and grammar school education who has no right to be in this world dominated by public school men.

He scowls. 'Is it? You seem to spend a lot of time sitting chatting with the nurses.'

'I discuss the patients with them,' she retorts, 'and—'

'Whatever.' He waves his hand dismissively. 'In any case, I would like you to do a review of the patients on the back wards.'

Janet squares her shoulders. 'The patients on the back wards are the senior house manager's job—'

'Actually, it's the job of whomever I tell to do it,' he retorts, his eyes almost begging her to dare to argue.

'But I—'

'Dr Humphreys, you've only been here for five minutes and yet already you're building yourself a bit of a reputation. Could you for once just do your job without everything needing to be an argument?' Dr Pauling straightens his cuffs and smooths his tie. 'Let's leave it there for today. I'll expect a report. And now, I'm rather busy.' He picks up his pen and carries on with his paperwork, studiously ignoring her. She stands and leaves without another word, seething, and stomps along the corridor back to the ward.

'Pompous idiot,' she mutters under her breath just as Dale walks around the corner.

'That didn't go too well, then.' Dale gives a knowing smile as he joins her on the way back to her office.

'You can say that again,' she says, opening the door and flopping down on her chair. 'There's no pleasing that bloody man. There's hardly a day goes by that he's not on my back about something. Now he wants me to sort out the back wards as well as everything else. I've just about had it with him.'

Janet opens the filing cabinet and yanks out a file and flings it on the desk, then plonks herself down on her chair. She picks up a pen and attempts to write, but it's empty. She throws it down with a grunt of frustration and picks up another, and another – none of them is working. 'Bloody NHS pens,' she grumbles, and hefts her handbag from the floor onto her lap. She turns out her keys, some tissues, a lipstick, a notebook and finally a pen. She scribbles on the blotter to make sure it works then throws everything else back in the bag.

Dale leans against the door frame, watching silently. 'Want to talk about it?'

'No point,' she says.

Janet sits cross-legged in jeans and an old jersey, her hair looking as though she forgot to brush it this morning – which wouldn't be entirely wrong. A pastel palette has been applied to the heavens this Sunday afternoon, a wash of soft grey, mauve and peach, with the odd gold highlight for effect. She watches a grey squirrel making its way down the branch of a huge elm whose trunk supports a whole universe of lichens.

Scattered around her on the carpet are the back-ward patient files that she's trying to arrange in some kind of order. She's been at it for hours and feels pretty overwhelmed. No real patient notes, just individual sentences, often separated by bald patches where nothing at all was recorded, as though the patient simply stopped existing for months at a time. Brief diagnostic and medication notes here and there. 'Septic foot. Bathe with iodine.' 'Impetigo. Paint with gentian.' Dosage details are encoded in Latin, which her tired brain struggles to remember.

How could anyone pull together a person's life from this? Sore throats and coughs, swollen ankles and ingrown toenails; the odd hallucination and a bit of difficult behaviour. But nothing that says anything about who this person really is – what they think, feel, do; where they came from, what hopes and aspirations they may have had, and may even still have. Years and years of signs and symptoms and nothing else. Is that all these people have become?

Janet stretches her neck and rubs her eyes. Perhaps she could review a couple of them each week . . . Even that, though, will take months. She sighs and makes her own brief notes in a bid to figure out where to start.

A man who tried to kill himself by lying on a railway line. Two traumatic amputations. Been here more than forty years. Oh, hang on – he was discharged years ago.

A woman from Auschwitz. Strange for her to be here. Ah . . . sent by the court. It appears she murdered a Mrs Müller in 1954.

A girl who was admitted at seventeen. It seems she was pregnant – a 'moral defective'. Though Janet remembers this term from her days as a medical student, she never imagined she'd actually see it written on a patient's notes these days. *God – she's been here since 1939.* Janet pulls the file out and puts it to one side, making a mental note to look up the legality around the incarceration of so-called moral defectives.

A man with an IQ of forty-nine, who seems to have had an

unlikely number of injuries – 'fell in the bathroom', 'bumped into a door', 'fell out of bed' – also, seems to have spent long periods in seclusion . . .

She also jots down the 'treatments' mentioned here and there. Cold baths, wet wraps, straitjackets, restraints, insulin therapy, sterilisation, unmodified ECT, continuous narcosis, psychosurgery – leucotomy, trepanning . . . on and on . . . She's never heard of some of it, although she does recall that someone in the USA in those days did psychosurgery almost as a travelling road show – lobotomy on demand in the back of a motor trailer. She shivers at the thought. She'll have to do some research. *Even more time I don't have . . .*

Hopelessness radiates from every yellowed page. She shuts the last file and slams it onto the pile. How can she even face these people who've been so abused and neglected in the name of medicine, let alone ask them to trust her? She stares out of the window again, unconsciously tapping on the sill. To be fair, what else could the doctors have done back then? What resources did they have? None of the medication available now. At least they were trying to do something at a time when many people just wanted the psychiatrically ill to disappear – or be euthanised. Anything to prevent them from being an embarrassment or their behaviour to cause a disturbance. *Although, what do we do now? Mostly just 'straitjacket' them with medication instead. And we still have psychosurgery . . .*

She leans back against the sofa, her eyes mindlessly following the progress of a robin around the garden, wondering what on earth she can do with all of this, when the door opens. Her husband, Ian, steps in and surveys the scene, his green eyes sparkling with irritation.

'Sunday afternoon and you're still working. I thought we were going out for a walk?'

Somewhere, at a distance, Janet is aware of his voice, but is still lost in her thoughts and continues to stare out of the window.

'Janet?' Ian raises his voice impatiently.

She snaps away from the window and looks first at Ian and then at her watch. 'Oh, sorry. The time ran away with me.'

'Something did, but I don't think it was just the time. You always find enough time for your patients.'

'Ian, don't st—'

'I'm not starting anything. Just wishing my wife would like to spend some time with me on the only day of the week we're both at home together. You've had two call-outs till God knows what hours this week – though how on earth that happens I don't know.'

She feels heat creeping up her neck. 'The SHO wasn't available.'

Ian's lip curls. 'Seems like he's often "not available".'

She sighs. 'Give me half an hour.'

'Just forget it. I've been waiting for hours already. I'll catch you later.' He turns and sweeps out of the room without another word, the collar-length hair she loves streaming like a lion's mane behind him. She hears rustling as he grabs his anorak from the hallstand and then the slam of the front door.

She closes her eyes and takes a few deep breaths, then stares into the space he just vacated and runs a frustrated hand through her dark hair, feeling unusually defeated. She sits up straight and sighs deeply. *What am I doing? I can't let this happen to us.*

But still she stares out of the window, biting her bottom lip, then her hand almost involuntarily wanders back to the notes of the woman who was admitted because she was pregnant and unmarried. She flicks through the notes again. Forty-two years of this woman's life in her hand. She pauses. Her heart hurts. She knows full well why this woman's plight has called to her.

She sighs again and places the file to one side. What she needs most, she thinks, is a strong cup of tea. And she'll call Martin. She misses him now he's at university. Nineteen. Where did all those years go? She wanders off into the kitchen and puts on the kettle, leaning heavily on her hands as she waits for it to boil. Her head droops forward as Ian creeps back into her mind, but the welcome bubbling of the kettle as it starts to boil rescues her and she breathes heavily and straightens up, reaching for the tea caddy. She swills boiling water round the pot to warm it and makes the tea, putting a tea-cosy over the pot to keep it hot, then stands still for a long moment, her own past bleeding into the present.

There but for the grace of God . . .

She rubs her neck and shakes her head, dislodging the

uncomfortable thoughts. She checks the time and heads for the sitting room with her tea tray.

Janet is awoken by the slam of the front door. She glances at her watch as she pulls herself up to a sitting position and pushes back the throw she'd pulled over herself on the sofa. Ten thirty. The files are in a stack at her feet. She looks around, confused, just as the sitting-room door opens.

'Janet, we need to talk,' Ian says, sitting down beside her.

A shiver runs through her. 'It's late, Ian. Not now.'

'Not now? It's always "not now". You're busy with this, tied up with that. There's never time for us.' He takes her hand. 'We don't even make love any more. I wonder if you even care.'

'I'm—'

'I know. You're busy. You're tired. But we have to make some time for us – some time to talk.' He glances at the stack of notes. 'I'm off to bed. Don't work too late, eh?' He kisses her cheek and turns to leave.

She grabs his hand. 'Ian, do you love me?'

'You know I do. But what's more to the point is, do you love me? If there's something that's bothering you, just tell me. We can work it out. Come to bed. Please.'

But she drops her head and avoids his eyes. 'Sleep well. I won't be long. I promise.'

Monday morning arrives after a restless night. The light edging its way round the curtains is flat and distinctly autumnal. Ian's arm is looped over her and Janet shifts a little, looking over her shoulder at her sleeping husband. Sadness engulfs her and she thinks, *Please don't let me hurt him.* She inches her way out from under his arm, trying not to wake him, and turns to really look at him, her heart aching. 'It'll be all right,' she whispers. 'I promise, I'll make it right.' But even as she makes the promise, she feels her mind drifting to her work.

She's in and out of the shower and part way through her breakfast before Ian emerges. She attempts a smile but his eyes slide over her as though she is just another appliance. He heads straight to the fridge, scratching his chin. Her eyes follow him as he takes out the orange juice, butter and milk. He grabs the marmalade from a cupboard and a couple of slices of bread, puts the bread in the toaster, pours the juice and takes a swig.

'Ian, I'm sorry – I just wasn't in the mood,' she says, but he leaves the kitchen, having successfully avoided meeting her eyes even once. Irritation now rises in Janet. *Well, two can play at that game.* She scoops the last few mouthfuls of her porridge into her mouth in double-quick time so that she can leave the room before his toast pops up.

They pass each other again in the bathroom as she cleans her teeth and he mops his face after his shave, then they head in different directions without a word.

They climb into separate cars with hardly a glance, then Janet rolls down her window. 'This is a stupid game,' she calls to him as he shifts into gear and starts to move off. He brakes and looks at her, his eyes empty.

'Then stop playing it,' he says.

Janet gives a wan smile. 'Don't work too hard.'

Ian doesn't smile, but at least he holds her eyes. 'You're a right one to talk,' he says. 'What time are you going to honour me with your presence tonight?'

'Six,' she says brightly, ignoring the burning sarcasm.

As he thrusts the car back into gear, he shouts back. 'I'll expect you at eight, then.'

Before Janet can respond, he drives off in a squeal of tyres. Janet hits the steering wheel and curses. She knows it's childish, but she hates it when he steals the last word like that. The whole way to work she is seething quietly; even the soothing tones of her favourite Bread track are unable to break through her mood. In fact, the lyrics just inflame her more and she slams off the radio.

She pulls into her parking space and turns off the engine, sighing into the sudden silence. There's no way she can go in feeling like she does now. She closes her eyes and forces herself to take deep, calming breaths until she feels ready.

Chapter Two

As Janet locks her car she glances up at the impressive Victorian façade of Hillinghurst Hospital. The September wind skirmishes with the crisp brown and gold leaves and abruptly changes, teasing her hair and snatching at the papers she hauls from the boot of the car so that she has to grip them extra tight. Weighed down with the files, she walks across to the annexe known as Rowan. Although this will be the first time she has entered this part of the hospital, since she started here she's wondered at the identity of the man – of course, it would have been a man – who named this beige relic from the post-war prefab era after the beautiful tree that produces dense clusters of cream flowers in May and scarlet berries in September. The door needs painting and the windows could do with some putty. It has the appearance of a hapless, neglected child standing alongside its ornate, stern Victorian mother. Janet takes a long breath and determines to feel hopeful about what she might find in there.

Her shoulder bag is caught in the crook of her arm and she tuts, backing up against the door, protecting her precarious cargo with both arms. But the door is lighter than she imagined and gives way, so that she almost falls inside, diving head-first into the familiar smells of urine, bleach and polish. A woman in a grey flared skirt and a pale green blouse approaches, hands outstretched. She's mid-forties, Janet reckons, with her mouse-brown hair short and well-behaved, her cheekbones high. She looks newly washed and shiny and her hazel eyes seem to dance. Her left hand bears a simple gold wedding ring and her face a welcoming smile. Her name tag states 'Ellen Saunders, Sister'.

'D'you need a hand?' she says cheerily and without waiting for a reply, Ellen expertly slices off the top two-thirds of Janet's pile of notes and moves towards another door. 'Dr Humphreys, is it?' she asks over her shoulder. 'Tea or coffee?'

Ah, hospital hospitality. 'Tea would be great, please. Milk, no sugar. And it's Janet.'

'Perfect,' says Ellen, handing Janet a steaming mug. 'Shall we get straight to it, then?'

'That would be great,' says Janet, then takes a sip of her drink and is pleasantly surprised at how good it is. Ellen must bring in her own teabags.

'It's hard to know where to start, so please tell me if I'm boring you,' says Ellen with a smile. 'Things have changed a lot over the years, with health-service reforms and such, but all of it too little too late for a lot of them. They're just burnt out, heaven help them. They couldn't exist outside now.'

'Is that the case for all of them?' Janet asks.

'Pretty nigh. Maybe one or two might still have a chance, but not many. This is their home now and most of them will be here till they die or until the government in its wisdom closes us down.' Ellen sighs regretfully. 'There was a big push to discharge people about ten years ago. Some were readmitted in a dreadful state, but so many of them just died – or committed suicide. It was a nightmare for all of us.'

'I bet,' says Janet.

They walk on, pausing every now and then for Ellen to greet one of the nurses and introduce Janet, then make their way to Ellen's office. Small and cramped, it houses a desk, one end of which is pushed against the wall to leave enough space for Ellen to squeeze between it, the filing cabinet, the medicine trolley and her chair. They both dump their piles of notes on the desk. The usual board with its safety notices, fire drill in pictures, staff holiday sheet and a variety of leaflets hangs on the wall next to the large clock.

'How are you settling in?' Ellen asks her as they sit themselves down.

'It's early days yet,' Janet tells her, 'and there's a lot to absorb between here and acute, but I'm sure I'll feel more at home soon.' Ellen gives her a commiserative look, and Janet pushes on. 'I was going through the patients' notes,' she says, 'but it's hard to tell what's going on with some of them.'

'At least you've looked at the notes – that's more than most people do. I know it's more interesting on acute for you doctors, but it's a shame that our lot are always at the end of the queue and rarely get more than five minutes of anybody's time. I know, we're not doing heroics here, but we're doing our best to keep them steady and give them a bit of pleasure if we can.'

'Maybe we could go through the notes together some time?'

'Wow,' Ellen says, looking at Janet with wide-eyed wonder. 'That would be fabulous. It'll be like a breath of fresh air to have somebody give a damn. Have you got time to meet some of them now?'

Janet smiles at Ellen's eagerness, but also feels a stab of sadness that a doctor showing interest in these patients is such big news. 'Absolutely,' she says warmly, getting to her feet.

'Great, let me show you around.' Ellen leads Janet out into the day room, where plastic flowers and crocheted blankets and cushion covers try valiantly to lift the air of resignation by injecting some colour and hope. Janet stops in her tracks as she looks around at the shells of women in the chairs that line the perimeter of the room, some tied down with restraints camouflaged as bandages. Most have bibs to collect dribbling saliva, their heads nodding, mouths chewing, eyes wandering or staring blankly. They're all wearing ankle socks that make them look like very old little girls; Janet feels her lips purse in irritation and wonders whose idea that was and what the hell they were thinking. She makes a mental note to confront that sometime, but not today.

Ellen leads her over to a white-haired woman who is picking at her skirt with one hand while rolling the fingers of the other in small circles, her eyes downcast. 'This is Elsie. Apparently, she suffered from a "nervous illness" since childhood, though what that was exactly, we'll never know,' Ellen says, her voice soft. 'She was diagnosed as "psychotic" and admitted here when she was sixteen. She had insulin shock therapy and repeated ECT. She rarely speaks, does exactly as she's told – never more nor less – and sits waiting for the next command: "pick up your spoon", "go to the toilet", "go to bed". She goes to art therapy but always just paints brushstroke after brushstroke in dark blue.'

Janet wonders what would happen if Elsie were instructed to use yellow, or red.

'And this is our Nora, Nora Jennings. She's been here for over forty years. Sectioned because she was pregnant and unmarried – diagnosed as moral defective.'

Janet stands perfectly still, aware of a lump in her throat as she looks at this small, shrivelled woman. Over forty years . . . Longer than Janet has been alive.

She blinks and forces her attention back to Ellen. 'Moral defective . . . Yes, I remember seeing it in her notes. I meant to look and remind myself of what that meant specifically, but didn't have time.'

'Alcoholics, prostitutes, unmarried mothers – that kind of thing,' Ellen says. 'They could all be detained indefinitely under the 1913 Mental Deficiency Act. It was only abolished in 1959. Can you believe it?'

Feeling winded, Janet stares at Nora, struggling to keep her composure. *There but for the grace of God* . . .

'Are you all right?' Ellen's voice registers somewhere far away.

Janet nods her lie, but thankfully Ellen seems satisfied and her eyes return to Nora.

'She's not a bit of bother – just institutionalised now. Doesn't talk much but I always have the feeling that there's more going on in there than we might think.'

They move on, though Janet's thoughts linger with Nora. 'And this is Joyce,' Ellen says. 'She's been mute for the last twenty-five years. Before then she was a "defiant young woman", according to her notes. Nobody seems to know what happened to her, but I suspect too much ECT.'

As they come to the end of the ward, Janet looks back. Her eyes drift back to where Nora sits still and silent, her head slightly bowed, her eyes staring ahead. *Is it really too late?* 'Ellen, could I start with Nora Jennings?'

'Absolutely. When?'

'Now.'

As Janet prepares to meet Nora Jennings, she knows this isn't going to be a walk in the park. From personal experience, she also knows that even a single hour-long psychiatric consultation can affect every aspect of someone's life, and that one mistake on the part of the doctor can be disastrous. She sits on her own in the small consulting room on Rowan, takes a deep breath and reminds herself of the aim of her work with Nora: to help her become the best she can be, regardless of the damage wrought by over forty years of incarceration. *No pressure, then . . .*

A timid knock on the open door interrupts Janet's thoughts. A stooped, elderly-looking woman with short, greying hair and wrinkled, sallow skin stands in the doorway, her head jutting forward a little, her eyes fixed on the floor. Her mouth follows the sagging contours of cheeks that eventually droop into jowls. She is dressed in a plaid skirt, woollen jumper, flat-heeled shoes and, of course, the incongruous white ankle socks. Janet stands and proffers her hand, her heart flooding with compassion. 'Miss Jennings, please come in.'

With short, nervous steps, Nora moves to the chair and lowers herself onto its edge, perching there for a moment before shuffling back little by little until she seems settled. She clasps her hands in her lap with a handkerchief crushed between them, and is finally still.

'I'm happy for you to call me Janet and I know that most people here call you Nora, so I wonder what you'd prefer that I call you?' Nora sits with her head bowed and makes neither movement nor sound. Janet breathes in sharply, hoping that asking Nora to make a choice wasn't her first blunder. Best just to continue. 'I'd like to have a chat with you, and see how you are, and if there's anything I can do for you. Is that OK?'

Nora's gnarled fingers begin to fidget with the handkerchief like a child with a security blanket. Janet presses on. 'I know you've lived here for a very long time, and you must have seen lots of people like me over the years. It's probably a bit of a pain to have yet someone else coming to talk with you.' She waits. 'If there's anything at all you'd like to ask me or tell me, it's fine, but don't worry if you've nothing to say today. We can just sit here a while and if anything occurs to you, you can ask me and if not, that's also fine because I'll be back again in a few days.'

The ticking of the clock is deafening in the silence. Janet decides to try a different tack. 'I always think it must be hard when someone new comes, and I want you to take your time and be comfortable. There's no hurry. I'm happy just to sit here with you, but if you want to go now, that's OK too.'

After a few minutes, Nora slowly lifts herself off the chair and walks to the door. At the threshold, she hesitates a moment, and Janet wonders whether she thinks the permission to leave might be repealed. Janet remains silent and Nora finally shuffles out into the corridor.

Janet sits for some minutes mulling over her first impressions. A clear case of institutionalisation if ever she's seen one. It breaks her heart. Ellen's words that there's little that can be done for any of them now echo inside her head. But Janet is always up for a challenge.

Chapter Three

Nora stands at the window. The pale sky tiptoes into morning and, as the low cloud lifts, it reveals a turquoise heaven. Trees step out of the mist and, behind them, layer after layer of hillside emerges, each a hazy echo of the one before, each calling the eye to follow as they extend out into the distance. Nora likes to imagine foxes slinking home after their night of prowling and birds coaxing each other into song, even if she can't see these things herself. And beyond those gates? Oh, how she used to long to see the outside world. But now . . . well, it's easier not to even think of all that. She's safer in her solitude, behind the mask her face has become in order to protect what's left of her from a cruel world.

A twinge of pain in her lower back breaks into her thoughts, and she realises she has been at the window for too long – her old body can no longer take standing for more than a few minutes at a time. She sits down on her bed, placing her hands together in her lap, and surveys the room. Though she has little space to call her own, with her bed, her chair and her locker, she's fairly content. Her three roommates keep themselves to themselves. She has some books, and a picture of a field with cows lying on the grass chewing their cud. She bought it in Oxfam and likes to sit and look at it. There's no violence now and, as long as she does what's bidden, she lives in a fairly companionable silence with the rest of the world. She is now the closest she's been to contentment since she was a young girl and doesn't want anything to change that. But now there's this new doctor.

Before she can probe her own feelings about this new

development, Sister Ellen appears and props herself on Nora's bed. 'How are you this morning?' she asks.

Nora peers up at her suspiciously. 'Fine,' she mutters.

'How are you feeling about seeing Dr Janet? Did you like her?'

Nora puts her head down, refusing to meet Ellen's eyes. But finally, the pressure to respond overwhelms her. 'She was OK.'

Ellen takes her hand. 'I think she'll be good for you, Nora.'

Nora remembers the trepidation she felt yesterday when she was told Dr Humphreys wanted to see her, and the fear that threatened to overwhelm her when Janet tried to talk about her past. *How was that good for me?* 'Why do I have to see her?'

'Well, she's just starting to work over here as well as on the acute ward, and she wants to get to know everyone.'

'Why?'

'Maybe she can help. Give her a chance, Nora.'

'What for?' Nora knows she's acting like a petulant child, but she doesn't care.

'Remember, I told you, you can't stay here for ever.'

'Why not?'

'Hillinghurst and lots of other hospitals like this will be closed. We already talked about that, remember?'

Nora blinks rapidly and starts to wring her hands.

'Now don't get upset, Nora. We're just talking. No need to get upset.'

But Nora's eyes are blinking faster and faster and her mouth starts to make chewing movements of its own accord.

'Nora, it's all right,' soothes Ellen. 'Nothing bad is going to happen. Calm down. Come on – count your breathing. One . . . slowly . . . One . . . yes, that's better. Two . . . Three . . . There you go . . . That's better. It's all right.'

Nora stops blinking and her hands are finally still, though she keeps them firmly clasped.

Ellen looks at her, the picture of motherly care. 'Nora, you know that when Joe was discharged, you could have gone too, but then you got so upset that you couldn't go after all. But soon you won't have a choice. Hillinghurst will close and you'll have to go somewhere else. We can't stop that happening.' Ellen pauses and watches Nora closely, and after a few moments she presses on. 'I think that Dr Humphreys can help prepare you if you let her. She's working with Audrey and all of us. And you can either work with the team and have some say in the matter, or else choices will be made for you.'

Nora's face clouds with confusion and her chest contracts like it does whenever she feels trapped in a small space. Breathing is somehow twice as difficult as it was a few moments ago.

'You have to decide whether you want to be part of the decision-making or not. I know you're not used to having much choice, but now you do.'

'OK. I want to stay here,' Nora whispers, her voice so quiet that Ellen has to lean in to hear her.

'I know, Nora, but soon you won't be able to,' Ellen says patiently. 'I'm sure that in that head of yours you've got lots of thoughts about it.'

Nora does have thoughts. She remembers when patients started to get an allowance or get paid for what they did. They were taken to the Oxfam shop and told that they could buy things. Nora could hardly believe it. She saw a china cup and saucer and allowed herself to be excited for the first time in years, but then the aide chose her a blouse and a skirt and took the money out of her hand to pay for them. *You see, they offer you choices, but in the end, somebody chooses for you.*

'All right,' she says, astonished herself that this word popped out of her mouth.

'Does that mean you'll see the new doctor? And try to talk to her?'

Nora nods, though she doesn't lift her eyes. Ellen reaches across and squeezes her hand. 'Good girl. Now come on, it's time for breakfast,' she says. With a final pat of Nora's hand, she gets up and leaves, but Nora stays where she is. She looks around at the other beds with their green blankets and white pillowcases. Each bed has a little shelf beside it for the few collected possessions – a photograph or picture, a little clock, a fairy sitting on a branch, a china mouse. Her own shelf has a little snow globe she bought at Oxfam with 'Blackpool' written on the base. She's never been to Blackpool, but that doesn't matter, she still loves the snow globe. She also loves her small figurine of a little girl tying her ballet shoes. The little china cup and saucer are also there – she finally did buy them – but the saucer got broken and the occupational therapist glued it together again for her. Her most treasured possession, her music box with its own ballerina, is packed away with her letters in case it should get broken.

This is her home and she doesn't want to have to leave it. But she knows she'll have to do as she's told in the end. And, she tells herself, if it all gets too scary, she already has things prepared for a final escape. Just in case.

Chapter Four

Janet shakes the rain off her coat and hangs it in the corner. Her hair is wet and her shoes are soaked. She shivers, but there's no time to worry about that now. She sits at her desk and opens her diary with cold fingers. She dials the ward and Dale answers. 'Any problems?' she asks, simultaneously leafing through her diary.

'No, all fine. Are you coming down?'

'Yep. Be there in a couple of minutes. I just have to phone Celia Fulton's GP. Sounds like Celia's off her meds and driving her neighbours mad. We might need a bed for her.'

'That'll be fun. OK – see you in a minute.'

Janet hangs up and then dials the number she was searching for in her diary. Celia's GP says that her neighbour is at the end of her tether, Celia having been hammering on the adjoining wall for days, apparently trying to create an escape route through the neighbour's flat for when hers is invaded by the people she believes are coming to kill her. She needs admission urgently. Janet puts down the phone and it immediately rings again. She picks up, sighing.

'Dr Humphreys,' she says, her eyes on the stack of mail on her desk. Then they flash with irritation. 'I asked you never to call me at work . . . No, I can't . . . I've already told you. I can't do it. I'm sorry . . . You're right. It's my fault, but I just can't. I want to try to make my marriage work. So please just leave me alone.' She replaces the phone feeling shaken. It rings again, almost immediately, and she grabs it instinctively.

'We need you. David Casey,' Dale says, the urgency in his voice unmistakable.

'I'm coming.'

But before she can get out of the door, the phone rings again, and she stifles a scream of frustration. 'Yes,' she almost shouts down the phone.

There's hesitation on the other end of the line. 'Sorry, you sound very busy,' Ellen says apologetically.

Janet sighs and forces herself to calm down. It's not Ellen's fault that her day got off to such a painful start. 'I am. But what can I do for you?'

'Just wanted to remind you about Nora, but if you're busy . . .'

Janet looks at her watch. *Bugger.* 'I'll be there as soon as I can, but there's an emergency this end. Has something happened?'

'Not really, it can wait.'

'OK, I'll be there ASAP.' She slams down the phone and hurries out of her office. As she runs down the stairs, she recaps David Casey's case in her head. A seventeen year old who became mute for several weeks following an episode of bullying at his boarding school that involved him being stripped naked, having his scrotum smeared with a chest rub and then being locked out of the dormitory overnight. As she arrives on the ward, it is immediately apparent that this morning his muteness has morphed into furious screaming. Though it's important that he hurts neither himself nor anyone else, Janet is delighted that he's finally letting it all out, and arms herself with a pillow that he can hit without causing any harm. *Here goes.* She takes a deep breath and enters his room.

An hour later, she backs her way into the nursing station, with David Casey's file tucked under her arm. Dale jumps up and gives her a broad smile. 'OK, let's try to catch up,' she says. Then glances at her watch. 'Oh, damn – just give me a minute.' She snatches the phone and dials hurriedly. 'Ellen? I'm so sorry. It's been a bit hairy here. Do you think you could apologise to Nora for me? I'll be there as soon as I can.'

'No problem. She's used to waiting around,' Ellen says. Janet can tell she's trying to sound breezy, but she doesn't miss the hint of disappointment and resignation in Ellen's tone. She can almost hear it – *I should have known she'd be just like the rest* – and can't help but feel stung. An uneasy pause ensues.

'I try not to keep anyone waiting,' Janet says finally. 'But sometimes—'

'It's OK. Honestly. Give yourself a break. I just don't want you to lose her before she's had the chance to start trusting you.'

'I don't want that either.' Janet carefully replaces the receiver and runs her hand through her hair. 'Sorry, Dale. Let's just organise things for David, then maybe we could go through the cardex and get ourselves on the same page?'

She completes requests for investigations for David then sits back, thoughtful. 'Dale, do you ever think about how patients were managed before we had all the resources and medication we have today?'

'I do. And it makes my heart ache.'

'Mine too. But can you imagine how it must have been for people like you and me when there was nothing they could really do? Awful.' She picks up her pen and taps it on the blotter, feeling glum, but she knows there's no room for wallowing during the day, and she forces herself to meet Dale's eyes with a smile. 'Right, I'm off. I'll be back later. You know where to find me if David kicks off again.'

Janet cycles the short distance to Rowan, enjoying the warmth of the sun on her face, though her mind keeps returning to the phone call of the morning. She knows she has to do something about that. But what?

She parks up her bike and walks slowly to the entrance, composing herself to see Nora. Ellen is waiting for her just inside and greets her with a smile.

'Sorry again that I'm late,' Janet says. 'You wanted to tell me something about Nora?'

'She's obviously been thinking and she seems willing to work with you.' She pauses. 'She's had so many disappointments and betrayals, Janet—'

'I'm not going to hurt her, Ellen.'

'I know you wouldn't mean to . . .'

Janet covers her impatience with a smile. 'Let's give it a go, shall we, and I promise I'll be careful.' They round a corner and Ellen points to the open door of a consulting room. Janet goes straight in and sits down opposite Nora. 'I'm so sorry I'm late,' she says, hoping that they will just be able to move past it. A few minutes later, however, Janet isn't feeling as optimistic. Silence reigns in the small room and Nora sits hunched in her chair, her eyes on the floor.

When the silence grows to the point that Janet can no longer bear it, she tries again. 'I'm really sorry to have kept you waiting. I promise I'll try not to do that again, but I can't guarantee that I'll manage to be on time for each session. I don't want you to think that you're less important, because you're not. But sometimes when things happen on the acute ward, I simply can't get away. I hope you'll forgive me for that.'

Janet looks at the top of Nora's head, which is the only bit of her that she seems willing to present today. She pauses. 'What I'd like us to do is to take a bit of the session every time we see each other to look at what's going on now, but I'd also like us to look at what happened to you before.' Nora doesn't move, and yet Janet has a feeling that she's listening attentively.

'I know your life has been really hard, and I feel sad about that. We can't undo what's been done, but sometimes with hindsight we can see it differently. That goes for the things people have done to us and the things that we, ourselves, have done too. And, since blame doesn't really help, and neither does guilt, hopefully, over time, we'll be able to banish both these things. If we can do that, it allows us to take responsibility for who we are and where we are, and that gives us the power to move forward.'

There's not a hint of movement from Nora. She could even be asleep, but Janet knows she isn't. Janet also knows this is a lot for her to take in, but it needs to be said, so she breathes deeply and presses on.

'Whatever happened, all those years ago, certainly never warranted what happened since. You never deserved that. And all the things that have happened must have changed you. I would really like to find out who Nora Jennings was then, and who Nora Jennings is now. And maybe also have a look together at a plan to help you be who Nora Jennings has been becoming all these years.' She pauses, watching Nora intently. Only the slow movement of her chest proves that she's even alive. 'Lots of parts of you haven't had the chance to grow, but they still could and we can find out what you want to do.'

Janet is determined to do her damnedest to give this woman the best possible chance of survival, but that's enough for today. Hopefully, there'll be plenty of time.

'Thank you for coming to see me,' she says gently. 'Ellen will tell you when I'm coming again,' she tells Nora, and watches as she shuffles out through the consulting room door.

All these people with wounds tracing back to their child-hoods. Lost potential. Lost relationships. Lost peace of mind. The ripples from long-ago traumas still disturbing the waters of the present.

Chapter Five

After several sessions, even though Janet has been beginning to wonder if they'll ever make any progress, Nora does at least appear less withdrawn. There are other subtle yet positive changes, too. She's less likely to stoop or curl up and try to disappear, and with every session she sits more upright in her chair. Today, though, they're ten minutes into the session, and while several times Nora has taken a deep breath as though about to speak, the silence continues. There's something different today that Janet can't quite nail down, and she's intrigued. She takes a deep breath and asks today's version of a question she usually asks. 'Is there anything you'd like to tell me – or ask me?' she says.

There's a long pause, but finally Nora looks up. Momentarily her and Janet's eyes meet before she lowers them again. 'You can call me Nora,' she finally whispers.

'Thank you, Nora,' Janet smiles, moved by this gesture of trust. Until this point, Janet has either called her Miss Jennings or, often, nothing at all.

Silence resumes, but then Nora begins in a small voice. 'Why are you nice to me?'

Janet pauses, taken aback. 'Aren't other people nice to you?' she asks, deflecting the question.

'Some are.' Nora twirls her handkerchief in her lap then looks out of the window. 'But when people are nasty to you, you know where you are with them,' she mutters.

'Well, I'd like us to know where we are with each other, but I hope that will be without us being nasty to each other,' Janet says. 'Maybe we could just make a deal to be truthful to each other, then we'll always know where we are.'

Nora continues to look out of the window, her face set.

'Is there anyone who's nice and you can still trust?'

Nora lowers her eyes. 'Ellen. Joe. And I could trust Peggy, but she died, and Dr Stilworth, but he retired.'

'I hope you will learn to trust me too,' Janet says, feeling carefully for every word so she doesn't stem this fragile trickle of communication.

'Sometimes people say nice things but then do nasty things.'

'Yes, I guess sometimes they do.'

The conversation seems to come to a natural pause once again, leaving a more comfortable silence in its wake this time. Nora looks around the room, then stops and studies her hands. Janet watches, fascinated – it's like watching a bud struggling to open.

Nora looks up. 'Aren't you going to write this down?'

'I don't usually write when I'm with people. I like to listen to what you have to say.'

Uncertainty crosses Nora's face and she fixes her eyes on the arm of Janet's chair before falling again into the silence. Janet simply waits, leaving a space for Nora to fill when she's ready. Eventually the words come out in an astonishingly articulate rush.

'They wanted me to behave like a tame rabbit,' she begins, her eyes down but her voice surprisingly strong, the words seeming to come from another place. 'If I behaved like a tame rabbit, people thought I was good. If I tried to say what I really wanted then I was told I was bad – a bad patient. In the end you behave in the way that makes them think you're good, but then you have to live with being a liar.'

Janet has to remind herself to breathe. 'I can see that. It does seem unfair.'

'I was put here because I might infect other people with my badness. I don't think I could. I'm not that strong. You are. You want me to talk, but you can make it bad for me if I say something you don't like. And if I *am* infectious, I don't want to infect you as well. You look kind. I never wanted to hurt anybody, but I did. I killed my mother.'

Janet stares, eyes wide. 'You killed your mother?'

'I sent her to an early grave.'

Janet breathes out in relief, then feels a flash of anger at whoever first told Nora that. 'How did you do that?' she asks.

'I did something terrible and she never recovered.'

'Can you tell me about it?'

There's a long pause and Janet waits while Nora's eyes flit around the room then back to her lap, seemingly weighing up whether she can trust yet another person who might just betray her. Without lifting her eyes, she begins to speak. 'I was wicked. I had a baby. She died. I never even saw her. I should have died. Sometimes I still want to, even if it's a sin. I got my just deserts.'

Janet is frozen, her eyes fixed on Nora's crown, trying not to allow her sadness and outrage to show on her face. This was all over forty years ago, and Nora has been here ever since. How could anyone ever deserve that?

'I'm so sorry, Nora,' is all she can manage.

Nora's head lifts slowly and she, too, looks shocked, but there's also something else, and Janet realises with a start that Nora is grateful. Her eyes seem to say that someone listened, didn't interrupt or try to make the story different. Made no excuse, nor impatiently looked at her watch. And for a moment their eyes meet and words are unnecessary. Then Nora pulls her eyes away and the moment is over.

'Nora, you didn't kill your mother,' Janet says gently.

'Yes, I did. And I also made my father very angry.'

'How did you do that?'

'I was a bad girl.'

'Were you?'

'Not all the time. Before I . . . did what I did . . . I think I was a good girl. Well, sometimes I wasn't, I suppose. My dad sometimes didn't think I was being good, but I didn't always understand why.'

Janet understands that very well. 'Sometimes we are being good and people misunderstand what we're doing and we get into trouble, but it's not really our fault.'

'But that time it was my fault. I committed a mortal sin and deserved everything that happened.'

'What mortal sin?'

'I tried to kill my baby and I tried to kill myself. Two mortal sins. And the wages of sin are death.'

Janet cringes inside. 'Then what happened?'

But before Nora can speak, something seems to switch within her and Janet watches helplessly as Nora gasps and clutches the arms of her chair, her shoulders lifting and her neck disappearing between them. Her brow knits together and her lips form a tight line. Janet logs every sensation and impression, remaining perfectly still until she has fully assessed what is happening, lest any interruption might be misinterpreted as an attack. *A neurological episode? A seizure?*

Nora twitches, squirming to the left, her hands coming up to cover her face. She whimpers and cowers, curling in on herself, minimising her external surface, obviously trying to protect herself from some sort of assault. *Ah, she's having a flashback*, thinks Janet. *No wonder she doesn't want to have to talk and remember.*

After a few more seconds, the episode appears to subside, and Janet starts to speak in a low, soothing voice. 'Nora. Nora, it's all right. You're here. You're safe.' But suddenly Nora raises her hands to cover her ears, her eyes tightly shut, and begins to wail.

Very carefully, Janet leans forward and, as she does, Nora lifts her hands and starts to beat her head and her face. Janet feels a dart of alarm, but tries not to let it show. Gently but firmly, she takes hold of Nora's hands. 'Nora, don't. Nora – try to look at me. Open your eyes.' But Nora still squirms, her breathing laboured as she rocks back and forth.

'Nora, open your eyes. You're here – you're safe.' And though Nora flinches, Janet maintains gentle pressure on her skin. 'Nora, it's OK. Come back . . .'

Then come the tears, streaming down her face and dripping off her nose. Janet shifts a little but continues to anchor Nora in this reality with the pressure of just one finger, resisting the urge to offer tissues in case that signals to Nora that crying is unacceptable. How she needs this gentle bathing of her soul.

Finally, the sobbing subsides, and Nora returns to the moment, her puffy eyes open and the tip of her nose red.

Janet smiles tenderly. 'Try to look at me, Nora. Take your time, but when you're ready, look at me.'

It takes a while, but slowly, Nora's eyes meet hers.

'Nora, this was a flashback, and you've survived whatever you remembered. You're safe now.'

They sit a while in silence as Nora recovers, wiping her eyes and looking around the room, dazed, trying to re-orientate herself.

Janet brings her a glass of water and waits as Nora sips it slowly. 'Nora, sometimes people feel really quite tired after a flashback, but if you can, it would be really helpful to try and find out what just happened. Do you think we could do that?'

Nora nods hesitantly.

'You looked frightened, Nora, as though someone was hitting you. Who hit you?'

'My father,' she whispers.

Janet breathes and checks herself. *This isn't about you, Janet.*

'How did he hit you?'

'Sometimes with his hand and sometimes with his belt.'

Janet breathes in sharply, but doesn't make a sound. She commands herself to slow down and be the professional; get her own emotions and her own past under control, and breathe. 'I'm sorry that happened to you, Nora. What did you do when that happened?'

'I don't know. Sometimes I didn't feel it, like I wasn't there.'

'And when you felt like you weren't there, where were you?'

'Up in the corner of the ceiling. I used to watch, but I didn't feel anything.'

'Nora, did anyone else hit you?'

'Lots of people.'

'Who?'

'Sister Cummings. And the aides when I wouldn't eat. Sometimes the night nurse. And the maid when I wet on the floor . . .'

Janet checks Nora's breathing. She's OK. 'I'm not surprised that you didn't want to talk,' Janet says. 'I understand. It does stir up old feelings and sometimes makes you have flashbacks. But it will also help you to understand and come to terms with what's happened to you if we keep on working at it.'

Now she hands Nora a tissue. 'How often does this happen to you?'

'I don't know,' Nora says shakily.

'When was the last one?'

'About a week ago.'

Janet pauses for a second, thinking. 'Something must have happened to trigger it. Was there something that reminded you of the past?'

'I don't remember.' Nora shakes her head and tears begin to leak from her eyes.

'No problem,' Janet says, glancing discreetly at her watch. She feels a stab of anxiety. She doesn't want to leave Nora now, but she's going to be late for her appointment with Dr Pauling. Damn!

She watches Nora for another minute or so, then touches her gently on her arm.

'Nora, I'm so sorry, but we're going to need to stop for today. I want us to come back to this next time so we both understand how you can move on from here. I'm going to give you a little book to write in, like a diary. It'll be *your* book and no one will look at it but you. You'll be able to share anything you want with me, but also know you don't have to if you don't want to. It'll be your private property.' Nora looks at her questioningly. 'Yes, Nora. Your own private property that you can bring to our sessions in case there's anything you want to remember to talk about.'

Nora lifts her eyes and nods, then steadies herself with her hands on the chair arms and stands shakily. Nora's eyes meet Janet's just for a moment and she mouths, 'Thank you.' And hobbles out.

★ ★ ★

As Janet steps outside, she is glad of the sharp breeze to help clear her thoughts. She knows she will need to really sit and look at all of her own father issues at some point. No time now. She pedals her bicycle as quickly as she can back to the acute block, wobbling as she tries to glance at her watch. He'll be livid.

By the time she arrives at Dr Pauling's office, Janet has just about caught her breath but lingers outside the door for a few seconds, bracing herself for a less than warm welcome.

'Sit down, Janet,' he snaps in just the same tone her father used to use when she had been naughty as a little girl. Her palms start to sweat and she feels the childish urge to resist, but catches herself at the last second. She sinks into the chair, glad of a moment of respite as Dr Pauling still has his eyes glued to the journal he's annotating. *He is not my father. He is not my father.*

Finally, he slams down his pen on the desk and looks at her with eyes like flint. 'What do you think you're doing?' His voice has the spiteful force of a tsunami, and Janet flinches. What is it with him? 'Did I ask you to create a lengthy investigation on the back wards?' he spits, his colour rising as hers ebbs.

Janet frowns, completely flummoxed. 'I'm afraid I don't understand,' she says, irritated at the tremor in her voice and determined to be her strong, professional self.

'That's very clear, though I wonder why not,' he sneers. 'You don't have time to waste hiding away on the back wards.'

Janet bristles. 'I'm not hiding away,' she defends, her voice now strong and clear. 'Nor am I wasting my time.'

'That's your opinion.'

She feels her chin jut forward, her face tipping slightly upwards. 'Yes, it is.' *Careful,* Janet . . .

She's back at the age of sixteen and standing in the room they called the kitchen but is really an all-purpose room to cook, eat and sit in the evening and watch the small black-and-white television.

Janet has asked permission to go to the cinema with her friend and is at stage two of the usual negotiations – first her mother who says, 'Ask your father', then to her father who asks, 'What did your mother say?'

'She said to ask you.'

'Are there going to be boys there?'

'I don't know. We're going just the two of us, though.'

Her father snorts. 'You're not going anywhere till I say you can.'

Then she makes the fatal mistake. Too late she's aware of the involuntary roll of her eyes. His hand is swift as it always is, and she gasps with pain and clutches at her already swelling cheek, yet again.

'You watch yourself, miss,' her father shouts. 'You're going nowhere. Get to your room.'

Her face stings and anger rises at the injustice of it. 'That's not fair.'

'One more word from you and you'll see what's not fair,' he growls.

But this time she can't let it go, despite what might – what is likely to – happen.

'Dad, I'm sixteen!' she cries, her eyes streaming with both pain and frustration.

'And as long as you live under my roof you'll behave as I see fit. Get to your room.'

The rest blurs as she's suddenly aware of Dr Pauling's voice. Janet blinks back into the moment, desperately trying to concentrate.

'The task I set should have taken hours, not weeks.'

Janet straightens her back and lifts her chin, forcing herself to focus. 'There are ninety-seven patients, many of whom hadn't been reviewed properly for years—'

'You feel qualified to criticise the work of those who preceded you?'

'I'm not intending to criticise anyone. Usually those wards have been looked after by SHOs or registrars who are on rotation, and I'm sure they did what they thought was right. Nevertheless, some medications have been continued for years without proper review. Some patients were taking up to six or seven different meds, some of which had interactions. They needed paring down and sorting out. Some of the patients are much more lively now they're off sedation, and I'm looking at who among them may yet have a chance of living independently. I—'

'That's enough. I will not have you neglecting the acute patients.'

Here it comes . . . Injustice always leads to her losing her cool. 'Do you have any particular acute patients in mind who have suffered neglect due to my work on the back wards?'

'That isn't the point—'

'With respect, I think it is. I've put in longer hours to accommodate the extra work, and have neglected nothing.'

'If you don't have enough to do . . .' he blusters. 'I want a teaching plan for the students on my desk in the morning,' he snaps.

'You will have it,' she says, rather too sharply.

'And you'll present at the journal club on Thursday.' His petulance matches her determination.

She knows it's almost impossible to prepare a presentation for the whole faculty in two days. But she also knows that she'll do it. 'Thank you for the opportunity,' she says, her voice brittle.

His eyes lock on hers and he stares but says nothing while she refuses to be the first to look away. 'That's all,' he says, and lowers his eyes.

Janet stomps along the corridor to her own office, fuming, not even returning the smile of Audrey – social worker, Earth Mother supreme, Angel of Hillinghurst Hospital – who flattens against the wall to let her past. She is marching up and down the short length of the room to calm herself when there's a tap on her door and Dale opens it a crack.

'You OK?' He smiles. 'Audrey said you had smoke coming out of your ears.'

'He's impossible,' she rants. 'Absolutely impossible.'

He leans against the door frame. 'Yep, but letting him get you wound up just means he's winning.'

'Stop being so sensible,' she grumps, but already she's having to make an effort not to smile. His eyes twinkle and there's that laugh, and she can't resist joining in. 'Don't you ever lose it, Dale?' she asks.

'Who, me? Never, darling.' He pauses. 'Of course, I do – and believe me, you don't want to see it when it happens. Not a pretty sight.' Then he becomes serious. 'But these poor buggers don't need my moods.' He touches her arm gently. 'And they don't need yours either. They've got enough on their plates as it is. I have the luxury of being able to let off my steam somewhere else.'

'Is that a dig at me?'

'Now, would I?'

Janet sighs. 'Point made.'

'Good. Now – cup of tea?' He turns to go, and is almost in the corridor when he pauses and looks back. 'Beware. Big Cheese rolling in,' he announces in a stage whisper.

She looks up and smiles. 'One of these days he'll catch you and you'll be out on your ear.' She laughs.

'Not with the power of the union behind me, my dear.' He laughs. But then his face becomes serious. 'He wasn't always like this, you know. Why don't you have a word with Audrey. She knows the full story.'

Janet looks at him, intrigued. 'OK, I will – thanks for the tip.'

She taps on Audrey's door and is greeted by a lovely smile. 'Thanks for making time to see me. I know you're very busy. Sorry I was in such a foul mood earlier.'

'No problem. It's lovely to see you.'

'I'm not asking you to breach confidentiality, but I'm having a real issue with Dr Pauling and Dale suggested I have a word with you.'

'Ah . . . come. Sit down.'

Half an hour later, Janet walks along the corridor with her heart full of compassion. How it must feel to raise a child to the age of sixteen and have him die of cancer she can only imagine. No wonder he's been angry with the world and everything in it. Poor man. She determines to do just as she would suggest to her patients and change her own attitude.

Chapter Six

Janet can't get the thought of Dr Pauling's overwhelming grief out of her head. Her mind drifts back to her own parents, and her own childhood.

She's four and the smell of newly baked bread and Victoria sponge cake make Janet's mouth water as her mother bends down towards her and fluffs out the gathered skirt of her new dress. She looks at herself in her mother's dressing-table mirror. Her hair is in ringlets and is crowned with a white bow that matches the collar of the dress. She likes the puffed sleeves. Her tan shoes are freshly polished and she has new white ankle socks. It's a very special day because Daddy is coming home from the war.

'You look very pretty.' Her mother smiles. 'Now, you won't forget what Mummy said, will you?'

'I haven't to be frightened if he has stitches in his face,' Janet recites.

'That's right. He will be tired and you have to be a very good girl and go to bed nicely in your new bed in the sitting room.'

'I want to sleep with you and I don't want to see him if he's got cotton in his face,' Janet says, halfway between anger and tears.

Her mother laughs. 'He won't have cotton stitches. And they might be gone anyway. And we can still have a snuggle in the morning.'

Janet looks down at her shoes. 'Will he like me?'

'I'm sure he's going to love you just like I do,' she says, 'but he's been very, very poorly and it might take him a while to get to know you – and to get to know me again too. I know you haven't seen him before, but I have hardly seen him since before you were born, either.'

'But I'm four now.'

Her mother looks out of the window for the umpteenth time. 'Well, he's been in hospital for a long time. He's a lot better now, but we still have to be very good and very quiet.' She turns back from the window. 'Not yet. He won't be long though.'

She bends down and gives Janet a hug then kisses her cheek. 'I know it's going to be very different but . . .' She looks away as a figure crosses in front of the window, then she runs to open the door. Standing there is a man in a khaki uniform with a big bag over his shoulder. She makes a little sound of surprise. He smiles. He doesn't have cotton in his face but there's a big lump under his eye and a funny bump on his head. Her mother puts her arms around him and they have a long kiss while Janet hides her doll behind her back and snuggles up to the backs of her mother's legs.

'And who is this?' the man says as he drops his bag and gets down on one knee. But Janet, suddenly shy, tries to hide in her mother's skirt and looks the other way. 'I brought you something, little Janet,' he says, and slowly she looks at him as he pulls a soft doll with dark woolly hair and a pink dress out of his bag.

Her mother reaches down and takes Janet's old doll out of her hand and swaps it with the new one. 'Well, look at that. She looks like you. What are you going to call her?'

But Janet is still watching her own doll and wants to cry. She's too shy to speak, and when her father stoops to pick her up, she feels afraid and stiffens and shies away from the scars on his face. And he smells funny. She looks back at her mother who is trying to smile, though her eyes look worried. Janet feels scared to see her mother so worried and she starts to wriggle and cry and wants to be in her mother's arms, not this strange man's, even if he is her father. He puts her down quickly.

'She'll be all right in a little while,' her mother says, giving a nervous laugh, 'it'll take time.'

Janet tosses around in the little bed in the sitting room and eventually falls asleep, but then is woken by her mother making funny noises like she's hurt, or maybe crying, or maybe talking . . . And then her father makes a strange noise too. She gets up and goes to the door to her mother's bedroom and opens the door just a crack. Her father seems to be hurting her mother. Then he looks up and sees her.

'Get out of here,' he shouts, and Janet runs back to her bed, afraid. She hates him.

The next morning, she doesn't know what to do. She can see that the sun is up but she hasn't seen her mother yet, even though she always gets up before Janet is even awake. She hopes she isn't dead.

She waits . . . and waits . . . and waits . . .

Then the door opens and out comes her father. He's wearing trousers and a vest and braces. He doesn't smile and goes straight to the toilet. Janet creeps to the door, terrified of what she might find. But there is her mother looking fine and Janet is staring at her, her forehead creased in a puzzled frown.

'Come and have a cuddle,' her mother says, and holds up the blanket so Janet can crawl in beside her. 'Come on. It's all right.' So, Janet climbs up onto the bed and into her mother's arms. 'Daddy will be back in a minute, then we'll all get up and have breakfast,' she says. She smooths Janet's hair and kisses her brow. 'Daddy had a very bad accident. A bomb went off beside him. We have to be very quiet and good and make sure we don't upset him.'

Her father enters the room and looks at them in the bed. 'Shall I make you two tea in bed?' he says. 'I could bring it on a tray.' Then looking at Janet, 'Would you like that?'

'Yes, please,' she whispers. This earns her another stroke from her mother.

'Right. I'll be back soon. Tea for my girls coming up.'

She snuggles down and curls up in the welcoming warmth of the eiderdown and the comforting, familiar smell of her mother's body, feeling safe and happy again. She won't ask about the funny noises in the night.

After breakfast Janet wants to help clearing the table as she always does. She stacks the plates – three now – and starts to pick up the pile. 'Just leave them, Janet,' her mother says.

'I can manage.'

'No, just leave them. I'll do that in a minute. Just put them back on the table.'

Janet turns with them and, as she does, one slips off the pile and falls, breaking on the lino floor with a loud noise. Her father spins round, startled, his face contorted, his hands trembling. Janet trembles too as she stares at him for just a split second before his hand contacts the side of her head, with a force that hurls her across the room.

'Do as your mother says,' he bellows.

'Jack,' her mother screams as she scoops Janet up off the floor. 'Just sit down. I'll deal with her.' Then all her attention is on Janet, who is too shocked even to cry. 'Are you all right, flower?'

'Of course, she's all right,' the voice thunders behind her. 'She needs to learn to do as she's told.'

Janet feels a hand on her shoulder and opens her eyes. Dale's beautiful eyes look directly into hers. 'You look exhausted,' he says as Janet flushes and sits up in her chair.

'I'm sorry,' she says, eyes darting round the room as she orientates herself. 'I *am* tired. Not sleeping so well.' And her mind shifts abruptly to Ian and the flush of her cheeks deepens with added shame.

Chapter Seven

Six months later

Janet, hair dishevelled, barefoot, in jeans and T-shirt, leans against the doorway between the sitting room and hallway. Her face is drained of colour, her eyes red and swollen. She clutches a ball of crumpled paper in her hand.

'Please don't do this, Ian. Nothing happened. Honestly.'

Ian pauses and looks up at her. His eyes seem dead; his skin dull. 'Janet, those letters aren't nothing.'

'I'm sorry. I love you. Please don't do this. Can we sit and talk?'

'I've been begging you these last months to talk. You've got to sort yourself out. I can't take it any more. You want him, then—'

'I don't want him. That ended months ago and I am sorting it out. Please don't . . . I'm sorry about the letters. I should have destroyed them—'

'You think that would have made it better?' he shouts, finally losing his temper. 'You should have told me. All those late call-outs with me sitting here waiting for you. All this flinching when I touch you. You can't tell me that there was nothing going on.'

'It's not like you think. I was flattered. I thought you'd never need to know.'

'Well, now I do, so just leave me be.'

'Ian—'

But he turns and carries on packing up his half of their life as though she wasn't there. She surveys the room. The bookshelves are bereft of much of their usually colourful content. They stare at her accusingly like empty sockets, while the books that remain lean at odd angles, as if offering each other much-needed support. The music centre, denuded of stacks of records in their colourful jackets, mocks her. The Bee-Gees, Bread, Beethoven and Bach are being dragged away in cardboard boxes and plastic bags. And from all the commotion of the day, a loud silence born of shock and pain is all that remains. She's pleaded and cajoled, shouted and cried, consciously manipulated, even, but nothing she has said has changed his mind. It's all she can do now to stand and bear witness, stunned, her breath coming in short gasps of pain and bewilderment.

'Do you want this?' His usually soft, Irish-accented voice is rough and hoarse as he holds out their wedding photograph – their younger selves looking at each other with such love and hope in their eyes.

'Of course I do, but take it if you want to.'

He throws in onto the settee where it lands in the arms of other rejected joint possessions.

'You can take it,' she mumbles.

'Make up your mind.'

'That's not fair.' She rakes her hand through her hair.

'Is anything about our marriage fair?' he shouts suddenly, and she jumps.

She turns away and walks into the kitchen, propping herself up on the counter with her elbows, crying into her hands. *How can this be happening?* The sound of yet another box being dragged into the hall makes her start. *He's actually going to leave* . . . She dashes into the hallway but he's already back in the sitting room with another black bin liner, stuffing a couple of cushions into it, dislodging some of the items thrown there, including the wedding photo which now falls to the floor. The glass shatters and they both stare at it, stunned.

All at once, fury burns within Janet. 'Don't do that,' she screams, pushing Ian aside so she can retrieve the pieces, piercing a fingertip on a shard of glass. She sucks the blood away as he makes a move towards her.

'Don't touch me!' She draws back as though from a snake about to strike.

'Have it your way, then,' he mutters under his breath, throwing the plastic bag down and grabbing one of the boxes. He heads for the open door.

Just as he reaches it, Janet turns, panic-stricken. 'Ian!' she cries, hurrying to catch up with him, wiping her streaming eyes with her sleeve as she goes. 'Don't go! Please. We can fix this.'

He shakes his head, eyes downcast. 'Janet, you're the psychiatrist. This isn't about me and probably not even about him.' He points at the letter she still clutches. 'It's about your father. That's what you need to deal with.'

'Stop it!' she cries. 'I'm trying to deal with it.'

'Is that what your patients say when you hit a nerve?'

Anger flares within her again. 'Fine, go. Get out,' she shouts. 'You only married me because I was pregnant, anyway – not because you love me.' There, it's out. The canker that has eaten away at her for almost twenty years and that she had determined never to declare, knowing it would mean the end.

He stops and stands perfectly still, then turns slowly towards her, his eyes glassy with hurt. They stare into each other's eyes, each offering the other a silent challenge. When he finally speaks his voice is low, crushed by her accusation. 'Is that what you think?'

Janet wants to take it all back, to say she didn't mean it, but she knows there's no going back now. She lifts her chin defiantly. 'The least you can do is admit it. You only married me because you had to. What do you think that feels like? At least I know he chose me for being me.' And she pushes away the image of this tall, handsome man with his flirtatious smile and dark eyes, who for a while made her feel desirable and out of her mind with longing.

Ian shakes his head. 'I didn't have to marry you. I'd have married you no matter what. You've been the love of my life ever since I laid eyes on you. But if that's what you've always thought then, I'm sorry, but all this is of your own making. And as for him, whoever he is, do you think he could ever know you like I do?'

Her heart shatters like the glass of their wedding photo at the finality of the lingering look, and only now does she understand that this really is the end. For perhaps the last time she drinks him in. He looks as if he's aged ten years in the last week. He turns and walks to the waiting van with leaden steps, and places the box in the back. He wipes his face with his handkerchief and turns again. He walks straight past Janet in the doorway, not meeting her eyes, returning moments later with the last box.

'I'll let you know where I am when I've found a place,' he says without stopping. 'I'll continue to pay the mortgage and if you need anything—'

'I won't,' she snaps, driving the final nail into the coffin of their marriage.

He climbs up and folds his beautiful, tall frame into the cab of the borrowed van that will take him out of her life. She can hardly bear the sound of the revving engine, or the sight of the vehicle as it reaches the end of the road and turns left. She stands in the doorway, arms folded over her chest, holding herself together, as the roses mock her with their perfect beaming beauty. Her eyes come to rest on a piece of paper that has lodged itself in the hedge. Absently, she steps out and crosses the lawn to pluck it out, an offending splinter in a wound. She glances at it – a scribbled shopping list in Ian's handwriting; must have blown out of one of the boxes.

She crunches it into a ball and adds it to the balled-up, incriminating letter already in her hand. How could she have been so stupid as to leave it where he could find it? But maybe that's exactly what was meant to happen. And he may never believe that she turned back and never consummated the relationship. Just a flirtation really. Good for her ego but deadly for her marriage.

With a final glance around the garden, she goes back into the house and shuts the door on everything – the day, the past, her marriage, Ian.

*   *   *

But the past will not leave her alone and, as she lies tossing and turning in bed, Ian's words ring in her ears. And her mind drifts back to that evening in 1962.

She and Ian have planned it as best they could in the circumstances, but Janet nevertheless nurses a sense of dread. As always, the fear of upsetting her father and causing either an outburst of aggression or, worse, a complex seizure because of his head injury, hangs in the air like a shroud. She has grown up with this tiptoeing around and trying to accommodate everyone, but Ian has a completely different take on how he should handle it. It's stupid to even hope that they can get away without some upset, and the worry of that adds to the tense build-up that makes it all the more inevitable.

Janet, her parents and Ian sit at the kitchen table having finished their meal, and Janet's mother stands to gather the plates. Janet gathers hers and Ian's and follows her mother to the kitchen sink to stack them for washing. She glances anxiously at Ian as she passes and he gently touches her back.

'I'd like to have a word with you,' Ian says to her father, and Janet's mother looks at Janet, a question in her face.

'Come and sit down, Mum,' Janet says, as her father moves from the table to one of the two fireside chairs. Her mother takes her place in the other one, and Janet sits back at the table beside Ian, who takes her hand. Ignoring the fact that Ian has spoken, her father reaches for his pipe, knocks out the ash onto the fireside grate and starts to refill it, tamping down the tobacco with his thumb. Ian waits, squeezing Janet's hand and giving her a quick, comforting glance.

Her father lights his pipe, draws upon it, then looks at Ian. 'So?'

Ian takes a breath then begins in a strong, even voice. 'Janet and I would like to get married.'

Janet's mother's face lights up as she looks at Janet, but then she reads the fear on her daughter's face. Her father looks up, his eyes flitting between Janet and her mother, but he says nothing. The silence stretches treacherously across the strained gap.

'We want you to know that Janet is pregnant,' says Ian finally. And the statement hangs there momentarily before it ruptures, splattering all four of them with its misery.

Janet's eyes flash to her mother. Her father's eyes bore into Ian then turn their fire on Janet. Her mother fidgets with her handkerchief. Ian looks at each in turn with a look of disbelief at this parody of a family.

Janet's mother breaks the silence. 'What on earth will the neighbours say?'

'There'll be no wedding from here,' her father pronounces, his voice like black ice.

'It's OK. We won't embarrass you in the village,' says Janet. 'We'll find a flat and marry from there.'

Her father glowers at her, eyes narrowing, stabbing through the air with his pipe. 'You'll do as you're told, miss.'

Janet squeezes Ian's hand, pleading through this contact for him not to push things any further. But he doesn't understand – or, if he does, he doesn't listen. 'We've talked about this. We're two adults who love each other and we'll find a place and be fine.'

'There's nothing fine about this,' Janet's father says flatly, to no one in particular. Then he taps his pipe on the grate and turns his gaze on Ian. He points threateningly with his pipe, and in a deadly calm voice says: 'And you – you'd better leave. You've done enough damage.' Then swings his attention to Janet. 'And you, miss, get to your room.'

Ian stands, still holding Janet's hand. 'If I have to leave, that's fine, but we'll go together.'

Janet's mother bursts into tears and Janet's anxiety bubbles over. 'It's all right, Ian,' she says, her voice trembling. 'I'll pack and you can come and get me in the morning.'

He looks down at her and Janet shrivels at the hurt in his eyes at this first betrayal.

'I don't think—' he begins, but she cuts him off, her eyes pleading as she looks away and towards her mother.

'Ian. Just go. I'll see you in the morning.'

His hand grips hers more tightly. 'Come with me.'

'I can't . . .'

Her father looks back and forth between the two of them while her mother cries. 'Look what you've done to your mother.'

Janet stands and shifts from one foot to the other, her eyes darting from one person to the other. 'Please, Ian. Just go,' she says.

His eyes search her face. 'Are you sure?'

'Yes. I'll be fine. Come for me around ten.' And she signals with her eyes that he should leave.

With one last pleading look, he turns, and Janet's eyes follow him, guilt flowing towards him like a stream to the ocean. *Please understand . . .*

The door closes. Janet feels bereft and she trembles with fear.

'Get to your room,' her father says. And as she closes her bedroom door, she hears her mother's voice. 'No, Jack.'

'You just get on with your knitting.' Her father's voice carries cold anger, and Janet shivers. She knows what is to happen next. As he opens the door, he is holding his belt.

The next morning, painful and sore, Janet packs her one suitcase, then comes out of her room, a welt across her arm and a bruise on the side of her face. Her mother is lighting the fire and looks up helplessly.

'I'll be leaving this morning,' Janet says, her monotone voice devoid of emotion. 'I'll let you know my address and the date for the wedding. You'll both be welcome if you want to come. But you both need to know that if he ever lifts a hand to me again, I'll hit him right back.'

Chapter Eight

1982
Forty-three years

Though she was determined to make it to work this morning, by the time Janet gets out of her car she is already struggling to breathe past the jagged hole in her chest where her heart is breaking. As she prepares for the day in her office, her eyes keep darting to the phone. She wants nothing more than to call him, just to hear his voice. But then what? They both need time. So for now, she must subdue the emotions she can't bear and that have no place here. Neither Nora nor any of her other patients deserve this.

She starts at a tap on the door.

'Janet, are you all right?' Dale calls gently.

'Just a minute,' she says, tugging on her skirt, patting her hair, smoothing her lips. She opens the door and tries to smile, but she can see from Dale's face that she wasn't very successful.

'Can I get you anything?' he says. 'Dorothy said you didn't look well when you came through reception.'

'I'm OK,' she says, her voice unsteady. 'But can you make my apologies? I'll be late for the ward round. Ten minutes max.'

'Done,' he says. 'And if there's anything else you need, just shout.'

A couple of hours later, the ward round out of the way without incident, Janet does a quick round of the acute patients, organises a couple of discharges, makes sure that those having weekend leave have their medication sorted and then toys with a sandwich in her office. She glances at her watch and finds that there's just time to get across to Rowan for their ward meeting – more low-key than the weekly round here that Dale refers to as the Friday Follies, but important nevertheless. There's excitement among the staff about Nora's progress.

'She's definitely more present and open,' Ellen offers, 'and she smiles more. Still pretty solitary, but she's eating and sleeping better too. And she's quite articulate when she gets going.'

'Yes, I have to admit that I hadn't expected the depth and breadth of her vocabulary,' Janet says, energised too by Nora's ongoing metamorphosis in a place where progress is usually measured in terms of stability rather than change. 'Her father was a solicitor and her mother a music teacher, so she was probably pretty bright, but still. What a life, bless her.'

'Great to have a bit of hope around here,' says Kit, a beautiful round West Indian nurse who seems to have been here for ever. 'Let's hope it'll rub off on some of the others.'

'Wouldn't that be lovely!'

'She seems eager to learn,' Ellen adds. 'She carries her diary everywhere.'

'Great. I know she's institutionalised but she also has serious complex post-traumatic stress disorder that could take a long time to heal. But she does seem motivated. Astonishing, really, after all these years,' Janet says. 'And she must still have fears about the future. But just to acknowledge that there might be one is a huge step forward.'

Audrey looks thoughtful. This is a woman for whom Janet has great respect. She's a wise and reliable sounding board. Widowed thirteen years ago, she's now proud to be the mother of two graduates making their way in the world. And at last, she's found love with Angus, a stout, lovable, dependable Scot, a widower who adores her. When Janet saw them greeting each other with such sweet affection in the car park one day, her heart stung for what she herself has lost. 'Has the topic of discharge been mentioned?' she asks. 'I know we're all concerned about the political situation and the imminent closure of psychiatric hospitals.'

Janet frowns, thinking back. 'I haven't broached the subject yet, but I think you might have done, Ellen?'

'I've mentioned it to some of them – including Nora – but I don't want to cause distress to any of them about it until we really know about Hillinghurst's fate,' Ellen says. 'I'm concerned that if we push Nora, we might lose her and she'll regress again.'

'I agree,' says Janet. 'Let's just keep going as we have been for the moment. I don't think closures are that imminent, anyway, but you never can tell with British politics.'

In the small consulting room later that afternoon, Nora sits alert, her hands clutching her diary. Janet smiles to herself. 'I see you have your diary.' Nora's grip tightens almost imperceptibly. 'It's OK, Nora. You don't have to tell me anything if you don't want to.'

Nora looks up, her eyes still full of doubt.

'Yes, really.' Janet smiles. 'Nora, you have rights that you don't even know about yet. Do you remember when we said we were making new rules until you were able to accept those rights as freedoms? Well, today's new rule is that you can say "no" to me whenever you want to.' And she wonders how long it will be before Nora has the courage to exercise that right. 'So, whenever you want to, you can share with me what's been happening or what you've thought about. But just to move us along a bit, I thought we could look at what happens when we get hurt and what we need to do to get better.' Nora raises her eyes a little to almost meet Janet's, though her grip on her diary remains. It's Janet who draws her eyes away. How much she herself needs this lesson today.

'Nora, if you had a wound on your arm, ideally you'd bathe it, examine it carefully to see that there was nothing stuck in it that might prevent it from healing, maybe put a bandage on it and rest it. And, even though it might hurt, it would eventually heal. It would leave a scar, but that would fade over time. If you didn't do those things it might get septic, it wouldn't heal properly, it would be very painful and you might even lose the ability to move your arm at all. You'd probably be scared that anyone might touch it because it's so painful.'

Nora tilts her head, listening attentively.

'Emotional wounds need the same amount of attention as physical wounds, but often we don't give them that,' Janet continues. 'We just carry on and try to forget about them; pretend they aren't there.' *But sometimes there's nothing else we can do*, she thinks, taking a long breath before she continues. 'But then we end up with all sorts of problems later. Parts of us don't work very well; we still have pain we hardly dare let anyone touch. We often feel confused about why we feel and behave as we do but can't seem to do anything about it. That isn't our fault. And since we're not bleeding and we don't have a bandage or a leg in plaster or whatever, nobody else can understand why we are as we are, either, and they don't know what to do with us, so we are often just left to get on with it, but that doesn't help us get better either.' She pauses. 'Are you still with me, or am I going too fast?'

Nora nods then shakes her head. 'Yes, I'm still here and no, you're not going too fast.' They meet each other's eyes and Nora gives a tentative smile.

'You're amazing, Nora,' Janet says with a smile. 'The good news is that we can always go back and have another look and do the same as we do with physical wounds – examine them and gently clean them up and take care of them till they heal. It might hurt as we do it, but it's the only sure way to get them to heal properly.'

Nora takes a deep breath.

'So . . . you can choose, Nora. We don't have to go there unless you're OK with that. You can say no. But if you can bear it, we can really look at what's happened and you can start to get better.'

She watches until Nora looks up with questions in her eyes. 'You can ask me any questions about any of this, Nora. So now I'll be quiet for a little while to give you time to tell me what you think, whether you'd like to try that or not. Remember, you can choose.'

Janet puts her hands in her lap and sits in silence, trying not to even look in Nora's direction, until, in a voice that's almost inaudible, Nora begins. 'Most of the time I don't feel anything any more. Then sometimes, like last time, it's different. I don't know what happens. I just get a funny feeling, then I'm scared and I can't think straight and I want to run away. Sometimes it stops, but sometimes it gets worse and I'm terrified that I'm going to scream.'

'And do you? Scream, I mean.'

'Sometimes . . .' She pauses and seems to curl in on herself. Then she looks up again. 'I used to, but then . . .'

'Then?' Janet coaxes.

'I'd get hit or have to have treatment.'

Janet shudders. That's a whole different can of worms. Best not even go there right now. She observes the bowed head, the drawn-up shoulders, the fingers entwined with each other, the in-turned toes, and her heart floods with compassion. It would be so easy to stop, but she knows she has to press on.

'I think it's about things that happened that for a long time hurt you too much to remember,' Janet says carefully – it would be dreadful to stifle this little trickle of communication by trying to go too fast. 'Memories always have several parts – an emotional bit, a physical bit and a psychological bit. And when something awful happens, we feel shocked, and the memory of it gets split into those parts and some of them seem to get lost altogether. Then we don't really know what's happened because we can't remember it properly. But actually, all the pieces are there somewhere. And, to get well, we need to find them all and see if we can put them back together again, so we can finally deal with what *really* happened. That's what I'd like you and me to do together, so you can let go of some of the awful things that happened to you and then be able to get on with your life.'

Even as she says this, Janet feels like a fraud. *Have I managed to do that myself?* Her heart yearns to be able to talk through some of that with Ian. But . . . he said he'd only talk about parenting stuff . . . nothing intimate. She drags herself back to Nora, whose eyes are still full of questions.

Janet presses on. 'You've still got lots of life left, Nora. Wouldn't it be nice if you could start to enjoy it? Maybe find out what you'd like to do, where you'd like to be?'

Nora stares uncomprehendingly. 'But I'm here.'

'Maybe you could be somewhere else.'

'How?'

'Well, maybe in the future you could live somewhere else and do something else with your life,' Janet says softly. 'Is there anything you always wanted to do?'

'You mean . . . before?'

'Yes. When you were young.'

Nora gazes into Janet's eyes as if trying to read something there. Then she shifts her focus. 'No,' she whispers. But Janet has glimpsed something different and that old excitement arises in her chest. This woman wants to live. *Yes!*

She smiles. 'There. You used your new word – "No!" – and that's fine. If there's ever anything you'd like to ask me or tell me, I'm listening.'

Nora shakes her head. It's not yet the right time.

'If you're tired and want me to stop, then that's fine, but I'm going to try to go just a bit further if we can. OK?' Nora nods. 'Sometimes flashbacks may still recur for a long time, and they can leave you feeling exhausted and sometimes embarrassed about your behaviour. But hopefully you'll learn to be patient with yourself and tell the pain that it's only a memory; that it's not happening now; that you've survived. Together, we're going to learn what your symptoms are trying to tell us, until you can speak about things and not have your body act them out. Still OK?' Nora nods.

'Right,' Janet says. 'We're changing gear a bit. I looked at your notes. It seems you'd been very quiet for the few days running up to that session and hadn't been eating very much. Ellen said you'd looked sad. What happened?'

Nora hesitates then finally says, 'I didn't feel very well.'

'What kind of not very well?'

Nora looks away then looks directly back at Janet, and the effort of doing so appears painful to Janet.

'That day, I was out for a walk. I was feeling OK. Then I saw Flo. Her family. Her granddaughter was pushing Flo's wheelchair and her daughter was pushing a baby in a pram.' She blinks, lowers her eyes and shakes her head a little and when she speaks again, her voice is barely a whisper. 'I was angry that she has a baby.'

Janet notes the wringing of her hands and a little agitated tap of her foot. 'I imagine it must still hurt that you couldn't have *your* baby, Nora.'

But Nora's eyes won't meet hers any more, and Janet knows she is already starting to shut her out. 'Nora, please don't run away now. Stay with me. I know it hurts, but just allow yourself to go into the pain. You've already survived it. Just breathe now, and let's look at the pain.'

Janet's breath catches a little. She knows what this feels like, to be on the brink and hardly dare inch forward. *Come on, Nora.*

'I can't.' Nora shakes her head and covers her face.

Janet desperately wants to touch her; to make sure she knows that somebody cares for her. But Nora has to do this bit by herself. 'You can,' Janet says, her voice a hoarse whisper.

Suddenly, Nora's body heaves and a wail fills the room as she rocks back and forth. 'They took my baby before I even saw her. My beautiful little girl . . .'

Janet looks on, blinking back her own tears as she watches this woman's struggle, knowing she mustn't rob her of this moment. Nora must emerge from this by herself.

Now the words spurt out of Nora's mouth like water from a faucet. 'I took quinine tablets. It was me who killed her.' She holds herself tightly as the tsunami of grief bursts forth, flooding every cell, leaving Nora quivering.

Janet waits until the sobs have subsided somewhat then she speaks slowly and quietly. 'She died, Nora, but you didn't kill her. You were only eighteen and did all you could . . .'

'I'm sorry,' Nora murmurs, dabbing at her eyes. 'I should be able to forget it.'

Janet shakes her head. 'The death of a baby is a major bereavement, and especially if the baby is just whisked away and the mother never even gets to see or hold the child. It's perfectly normal that it comes up for you, and especially when you see other women with their new babies.'

Nora looks up, swollen-eyed. 'They told me to just forget her. I thought she'd been adopted, and I tried to think of her being happy and healthy out there somewhere, with new parents who loved her, but then I found she'd died the same day as she was born. But she was alive, Dr Humphreys, I know she was alive. So, if it wasn't the quinine, why did she die?'

Janet freezes. She knows what used to happen. What can she say?

As Nora recounts her memories of the birth, Janet listens, aghast. By the time Nora finishes, her voice is hoarse. 'Even though I never even held her, I called her Angela when I found out later that she was a girl.'

Janet turns away slightly to compose herself. No matter how often she witnesses a catharsis, it always gets her. But if it no longer affected her, it would mean she had lost her humanity and would be no use to anyone any more.

'Even though it's many years ago, your grief is still as fresh as though her death happened just yesterday.' Janet reaches out and gently places her hand over Nora's. 'I'm so sorry, Nora.'

Nora weeps silently, and when she eventually lifts her face she looks ravaged yet somehow at peace. 'I've never been able to talk about any of that. Nobody ever asked me how I felt about it. But I don't think I could have told them anyway.'

'I'm honoured that you were able to talk to me,' Janet says, squeezing Nora's hand.

Nora looks down, then a whisper creeps out of her mouth. 'They did something else.'

Janet tenses. What else could have happened to this poor woman? 'What else did they do, Nora?'

'They said I was having my appendix out, but that's not what they did. They did an operation so I could never get pregnant again, so I could never have had another baby, even if I'd wanted to.'

A flame of rage flares in Janet's heart. And she can hardly maintain her composure. But she breathes and tries to settle down since that would be of no use to Nora. 'I've heard that that happened and I tried not to believe it could be true. No one ever had a right to do that to you, Nora. I hardly know what to say except that I feel ashamed of anyone of my profession who could countenance such a thing.' She squeezes the hand she's still holding as Nora's eyes flood with gratitude and hold her own.

For what seems a long moment, Janet is speechless, then she sits up straight.

'Nora, I have an idea. I think that there might be something we could do. Nothing can bring Angela back, nor undo the dreadful things that you suffered, but . . . let's see . . .' Nora looks at Janet sceptically, but there's also a question in her eyes and Janet pushes on. 'Back then, you weren't able to have any kind of ceremony to mark either Angela's birth or her death.' Janet pauses, keeping her voice steady. 'But maybe you could have one now.'

'A funeral?'

'Well, not exactly. Maybe more like a memorial ceremony.' She gauges Nora's reaction before continuing. 'You could do something really beautiful – whatever you want to do, in fact.'

'How?'

'Well, I don't know right now. It needs to be something that *you* would like. For instance, you could have some candles and flowers and say some lovely words.'

'Prayers?'

Janet looks at the small, hopeful face and feels suddenly hopeful herself. 'If you like. Or just whatever you might want to say.'

'Would you do it with me?'

Janet smiles. 'Yes, if you'd like me to. Or, if you'd prefer, you could do it by yourself.'

'No. I don't think I could do it on my own.' Her voice takes on an anxious edge.

'Well, maybe you'd like to think about what you'd like to do and we can discuss it next time. How does that sound?'

But Janet can already see the cogs whirring behind Nora's eyes. 'Could we do it on Angela's next birthday – 30 April next year?'

Janet smiles. 'Yes. I think that would be a lovely idea. I'll make a note in my diary.'

Nora looks wistful but at peace as she stands to leave, but just as she opens the door she hesitates and turns back. 'Even though she wasn't baptised, do you think Angela could still go to heaven?'

'I'm sure she could.'

Chapter Nine

1983
Forty-four years

Nora wakes early in her narrow bed and, for a split second, wonders why today feels so different. Then she remembers: it's the last day of April, the forty-third anniversary of that wonderful but dreadful day when Angela was born. She pushes against the anxiety that immediately threatens to engulf her. Historically this anniversary has always sent her on a downward spiral. She tries desperately to maintain every inch of solid ground she's fought so hard for, while the usual dark squadrons of memories gather to torment her and the voice she's tried to quash refuses to be silent.

You're stupid. You're wicked. You don't deserve anything.

But then there's that blessed new voice. *Nora. Stand up. You can do this.* It sounds a bit like Janet.

She sits on the side of the bed and clasps her hands together, her lips resting on her fingers. She notices that they are trembling. 'Please, Lord, let it be OK,' she mutters.

She glances at the clock and her heart lurches. She could make it there and back before breakfast if she hurries.

She makes her way through the walled orchard garden, then squeezes through the narrow gap leading out to the woods, disturbing a frolicking squirrel and a wriggling earthworm trying to hide its nakedness. The scent of bluebells and periwinkles assails her, and she pauses to draw in a deep, calming breath.

She kneels at this place she knows so well and presses her hands to the earth as though to touch Angela's body sleeping below. 'Hello, my love,' she whispers. 'I have lots to tell you. We're going to have a birthday celebration for you today and I'm bringing some nice people to see you. So, I'm just going to tidy things up a bit.' She takes deep breaths in and out, in and out, steeling herself to say what she knows needs to be said. 'Angela, I think at some time, I might be going away . . . I don't know yet, but maybe. But I want you to know that even if I do, I'll never leave you really, and I'll always love you and always be your mother.'

Then, tenderly, as if not to wake her, Nora clears the leaves and twigs that have accumulated since the last time she was here, and traces a little heart-shaped area with pebbles she brought in her pocket – she hopes no one saw her take them from the gravel path.

Now everything is prepared. She smiles at her handiwork, kisses her soiled fingers and presses them to the earth, then hurries back to the ward to change – today deserves her best clothes.

An hour later, Nora waits close to the entrance to the ward in her navy skirt, green blouse and cardigan, her raincoat draped over her clasped hands. Audrey is coming at ten to take her to the flower shop and, for the umpteenth time, she counts the money in her purse, hoping she has enough for the flowers she wants.

Ellen comes and sits with her. 'Big day, Nora. Are you excited?'

She nods. 'But a bit scared as well.' She pauses. 'What time is it?'

'Just twenty-five to. I'm sure Audrey won't be late.'

Nora smiles. 'Yes. I'm sure. And if she is, I'll just be patient.'

Ellen touches her arm. 'Nora, you're always patient. I don't know how you do it.'

'I've had years of practice,' she says.

As Nora finally approaches the florist, she is hit by a wall of fragrance that steals out of the door to lure passers-by with the promise of scented and visual delights. A riot of colour awaits them as agapanthus jostles with lily of the valley; carnation competes with campanula and gerbera rivals gladiolus. Roses preen, certain that they are supreme. But Nora wants none of this. She stands still, grateful that Audrey is hanging back, giving her the time and space she needs.

Finally, a smile breaks over Nora's face as she spies the smaller flowers in a little galvanised bucket on the floor. Anemones – purple and pink and blue. Just right. She smells them, opens her purse and hands the exact money to the assistant.

'Shall I wrap them for you?'

'Yes, please. Do you have any pink paper?'

'I think I can find some.' The motherly woman smiles. 'Let me see. Yes. How about this one?'

'Perfect, thank you.' Nora watches as the flowers are swaddled in the pretty tissue paper.

'Are they for someone special?'

'Yes. Very. They're for my daughter.'

Audrey blinks and turns away.

'I'm sure she'll like them,' the woman says.

Nora, composed, smiles. 'I'm sure she will.'

Nora carries her bunch of anemones, Audrey holds fragrant pink carnations, and Janet has yellow freesias, as well as tea lights and matches. Joe, in his best jacket and a white shirt, wheels himself alongside Nora until the wood becomes too wild, and then she takes over pushing his chair. She tries to avoid the tiny star-shaped scarlet pimpernel that hovers close to the ground, then manoeuvres the chair around the buttercups that nod to each other in the gentle breeze stirring the flowering grasses. Eventually, the group is in the woods, and spread out before them are masses of bluebells. Despite everything, Nora can't think of a more beautiful resting place for her baby.

The little party slows as it approaches the weathered marker on the spot where her baby was buried forty-three years ago.

Nora and Janet create a circle of candles on the cleared area around the grave, and Nora kneels to light the first one.

Her voice is strong and steady. 'I light this candle for you, Angela –' Nora's voice catches – 'my daughter. Happy birthday. Know that I've always loved you and always will.' She gently places her flowers, then wipes her eyes and takes her place back in the little circle of people who care for her.

Janet goes next. 'I light this candle for Angela and Nora, that they will both have peace and know that they are loved. Happy birthday, Angela.'

Audrey places Joe's candle for him as he takes a paper from his pocket and reads in a quavering voice. 'There's a time to be born and a time to die. Sadly, Angela lived just a little time in between. I wish I could have known you, Angela, because I know your lovely mother. She's a good woman and my friend. I hope you can both rest now, and that the pain will finally go away.'

Nora puts a gentle hand on Joe's shoulder, and he covers it with his own.

Audrey lights her candle and her eyes take on a new softness in its light. 'I dedicate this candle to all the mothers and children who, like Nora and Angela, have been separated by death. May they find solace and peace and healing for their broken hearts.'

The gentle breeze toys with the tiny flames and Nora weeps silently. Janet puts an arm around her shoulders. 'Can you read your poem?' she whispers.

There's a pained pause but then, in a soft but clear voice, Nora begins.

I never got to hold you, but right from the very start
I've held you always, but only in my heart
I'm sad I never heard you laugh, or heard you chatter and play
But I've seen in my own mind's eye and know it would be that way.
I never had chance to see your eyes, but I know they'd be deep blue
I never was able to touch your face, but . . .

Her voice falters and she scrunches up the poem and kneels down. 'I love you, Angela. I'm sorry I could never say that to you in person, but now I know you'll know.' And she crumples, her forehead almost touching the ground. 'Happy birthday,' she whispers.

Janet takes a small oval stone from her pocket, upon which she has written: *Nora and Angela, parted for a while, together for ever.* She touches Nora's shoulder and – from her flat palm – offers her the stone.

Nora looks at it and then directs her gaze into Janet's eyes. Though she says nothing, Janet understands the depth of her gratitude. Nora takes the stone, rubs it gently, then without a word, digs a little hole with her fingers and buries it close to the marker.

Joe blinks and gives a gruff cough, then reaches for Nora's hand, which he squeezes gently. 'Nora, I brought you something else.' As though performing a magic trick, Joe produces a cassette player. He presses a button and the soaring notes of 'Ode to Joy' fill the clearing. Her eyes hold his and a gentle smile lights up her face as silent tears stream down her cheeks.

Chapter Ten

Something's amiss. Nora, who has, over the last few months, learned the value of the social smile, walks into Janet's room with a stiff face, trailing a cloud of anger. She takes her chair without a word of greeting and folds her arms. If it weren't for the wrinkles and the greying hair, she could be a petulant child. 'You told me I could trust you,' she blurts out, her eyes stone cold.

Janet looks back, astonished, but also glad that Nora has come far enough to confront her about something. 'Did I?'

'Yes. Well , you made me think I could. And now you might leave me.'

Janet's heart falters, but she tries her hardest not to let it show. 'Who told you that?'

'It doesn't matter. Are you leaving?'

'Not at present, but even if I were, that wouldn't mean you couldn't trust me.'

Nora stares mutinously at Janet, and Janet feels a flicker of impatience.

'Nora, you're part of my life, but only part of it. Everyone should have the right to live their own life without judgement from anyone else. I know it hasn't been like that for you, and I'm sorry that's so, but we have to learn to give other people freedom to be who they are, and the opportunity to do what they want to do.' Nora still looks like thunder and Janet watches this new face she hasn't seen before. She tries again. 'The fact that we have different things to do and different places to be doesn't mean that we don't care for each other.'

The tension in Nora's tightly clasped arms eases a fraction and she tilts her head slightly and peeps upwards, like a curious little bird. 'Do we care for each other?'

'Yes, I think we do, though I'm not your mother, I'm not your sister and I'm not really your friend. I'm your doctor. But as long as I'm able, I'll support you in whatever feels right for you to do. But I will also live my own life, and I don't expect to have to explain that to you again.'

Nora pouts. 'You sound angry.'

'No, I'm not angry, I just want to be very clear.'

'When you say you'll support me in whatever it seems right for me to do, does that mean that you can choose what I can do and what I can't?'

Good for you, Nora.

'No, not at all. But if I thought that you were going to do something to hurt yourself – like, you were going to take an overdose, for instance – I wouldn't support that. But in most other things, yes, of course, I'll support you.'

'But why can't I choose what I want to do?'

'You can. But there are consequences to every choice we make. And the other thing is that, though I will accept what you choose, I don't have to like your choice and, as I said, if I thought it was dangerous or misguided then I'd probably try to dissuade you.' She takes a breath and studies Nora intently. She can see she has confused her, and compassion flows through her. This must be a lot to have to deal with when you've hardly been allowed any power over your own life since you were an adolescent. Janet tries to soften her tone. 'I know that for much of your life you haven't been able to, but that doesn't mean it will always be like that. I think you do have choices now about some things and, bit by bit, you need to start making them.'

Nora scowls. 'I don't think I want choices. You should just tell me what to do.'

'No. I can't and won't tell you what to do,' Janet says,

impatience creeping into her voice again. 'You have all the answers inside yourself, somewhere.'

'No, I don't,' she snaps. 'I need you to tell me.'

'Nora. Listen to yourself. I think you've hated always being told what to do, and it's left you sometimes unable to think for yourself. But you *can* make decisions. And, as far as I can, I'll try to guide you if you ask me, but I want you to grow and live your own life.'

'I don't have a life,' Nora screams suddenly. 'What do I have to live for?' And just as quickly as it flared, her anger turns to tears and she slumps in her chair, her face in her hands.

Janet sits silently for a moment, giving Nora time to settle. 'Nora, I'm hoping you can build a life now and find something to live for,' she says gently.

'Like what?'

'I don't know. But I hope you'll make friends and find something to do that pleases you, and that you'll learn to enjoy yourself. There was a time, albeit a very long time ago, when you knew how to enjoy things.' But even as Janet says this, she knows it's not that easy. She herself is trying to restructure her own life and fill a hole she never expected to find in it. Her heart aches. But that doesn't belong here this morning, and she forces her mind back to the task at hand.

'Nora – let's look at what it means to make choices. You're making them all the time. You made a choice to come this morning.'

'Well, it's my appointment. I have to come.'

'Yes, kind of . . . but you still could have chosen not to come.' Nora looks baffled. 'But that might have made you angry.'

'Yes, it might. And we wouldn't have been able to have this conversation. Those would have been the consequences of making a different choice.'

'But that's not fair.'

Janet smiles and makes a helpless gesture with her hands. 'Yep – I agree it doesn't always seem fair. But it's still your choice.'

Nora throws up her hands in angry despair. 'That's stupid.'

Janet laughs. 'Most of us are making choices all the time and nobody else has to like them. But with the freedom to choose comes responsibility. You can't have one without the other.'

'So . . .' says Nora, in a tone bordering on patronising, 'you see, it's safer if you just choose for me.'

Janet laughs again. 'Maybe so, but I'm not going to do that. Deep inside yourself you have a voice. Listen to that voice. Listen and do what you know you need to do. And then we can talk about how, if you'd like that.'

Nora tosses her head like a horse trying to swat off a fly, and Janet tries not to smile. She really likes this newly revealed bit of Nora that will get into a skirmish and not let go. Bravo.

'So, really – you're not leaving?' she asks finally.

'I told you – not at present, and if ever I am, I'll give you plenty of warning. OK?'

Silence, then a tiny, 'OK.'

Janet arrives home ready for a quiet evening, and maybe some TV. However, no sooner has she settled down with a tray on her lap than the phone rings. She heaves a sigh and picks it up.

'OK,' she says, looking mournfully at the pesto pasta that she knows is destined for the bin. She should have known better on her on-call night. 'Give me an hour . . .'

The drive back to the hospital is fraught with slanting sleet and treacherous roads, all courtesy of an icy wind from the east, and in the end it takes her almost two hours to do a journey she can usually do in forty minutes.

Ben, the night porter, tips his cap. 'Dr Janet.'

'Ben.' She nods as always, and she moves on with a smile at what has become a bit of a game between them. Sometimes she wonders what he'd do if she stopped for a natter.

Her boots clatter on the marble floor, creating a cadence of echoes in the corridor. Besmirched by a century of suffering, the pain of hundreds of patients still clings to the walls. This place requires a strong constitution at night; in spite of herself, Janet shivers.

Ash ward is illuminated by a flash of lightning as she enters, revealing row after row of ageing women waiting to make their final escape from their tortured lives. Janet sighs and fights the sinking feeling in her chest. She refuses to let Nora end up here.

She examines Sarah Golson quickly. Crackles in both lungs – not much longer for her to suffer. The odour of death already surrounds her. Janet picks up the cold, skinny hand and holds it gently, then lays her other hand on the high forehead with its waxy skin, pale violet veins weaving across it.

'Sarah,' Janet whispers. 'Sarah.' There's the slightest of movement of her eyelids. 'Just rest, Sarah. Well done.' She hopes that this old lady, almost at her journey's end, will hear the caress in her voice and know that she's not alone.

Kumar appears at her elbow. 'Thanks, Janet.'

Janet smiles and turns to Kumar, whose brown face is gleaming. He simply nods.

'It's quiet,' he says. 'I'll stay with her as long as I can.' The soft light throws shadows onto the far wall as Janet gently squeezes the hand she holds and then grips Kumar's shoulder gently. She knows Sarah is in good hands; Kumar has been here for decades.

'Let me know,' she says.

As she prepares to walk away, Janet glances at the old lady's locker. Here, in this little steel cabinet, is all of Sarah's life. Atop it is an old sepia photograph. A perfectly poised woman sits holding a pudgy baby on her lap, a hand under each chubby armpit. At her side stands an unsmiling light-haired girl of about three, with an arm stretched up to rest her hand on her mother's shoulder where the photographer no doubt had placed it. The woman looks serious, handsome rather than pretty, her dark hair drawn severely back and upwards. No smile, staring straight into the eye of the camera, doing what she's told. Janet studies it. There's no intimacy, no emotion. Just three separate pieces of a family arranged together for posterity.

Janet glances back at the shrunken and wrinkled face as, with toothless mouth gaping, Sarah struggles with her last breaths. Is the woman her? Or the serious child? She wonders if anyone here knows.

*   *   *

By the time she reaches the car, the first tinges of the dove-grey of dawn are appearing, revealing the black silhouettes of the distant hills. Clouds like shards of granite point eastward, harsh and accusing. Her tyres crunch the hills of frozen slush as she pulls the Clio into the parking space outside her home. The house, rising above her, tall and beautiful, begins to reveal itself to the morning. There's just enough light to pick out the vigorously pruned roses; they look sad now, but in the summer will once again be riotous clad in scarlet, with their perfume drifting down the road to meet that of their sisters in neighbouring gardens. It was never her plan to live here alone and, as she gazes at her once-happy home, her loneliness pierces her like a knife. She still misses Ian so much it physically hurts.

She turns off the engine and pulls her coat more tightly around her. She tucks in her scarf, stretches her neck and rolls her tired shoulders, then leans forward onto the steering wheel. The feelings she has been suppressing so successfully finally well up and she crumbles as tears fall. Tears for her child self, tears for Sarah, tears for Nora, tears for her own aloneness, which is no longer chosen solitude, tears for Ian and for Martin, who is so upset and confused about what's happened to his parents. And for her own mother and father, so long estranged from her . . . Just tears, and more tears.

Finally, she gathers herself together and opens the car door. As she steps out, her foot slips on a patch of ice. Her right knee twists, and she puts out her hand to try to save herself, but she hits the frozen ground hard and lies for a moment, gasping. She moves her knee experimentally and winces with the pain. Suddenly she feels very tired.

Lying on the road with her left foot still in the car, she tries to work out how she's going to get up. It'll be hard to gain traction on the ice. She checks herself over again, more cautiously this time. Sore right wrist – sprained probably; best not to try to put too much weight on that. She pulls on the door frame with her left hand and tries to lower herself completely onto the road. As she does so, her handbag falls and its contents scatter about her.

Her left foot comes neatly out of the car and promptly kicks her lipstick which, as though in slow motion, rolls the last couple of inches towards the drain and descends between the bars with an elegant finality. She hammers her good fist on the road.

'Fuck!' she screams as she lies on the ground, wondering how on earth she'll make the few metres to her front door.

Chapter Eleven

Janet's knee is hot and swollen and she winces as she shifts a little. Her mouth is parched and she longs to brush her teeth, but remembers the fiasco of getting to the bathroom earlier and tries to settle down. But half an hour later, she has to accept that she's going to need help. She glances at her watch – seven thirty. Is this an OK time to call a working woman with a family? It's going to have to be.

'What's up?' Audrey's gentle voice is already laced with concern, this being the first time that Janet has ever called her out of hours.

When Janet has finished telling Audrey about what happened, there's a short pause at the end of the phone before Audrey says, 'Sounds like you won't be in tomorrow either.'

'No. Probably not.'

'Do you need somebody to have a look at it?'

'I suppose I do.'

'OK. No problem. Just give me time to make a couple of phone calls and I'll come around and pick you up.'

Janet sighs with relief and gratitude. 'I always said you were an angel.'

'Oh, don't say that, or it'll be hard to keep my feet on the ground.' She laughs. 'I bet you haven't even been able to have a cup of tea, have you?'

Janet manages a smile. 'No, I haven't. And I've got withdrawals.'

Audrey chuckles. 'OK. That'll be my first job when I get there. Just stay where you are. I'll be as quick as I can.' Janet smiles, replacing her phone in its cradle. She's always amazed at how gracious people are when you need help. Tears of relief aren't far away now she knows the cavalry is coming.

As soon as Audrey arrives and sees Janet's knee, she insists they go to casualty. Though Janet protests, she knows it's the right thing to do, and gives in after only a short while. Audrey helps Janet out to the car and Janet tries not to show how every bump in the road causes pain to shoot through her leg.

They hobble in, and Janet looks with dismay at the scene. Is there ever a time when casualty is empty? Audrey deals with the business of registration, then parks Janet in a wheelchair. Heaven knows how long some of these people have been waiting. But moments later a nurse calls Janet's name, emphasising the 'doctor', presumably to mollify everyone else as Janet jumps the queue. She squirms as she raises her hand.

'So, doctor, what have we here?' The junior doctor wears his crisp white coat with panache and his eyes are soft and kind, with irises the same brown as his skin, but they look glassy with tiredness. Janet wonders how long he has been on duty and remembers her own days on a punishing on-call rota. She doesn't miss them.

Within an hour, the diagnosis of a torn medial meniscus is confirmed, a date for meniscectomy made, and Janet and Audrey are good to go, with strict instructions regarding bed rest. 'At least three weeks, I'm afraid, Janet. And no cheating.' The consultant smiles. 'We all know that we doctors are the worst patients.'

Once Janet is safely in the car, Audrey turns to her. 'You'd be very welcome to come to us,' she says. 'But if you prefer to be at home, then I'll come around every morning when I've got the children sorted and between us we'll manage.' She smiles. 'Can I trust you to be good?'

'I don't think my knee will let me be otherwise. And I don't want to put you to any trouble, but yes, I'd prefer to stay at home, if possible.'

'It's no trouble.'

The next few weeks are the slowest of Janet's life. She isn't used to inactivity and now that she's alone at home, feeling vulnerable and lost, she finds his absence especially difficult to bear. Several times a day during the first week her heart strays to Ian and her hand to the phone, her pulse racing at the thought of hearing his voice. She wakes in the night, her knee throbbing and her arm searching the Ian-shaped space beside her, longing for his warmth, his touch, his familiar smell. She hugs her hot-water bottle for comfort and somehow drifts back into a shallow, troubled sleep, proud that she has managed not to call him but aching for him nonetheless. It's all the more tempting because she knows that if she did call, he'd come. But she doesn't want her neediness to be the reason he finally comes home. Still lurking somewhere in her mind is that old belief that he only married her in the first place because she needed him.

The days pass in a sluggish blur of restless routine and, at the end of it all, she wonders how on earth she managed to get through it without going mad. The night before her return to work, she feels jittery with excitement and energy.

The next morning, Janet pulls her car into her parking space by Rowan. She spies Nora looking out of the window and smiles, but Nora's face remains immobile, her eyes flat with a hint of accusation. Then she's gone.

Janet sighs and gathers her things, opens the car door and stands her crutches out on the road propped up against the car, then pulls herself upright. Only then does she notice that Nora is now leaning against the front offside wing, her eyes looking straight ahead and away from Janet.

Ah, that's the game.

'Hello, Nora,' she calls, but she's met with a stony silence. Janet steadies herself. Nora hasn't moved, though Janet can feel she's longing for contact. 'Good morning, Nora,' she says again, her tone light and questioning. 'Are you going to speak to me?'

Nora studiously ignores her, but as Janet starts to move, Nora finally sees the crutches and looks horrified, but Janet also detects a flash of relief in her eyes. 'Oh, you're hurt!' Nora's eyes fix for a moment on Janet's leg. 'I thought you'd gone away.' Janet feels amused that her being hurt is obviously the more acceptable option.

'I fell and had to have a little operation on my knee.'

'Nobody told me.'

'Didn't they? Are you sure?' Janet knows full well that Ellen has tried to explain to Nora.

'No. They said you were off sick.'

'Well, I was.'

'But it was a long time . . .'

'Just three weeks.' Janet smiles. 'Nora, I told you, if – when – I have to go, I'll give you plenty of warning.' She hobbles into the building. 'I'll see you later.'

Ellen is dealing with a patient in reception, and Janet hovers until she is finished. 'Oh, that still looks painful,' says Ellen.

'Too much dancing in my teens,' Janet quips.

Ellen pulls up another chair so that Janet can put up her leg. 'How was Nora?'

'Well enough to punish me.' Janet smiles.

'Thought she might. She's hardly been eating and hasn't slept well.'

'Those old abandonment issues take a long time to heal, don't they?'

'If ever.' Ellen looks thoughtful. 'It's a tightrope you walk, I guess, when you work as you do – when you let them get close to you . . .' She trails off, her face serious.

Janet doesn't miss the hint of disapproval. 'I just can't do it any other way,' she says. 'Well, that's not altogether true. I do manage it differently with people who simply can't take emotional warmth. But others . . . I want them to have the chance of knowing they're special and cared for. Sometimes it's the first time they've ever felt that.'

'And when you leave, do you not just give them another bereavement?' Ellen's eyes are kind but the words sting.

'I hope not. Oh Ellen, I hope not. I believe that nothing's ever lost. Even though they may be sad at parting, they'll remember that they were valued.'

'Maybe.'

'You don't sound too sure.'

'I see what's happened with Nora, Janet, and I've seen what's happening with others you work with too. It's amazing to see how quickly they can change, but I just wonder what happens afterwards.'

'Afterwards?'

'When you move, as of course you will. What then? You can't follow up with everyone.'

Janet sighs and worries at some loose skin on her lip. 'No, I can't. But do you think it would be better for them never to have had anyone really caring for them?'

'We all care for them, Janet. Well – not everybody. But many of us do. Maybe we just don't show it like you do.' She looks at Janet's crestfallen face. 'Janet, don't get me wrong. What you do is great and you obviously get results, but make sure you don't just leave a trail of broken hearts behind you.'

'That's not fair,' she protests.

'Isn't it?'

There's an uneasy pause. 'I'll be careful,' Janet says.

The older woman smiles. 'I know you will – just checking.'

Catching up on acute, Janet flicks the patients' cards on the Rolodex.

'Oh . . . Miles Little is in?' she says, and looks up at Dale. 'His cycle's getting quicker. It's only been about a month since his last admission.'

'Not even a month,' says Dale. 'He was dishevelled and suicidal when he came in. He's a bit more stable now, but only just.'

'Poor man,' she says. 'Was he taking his meds?'

'His parents seemed to think so, though they said they couldn't be sure.'

What a tragedy – this courageous man with a brilliant mind, whose life has been stolen by this awful illness. His once promising banking career lost after two hypomanic episodes, during one of which he assaulted his boss. Early retirement with a generous pension was the best thing on offer. But now, in his forties, he has little or no prospects. His marriage ended a few years ago and he's back living with his elderly parents, who love him, but are constantly worried about what the next day will bring.

Janet heads for the ward and has a long chat with Miles. There's not much left in her armamentarium but depot medication and ECT, both of which he refuses to consider. And once again, his mental state has switched very quickly and he does seem stable again for the time being. When he begs for discharge, Janet can't make a good case for refusing to let him go home, apart from the fact that his parents need a rest. They discuss the necessity for him to take his medication but she knows he'll have difficulty adhering to his promise if he gets high again. So she remains uneasy. With Miles it's never simple and she prays she's made the right decision.

Back in her office, she picks up her Dictaphone to record a discharge summary for Miles when there's a sudden crash of thunder and the sky opens, releasing its long-held burden. *Par for the course. I knew I should have brought my umbrella.* There's a soft knock on her door.

'Come in,' she says absently. Then, when there's no response, she calls irritably, 'Come in,' and hobbles to the door. 'Come in,' she says again, as she opens it herself, her attention still elsewhere.

There stands Nora, her new handbag hooked over her arm and her gloves clasped in her hand, wearing her new Oxfam coat. Her eyes are lowered. 'I was going to go for a walk but it's raining.'

For once, Janet is speechless. *What's this about?* 'Come in, Nora,' she says, standing back to allow her to pass. She hopes that her irritation of seconds ago did not come across. The last thing Nora needs is to think that she has to rescue Janet, or to feel somehow responsible for her. Nora doesn't need to know how hard Janet, herself, has found it to stand up, or how often she still has to steel herself to do so.

Thankfully, Nora sits down, but says nothing. Her brows are knitted together as though she's trying to get her thoughts in order before she speaks. Janet waits and wonders about Ellen's words.

'I want to say I'm sorry,' Nora says finally.

'For what?'

'For not trusting you.'

'Oh.' Janet smiles.

'I didn't want to take up your time. I just wanted to tell you that I *do* trust you.'

Janet smiles. 'Thank you. I thought you'd come to tell me you're leaving . . .' she teases.

Nora looks shocked. 'Me? Why?'

'You have your handbag.'

Nora rewards her with a rare smile. 'No, I wasn't, but I promise you I'll tell you when I'm going to.'

It takes Janet a moment to realise that Nora is parroting her own words back at her, and she smiles widely. 'You made a little joke, Nora!'

Nora pauses and then looks at Janet, a smile spreading across her face. 'I did, didn't I?'

Chapter Twelve

Nora shuffles around the ward, her eyes searching. She needs to find a newspaper. She's desperate to find out whether what she overheard the nurses talking about this morning is true. She finally sees one discarded in the day room, and she grabs it and dashes into the toilet – her only private space. She searches page by page, and there he is. She can hardly breathe.

Robert Harcourt's impassioned plea for rights of mental hospital patients

While addressing his South London constituency yesterday, Robert Harcourt returned again to the topic that won him considerable popularity in last year's general election. Though his views are controversial, the topic of the closure of mental institutions has nevertheless gained much attention of late.

He reported that, in 1920, there were 2,783 unmarried mothers in workhouses in England alone. In 1913, the Mental Deficiency Act had deemed them morally defective and, within that law, they could be certified and committed to mental institutions.

'It is to our shame that many of them have remained there, without rights, for forty or fifty years or more and have suffered prejudice and a form of imprisonment, by no means commensurate with deeds that would nowadays be accepted perhaps as being unfortunate, but as the new norm,' he said. 'We have talked of community care for the last twenty years, and yet the number of patients in our large institutions has continued to increase. Adequately funded care in the community must become a reality so that those who remain vulnerable and unable to tolerate the stresses of modern life can be properly catered for.' He went on to say that our mental institutions are a

public disgrace and an atrocity against humanity that must no longer be tolerated. He blamed underfunding and mismanagement and said that both for the health – mental and otherwise – not only of the patients, but also the staff who man these hospitals without adequate resources, action must be taken now.

He underlined that the closure of old-style mental institutions is essential, but must go hand in hand with a commitment to adequate community and domiciliary care and that this 'heinous situation' bequeathed upon this generation by the last should not be allowed to visit future generations also.

Nora gazes at the photograph of Robert, then slowly closes the newspaper and holds it to her chest. She shuts her eyes and tries to see the older man in this photograph as she knew him, in the vibrancy of his youth. Her eyes fill with tears, though this time tears of joy.

Janet parks her bicycle outside Rowan. She hauls her bag out of the basket when she hears Ellen tapping on the window, gesturing enthusiastically for Janet to hurry, and also be very quiet. Though she's cold and her knee feels stiff and sore after just a short ride, Janet does her best to comply.

'What's going on?' she stage-whispers as she pokes her head round the office door.

Ellen points to the observation window. 'Come and see.'

Unusually for this time of the morning, the ward is deserted, except for one figure. Nora is standing by the piano, staring down at it. A discarded newspaper lies on the top of the piano.

'She's walked to it, then away, then back several times,' Ellen says excitedly. 'Do you think she's going to play?'

'Dunno,' Janet says, shrugging her shoulders and leaning closer to the window as though that will help her see more. 'How long has she been there?'

'Well, I've been watching for maybe five minutes, but I don't know when it started.' And together they watch, excited little girls whispering while waiting for a performance to start.

Nora gingerly caresses the piano lid. Janet watches, almost holding her breath in case she disturbs what looks like a miracle unfolding. She reaches for Ellen's hand and squeezes it.

Slowly, Nora lifts the lid and runs her hand gently across the keys and then pauses, perfectly still. She seems to be looking at her hand.

'Something's happening,' Janet whispers.

Nora looks down at her ageing right hand. She slowly lifts her head and, standing erect, closes her eyes.

Now she sees her hand, soft-skinned, plump and pale, with a fine gold ring bearing the Sacred Heart of Jesus on its little finger. Her peach taffeta dress is draped over the piano stool, its puffed sleeves revealing smooth, sculpted arms. The bodice drapes perfectly, then narrows to a trim waist. Her hands fly skilfully over the ivory, raising elegantly from her wrist, then lifting forward to the ebony, coaxing the melody to unfurl. Bold forte, shy pianissimo, perfectly executed grace notes, her body gently moving with such passion and tenderness, stirred as she is by emotion as the music flows through her. And now she opens her throat to sing, her voice lifting, high and clear, effortless, her heart hardly able to contain the beauty of the moment. Robert, young and golden-haired, stands to her right, ready to turn the page. She can feel the warm beam of his smile at her shoulder.

She can almost hear the breath of her family and assembled friends as she bathes in her parents' pride. All she loves is assembled here, and she thanks God. The last chord is played and there are sighs of admiration, gasps of joy, eruptions of congratulation and delight, and she allows herself to look at Robert and receive that smile that starts at his eyes and ends at his lips.

'Wonderful,' he mouths, and now it's complete. She has all that she needs and more.

And later ... it was so simple, so beautiful. Together ... A gentle awakening ... A perfect unfolding ...

Nora blinks. Her hand moves in its crepe, age-spotted skin, under which knotted veins snake blood back to her heart – her tired, aching heart. Her head droops and she folds into herself, weary. Her hand falls away from the keys.

Janet looks at Ellen, concern etched upon her face. 'What do you think happened?'

'I don't know,' Ellen whispers. While these two women – so invested in Nora's recovery – wait, Nora closes the piano and pulls her cardigan across her chest. She seems to have aged ten years in front of their eyes. She adjusts her body, picks up the newspaper and slowly walks away. Her eyes are moist, and Janet's too.

Janet exhales. 'I feel so sad,' she says.

'Me too,' says Ellen.

'Something happened then.'

'Yes.'

Nora sits on her bed. None of the other women is here, so she is enjoying a rare moment of peace. She spreads out the newspaper and reads the article again, then carefully tears out the photograph. She stares at it for a long moment and then folds it and places it in her Bible.

She sits staring ahead, then looks at her picture of the peaceful cows chewing their cud and closes her eyes.

As they settle in Janet's office, she notices that Nora looks subdued. 'What would you like to talk about today?' she asks, hoping that she might open up her feelings about the piano, but it takes a while for Nora to respond.

'When you ask me to talk, I feel afraid that if I do – if I really do – you'll have the power to keep me here for ever.' She pauses, watching for Janet's reaction, though there appears to be none. 'It's not that I don't trust you,' she goes on quickly, 'it's just that that's the way it's always been – you can't trust anyone. But there's something else as well. I don't want whatever it is that people thought I could do to hurt you or anyone else. They said I could infect people.'

'Nora you aren't going to infect me or anybody else,' Janet says.' That theory was a kind of fashion at the time – that's what people believed. But we know more now. And in any case, you're not sick any more and—'

Nora's head snaps up and there's anger in her eyes.

'—I never was sick,' she flashes. 'I was pregnant, beaten and taken from my home and nobody wanted me. I was shocked and heartbroken. And when I was told that I'd never go home again and never leave here, I just didn't know what to do. It was awful. Then my baby . . .' Her voice breaks, but the anger remains. 'How could all of that happen? I was sure my mother or my cousin would come and save me, but they didn't.' And now she's crying with frustration. 'My cousin came on Christmas morning but he went away without seeing me, and I was banging on the window hoping he'd hear me but he didn't. I was screaming trying to reach him. Then I got a good hiding because I was angry. That's not fair.' She crumples forward, her face in her hands.

'No, it isn't, Nora.'

'People would hit me or tie me down and do awful things to me. How dare they?' She bangs her hand on the arm of the chair. 'Wouldn't you be furious?'

'I would,' Janet says quietly.

'But after a while, I stopped. In the end I learned to play the game like everyone else – be quiet, keep your eyes down, don't argue. But then everyone assumes you're sick. Or useless, or without a mind of your own, when really you're just trying to survive and stay sane.' She looks up. 'Isn't that funny? You have to play at being stupid in order to stay sane?' There's a shrill edge to her voice. 'Then I got to the point that I hoped I would just die. But because I was young and healthy, the only way that was going to happen was if I did it myself. But that then got me into more trouble. If you do that, they come with ECT. There's no way out . . . No way out.' Her voice falls to a whisper, but then she lets out a bitter, sad little laugh.

'Once, we did a play for Christmas. It was the best time we'd had for years. The staff were amazed that we could learn lines.

They kept looking at each other and asking how on earth we'd been able to do it. No one ever seemed to have considered that we might have brains and could think and learn. They thought we were only fit to work, or wait for the next meal or the next cigarette or to be told what to do, or for it just to be time to go to bed. We had no hope, no responsibility – just waiting, bored, lost, for years and years.'

Her eyes fill up with tears, but she dashes them away with an angry hand. 'Every now and then it became so frustrating that one of us blew a gasket and then they thought we were even more sick, and so we had to have drugs or "treatment". No wonder I still get in a panic even at the mention of the treatment room. I know what that used to mean. We'd be told it was going to be a "talk" so that we didn't kick up much fuss. But when we got there they could do anything. Maisie was taken to the treatment room for a "talk" one day and they held her hand up against the iron because they said she'd stolen some soap.'

Janet listens, transfixed.

'We could never decide anything – not even what to wear or what to eat – so we became like dogs that just sit when someone says "sit", and walk when they're told to walk, and the rest of the time just lie about. Maybe once in a while they get up and have a mad half-hour. But when we have a "mad half-hour", it's thought to be just that – that we're mad.'

Her nails dig into the arms of her chair. 'I – was – never – mad,' she shouts, emphasising every word with a bang of her hands on the chair. 'There were times when I was sleepy and hardly able to talk because of the medication. I was dragging my feet around the place or sitting there drooling, listening to people discussing how sick I was. I was frightened that no one would see me or hear me inside the lump I'd become.' She pauses for breath. 'No one except Dr Stilworth seemed to see me. He did, though. I know he did. He was so kind. It was awful when he retired . . .'

She frowns, eyes dry now, and looks Janet straight in the eye. 'I used to be scared that people might think I was dead, when I was just slowed right down. It was so frightening. It made me think of the people with the plague who woke up in their graves and tried to scratch their way out. Did you know that they were eventually buried holding bells, just in case?' She smiles sadly. 'I often wished I'd had a bell – but I'd probably have been given ECT for ringing it!'

She stops for a moment but, though she hesitates and looks anxious, as though worried she may have said too much, she's not spent yet. Janet sits perfectly still, praying she'll continue.

'The worst thing was to look around and see that we were all the same. We all looked sick and stupid. Maybe none of us was at the beginning. But in the end, it was safer to let them think we were.'

Janet feels a sick swoop of shame that she, too, had assumed that Nora was incapable of such clarity. But here she is, intact, articulate, spirited, despite years of being denied any kind of intellectual stimulation. 'Nora, if anyone tried to tie me down, I know I'd fight. And if anyone locked me away and took away everything that made me who I am, I'd scream. And I'm so happy to hear you finally complain about such abuse. I'm so sorry all this happened to you, Nora, and so glad that you're angry about it.'

'It isn't your fault,' Nora says quickly. 'You won't give me ECT for being angry, will you?'

'No, Nora.' Janet reaches out and touches the back of Nora's hand. 'I'm still sad about all that happened to you, but it's wonderful that you've survived in one piece.'

Silent tears stream down Nora's face. 'But I didn't. I daren't even make a choice when you ask me to.'

'But you will, Nora. You will.' She pauses for a moment until Nora's shoulders fall a little and she stops crying. Nora lifts her eyes, still looking drawn and sad. Janet tilts her head a little and smiles. 'You're amazing, Nora. Something kept you alive, kept you going all that time. What was it? Do you have a secret formula for survival that you can share with me?'

Though Nora initially looks puzzled, she finally starts to smile, too, with an unusual twinkle in her eye. 'Once, when I was starting to get better after feeling so low, I remembered a teacher at school,' she smiles. 'I must have been about fourteen. She was teaching us about posture and deportment, and how if you stood up tall, you'd feel better. She had us walk around the classroom waving our arms and hands at each other, and smile even if we didn't feel like it. It was amazing how good it felt. So . . . I thought I'd try it, but I didn't want anyone to think that I was having some sort of new problem, so I used to go and do it in the lavatory.' She glances at Janet. 'I would stand by the lavatory bowl and stretch very tall, wave my hands up in the air and put my face into a grin then check myself out, and I did feel better. Sometimes I even felt a bit giggly.' She laughs straight into Janet's eyes, looking a little proud of herself. 'Then I'd sit down and watch my breath all steamy while my bottom was so cold.' She puts her hand over her mouth. 'Oh, I'm sorry.'

'What for?'

'I was being rude,' she whispers.

'No, you weren't.'

'Oh.' She looks unsure.

'Go on, Nora,' Janet says encouragingly.

'One day I was in there a long time and Sister Cummings must have realised because she shouted, "Jennings, what are you doing? Get out of there." Then I had to walk back out looking miserable, just in case she thought I was now high or something!'

And the laugh becomes a giggle and Janet, caught up in the joke, laughs too. 'Are you high now?' she quips.

Immediately Nora's chin and eyes drop and she curls in on herself, as though preparing for an attack. 'I'm sorry,' she whispers.

Janet blushes, stricken. 'No, no, Nora. It's I who need to apologise. I'm so sorry. I meant it as a joke, but it was insensitive. Please go on. I love to hear you talk and tell your story. It's wonderful that you can make light of things. And you teach me so much that I don't know.'

Nora pauses a while longer and then continues, her voice sombre now. 'For years I longed for someone like you to talk to. Someone I could tell when I was sad or grieving and not be given treatment to get rid of it. I wanted to have emotions – even if they were hard ones to cope with. I wanted to be able to solve my problems and make amends for what I'd done wrong. I wanted to think, and do things. I wanted to try to become me as an adult. I came here when I was nothing but a child really. I don't know how to be grown up.'

'Oh, Nora, you do. You're an amazing adult and I'm honoured that you talk to me. You inspire me.'

'*I* inspire *you*?' Nora looks shocked.

Janet nods sincerely. 'Nora, you're very inspiring. You've survived what many people wouldn't have been able to survive. People weaker than you probably succumbed long ago. I'm so thrilled to hear your thoughts and ideas. And I love it that, despite all that happened to you, you can tell me sweet and funny stories. Please don't stop. We can talk about anything you want to talk about.'

But Nora's eyes remain downcast and there's a painful silence. Janet waits with bated breath, respecting Nora's need for time but hoping that she has not lost her for today.

'Nora, what would you have liked to do with your life?'

Slowly, Nora lifts her head. 'I would have liked to have had a family – four children, maybe. And a life of ideas, of being able to find out about things. I would have liked to know more about the world, and different people . . . and myself. I'd like to know who I really am – why I was born.' She pauses and gives a little smile. Her eyes are regaining their liveliness by the moment. 'I can't believe I was meant to end up spending my life in a hospital and not do anything useful. But maybe thinking that is conceited and sinful.'

Janet marvels at such courage and grace. 'Nora, you're certainly neither conceited nor sinful. You're wise and astute despite a lifetime of being disallowed your right to opinion or freedom—'

'I've often wondered how I got here – really. I know I did something that people considered dreadful and that I was an embarrassment to my family, but . . .' And her eyes wander to some far-off place to which Janet has no access, then back again. 'You know how you say that I can choose what I want to do now?'

'Yes.'

'What did you mean?'

'Is there anything you would like to do with your life? Maybe . . .' and though she is about to make some suggestions, she watches Nora gather breath and courage and Janet stops short, leaving space for her to speak.

'I know what I want . . . but . . .'

'But what?'

'I'm frightened. So many times in the past, what I really wanted has been used against me. I used to sometimes try to play the piano, but when it was seen that I liked it, I was forbidden to touch it.'

'That isn't going to happen this time, Nora. Take a chance on me.'

'I'd love to sing.' Nora's words come out in a rush.

'Sing?' Janet is taken aback, but feels the hope and yearning in those few words.

'Yes. I want to see if I still can. Do you think that's stupid?'

'No, Nora. I think it's wonderful. Tell me more.' Janet leans forward in her chair, like a fellow conspirator in a child's game.

'I used to sing all the time. I was in the church choir. I used to give little concerts at home when I was very small. I used to sing when I was just doing ordinary things, like washing up. It made me feel wonderful. I used to play the piano, too.' Her eyes take on a new, dewy softness.

Janet lets out the breath she's been holding. 'Go on . . .'

'On Sunday evenings we would all sing together. Sometimes I'd sing for people who came to visit my parents. And Robert – my cousin – and I would sing and play the piano together.'

She steals a glance at Janet, but seems to find eye contact too difficult to manage. 'I wanted to sing and teach music when I was a girl until . . .' Her eyes fall towards her lap and she fidgets, her two forefingers wrapping round each other, twisting a piece of her cardigan between them.

The pain drops into the silence and Janet gives it time and space. She knows what it is to have young hopes dashed. But she clears her mind of anything that's hers. She needs to be a clean slate upon which Nora can write her own story. At last, Nora draws breath and looks about to speak. Janet's heart lifts, but when Nora begins, her tone has changed.

'I mustn't even think about those things. I can't do anything now. My life's nearly over.'

Janet feels a pang of dismay. 'It isn't, Nora. I think you still have lots of life yet.'

'No.' She puts up her hand. 'I'm too old.'

'No, Nora, you're not. I know it's been awful. I doubt that I'd have coped this far if I'd had your life. But you have. You're still here. You still have time. Don't throw it away. Much of your life's been stolen, I know. And that's dreadful, and we can't change that. But now you can do something with what you have left. Or choose to let all of those who abused you over the years win. Stand up, Nora. You can. I know you can. You're not dead yet. Use what life you have left. I'll help you, but I can't do it for you. The next move has to be yours.' *Janet, take a step back. She'll only find herself if she stands up on her own.*

But she can't just yet.

'I have a favourite quotation, though I don't know where it came from,' Janet says. 'It goes like this: "the measure of our greatness is in how we stand up after we fall".' Janet reaches towards Nora and places a finger under her chin and lifts it gently. 'Nora, you have to stand up – to get out of this on your own. You have to make the decision. No one can make it for you.'

And now Nora's eyes lift to meet Janet's. She mumbles something in a very low voice, then looks away.

'I can't hear you, Nora. What did you say?'

Nora looks back, with a tinge of defiance. 'I said, I want to sing.'

'Good,' says Janet with relief. 'Then sing, you shall.'

When Nora leaves, Janet sits back and takes a deep, shaky breath. She knows what she needs to do. She lifts the phone and dials. 'Hello. It's Janet . . . Great . . . Susan, are you still giving singing lessons?'

A few minutes later, Janet puts down the phone and calls the bank.

Chapter Thirteen

1985
Forty-six years

Janet pops to Ellen's office on her way to her session with Nora and finds Ellen doing a training session with a couple of young nurses. Ellen greets her with a broad smile.

'Ah Janet, I was just telling them about Nora and how excited we all are.'

Janet smiles. 'Yes, she's doing so well. A good reminder to us all never to give up hope.'

She looks at these raw young recruits and hopes that they can start with a positive attitude to mental illness. 'It's amazing, after so many years here and almost being written off as hopeless and helpless, that change is still possible. It's a bit like tending for a plant that hasn't been watered, and as soon as you give it what it needs, it blossoms again.' Then she focuses on Ellen. 'Just popped in to see that everything's OK. My plan is to start to talk about the option of discharge today. Are you all right with that?'

Ellen looks surprised and Janet realises that she's thoughtlessly cornered her. She continues quickly. 'Sorry, Ellen, I should come and chat with you about that again later. Maybe we could find a bit of time, especially bearing in mind this morning's news.'

Ellen gives her one of those looks and Janet steps back. 'Don't worry, I'll pop across again later.' Then she smiles at the young nurses who look bright and enthusiastic and all agog. 'Listen to every word of wisdom Sister utters. And have fun.'

Janet retreats and heads for the small consulting room, where Nora is waiting patiently for her, as always. Once they are settled, Janet takes a deep breath to start, but Nora gets in first.

'I've been thinking about everything, and I think I should just stay as I am.'

Janet holds her breath. 'Why?' she says eventually.

'Well, I used to let myself dream about all sorts of things, but it just hurts in the end. So, it's just safer not to want anything.' She looks down. 'Sorry, Janet.'

'Nora, I don't think we should ever give up hope, but then I haven't suffered like you. I think you can still do all sorts of things if you really want to. But if you choose not, that's fine, and you don't have to apologise to me. I know we talked about the fact that the hospital will eventually close down, and maybe that will be sooner than we'd thought, so I've been thinking too. Can I share it with you?'

Janet knows she must go slowly. Nora's life has been endlessly precarious, and she must remember that at every stage.

'I think that if we work hard, there really can be a time when you can go home if you want to, rather than maybe going to live in another hospital when Hillinghurst closes.'

'But I don't have a home,' Nora says, baffled.

'No . . . Sorry. It would mean you'd have to have a new one.'

'How?'

'Well, we'd help find you one – probably with some other women to start with. And Audrey and I and the rest of the team would support you.'

'No.' Nora shakes her head. 'I'm too old.' There go the fingers fidgeting in her lap. Janet reaches out and puts a finger on her arm.

'Well . . . I don't know about that, Nora.'

Nora looks directly at Janet, hope and doubt in equal parts in her eyes. 'Do you really think I could?'

'I do.'

'Leave here? And maybe sing?'

'Yes. I know that, sadly, it isn't the right environment for you to sing here – but when you leave, I don't see any reason why not.'

She pauses, but only for a moment. 'Then that's what I want – to find a new home and sing.'

Janet's heart leaps. 'Wonderful, Nora. Now we start to plan!' She rubs her palms together.

The clinic out of the way, Janet calls in on Ellen before they both head off for home. Ellen looks grave. 'I see that we're on the list for closure.'

'We knew it might be coming at some point, but yes, this is earlier than we'd expected. So it means we've got to get a move on. But I guess it's really hard for you, Ellen, and the rest of the staff who've been here for years.'

Ellen looks sad and older than she did this morning. 'I'll retire. I'm like Nora – too old to transplant.'

Janet gives her a compassionate smile, though her heart sinks. 'Ellen. You've given years of service here, and if retirement feels like the way to go, then I wish you every happiness with that. You've earned the rest and I hope you'll enjoy it. But I don't think Nora's too old to transplant, nor you either. I did talk to her about it today and she was very positive in the end, so it's up to us to help her keep that attitude. That will make the difference between her succeeding or ending up as many others who were institutionalised did in the past. So I'm going to get all the team together and let's really give her the best shot.'

Ellen tries to smile, but obviously isn't convinced.

Nora lies awake in her shared room, and though her eyes remain closed, she's alert as she explores the morning with her other senses. Something has changed. Her heart feels lighter. A weight has lifted from her chest. She places a gentle hand over it, feeling her ribcage rise and fall, rise and fall, then her eyes spring open and dart their way around the room, unable to settle on anything.

Could it be true? Did I dream that conversation? Could I really go home?

The light peeping in around the edges of the curtains has the quality of sunshine. She wonders what time it is – these summer mornings, it's difficult to tell. It feels very early – maybe four o'clock? Her mind is confused yet oddly clear. It doesn't make sense. She blinks. Then again, and listens.

Apart from the dawn chorus as birds start the business of their morning, there are the usual breathing noises, plus some snoring and grunting as someone turns over, surfacing from a dream, perhaps. Four women sharing a room – especially in these circumstances – must develop tolerance of each other's jabbers, mewls, and eructations. But above all the usual background noise, Nora can hear something else. She looks straight up to the ceiling and cocks her head on the pillow.

She could have sworn she heard music. She blinks again, wondering if she is just dreaming. But even if it is a dream, it's amazing. She can't remember the last time she had a dream accompanied by such sweet music. Years. She closes her eyes again to try to capture it. It was there. She knows it was there. *Please let it come again.*

But it doesn't. It's gone. Tears swell and collect until they could burst both her head and her heart with the force of their grief. She squeezes her lids shut, balls her hands into fists under the blanket and prays. How long since she's done that ... ? *Please let me have the music back.*

But there's silence. Nevertheless, she knows that something has changed. Maybe it will come again.

She tries to relax. *Breathe. Let your body go. Breathe.*

It was so precious to her that she could always hear music when she was a child. She could hear a song and sing it; hear a tune and play it. But many a time, after she came to Hillinghurst, it would taunt her until she cried in frustration and begged it to go away and leave her alone. And it did. But, oh, how she then grieved it, searched for it, yearned for it. She relaxes the muscles of her face, unfurls her fists and stares up towards the ceiling, and lets the tears come, pooling in her ears. *Please ...*

And there it is. She opens her eyes wide and shifts her head, tears spilling onto her pillow. She listens.

Yes. It's there. I can hear it.

She hardly dares breathe. She hears the swell of the organ, the very breath of the choir, the hush before the first note. She can hear the movement of the choir master, even as he lifts his baton and places the forefinger of his left hand on his lips, signalling to the singers. *Wait. Prepare. Put your weight squarely on your feet. Lift your heads. Let it come. Ready . . .*

His finger leaves his mouth and his forefinger and thumb come together, his other fingers elegantly fanned. Then, as if his baton were a magic wand, he parts the air with it, silently calling to them. *Lift . . . And . . . NOW.* The whole choir exhales that first perfect, crystal-clear note into the body of the church and it ascends in praise.

And there it is – she can hear her own voice blending into the matrix of concordant sound, part of the whole and yet individual. She can hear it in her chest, in her head, all around her, and the emotion in her heart lifts her further. She's at one with the music, and she listens as tears now soak the pillow at each side of her head and she frees her body to cry, her throat to allow the sound of her sobbing to be heard, her chest to feel its breathing, her back to feel itself on the bed, and her legs to feel straight and strong.

I'm alive!

She wants to tell someone. To shout. But she doesn't want anyone to snatch it away from her. She whispers very quietly to herself, *'I'm alive.'*

What was it the choir master used to say? 'Once you can feel that you become the music, then – only then – can you truly sing. When nothing else exists but the music coursing through you and lifting you out of your body, leaving it to do whatever it needs to do, while you – the music – are simply being.'

She sighs and breathes as her tears eventually subside and she knows – truly knows – that the music will never leave her again. She can hardly wait to tell Janet. She's the only person who will understand.

Chapter Fourteen

1986
Forty-seven years

Ellen glances around the room at the case-study team of professional, compassionate women, all with Nora's welfare in mind.

'So, it looks like we've at least got a sketch of a plan,' Janet says.

'I think so.' Audrey closes the notepad in front of her.

'Does anyone have anything to add?'

Ellen shifts in her chair and twiddles with a pen on her desk. Janet glances at her, eyes questioning. 'Ellen. What about you?'

Ellen hesitates, not quite meeting Janet's eyes. 'I do have some reservations, as I've already said. I just don't want to see one more patient get into difficulties and do something . . . well, unfortunate.'

'I know how you feel.' Audrey nods at her. 'I was just starting off in social work when there was all that hurried discharge without proper preparation. And the suicides! For weeks we seemed to be expecting at least one person to be either readmitted or found dead on a park bench or hanging in some hostel bedroom. I remember wondering if I really wanted to be doing this work at all.'

Janet glances at Ellen who is playing with her pen again, her brow creased and her teeth worrying at her bottom lip while the rest of the team falls into silence.

'I know I wasn't here then,' she says, 'and I feel for everyone who was. It must have been dreadful. But hopefully everyone has learned from that experience and that's why we're having meetings like this and preparing her as well as we possibly can.'

Ellen looks at Janet, clearly unconvinced.

'I know she's been here for years,' Janet continues, 'and I'm not underestimating how hard it will be for her. But let's look at the options. A while ago it just so happened that the SHO was sick and I had to do the death certificate for Sarah Golson. She'd been here pretty well all her life, just like Nora. In fact, it could have been Nora. It was heartbreaking.'

It could have been me, too . . .

Janet is flung back again to that moment when she read Nora's notes and was faced with the fact that the legislation that held Nora captive all these years was still in place just a few years before she herself became pregnant out of wedlock. Though it hadn't been used to condemn unmarried mothers for some years, it was still legally possible until 1959. The 'crime' hadn't changed. If Nora was guilty, then so was she, and a wave of indignation surges up from her belly to her throat. A new fire burns behind her eyes as she looks around the table. Ellen has stopped playing with the pen and her eyes finally meet Janet's.

'It's a travesty that she has been kept here so long with her rights denied and without hope of reprieve, and I for one will do everything I can for Nora and anyone else who actually still wants a chance to try to live independently. As I said, I'm not underestimating the risks, Ellen. But we'll prepare her well and supervise her every step of the way. Let's at least give her a chance.'

After a few tense seconds, Ellen nods and the atmosphere lifts.

'We'll watch her carefully, Ellen,' Audrey says gently. 'I don't think anyone wants to see her pushed, but we need to be realistically optimistic and keep moving forward, if we can.'

'It would be crazy to expect it to be all plain sailing,' Janet concedes. 'It won't be. But she's an amazing woman and I think she can make it.'

The meeting over, and everyone seeming to be clear as to what needs to happen going forward, Audrey leaves while Kit hangs back waiting for Janet, those beautiful West Indian eyes full of wisdom. As they leave the room together, she puts a warm arm round Janet's shoulders. 'You all right?' she says.

Moved, but also disarmed, Janet tries to smile, the wound opening to bleed now it's touched. 'So-so.'

'You give me a call if you need anything, right?'

Janet nods, but tears are welling in her eyes and she knows she has to be on her own. 'I'll be OK.'

'I know you will. But you don't have to do it all on your own, you know.'

They're at the end of the corridor now and need to part ways. Kit's round, fat arm grips a bit more tightly for a moment, and then she lets go. Janet smiles but is glad to be not far from her own office where she can hide. It's still all too raw to deal with here.

She hurries in as quickly as she can and then leans her back against the closed door. Her chin falls to her chest. She takes a long breath, bites her lips together and lifts her head. She can do this.

Her eyes scan the room and come to rest on her bookshelf. There are various heavy books on psychiatry, then a section that she often lends to patients. She reads the spines of the first five books that stand adjacent to each other on that shelf. *Living, Loving and Learning*; *Listen to Love*; *Finding Each Other*; *The Courage to Heal*; *Soul Mates*. She smiles. That's her story with Ian right there. It will be fine. She just has to trust and keep going.

She lowers her eyes and listens to her own heart beating, a cloak of sadness heavy on her shoulders. Then her eyes stray to the window and the trees swaying in the wind and she remembers a conversation she had recently with one of the nurses who was complaining about the behaviour of another.

'If she were a patient, would you be complaining?' Janet had asked.

'Of course not. But they have a reason to behave like that. They're sick.'

'Maybe she's not well either,' Janet said. 'Might it be worth asking her if something's wrong, rather than just being irritated by her behaviour?'

How she wishes that she was big enough to take her own advice and acknowledge that she, too, is a carer who is one of the walking wounded; like so many others, she doesn't share her issues, even though on a daily basis she expects those in her care to do so. She is a hypocrite.

The image of Ian's tall, sad frame receding down the path all those years ago as he left their home still haunts her. She's been so full of her own pain and patients' pain that she hasn't considered his pain – and how alone he must feel in it. She wonders how alone he felt even when they were together, while she had her head and heart buried in her work. A wave of love and regret floods her and she wraps her arms around herself and she sends Ian a silent apology.

Feeling chastened, she pulls out her little lipstick compact, checks her hair, reapplies her lipstick. She must be fully prepared for this crucial session with Nora. She makes her way to the small consulting room, and there is Nora, waiting patiently as always. Even before Nora sees her, Janet can feel the sense of calm in the room. Something's changed.

Nora turns and smiles, her face lighting up. 'I dreamed about music again,' she says, 'and I could actually hear the choir singing.'

Janet's heart lifts and her smile matches Nora's in breadth and brilliance. 'That's wonderful!'

'Yes, it is. I hadn't been able to hear it for years, but that's two lovely dreams I've had now. And today if I close my eyes I can almost hear it. So I'm ready to go home now.'

Janet does her best to equal Nora's enthusiasm, even though her heart still feels bruised from her own troubles. 'Ah, that's so good to hear, Nora. In that case we have to keep up our work and make sure that everything's as good as we can make it. OK?'

'Yes,' Nora says, her head held high and her voice strong and steady.

'Right. Then today I want us to come back to our last session, if that's all right with you. It's time to look at the good things in your life. You know, before all of this happened. It sounds as though you had a nice family. I know that your father was strict, but there were also lovely things happening, with church and your family, your friends and your cousin.' Janet notices Nora's flinch, but ploughs on. 'And I know between now and then, all sorts of things have happened to hurt you and you've had terrible loss. But if we can pick up the good things and happy feelings you had as a child, we can build on that. Because, as long as you had times when you were very little when you knew you were loved by your mother, no matter what happened next, that inner security can be resurrected at any time in your life. We can help it recover. It maybe won't ever be what it might have been had you not had all of this terrible stuff in the middle, but I'm sure that if we work hard, it will improve, and you're going to need that when you're living outside.'

She pauses, watching. Any reaction from Nora would be helpful, but even though her eyes are attentive, she gives nothing away. Janet thinks sadly of all the years that Nora probably didn't dare speak, and how hard it must be to start now. She presses on.

'As we grow up, ideally we develop a part of us that we could call our "inner parent". Its job is to always champion and take care of that vulnerable child part of us, whatever happens. Once we develop that, we'll always be OK.'

Nora's eyes shift a little and there's a tiny movement of her head and a tension in her brow. She's engaged.

'When your inner child feels scared and lost and like she can't cope, your inner parent can kind of put her arm around her, and comfort her. That part of you – the part that can take care of you, what I've called your inner parent – started to develop when you were only thirteen or fourteen, long before you came into hospital, so we need to find it and help it to get strong.'

Nora looks uncertain.

'Don't worry, it's not as complicated as I may have made it sound.' Janet smiles. 'The thing is, if we had harsh parents or other authority figures, we tend to become critical about ourselves, and instead of our inner-parent part taking care of us, cherishing us and treating us lovingly, it can often shout at us, say awful things – like that we're useless or no good. Are you with me?'

Nora nods, and Janet gives her a reassuring smile.

'So, what we really need to do is to take the very best of each of our parents, and mould our inner parent from that. And we can also add bits we've learned from other people too – people who show us a way to be kind to ourselves.'

'Like you?'

'Erm . . .' Janet hesitates, her cheeks reddening. 'Well, that's not quite what I meant . . .'

'But could I use bits of you?'

'You could use some of the ways I am with you if you like, but really I'd like us to also have a look at your real parents, and the nice things you remember from long before any of this awful stuff happened. So, can you think of some of those nice things?'

Nora pauses and looks out of the window to where the morning has ripened into a beautiful, blue-ceilinged day, and suddenly she's in a different morning . . .

Leaves are aflutter, flirting with pink cherry blossom, while the trees tell the saplings stories of what they've seen and what they've heard; of seasons gone by, of children now grown, of maypoles and cricket on the village green.

Her father is in his whites, with that red stain on his thigh where he polishes the ball. He runs up to the wicket with that amazing Catherine wheel of an action. There are cries of 'Howzat?', then a polite nod to the umpire. Later, he's tying on pads, carrying the sacred willow as he strides to the crease. Her mother is sitting on a tartan blanket spread out on the grass, her face rosy from the sunshine, watching him carefully, with such pride, as she clicks her knitting needles, teasing out the wool from its nest in her bag, hardly glancing at the ever-growing length of the jumper she's making. She's wearing a bright yellow wrap-around dress she made herself. It has brown buttons right to the hem of the skirt. As the sun lights up her hair, which has come a bit loose and strays gently across her cheek, Nora thinks she must be the most beautiful woman in the world.

Little girls are having a dolls' tea party, and Auntie Isabel is walking towards them from the pavilion, balancing a tray with cups of tea, a Victoria sponge and some scones and butter. 'Nora, would you like to come and help me?' she calls, and Nora skips up and runs, light-footed on tanned legs. She takes the scone plate and carries it proudly with two hands.

'You're a good girl,' her mother says.

Then she's back in Janet's room.

Janet watches, enraptured. 'That looked as though it was something nice,' she says, as Nora draws back her gaze.

'Yes,' Nora says slowly. 'It was.'

'Then maybe you can store it again – in a new file of good memories. In fact, I think it calls for a new notebook – a "nice-memory book".' Nora smiles. 'None of those memories are lost, Nora, any more than the nasty ones are. Sometimes we're so busy trying to forget the nasty stuff that we forget there was also a lot of good too. We can find those good bits again, and even now, despite all that happened between, the nice memories can heal us, and also help us learn how to be kind to ourselves as we remember how people were kind to us and each other.'

'A lot of the things I remember were about music – and my cousin. We used to sing together and play the piano together. He was my best friend as well as my cousin.'

'That sounds lovely.'

'It was . . .' but then a shadow crosses her face. Janet had planned to stay with the good stuff today, but this is an opening she can't ignore, so she leaves a silence for Nora to fill with whatever is on her mind.

'You know, there was something confusing about my parents.'

'Oh?'

'After my grandma – my mother's mother – died, and when my mother was so sad and crying, my father seemed so lost, wandering from room to room with his newspaper folded and held between two fingers. He would occasionally tap a piece of furniture with it, pause, look very thoughtful, then walk on again, as though he'd forgotten where he was going or why. Sometimes my mother would be crying in the night and Dad would shush her like a baby – so gently and with so much love in his voice. They really did seem to love each other then. He wasn't a man to hug much, though sometimes he used to touch Mum so gently. I loved that. I used to watch silently. It was so beautiful. Just the odd touch of his hand that he seemed to leave there for just an extra second . . . And she would say nothing, just be still – well, not always. Sometimes I could feel her just lean in towards him – kind of meeting his hand and touching him back with her body. I always thought it was proof that they loved each other even though they never said so. Well, maybe they did, but never in front of me.'

Nora's voice dances at the semi-forgotten sweetness. 'When he was going off to work in the mornings, she would straighten his tie, even though it was already straight – she just tweaked it a bit and then smoothed down his collar and brushed imaginary hairs from the shoulders of his suit with her hand. I wanted them to kiss each other, but they never did, apart from a tiny peck on the cheek. But one night there was a huge row. I must have been about fifteen. My mother was so angry. She was screaming at Dad. I ran into the parlour to see if I could help but my mother stopped mid-scream and Dad looked sad and tired. She told me to go to my room and that she'd come up in a while, but as I was going back upstairs, I heard her tell my dad that she'd never forgive him. He was begging her to understand something . . . said something about only having supplied what was needed, without contact . . . I didn't understand it at all – still don't. She was shouting again that he should have asked her. It doesn't make any sense because then she said if he had done, she would have said no, that it was disgusting. Then there was something about her being less important than doing it – whatever "it" was. Then Dad shouted something about Robert, but I couldn't hear it all because Mummy ran into the hall crying and saw me on the stairs and I tried to run up to my room pretending that I hadn't heard anything.

'I did hear, but I've never understood what it was all about, and I've always been puzzled by it. Then, one night – it must have been weeks after that – I left a book downstairs that I needed for my homework and I tiptoed into the sitting room so I wouldn't disturb anyone. My father was sitting in his chair by the fireplace, leaning forward with an elbow on each knee. I couldn't see whether his eyes were open or closed, but he obviously hadn't seen me. I wanted to disappear without him knowing I was there because I thought he was crying. There wasn't any sound, just he looked so sad and defeated. I didn't know what to do. I stood stock-still in case he saw me. But he put his head in his hands then and I hardly dared breathe. I always wished I'd gone and hugged him.

'It was never the same after that. Mummy didn't bother smoothing his tie or brushing his jacket any more. One day he was ready to go and he just stood in front of her, looking sad, and he took her hand and held it on his chest. She looked up at him but she didn't smile and then she pulled her hand away.' Nora shakes her head in bewilderment. 'He'd always been a bit aloof, but he became really distant after that and got angry so easily. Mummy changed too, and – well, it was all just different.' She pauses. 'Then, of course, I did what I did, and . . .' She looks wistful. 'I look back now and wonder if whatever happened between them hadn't happened, would it have been different when I got into trouble.'

'And?'

'I think Mummy would always have been disappointed and my father angry, but I don't think it would have been like it was – that they never tried to see me or take me home.'

'No,' Janet agrees softly.

'I know what I did was wicked.'

Janet sighs. 'Nora, it wasn't wicked. You were a normal young girl falling in love. It's what young people do.'

'Did you fall in love?' she blurts out.

'Yes, I did.' But Janet is unwilling to say more, lest her own pain should overflow and jeopardise her professionalism. 'But this is about you, Nora, not me.'

'I'm sorry.'

'Nora, I'm going to ban "sorry" from your vocabulary,' Janet says, though she smiles reassuringly to offset the exasperation she can't keep from creeping into her voice. 'You've done nothing wrong. You don't need to apologise. We all do our best, but sometimes we only realise the effects we've had on our loved ones years later. I'm sure that a time came when your mother and father realised what they'd done.'

'But they still never came . . .'

'No. They didn't.'

Chapter Fifteen

Janet can hardly believe that today may be the team's final pre-discharge meeting before Nora will finally be free. She arrives early at Audrey's office and, as usual, marvels that it's almost as elegant as Audrey herself, with personal touches in vibrant colours that raises an ordinary NHS office to a thing of beauty. The sound of hearty laughter coming down the corridor heralds Kit, with some of the other women in tow. 'Here they come,' says Audrey.

There's a tap on the door and Kit's huge jolly presence enters the room, Ellen in her wake. 'Janet,' she cries, 'what you been doing, girl?' And she envelops Janet in big strong arms.

They settle down around a low table, in front of each of them their 'NORA' folder, so that everyone can share their part of the teamwork. Janet notes that Ellen is quiet, but she passes that off as her being tired.

'Daily living assessment is in,' says Iris. 'She did well. I think she'll manage – she hasn't really needed much supervision for a long time now.'

'What about money?'

'Yeah. Handling money – budgeting and such. She'll need quite a lot of support with that, but we still have some time and I'm making sure she gets out regularly and learns to spend – and save. I know they have regular community meetings at the group home and work out budgets and menus, so she'll have quite a bit of input. Mrs Singh's quite into that.'

'Great.' Janet smiles around the room. 'Ellen, what about you?'

Ellen looks uncertain. 'She's been pretty stable for a long time now but she's never been on her own – ever. I just have an uncomfortable feeling.' She shakes her head as if to clear it. 'I know we have to take a chance. She'll have the others and lots of support. And the home's great. Have you seen it yet, Janet?'

'No, but you have, haven't you, Audrey?'

'Yes. It's lovely, and she's going to have a really pretty bedroom. And Mrs Singh's an angel. I think she'll be OK. I'll visit as often as I can and she'll have her CPN too.'

'Which one?' Janet asks.

'Evelyn.'

'I tell you, these community psychiatric nurses are just amazing, and Evelyn is one of the best. She's so grounded and funny, too. I think she and Nora will get on well. Sorry I didn't copy her in about this meeting. Will next time.'

'Which next time?' Kit laughs. 'This is it, girl.'

'She and Nora have had a couple of meetings and it seems fine,' Audrey says. 'In fact, Evelyn came in and we all had a chat on the ward. I think you got feedback on that, didn't you, Ellen?'

'Yes, it sounded as though it went really well.'

'But you still sound concerned.' Janet peers into Ellen's face.

'I feel a bit better since we had our meeting yesterday. And maybe I'm always a bit anxious when people leave after such a long time. My gut still feels uncomfortable, but I really don't think that Nora could be any better prepared than she is.'

'What about meds, Janet?' Audrey asks.

'Well, she's off pretty well everything now and seems to be coping. She might need some occasional night sedation, but maybe not. I'm keen to get her to use simple things, if she can. Not dependently, but just ad hoc. Things like Rescue Remedy would be good for her too for daytime use, just to have as a safety net in case she needs something. She could even use that at night, on occasions. What I don't want her to have is anything containing valerian. That can give people awful nightmares, and she already has more than enough of those without any help from us. I think she's sleeping well now though, isn't she, Ellen?'

'Still the occasional disturbed night.'

'There's always someone to chat with her here, though.' Janet laughs suddenly. 'We could try to clone Kumar. Who wouldn't want him to chat with at night?'

'But there's Mrs Singh,' says Audrey. 'She lives there, albeit on the top floor, and though we don't want to set up a night-time service, at least Nora will know there's someone she can talk to, should she really need to.'

'I think we could go on planning for ever,' says Janet. 'But I believe we've done all we can and just need to get through this last little while. Let's hope it goes smoothly.' Janet looks around the table. 'OK – anything else?'

There's lots of shaking of heads and nods of agreement.

'So, I guess that's just about it. Thanks, everybody. I'll be seeing her later and, if there's anything, I'll make sure everybody's involved. Got to dash now, though, I want to see Nora and I've got outpatients too.'

Fired up by the team meeting, Janet has high hopes for a good session with Nora, the plan for today being to talk about the details of discharge and thereafter. However, as soon as they sit down, it is clear that Nora is in a strange mood. She doesn't want to hear anything about the group home or the arrangements that are being made, or even new shopping expeditions that Janet had hoped would be fun.

Janet can't help feeling a little irritated. 'Nora, I know you're scared, but you really need to play an active part in all of this. We're trying to ensure that you have all the support you need and that any questions you have can be answered. So, the more we can talk about it, the better.'

'I don't want to talk about it,' she says, an unusually petulant tone to her voice.

'All right. What *do* you want to talk about?'

The silence lengthens and Janet's irritation subsides as she watches Nora's face. Compassion wins. 'Nora, deep down you know how to do this. You knew when you were a girl. You knew how to think, make decisions – how to live. And somewhere, you still know how. Now you have to have the courage to remember. I'm not saying it isn't hard. I think it's a very courageous thing to be doing and you should be proud of yourself for getting this far. You can do it—'

'I can't,' Nora snaps.

'Yes, you can,' Janet says firmly. 'Nora, you can live again, or stay where people have put you – and I don't mean Hillinghurst. I mean in that place inside you where you hide. That place is too small for you now. You've outgrown it and you need to come out.'

Nora casts her eyes down. 'It's safer here.'

'Not any longer. Not now you know a new way.' Janet smiles, knowing that what she's about to say is manipulative, but on this occasion the means justify the end. 'And not now you have your music back . . .'

Nora frowns. 'That's not fair.'

'Maybe not. But sometimes life isn't fair.' Janet pauses, watching and willing Nora to take the leap. 'If you don't grab it now you have the chance, you'll be doing yourself an injustice. Those who used to abuse you have gone. The war's over. Don't become your own abuser. If you don't step out now, you'll have missed your opportunity. But it's your choice.'

'But you're forcing me, so it isn't my choice.'

Janet scans Nora's frightened face. 'You're absolutely right. I'm sorry. I'll try not to put any more pressure on you and just be here.'

Nora's eyes widen in surprise. 'But I want you to . . .'

'Nora, you can't have it both ways.'

This is the make-or-break moment. Janet needs to step back and swallow her own earnest desire for this woman to stand up and walk out. In the end, it's not her business, even though her heart aches. But she can't help herself from giving one last push, all the while praying that she won't get it wrong.

'OK, Nora. It's fine. Let's close for today,' she says, her voice cold and hard.

'But—'

'No. It's enough now. It's fine. No problem. Come on, let's go.' And she looks at her watch and smiles distantly. She hates what she's having to do. 'Come on, Nora,' she says sharply. 'I have someone to see at the outpatient clinic. I'll see you on Wednesday, at our usual time.'

Nora looks alarmed, sad, confused. Janet breathes, praying that this paradoxical intervention will work. She stands and busies herself, stacking the notes on her desk, unable to look at Nora any longer. She turns and glances back. Nora is still seated. 'Nora,' she says, her voice louder, her tone cold. 'It's time. I need to go to outpatients.'

Nora finally stands, her back bent into the old curve.

'And don't slouch,' Janet says. 'It makes you look old.' She turns away once more and waits for the door to close. But when she turns back, Nora is still standing there. 'Nora, I'm late,' she says impatiently. 'I have to go now.'

Nora leaves without another word.

A few hours later, Janet is sitting in her office writing up outpatient notes when she's interrupted by a firm knock on the door. The person doesn't wait for her response to open it.

'Janet,' the staff nurse looks harassed. 'You're needed on Rowan – urgently – a problem with Nora. Extension 372.'

Anxiety rises like a volcano in Janet's chest and she struggles to maintain her calm, cool exterior. 'Thanks,' she says, turning away and picking up the phone. 'Hi Ellen – what's the problem?'

She listens, her face frozen with her mouth slightly open. 'I'm coming.'

She bangs down the phone and she's caught for a split second in a freeze-frame before adrenaline surges and she's sprinting, taking the shortest route between the outpatient building and Rowan. She slides a little on the lawn, startling a couple of patients who are enjoying the winter sunshine, then swiftly corners on the footpath that leads to the ward.

Janet crashes through the doors. 'Where is she?' she shouts to one of the nurses.

'In her room—'

And Janet keeps on running. She arrives sweating and breathless to find Ellen and one of the nurses outside Nora's door.

'Don't know what she's got up against the door, but we can't get in.' As their eyes meet, Janet knows this is exactly what Ellen had feared would happen. Janet pauses, catching her breath and steadying herself so that her guilt and concern don't show in her voice. She can only imagine how angry and frightened Nora must be that she's regressed to the adolescent who was admitted all those years ago. She can hear the rare sound of Nora crying, and her heart aches.

When she feels that she can talk normally, Janet takes one last, deep breath and knocks on the door. 'Nora. It's me. Let me in, please. We can sort out whatever's going on. Come on – let me in.'

The sound of crying subsides and the voice, when it comes, is muffled, but there's no mistaking the anger it contains. 'Go away.'

Janet softens her voice as much as she can. 'Nora – it's OK. Please. Come on. Let me in.' As she waits and hopes, a memory tugs at her mind.

She's sixteen and her body hurts from the beating of the previous night. She's angry. Very angry, and no matter how much it hurts, she drags everything she can and stuffs it against the door, then sits on the floor, her back against the upended chair she used to complete the barricade. Then, finally, the tears come, and she shakes with that powerful mixture of rage and impotence, until at last she's spent. She chose to do this while there was no one else in the house to hear her, apologise to her, beat her, plead with her to come out or in any way cheat her of this release. What she needed to know is that she could do it. A wave of humiliation threatens to drown her as she realises the futility of her protest – but then she allows a little ripple of pride to creep in. She did it, and she knows now that she will be fine. Stiff and painful as she is, she drags one piece of furniture after the other back to where they belong. She remakes her bed, hangs her clothes back in the wardrobe and sits down. She initially feels even more helplessness than before, but then she stands up and walks out and switches on her music and starts to dance.

Nora's voice pulls her back to the moment. 'Go away,' she shouts. 'I don't need you.'

Janet, relieved at the strength of Nora's voice, breathes easier, though her heart still pounds at the vividness of the memory she just relived. She places her trembling hand against the door. 'I know. But let's talk a bit. Can I come in?' The pause of a few seconds feels interminable.

'No!'

There's another tense pause. Janet holds her breath and exchanges a worried glance with Ellen. 'Nora, open the door.' She leans her face towards it. 'Nora, come on.'

The sound of movement from within the room floods Janet with relief. Then the sound of something heavy being dragged away from the door is replaced by silence. Janet pushes the door open and looks around the room, aghast. It must have taken some strength for a sixty-five-year-old woman to have shifted all four beds and lockers. All stand askew. Nora's clothes are strewn around, some of them torn. Blood-spattered pillows and sheets lie wherever Nora has thrown them. There's blood on the floor, Nora's bed, the walls, and streaming from her left wrist as she stands in a corner, head up, pale, angry and defiant. *Good. Not the victim lying on the floor.* Janet glances quickly at the bleeding wrist and, though she feels that her heart will break, she knows that she has to push this through now. *Be strong, Janet.* She approaches swiftly but carefully, all too aware that she can't yet see the tool Nora has used. 'Let me see your wrist.'

Nora stands pale but defiant, her chin up and her eyes averted – not from the wound or the blood, Janet realises, but from her. She makes no attempt to stop Janet examining it, though. The horizontal cut is deep and needs to be sutured. 'Ellen,' Janet calls, willing her voice to remain steady. 'We need a dressing tray.'

Janet looks again at the wound. 'Nora, we need to have this stitched. What did you use?' Nora opens her right palm to reveal a bloody razor blade. Janet takes it and places it carefully out of reach. 'Let's get this seen to. Do you have anything else to hurt yourself with?'

Nora shakes her head.

'Good. You know we'll have to do a search.'

'There isn't anything else,' Nora says, her voice strong and unrepentant.

Janet knows she now needs her own strong voice again. 'How dare you behave like this? Like a spoiled child who didn't get her own way. One of the nurses will dress your wrist, then we'll have you off to casualty. You'll clean this mess up yourself when you get back – no one else is going to do it for you. And if you want to stay here and revert to how you were, then that's fine. But you'll do it on your own.'

As Janet turns, Nora shouts, 'You should just have left me alone, but you've woken me up. And now you expect things from me. I can't do this.' Her voice descends to a whisper. 'I'll disappoint you, and then you'll be just like everyone else.'

Janet winces. *Am I just like everyone else? A do-gooder who goes home to sleep at night? Someone who just walks away when things get too difficult to follow through?*

Nora's energy seems to collapse, all the fight draining from her before Janet's eyes. 'I'm sorry, Janet,' Nora mutters. 'I didn't mean that.'

Janet sighs. 'You don't need to be sorry, Nora. Maybe you're right. Maybe it's just too late. Maybe you don't have what it takes. Maybe I misjudged everything. We should just forget it and you can go back to being who you were. That's just fine.'

She can almost see the reality of the situation clicking into place in Nora's head. And suddenly, Janet knows that it will all be OK.

Nora stares into her eyes. 'You did that on purpose, didn't you?' she says finally.

'Who, me? Did what?' Janet's mouth curves into a smile. 'I'll give you a tip in case you ever need it – when someone is in a self-pitying mess, there are two ways of getting them out of it. One is to make them angry and the other is to make them laugh. Better still, use both.'

Nora's face is like thunder, but her anger gives way suddenly to a wan smile.

'Feeling better now?' Janet says.

Nora nods.

'You know what needs to happen next.' Janet turns to one of the nurses standing by. 'Caroline, there's a blade there that needs to be disposed of,' she says. 'Would you have one of the nurses do a search, please? I'll just do a quick referral letter, then we can get Nora to casualty.'

Suddenly she feels shaky, and an overwhelming weariness assaults her. Without another word she walks directly to the nursing office, desperately trying not to cry. Only when she is through the door does she realise she is not alone, but it would be too awkward to leave now.

Ellen looks up. Janet flops on a chair and closes her eyes and breathes. *Please don't say anything.* Minutes pass and she feels the tension slowly ebb from her muscles.

'Cup of tea?' Ellen's voice is soft and kind and perfectly timed.

Janet nods with her eyes still closed, and Ellen bustles off to make it.

With cup held in both hands to hide her tremor, Janet takes small, grateful sips, not ready yet to say anything. She knows that Ellen's wise enough to give her time. Eventually, she sighs. 'Let me write the referral, and then she'll need transport.'

'I'll sort that,' says Ellen, lifting the phone.

'I was awful to her,' Janet says.

'No, you weren't.'

'I was.'

'This could go on for ever,' laughs Ellen.

Janet drains her cup and places it on the desk. 'I'm sure she can do it,' she says.

'I'm sure you're right.' At last, Janet lifts her eyes to those of this nursing sister whom she trusts so much. 'Don't worry. I'll watch her,' Ellen says.

Janet nods. 'Best I go.' It's both a statement and a question.

'Yes, I think so.'

'OK.' Janet stands, and suddenly the overwhelming weariness returns. 'Do you think—?'

'No,' Ellen says firmly. 'Go. Rest a bit. We'll take care of things here.'

'Of course you will.' Janet smiles. 'I have no doubt.' And she walks out into the ward, and out into the clean air.

Janet really could have done with an early night, but by seven o'clock she knows it's not going to happen. Outpatients runs late and she can't leave without completing the paperwork with Nora, who is now bandaged from fingers to forearm and looks shamefaced, but at least attempts a smile.

'Shall we talk about it?' says Janet.

'I'm sorry,' says Nora, though she avoids eye contact. 'I cleaned up my room.'

'Good. You know I have to ask some questions, so let's get that bit out of the way. Are you ready?'

She nods.

'Did you want to kill yourself?'

'No.'

'Do you want to kill yourself now?'

'No.'

'Did you plan this?'

'No.'

Janet cocks her head on one side and looks at Nora from under her brows. 'Yet you had a blade?'

'I've had it for a very long time.'

I won't ask for how long. 'Where did you hide it?'

Nora avoids Janet's eyes. 'In the hem of the curtain.'

'Clever . . .' and Janet can't hide a wry smile.

'I hoped I'd never need it.'

'You didn't.'

'No. Well . . .'

'Nora, you haven't done this for nearly twenty years – at least, according to your notes.'

'Sister Cummings beat me for doing it. I never did it again.'

Janet reaches across and lays her finger on Nora's right wrist. 'Well,' she says, 'no one's going to beat you now, but please don't ever do it again. This is now a behaviour of the past.'

She shakes her head and looks back at the form she has to complete. 'Are you depressed?' *What a stupid list of questions.*

'No . . . Frightened, I think. But not depressed.'

There's a short pause and Janet looks at her keenly. 'Why are you frightened, Nora? Is it just about leaving the hospital, or is there something else?'

Nora stares at her for a moment, and looks unsure as to what she really wants to say. She drops her chin, then lifts her face again, her eyes on Janet's.

'That I'm too much for you. And that when I'm gone, you'll forget me,' she says, then drops her gaze till her eyes fix on the leg of Janet's chair.

Janet has to lower her own eyes for a moment. 'I've told you before, Nora. I'll never forget you. And you're not too much for me, either. You could have asked me that without hurting yourself.'

Nora nods. 'I'm sorry.'

'You don't have to keep saying sorry to me. I know it's a difficult time, but I also know that you've come such a long way and it would be a shame to go backwards now.' *Enough said.* 'OK.' Janet lightens the tone. 'What have we learned?'

'To think and talk and act rather than react,' Nora recites.

Janet nods.

'To clarify confusion with questions.'

Janet nods.

'That I don't need razor blades.'

'No . . . You don't shave, do you?' And they both smile. It's over.

But Nora swiftly lowers her eyes again and Janet focuses on

the crown of Nora's bowed head. 'Nora, why don't you look at me?' Slowly, she lifts her head. 'When people who care for each other have an argument, or something difficult happens, ideally when they get to the point that both of them can say sorry, then it's over. So, I'd like to say I'm sorry, too. Sorry that I scared you earlier and sorry that maybe I could have explained things better. And also that you felt the need to harm yourself. I want you to know that, for me, we are just where we were, except that we've both learned something. So now, we start just where we left off and I'll see you tomorrow. OK?'

Janet can feel Nora's eyes searching her face, as though unable to believe her luck. Then slowly those green eyes moisten, and she looks twenty years younger. She doesn't blink, though a couple of tears escape silently down her cheeks, and as Janet watches, she knows she did the right thing.

'OK,' Nora murmurs.

Chapter Sixteen

1987
Forty-seven years

The weeks pass in a flurry of activity, with Nora no longer a passive bystander but fully engaged in her own future. She's visited the group home several times and has seen the room that's going to be hers. She can hardly believe it. A room of her own! And tomorrow she will leave Hillinghurst for good. She's done some packing – all her possessions fit into a small brown leather case – and she sits on her bed this last evening, hardly able to be still and yet simultaneously hardly daring to move. She just has to get through tonight.

There's a soft knock on the door and she starts. It's nearly nine o'clock. No one comes to the rooms this late. None of the other women stirs, so Nora tiptoes to the door.

There stands Janet, smiling, with an envelope in her hand.

'I brought you a card,' she says softly, stretching out her hand and peering past Nora at the sleeping women. 'I thought it would be nice if we just had a few minutes together because you'll be so busy in the morning. Shall we just walk down the corridor for a while?'

They stroll in a companionable silence until they reach a window and stop, looking out into the night. The moonlight sparkling on fresh snow has created a wonderland across which a fox has walked, its footprints in a perfectly straight line directly towards and out, through those gates that Nora felt would always imprison her, to the freedom beyond – the path that Nora will follow in just a few short hours.

'Nora,' Janet says, 'I want you to know just how proud I am of all you've done, but the most important thing is that you're proud of yourself. I know you can do this. It won't always be easy, but just keep remembering how far you've come, and keep going.'

And as easily as if it had always been, Janet slips an arm round Nora's shoulders and squeezes while they both continue to look straight ahead, as if into the future.

'I'm inspired by your courage, to say nothing of your wisdom and your beauty as a human being. Sometimes places like this destroy those things, but even though you've lost so much, here you are, whole, standing on your own. From tomorrow, you can choose.'

Janet holds her palms together, steps back, nods again and is gone.

It's five in the morning, and Nora has been awake for hours. A spark of excitement dances somewhere deep within her and she can hardly believe that this is the last time she'll wake up here. She doesn't want to disturb the others, so she grabs her cardigan and wraps it around her shoulders. She folds her arms then silently moves to the window where, with a single finger, she lifts the curtain. She knows that when she goes through those gates this morning, she'll be leaving much more than Hillinghurst behind her. There are almost fifty years of memories here, the shadows of people long gone: Peggy, Joe, Gladys, Stan, Dr Stilworth, Dr Mason, Sister Cummings and many more. Recollections of pain, and some pleasure too. And Angela . . . She'll be the hardest to leave.

Fenshaw still twinkles in the distance. Whenever she's allowed herself to think that leaving might be possible, she's imagined returning home there. She'd fantasise that her mother would be so happy that she'd cry; her father would have forgiven her and would hold her in his arms for a long time, his cheek on the top of her head, saying nothing, but breathing her in with the pride she always knew he felt. And they'd sit around the table and eat a special meal and tell stories and laugh. Then, after dinner, they'd play the piano and sing. Robert would be there, and Auntie Isabel, too. Mrs Lampeter would live in the same little house on the outskirts of the village where, as a child, Nora would go if she needed to hide.

But she won't be returning to Fenshaw. Not ever.

She lets go of the curtain and surveys the room. The other three women are dark mounds of sadness, proof of life lost. At some time, they must also leave, but Nora knows that none of them is as well or as lucky as she is, and she wonders what will become of them. She hopes that they will all survive.

Under her mattress, she has a collection of tablets, wrapped in sheets of toilet roll. Her dilemma is whether to dispose of them or take them with her. Like the razor blade, they've been her insurance policy and her potential escape route for years, and knowing they were there has helped her cope. They've been moved to so many different hiding places, and she's amazed they've never been discovered – how they escaped attention when her room was searched recently, she'll never know. In fact, she's had them for so long that they probably wouldn't work anyhow. She'll flush them down the toilet.

It's hardly light when Nora sneaks out, her coat wrapped tightly around her and her woollen hat pulled down. Her gloved hands are buried in her pockets and her head is bowed, butting into the frosty morning air. She walks as fast as she can, enjoying the squeaking and crunching of snow beneath her boots. She's on a mission and doesn't want to be seen, but she can do no more about her tracks than the fox could about his.

She puts her weight against the door through the garden wall and snow falls from a swaying branch onto her head. She shivers. Not far now.

Under the trees, there's not much snow, and all the little markers proudly poke their heads above it. Her feet know the way, and the rest of her takes in every bit of what might be her last visit here.

'Angela, I'm not really leaving you,' she says as she clears a space around the marker with her gloved finger. 'I'm taking you with me in my heart.'

She kisses her gloved hand and puts it flat on the very spot she imagines Angela's heart to be. From under her coat she produces her snow globe, which she shakes, then stands it on the grave. The snow covering Angela and the snow in the globe seem to mingle. She holds her hand flat on the grave for one last time, then she turns and heads back to Rowan, hoping she hasn't been missed.

Audrey's car turns north. Nora looks out of the back window at the gates she has been behind all these years, and now, at last, they are behind her. Then she gazes back down the road beyond the gates, in the direction of Fenshaw. A single tear runs down her face and she brushes it away smartly as she catches Audrey's eyes upon her.

'Are you all right?' Audrey asks, smiling gently.

'Yes,' says Nora, though her voice is breathy and uncertain.

'It's going to be fine,' Audrey encourages.

'Yes.' She lifts her hand and places it flat on the car window in a gesture of goodbye. She bites her bottom lip, determined not to cry. She managed to stay dry-eyed throughout the farewells from staff and patients alike, but was glad that she and Janet agreed yesterday that there'd be no goodbye today since they'll see each other in a couple of days when Nora comes for day care.

Now she sits stiffly, staring straight ahead, hardly trusting herself to even look out at the stark trees, beautifully back-lit by the low March sun, their spartan trunks rising proudly out of the snow-covered fields. On her lap, carefully wrapped, is her music box. Her letters, painstakingly sorted into date order, are with all of her other belongings in the little brown case. She also has a new handbag and a blue purse, a twenty-pound note and some coins, and is wearing her warm coat and new shoes that aren't very practical but look better than her wellington boots.

In the last month, Nora and Audrey have taken this drive several times, initially going back to Hillinghurst in the afternoon. However, twice now Nora has stayed overnight at the group home, to get used to her new bedroom with its sunny yellow paint, its pine bed covered with an orange and yellow candlewick counterpane and white-painted chest of three drawers. The wardrobe has a mirrored door, just like the one she had when she was a girl. Six coat hangers are waiting. Her letters will go in the drawer of the little wooden cabinet by her bed.

In her mind, she reruns Janet's words of last night and smiles as she glances down and frees the hand cradling her precious ballerina to tug on her sleeve and hide her wrist. Her fingers stray to the healing scars. Interesting that Janet wasn't really angry. Not like the last time. But it hasn't been mentioned since each of them apologised the next day, when the stitches were removed and papery tags of skin were still trying to dislodge themselves as new cells pushed up from below. Janet said that, just like that, there'll still be parts of herself that need to be dislodged before she can be truly healed of Hillinghurst, so they're going to continue to work on that.

She pulls Janet's card out of her handbag and reads it again.

> *Thank you for the journey so far. You're one of the most inspirational women I've ever met and you've graced my life. Go out now and grace the world. You can do this, Nora.*

She blinks and looks straight ahead.
Yes, I can.

Nora sits on her bed in her yellow room, where the counterpane has been drawn back in welcome. Her ballerina is perfectly poised opposite her, beside some fresh daffodils. She kicks off her shoes and lies down, staring at the ceiling, then whispers into the room, and to whomever might be listening, 'Thank you.' She closes her eyes and allows silent tears to run down and well in her ears.

After forty-seven years and four months, she is free.

Chapter Seventeen

Nora is amazed at how quickly she is able to establish a new way of life. After years of regimentation, rules and rigid discipline, she has made a fairly smooth transition into a new groove that's still being carved out for her. There have been moments when doubt has grabbed her by her ankles and tried to pull her down but, in the main, she's coping well. However, the oddest things can thrust her back into the past, and into a murky puddle of memories she'd prefer to forget. But similarly, minor miracles thrill her. Someone being cheerily kind on the bus; the conductor who greets her with, 'Good morning, young lady,' as she pays her fare; the robin that seems to wait for her in the mornings, sitting atop one of the concrete posts at the entrance to the front garden; the hedgehog in residence in the back garden, watching with her; and the gymnastics of the squirrels as they try to get into the bird feeders.

Nora, aided and abetted by Mrs Singh's children, Dakshar, aged four, and Maaran, a sturdy boy of seven, has taken over the job of filling the bird feeders with seeds and peanuts. The children warm her heart every time she sees them, in their bobble hats with ear flaps and snuggly gloves, brown faces glowing with delight. They've named the collective feeders 'The Singh Breakfast Bar for Birds', and they report to each other daily about how many regulars and how many new visitors show up.

Nora often watches Mrs Singh with her children. These are the first children with whom she's been in close contact all these years, and they're helping her to remember some of the sweetness of her own childhood. The gentle pleasure of picking strawberries with her mother; shelling newly gathered peas for Sunday lunch; burying their noses in the sweet peas and sniffing their wonderful perfume until she felt quite dizzy. And sometimes good memories of her father too. Collecting pine-cones – some to decorate, and some to light the fire and fill the house with their crisp fragrance; his pride as she played the piano. And, of course, she thinks about Robert. Dear, lost Robert. Snatches of conversations; giggles as, at ten and eight respectively, they practised duets on the piano and fell into riotous laughter when their four hands seemed to get into a tangle. She's rewriting her past, nurturing her child and adolescent self, and trying to forgive herself for having set in motion the dreadful avalanche that concluded in the destruction of their family.

But, of course, sometimes she still lies awake in the silvered moonlight, imagining what could have been – how old Angela would be now; how she would have looked at Dakshar's age. She might even have had grandchildren by now. Such mischief of her mind offers pleasant warmth initially, but if she lingers too long, the memories of what she has lost start to burn.

'Nora, are you going to live with us for ever?' Dakshar asked last Sunday.

'I don't know,' Nora replied, and that simple question opened the door to the breathtaking possibility that maybe, just maybe, she could some time have a flat – a home – of her own.

There are still times, of course, when the pain rears its head again, though they're less often these days. Whenever it does, she wraps herself in a crocheted blanket, curls up with her feet up beside her – now there's no one to say she mustn't – and watches television. And no one shouts at her when she sits all day working her way through a shelf full of books. Paradise!

Mrs Singh hovers occasionally and makes that wonderful Indian movement with her neck and frowns, 'Nora, Nora, no smile tonight? I bring you some hot chocolate,' and pads off into the kitchen; always spoils her with a biscuit too. Whenever this happens, Nora is reminded of the beautiful Peggy and a very special biscuit that changed her life.

She concentrates on the joy of hot showers, scented soap and soft, colourful towels that don't tear at her skin, and hopes she'll never become complacent and forget how lucky she is.

And she has her routine. Off to catch the eight twenty-five bus to Hillinghurst for day care on weekday mornings. With Iris's help she's making a sampler for Janet, rekindling her adolescent love of embroidery. She's also learning to paint and has sessions with the art therapist, who sees things in Nora's paintings that Nora herself had never thought of. Then, twice a week, she has an appointment with Janet. At the group home she takes her turn on the evening cooking rota and, on Sunday mornings, she helps with the baking. Last week, she made a cherry cake according to a recipe that she'd copied into her notebook before she left Hillinghurst. Mrs Singh was very complimentary and asked if she might take a slice upstairs for each of her children, which thrilled Nora immensely. This weekend Mrs Singh is going to teach her to make a curry, something she's never tasted, though the smell of the spices tantalise her when Mrs Singh is cooking. Life is better than she could ever have imagined, as long as she keeps busy and doesn't think too much.

This week, Nora's appointment with Janet has been moved to the acute unit since the other office isn't available. Nora is almost at the door but, suddenly, she stops in her tracks. There in front of her, aged but still recognisable, is a face from the past. Her mouth opens and words tumble out before she can stop them. 'Bill Oldbury? Good heavens.'

He peers at her through smudged, speckled glasses that Nora itches to clean. Then he frowns, clearly trying to place her, and she can see on his face the moment he does. 'Nora Jennings?'

'That's right.' An elated laugh escapes her as she struggles to reconcile her memory of him with the man standing before her.

'Good God. It must be forty years.'

'Nearer fifty . . .'

'I thought you'd left the area years ago. Are you back here now?'

'Er, y-yes,' she stammers. 'Yes. Yes, I am.'

But now, even though this tall, thin man actually bears little resemblance to the beautiful boy she remembers laughing with her and Robert at the church gates after choir practice, elation morphs into panic as memories start to swirl in her mind, dredging up with them emotions long repressed. With them comes that sickening, dizzying surge of nausea and the desire to escape. She puts out a hand to the wall to steady herself.

'What are you doing here?' he asks but, without waiting for an answer – for which Nora is immeasurably grateful – he goes on. 'I've been here ages. I got really sick and they brought me in here, but I'm about to go home any day now.'

Of the many questions she may have wanted to ask, only one emerges. 'Are you better, then?'

'You wouldn't believe it,' he says.

She tries to smile, despite the fact that she's losing her grip by the minute. *Neither would you.*

'A couple of months ago I thought I was dying. My thyroid had packed up. Amazing what they can do these days. But I'm going to complain that they put me on a psychiatric ward – there's nothing wrong with my mind.'

'They must have thought there was,' she blurts out, and then blushes at her own rudeness. But he doesn't seem to notice.

'Have you caught up with Robert since you got back?' he asks.

Nora feels as though the air has been sucked out of her lungs, and she can't speak or even breathe, but again, Bill appears to be completely unaware.

'I haven't seen him for a long time,' he goes on.

'Nor me,' she somehow manages, the world now spinning.

'He's far too big for us now.' His mouth turns down in a spiteful grimace. 'They say he'll be a minister in the next shuffle.'

Nora desperately wants to leave, to run. 'I'm . . . I'm sorry, I have to go now,' she says, and tries to turn, pressing against the wall for support.

'I thought he was better than that,' he presses on, and the judgement in his tone slithers into her brain and ignites a fire that shocks her back into the present. She turns, bristling, her chin jutting forward. 'Better than what?'

'Well, we picked up again maybe thirty years ago. All that kids' stuff between us was over.'

'What kids' stuff?'

'You know – choir boys and all that. A bit of . . . well – you know.' But he watches Nora pale. 'My God – you didn't know, did you?' He laughs incredulously, spite in his eyes.

The room is spinning again and Nora's breath catches in her throat. She doesn't really want to know what he means, yet maybe she does. She wants to scream at him, or even hit him. She searches the corridor, hoping for help, needing to escape.

She catches Dale's eye through the observation window and he's on his feet immediately and hurrying through the office door towards her. 'Are you all right, Nora?'

'I'm, er, I'm, I'm . . .'

'Bill, why don't you go along?' Dale says with a flick of his head to encourage him into motion. 'And Nora, come with me for a minute.'

But Bill doesn't move. 'I know her. We were kids together,' he says. 'I had a fling with her cousin, that's all. But she's a prig, like all of that family.'

Nora looks away, clutching her hand to her mouth as tears start to brim.

'All right, Bill, all right,' says Dale firmly. Then he turns to Nora and puts an arm around her. 'Nora, come.'

Once in the office, Nora sits perfectly still. Dale has plied her with a cup of tea, stronger and with less milk than she prefers. She doesn't usually have sugar, but the sweetness is just right. The last five minutes have changed everything, opened doors to ideas she'd never even considered. She's known Robert all her life – how could she not have known that he . . . ? But, at last, so many things make sense. *Yes, it all makes sense.*

In all these years, she's forgotten nothing of him. From the last time she saw him, that first Christmas morning here, she's followed him as best she could – from his time in Stoke Mandeville Hospital to what she's been able to pick up about his career and his political profile. She's seen his handsome, if ageing, face in the tabloids, and more lately on television, and has gone through phases of resentment, anger, and even some bitterness on the way, but the love has always remained. But now, this feels like finding the last piece of a jigsaw she started fifty years ago.

She allows her mind to go back to those very young days – the beautiful golden boy who all the girls loved, though he never seemed interested. To their first kiss that was full of sweetness, but not passion. And she always wondered why he never made any attempt to make love to her again after that one night, even though she knew he loved her. But now she realises: not like she loved him. She'd been confused and upset that, in the weeks that followed, before she found she was pregnant, he had seemed to avoid her – like when she searched for him at church, the Sunday before she was first taken to Hillinghurst. For the first time in decades, she allows herself to remember the full force of the betrayal she felt when he didn't come for her. Her anger, her shame, her sorrow. But now, finally, she understands. He must have been terrified of anyone finding out – including her. And a tiny, shameful part of him might just have been relieved to have avoided a future in which he would have been forced to marry her and live a lie. Although she is not quite able to forgive just yet, she is grateful to finally understand.

She feels Dale's eyes upon her face and shifts her gaze to him.

'Nora, are you sure you don't want me to get Janet?'

'No, thank you. It's all right. I'm OK now. I have to catch the bus,' she says, her face slack with shock, but her eyes clearer.

Dale looks at her askance. 'I'd rather that Janet had a look at you. And you have an appointment with her shortly, don't you?'

'No . . . I mean, yes, but I . . . I'm OK, really.' She gives him a gentle smile. 'Please just tell Janet I wasn't feeling very well and I had to go. I'm fine.' She hurries off, leaving Dale in her wake, his brow furrowed with concern.

She's part way down the corridor when Bill Oldbury calls after her. 'There's a lot more I could tell you about him. He's not all he makes out.'

Nora turns, anger flashing in her eyes. 'You know nothing about him,' she says.

'I know more than you think,' he retorts. 'He used to come and play chess with me – and other stuff,' he sneers. 'Then he fell for some guy in London and he dropped me like a stone.'

Nora stands statue-still, her eyes locked on his, wanting to make some retort, but speechless.

Dale's voice booms down the corridor as he hurries towards them. 'Bill. I'd like you to leave Nora alone. Go to the day room and I'll see you there. I will not have you upsetting other people.' He puts his hand on Nora's arm. 'Nora, are you OK?'

Nora looks at him with her head high and her eyes sharp. 'Yes, I am, thank you,' she says, and smiles. 'I'm really fine. Honestly.' And she walks out into the fresh air and breathes deeply, and with every breath out, she lets go of things that have haunted her for almost fifty years.

Chapter Eighteen

Janet is devastated. Last evening Miles Little threw himself in front of a train. Again and again, she has imagined him in those minutes between him absconding from hospital and making it to the station. Those crucial minutes when his mind was made up and possibly finally at peace. Nearly over. No more shame. No more pain. It would be finished; granting his parents a peaceful retirement at last. But it's the loneliness of it that tortures her. Before she left last night, she told all the acute patients about the situation in the presence of Dale and the other nurses, who could then support anyone in need. Extra observation was made available to anyone who themselves may be suicidal – a string of copycat attempts would not be a good thing. Today there needs to be a second round of support, since feelings will have changed overnight. Janet will have to present herself for scrutiny as well. It would happen when Dr Pauling is away for a few days – what a thing to return to.

She arrives at work and only discovers when she visits the Ladies' before her meeting that she's forgotten to apply her makeup. She scrutinises her face – pale and drawn with puffy, red-rimmed eyes. She sighs and splashes water on her face and pinches her cheeks. She really would prefer to see no one today.

Back in her room after the gruelling enquiry with three senior consultants, Janet closes her door, but no sooner has she sat down than one of the nurses taps upon it and opens it a crack.

'Janet, are you OK?'

'Not bad.'

The door opens wider. 'These came for you.'

'Flowers?'

The card reads:

Thank you for all you did for Miles. We always knew that this was inevitable, though of course we will miss our beautiful son for ever. Albert and Annie Little

And once again, the tears come. Tears for Miles, tears for his parents, tears for all those tortured by mental illness and also for her inability to help more, despite her passionate attempts to do so.

Half an hour later, Janet still sits with the flowers in her lap, staring out of her window, when there's another knock on the door. She doesn't respond, but then it comes again, this time with Dale's special rhythm code, and she calls to him to come in.

'You OK?' he says as he enters.

'So-so.' She sighs. 'I think I'm going to take myself out for lunch.'

'Why don't you just sit for a while – or even take the afternoon off?'

'I've got a lot to do. I just want to walk a bit. I'll be all right, I promise.' She manages a smile but both of them know there'll be more tears between here and there.

'Are you sure?'

'Dale, you're starting to sound like my mother.'

'All right. Promise me you'll call if you're not.'

'I promise.'

'Where are you going to go? They tell me that new Italian's quite good.'

'OK. Maybe I'll try that. But I don't have any appetite. I just need to be on my own a bit.' Her eyes fill with tears.

Dale steps closer, but she puts up her hand. 'I'll be done for if you hug me,' she says, her voice cracking. The phone rings. Janet looks at it but doesn't move.

'Do you want me to take it or just ignore it?' Dale says.

'Better take it.'

He lifts the phone. 'Dr Humphreys' office ... Er, just a moment, please.'

He puts his hand over the mouthpiece. 'It's Dr P. Do you want me to make an excuse?'

She shakes her head and reaches for the phone.

'Dr Pauling?'

'Janet, I wonder if you could pop into my office when you have a minute?'

'I'm free now.'

'So am I. Shall I order you some tea? And a sandwich?'

'Just tea would be perfect, thank you.'

She hands Dale the phone, and he replaces it on its cradle. 'Looks like I'm not going to get any peace, after all,' she says, sighing and checking her face in her pocket mirror. A little red around the eyes, but nothing she can't blame on a bit of a cold. She gives Dale a wry smile, and heads off to Dr Pauling's office.

When she knocks tentatively and opens the door, she finds Dr Pauling sitting on one of the easy chairs looking uncharacteristically relaxed, with a pot of tea, cups and biscuits on a small table beside him. He has certainly been different of late, but she still feels wary.

'Come and sit down, Janet.' He smiles kindly while pouring the tea and, perhaps for the first time, she can see how he might be with his patients and she finds herself unexpectedly moved. 'You're having a bit of a hard time, aren't you?' He pauses. 'Milk? Sugar?'

'Just milk, please.' He complies and hands her the china cup on its saucer.

'Biscuit?' He offers the plate.

She shakes her head. 'No, thank you.'

'Janet, I know things haven't been particularly easy between us and I might be the last person you'd be inclined to talk to, but I do try to support my staff. I don't want you to be dashed by the events of the last twenty-four hours.'

Janet lowers her eyes, feeling unsure and vulnerable.

'I had a chat with our colleagues after your meeting this morning. They were as impressed by you as I am. Janet, I know that you did everything you could and this is neither your fault nor your responsibility. Sadly, these things do happen. I trust your judgement.' He tries to smile, but is clearly as uncomfortable as she is with this break from the normal confines of their relationship. 'You did what you thought was right, Janet. That's all we can do.'

'And Miles is dead,' she says, so quietly it's almost a whisper.

He pauses, looking directly into her eyes. 'You have my compassion. I remember the first patient I lost to suicide. It was dreadful, and no matter what anyone said or did to try to help, I just had to work through that in my own time. You will too.' He smiles. 'You never take time off, do you, Janet? We're working day after day, with people who are suffering in all sorts of ways. Sometimes we just need to take the odd day to rest.'

'I always think I'm better working.' She stares into the tea that she's hardly touched. 'Thank you for taking time to talk with me,' she says. 'I'm very grateful.' She fights back tears.

He clears his throat, returns his eyes to hers and changes the topic, for which she is grateful. 'Your work with Nora Jennings seems to have caught the imagination of the nursing staff,' he says, no longer looking at her but playing with his spoon. 'Of course, I'd have expected no less from you.'

Janet really wants to leave, and yet it feels as though he's not quite finished. She looks at her hands and waits for the bomb to fall. It's been all too easy thus far. Best get it over with.

He clears his throat yet again. 'Janet, this may not be the best of times to mention this, but . . .'

Here it comes. She raises her eyes, narrowing them a little, girding herself for the onslaught. 'Whatever it is, I'd rather you tell me now,' she says.

Something flits across his face that she doesn't quite understand. Shock? Amusement? Mischief? Whatever it is, she'd rather he just got on with it.

'I wanted to have a word with you about a consultant post that's coming up in London. Ben Wales is retiring, so it'll be a general adult psychiatry position and I have no doubt whatsoever that you'd be a good candidate. I also feel you're more than ready. So, if you do happen to consider applying, I'd be happy to be a referee. Though we may have had our differences, your work is of the highest calibre and I'm impressed with what you do both here and on the back wards.'

Janet blinks. Did she hear that properly?

Dr Pauling reads her well – he is a psychiatrist, after all – and his eyes dance with amusement as he treats her to a broad smile before he becomes serious again. 'And if it's somewhere in your consciousness that this might be my way of trying to distract you from your grief about Miles Little, I'd like to disabuse you of such a notion.' He stands, and Janet follows suit. 'Think about it, and maybe we could talk another time. If I were your psychiatrist, which I'm not, I'd advise you to take the next couple of days off. Take your time. Relax and think.'

Nora, busy in the art therapy room, pauses with her brush dripping paint onto her paper, while she listens.

'Yes, and you know how she loves her patients,' Iris says to Audrey as they both lean back against the counter, shaking their heads sadly.

Nora listens intently.

'But she won't hear of taking time off. I don't know how she's coping. She's had such a hard time with Ian and everything.'

Nora stands up abruptly and almost knocks over her stool.

It's mid-afternoon by the time she gets her first sighting of Janet walking in the grounds, looking distracted and sad and without her lipstick – a sure sign that something's amiss. Nora remembers the day, many years ago, when Nurse Turret was distressed about losing her baby, and she wonders how Janet really is and who supports her when something painful happens.

*   *   *

Janet walks with her head down, and doesn't see Nora approaching until she's there on the path, emanating an unusual sense of purpose, one hand behind her back. Janet stops and tries to dredge up a smile.

'I was looking for you,' Nora says.

'Oh?'

'I wanted to say that I'm sorry about your patient and I brought you these.' She thrusts out a hand, bearing a posy of flowers. 'One of the gardeners said I could pick them. There's a note.' And with that she turns and scurries away.

Janet stares at the marigolds, lavender, daisies and nasturtiums. 'Thank you, Nora,' she calls to her retreating back. 'They're beautiful.'

Janet tugs at the little note stuck in the twine and opens it.

I'm sorry something awful happened. Now I know that I could never kill myself so please don't worry about me.
Thank you.
Nora

For a moment Janet stares after Nora, so healthy now, hurrying back to the day unit, and allows tears once again to run down her cheeks.

Chapter Nineteen

Janet lies on her bed, staring at the reflection of the almost full moon in her dressing-table mirror, her mind taking her back twenty-five years or more.

She and Ian stand against the rail of a ferry, taking them back across the river as they watch the reflected moon dancing in the ripples on the water. Ian has his arm around her and her head rests so perfectly in the hollow of his shoulder. It feels blissful. She wishes it would never end. He is caressing her hair with his lips and she raises her face to his and they kiss hungrily, yearning for each other.

'I think we should get married,' he whispers.

She draws back and looks at him. It's only a matter of weeks since they met.

He reads her eyes. 'I already know,' he says, kissing the tip of her nose. 'Time isn't going to make any difference. I'm in love with you and that's that.'

'But we—'

'You don't have to say anything. Just take your time, relax and think. It's fine. I'm not going anywhere unless you tell me to.'

Outside her bedroom window, the wind suddenly picks up and a briar of the climbing rose lashes across the reflection of the moon, tearing it in half.

An hour later she's in the sitting room, curled up in her dressing gown, a cup of hot milk on the side table beside her, reading lamp focused over her shoulder on the *British Journal of Psychiatry* that is open on her lap. The advert for the consultant post stares back at her. She reads it again and closes the journal, staring ahead, her stomach churning and her skin tingling.

Take your time. Relax and think . . .

Am I ready? Do I want to be in London? What about Ian? What about Nora?

Abruptly she swings her feet off the sofa and onto the floor, grabs her cup and the journal and takes them both into the kitchen. She places the cup in the sink and runs some water into it, picks up the spoon and the milk pan and places them in the sink too, then switches off the light and heads for her bedroom.

Take your time. Relax and think.

It's still early, not quite dawn. She startles her friend the urban fox as she walks along, taking her time, envelope in hand. She feels quietly at peace, for the first time in months. The kaleidoscope turns. The pieces fit into a new pattern. All will be well.

She approaches the post-box and pauses, taking her time . . . She looks at the envelope, rereads the address and takes it right to the lip of the mouth of the letterbox, then draws it back, lifts it to her mouth, kisses it and quickly drops it in the box.

She turns and picks up her speed, first to a jog and then to her running pace. She's back in gear.

Janet has been dreading this afternoon for some time. She swallows hard as Nora takes her seat for today's session. The niceties out of the way, she decides to get straight to it, to allow maximum time for Nora to process it. 'Nora, I have something I need to talk to you about. You know I told you that I couldn't stay here for ever? Well, I've been offered a consultant post in another hospital and so I'll be leaving Hillinghurst in a couple of months.'

She pauses a moment. Though Nora hasn't said anything, she's tapping her foot and fiddling with her fingers in a way that Janet has come to recognise means trouble.

'I've talked to Audrey and Evelyn. Your day care will still be as it is until you're ready for that to end, so they'll be continuing to see you regularly here, as always. But I want to talk about how you and I will continue – or not.'

Nora inhales sharply and she lifts her face, anger vying with hurt in her eyes.

Janet continues. 'I'll be very happy to see you as an outpatient – that's if you'd like that, but if—'

'Why don't you just let me go?' Nora interrupts.

Janet's heart freezes. 'What do you mean?'

'You don't have to stay here and look after me. I'm not a baby,' Nora snaps, turning her body away from Janet and folding her arms.

'I know,' Janet says, now on the defensive.

'So why don't you just go?'

'My new job doesn't start for a while yet, which is great as it will give us time to talk about it and make plans about what we both want to do. And I want you to be able to say anything you want to say about me leaving.'

'Why?' Nora pouts. 'Would it make any difference?'

'Not to my leaving, no. But it might help for you to tell me what you really think about it, and be angry if you need to be.'

'Help who?'

'Both of us.'

'Why do you need help?' Nora snaps.

Janet looks at her intently. 'I want to make sure that your care is ongoing for as long as you need it and that you have the opportunity to really express your feelings,' she says.

'Why, when my feelings don't count?'

'Nora, they do count.'

'Well, they're not going to make any difference. You'll still leave me anyway.'

'I'll be in a different hospital. I'll be further away – but that doesn't mean that I'm *leaving* you.' Janet feels lost in the nuance of this herself, but she tries her best to look reassuring.

'Yes, it does.'

'As I said, if you'd still like outpatient appointments with me, we can arrange that. It just means that it will be further away.'

An uncomfortable silence descends until Janet can bear it no longer. 'Nora, the point is that you have a choice, even though the options might be limited. You could decide to see me, or, if you prefer, not to see me. Somebody else will be taking over my job here, and if you'd prefer to see him, that's absolutely fine.'

'Him?'

'Yes. Dr Bradley Newton is coming to take over my job here. I know him quite well and he's a good man and a thorough psychiatrist. So, if you want to, you could choose to do that instead.'

'You see, it doesn't matter to you,' Nora fires.

'That's not what I said.'

'I don't want to see anyone else,' she says petulantly.

'That's fine then. Since we've worked together for so long, I thought that it would probably be better for you that we continue to see each other, but I want you to be able to choose.'

Nora's mouth hardens into a thin line.

'Maybe you'd like to think about it – and please don't worry about hurting me,' Janet says.

'Why? Don't you care?'

'Nora, I care a great deal,' she says patiently. 'That's why we're talking about it rather than me just walking away.'

Despite herself, Nora squints from under her brows, reading Janet's face, but says nothing. And then the drawbridge is up and Janet knows she won't be granted access again today. They sit in silence for a few minutes. Then, without a word, Nora lifts herself off the seat and walks towards the door.

'Nora?' Janet calls, but Nora continues to walk. 'Nora! Just think of all the times that you've wished you could have the opportunity to talk about what's going to happen. Don't walk away now.'

Nora stops and turns. 'I'm taking the time you said I could have to think about it.'

'Good,' says Janet, with a reassuring smile. 'If you come to a decision, maybe you can let me know.'

It's late in the afternoon and Janet is tidying up ends before she leaves the office, shuffling things around and not making much progress, her mind on Nora. She hears her mother's voice. *The right way isn't always the easy way.* At some point she has to trust that Nora can make decisions for herself and step back to allow her to do so.

Her hand wanders to the phone, and she dials almost subconsciously. 'Ellen. I talked to Nora about me leaving.'

'How did she take it?'

'She was a bit angry, which is healthy. I offered her the option of continuing to see me as an outpatient or seeing my replacement. She's thinking about it. I think she's OK, but just in case, will you keep an eye on her? I'll be off shortly and I'll pop in in the morning. But give me a call if you need anything.'

'I will, but she hasn't come back to the ward. She usually comes back to collect her bag and check out.'

The hairs on the back of Janet's neck stand up. 'It's almost two hours since she left me.'

'Leave it with me. I'll get someone out to find her.'

'Oh, God . . .'

'I'll call you back,' says Ellen, a new urgency in her voice, and the line goes dead. Janet stands stock-still, the phone in her hand. Her heart fills with dread. Then, as quickly as she can, she dials the nursing station. There's a tap on the door.

'Come in,' she calls distractedly, still listening to the ringing tone. *Pick up, somebody!*

The door opens and there is Nora. Janet puts down the receiver and closes her eyes. She says nothing, just breathes in relief, giving her pounding heart a few moments to recover.

'I'd like to come and see you at your new hospital for my appointments, if that's all right.'

'That's just fine, Nora,' Janet says, hoping her voice sounds calm and steady. 'Just fine. We'll sort out the details when we see each other next week.'

Nora nods and, without another word, turns and leaves. Janet slumps back in her chair and closes her eyes. 'Thank you,' she murmurs, her eyes upcast.

'Ellen, false alarm,' she breathes into the phone. 'I think she'll be on her way back to you now. She's OK.'

Chapter Twenty

Even though she has been in her new consultant's post for over a week now, Janet still has a thrill when she walks into her office. In many ways it feels as though she's always been here, and she is certain that this is what she's meant to do. But this morning she has a heavy heart, having received a call from Dale last night to say that Nora was readmitted on Friday in a regressed state, refusing to eat or get up out of bed, and being more than the group home could manage. All the old doubts about how she can manage to continue Nora's care from a distance came flooding back in an instant, and she has been brooding on them ever since. She picks up the phone.

'Hi Dale, how are things this morning?'

'Not much change, I'm afraid. She did have some tea this morning but refused to eat anything. Kit's coming across to see if she can get her into the shower and coax her to have some toast in a little while. If anyone can do it, she can. Don't know whether I mentioned that I called Joe on Saturday morning and he came in to visit, but she wouldn't even look at him, let alone talk.'

'Ugh! I hate to think of her like this. Was there any warning?' she asks, feeling even more guilty.

'Evelyn mentioned maybe on Wednesday that Mrs Singh had called in to say Nora wasn't coping so well, but by Friday, she'd got a lot worse and Mrs Singh felt that Nora needed to come in.'

'Wish I'd known,' Janet grumbles.

'Why – what would you have done that we couldn't?'

'Ouch, a bit harsh, Dale,' she says, irritated. 'I know you can deal very well with bad behaviour.'

'And is that what you think this is, Janet? Bad behaviour?'

'Well, what are you calling it?'

'Heartbreak. Not a very professional term, but I think that's what it is, nevertheless.'

All at once, clarity dawns on Janet and her face crumples. 'Oh Dale, I'm sorry. I've only been gone ten days and have an appointment with her later this week, so I didn't think. Would it help if I come down?'

'At this point I think that would be helpful,' he says, his voice softer now. 'But I know you're all tied up there so there's no easy solution.'

'I'll juggle a few things around and try to get away mid-afternoon, but I need to clear that with Dr P and also Brad. Don't want to step on anyone's toes.'

There's a slight pause, just enough to tell Janet that this isn't all the difficult news Dale has to deliver. 'What else do you need to tell me?'

'Yes, well, I'm afraid you're not the most popular bunny here at the moment,' he says.

'I can imagine. How bad?'

'I guess when the baby still cries for Mummy when Daddy is doing his best to pacify it, he gets angry about being a poor second best . . .'

Janet closes her eyes. 'Understood. I'll wear my flak jacket and tin helmet.'

'Good idea.'

It's almost five by the time Janet arrives. Nora lies curled up like a little caterpillar, facing the wall.

'Hello, Nora,' Janet says.

Silence.

'Nora, I know you can hear me. It would be really nice if you turned over so we could talk.'

Nothing.

'I'm sorry you've not been feeling well.'

'Leave me alone,' Nora whispers, her face still towards the wall.

Well, at least that's something.

'Nora, I'm sorry it's hard for you, but coming back into hospital isn't going to solve things. Can we talk and see if we can find a good way forward?'

'Go away.'

Janet walks over to the next bed and stoops to collect a chair, when suddenly Nora jerks upright, her eyes searching until they finally come to rest on Janet. 'I thought you'd gone,' she says in panic.

'No. I'm not going anywhere until we've talked,' says Janet, placing the chair by the bed and sitting down. 'Nora, I can't give you any guarantees about how your life is going to be. I can't, in truth, say it's going to be fine or that it's going to work. But I do know that this isn't helpful, and I think you know that too.' She pauses. 'Do you remember when you cut yourself and I said you could have told me what you wanted to say rather than act it out? Well, you're acting this out too. I'd like you to talk to me, like the amazing woman you are, so we can discuss how we can make it feel better for you.'

Nora turns back to the wall.

Janet waits, trying to be patient, yet she knows that this needs a different approach. 'Nora!' she barks. 'At least look at me so I can talk to you. Your soul is awake now, Nora, and I, for one, am not going to give it permission to go to sleep again. You've come so far and I'm not going to sit here and let you destroy it all. So, I want you out of that bed, into the shower, dressed, and I'll see you in Dale's office in half an hour.' She stands up.

'Go away.'

'I am going away,' Janet says sharply. 'Thirty minutes. Dale's office.'

And, though she hates seeing Nora like this, she knows that she must walk away. She nods to Dale on the way and signals with her eyes for him to follow. He catches up with her at the end of the corridor. 'How did it go?'

Janet sighs. 'I don't know yet. Can I use your office?'

'Sure.'

'I've told her I'll see her there in thirty minutes.'

'OK. So, I guess the ball's in her court.'

'Yes. I hope to God she does something with it, because I haven't got anything else up my sleeve.' She sighs and leans into Dale, who puts a warm arm around her shoulders and smiles down at her. 'Well now, it just so happens that today – and for one day only – I have a special offer running: any guest using my office gets room service. Tea?'

'Dale, you're such a blessing. I want to put you in my pocket and take you to my new place.'

'You'd need a very big pocket.'

'That could be arranged.'

And he laughs as he walks away.

Janet sits in one of the two chairs at the front of the desk, quite still, eyes closed, hoping against hope that Nora will appear. She's already drunk her cup of tea and has nothing to do but wait. She's well aware that she must keep to her word and, on this occasion, thirty minutes has to be exactly thirty minutes – or less, but not more. She looks at her watch for about the tenth time. Twenty-eight minutes. She sighs, drumming her fingers on the desk. *Nora, please.*

There's a tap on the door.

'Come in,' she shouts. The door opens and a newly washed Nora stands there, hair wet and plastered to her head, eyes cast down.

Janet stands – she'd love to give Nora a hug but decides against it, for now. 'Lovely to see you, Nora. Come and have a seat.'

They both sit, but neither says anything for a while. Janet eventually breaks the silence. 'Nora, as I said before, I know it's very hard for you. And I'm sorry. I would love it if we can look at what might make things better for you.'

For a moment, it seems that Nora might not even have heard. But then she lifts her head and looks at Janet. 'I'm sorry,' she says. 'I know I have an appointment with you soon, but I thought you didn't really mean it and you'd cancel it and not see me,' she says.

'Why would I do that?'

'Because I'm a burden.'

'Not to me. You know, it feels like you wrote a little play in your head, then played all the parts and got to the end where you're abandoned, and that was that. But no one else had the chance to say anything before you acted it all out. I have no intention of cancelling your appointment – in fact, I'm really looking forward to seeing you and hearing all your news. And Audrey is all set to accompany you until you feel confident to come alone. And she's excited too.'

'Really?'

'Yes, really.'

'Oh . . .'

Janet peers wistfully at the leafy lanes around Hillinghurst as she drives back to London. She keeps coming back to what Ellen said about the relationship between doctor and patient often becoming the most important thing in the life of someone who feels they have nothing. A huge responsibility for the clinician. Nora's emergence into the light of life, having been buried years ago when she was just a child, has been nothing short of spectacular. Janet knows that Nora couldn't have done it without her, but the last thing that Janet wanted was to create dependence. She sighs, knowing there is no simple solution. All she can do is hope that the continued love and support of those around Nora will carry her through.

Chapter Twenty-One

It's a big day for Nora. After several accompanied visits to London for her appointments with Janet, today she's travelling alone by train. She has a packed lunch – a ham sandwich wrapped in greaseproof paper, a banana and a Thermos flask of tea – and she's loving watching the world go by from the comfort of her window seat. She is fascinated by her fellow passengers.

Sitting opposite her is a man of about forty. His eyes are closed, while the long fingers of his right hand tap rhythmically on the seat beside him, as though he may be silently humming to some nostalgic tune. His slight, contented smile intrigues Nora, and she wonders what memories are being evoked by the music. His left hand, bearing a wedding ring, rests on his open wallet balanced on his thigh, and between his fingers Nora can see slivers of a photograph. Nora also has a photograph. It's the one of Robert she tore from the newspaper. It's tucked safely inside the notebook that she carries with her everywhere.

The man opens his eyes abruptly and looks directly at Nora, who quickly averts hers, a blush creeping up her neck and pinking her cheeks. She blinks. Then her eyes are drawn back to the man, shocked to find him still looking at her, smiling – at her blush, no doubt. A woman in her sixties, blushing!

He moves his hand to the side, revealing the picture of a beautiful woman. 'My wife,' he says, as though those two words explain everything, then he closes his eyes and resumes his tapping, leaving Nora with the kernel of their story – the man, his wife, their love and their music.

Her own love story, which has slept curled up in her heart all these years, creeps to the surface. Within it are the beauty, the longing, the grief and the lost potential of a seventeen year old in love who, with all of the finesse of a blind mouse, tumbled into a doomed pregnancy. She remembers also *their* music and knows that she too has been loved.

Tidy fields and Friesian cattle rush by, losing themselves behind the train. Yet, as she sits still, more countryside constantly opens up before them, embracing the train as it cuts its path. Could her life still be like that? New fields to walk in, new flowers to pick? New people to meet? And she murmurs to the glass pane the mantra she's been using these last days as she prepared for this journey. '*I can live. I can love. I can be.*'

As she reaches her destination, Nora views herself in the mirror in the foyer, wanting to look nice for Janet. Far different from the girl who stared back on that dreadful night when she was seventeen, but better than the version of a couple of years ago who appeared to be dying from the inside out. Her hair is longer, more grey than chestnut, but it's resumed its natural bounce. There's a web of lines at the corners of her mouth and eyes, but there's a liveliness that was lost during those years in the parched wilderness of her life.

Janet's secretary's office door is open, and Nora taps as she enters, giving the bespectacled, middle-aged woman there a shy smile. She takes in the wine-coloured jacket, soft pink blouse and pearls. A three-stoned engagement ring nestles in an accommodating fleshy indent beside a wedding band; Nora imagines those hands caressing grandchildren.

'Maybe you'd like to take a seat in the waiting room. Dr Janet won't be long.'

The waiting room is welcoming, with women's magazines laid in neat rows, along with one men's magazine bearing pictures of motorbikes. A thin, pale woman fidgets with the corners of the pages of a magazine – ruffling them, twisting them between her thumb and index finger while her eyes seem lost elsewhere. Maybe she's worrying about paying the rent, coping with her children or her husband having an affair. Nora hasn't had to deal with any of those things and, even though her life has been restricted, her basic needs have always been met without her having to worry. In fact, when it was decreed that patients should have some recompense for the work they did, Nora – being a non-smoker – didn't really have anything to spend money on. But then Joe changed that.

He had a gramophone. For weeks before her birthday he'd teased that he had a secret plan. They had agreed to meet in the gardens and he appeared with a big smile, wheeling himself as quickly as he could, signalling that she should follow, then when they were out of sight, he had whisked the blanket off some kind of box on his lap upon which was a large packet, which he handed to her.

'Open it,' he said, his face suffused with happy anticipation.

Excitedly she had unveiled the sleeved vinyl. 'Beethoven's *Ninth Symphony.*'

'Happy birthday,' Joe had said, smiling while she stood frozen. 'Nora. It's for you. For your birthday.' And he had taken it out of her hand, slid it out of its sleeve and placed it on the turntable of his gramophone right there on his lap.

From then on, she'd known what to spend her money on. When men and women were finally given permission to share a day room, Joe and Nora would sometimes play their music there; even the staff would come to listen.

The gloved hand of a fellow patient shoots past Nora's nose to reach the magazine rack next to her, startling her back to the present. Nora studies the woman. Her head has what would have, at one time, been called a noble bearing. Her finger taps unconsciously, occasionally stilling whenever she becomes aware of it. She gathers her beautiful coat that has spilled over the seat around her and repeatedly slaps her leather gloves into her palm. Nora taps her own fingers to the rhythm.

The door opens, Janet appears and Nora's heart leaps. She stands and, simultaneously, so does the woman.

Janet looks quickly back and forth at both of them. Nora sits down, eyes to the carpet, her colour rising. She must have made a mistake. Janet looks directly at the other woman and smiles.

'I'm so sorry,' says Janet. 'Maybe we have an administrative error. I'm afraid your appointment was yesterday.'

Tears spring to Nora's eyes. 'It's OK,' she murmurs, gathering her things together to leave.

'I don't think so,' the other woman says coldly, and Nora's head springs up.

'I have a cancellation at twelve, if you'd like to wait.' Janet smiles.

'No, my appointment is now.'

'I'm afraid you're mistaken. It was yesterday. I dictated a letter to you last evening, enquiring after you since you hadn't attended, and suggesting you call for another appointment.'

'Well, I . . . I don't have time to wait . . .' She makes an exaggerated play of looking at her watch and huffs angrily.

'Then if you pop into my secretary's office, perhaps she can help find a slot that's mutually convenient,' Janet says, then turns to Nora and gives her the fullness of her smile. 'Miss Jennings,' she says, and shepherds Nora into her room with a hand hovering somewhere in the region of her back.

'It's all right,' Janet says as she closes the door behind Nora. 'This is your appointment.' And she opens her arms for Nora to enter and they hug. 'You made it on your own, Nora! Wonderful. Well done.'

Though Nora says nothing, she notes with joy that Janet seems proud of her and, for the first time, she understands. It will be all right to leave at the end of the session; they will be seeing each other again.

On the train, Nora rests back in her seat, feeling more relaxed than she has since Janet left Hillinghurst. She watches the green blur of fields and listens to the train's rhythm thrumming in her head. Huge white clouds busy themselves across the cornflower blue sky and she's suddenly aware that she's smiling.

Chapter Twenty-Two

1990

Nora stands in the middle of the room, motionless except for her eyes, which roam around in excited disbelief. She can hardly contain the squeal of delight that longs to burst from within her. Here she is, in her very own flat, where she will live alone for the first time in all her sixty-eight years. It's three years since Nora was discharged from Hillinghurst, and today, with the support of Audrey and Evelyn, she moved into this flat owned by a Christian charity and reserved for people just like her.

All of her belongings are here around her. The ballerina on her music box pirouettes to the strains of *Liebestraum* as the beauty of the music fills the space, touches the walls, permeates the fabrics and thrills Nora's heart. She holds her hands as if in prayer, her fingertips to her lips. Her breathing is shallow, her elbows tucked in. She closes her eyes, and tries not to free the grin that she feels could break her face in two.

'Thank you, thank you, thank you,' she whispers.

She lifts the curtain that hangs between the sitting room and the tiny cupboard of a kitchen, with its two-ring stove and her new kettle. Two mugs hang on hooks and she straightens them a little, then steps back again to survey her new domain. She closes her eyes and blinks back tears of joy. Her back aches with the carrying of boxes up two flights of stairs and she's tired, but cannot think of going to bed.

Suddenly, a wave of anxiety threatens to sweep her away. She's completely alone for the very first time since she was seventeen.

Come on, Nora, keep busy!

As she bustles to the kitchen and puts on the kettle, she comforts herself by remembering that, two weeks from today, she'll have her first very special invited guest.

Though Janet is no stranger to visiting patients' homes, she's not usually bringing flowers and coming because of an invitation to tea. Yet, ignoring her traditional schooling on professional ethics, here she is, climbing the stairs to visit Nora.

The door opens almost before she's knocked upon it and standing there is Nora, her hair now almost silver, her face glowing with delight. She's wearing a simple, short-sleeved cotton dress with a buckled belt, and a necklace of brown glass beads hugs her throat. Delight shines from every pore of her beaming face.

'Nora,' Janet smiles, 'you look wonderful.'

Nora opens the door more widely. 'I'm so happy that you came. Please come in.'

Nora accepts the proffered flowers with unadulterated joy. 'Oh, they're gorgeous,' she says, burying her head among the pink carnations. 'I'll stand them in water in the kitchen for now.' She disappears behind the curtain.

The room is small with a blue two-seat settee and one matching chair separated by a rose-emblazoned fireside rug. The small grate holds a pretty china bowl containing a few dried flowers in pinks and purples, and the narrow mantelpiece is home to a small figurine of a woman and child clinging to each other and for ever entwined, tethered as they are in a piece of green soapstone. Janet's eyes linger upon it. She feels a lump in her throat and blinks quickly, hoping Nora hasn't noticed. Atop the small chest of drawers that doubles as a sideboard stand a few books, Nora's music box, and a bunch of wild flowers in a glass jar.

In a corner between the settee and the curtain stands a small drop-leaf table, draped with a pink-checked cloth, perfectly positioned with a point hanging down towards the floor. Two chairs with black leatherette seats are somehow accommodated in the tiny gap between the settee and the table. Nora re-emerges from behind the curtain, smiling and looking deceptively young. It's obvious that she has taken pains to make this special – from the presence of the little rose-painted jug to the ironed handkerchiefs that are standing in for napkins. The crockery is a collection of odd pieces, but all share the common motif of roses. The scones are home-made, and the little pot of jam is topped with checked gingham. 'May I take your jacket?' Nora says, her voice soft yet confident. She hangs it on the single coat hanger suspended from a peg on the wall.

Nora returns with a teapot in a hand-knitted cosy, then she hovers for a moment, her expression anxious. 'Oh, sorry, I'll have to move you,' she says.

'No problem.' Janet stands and moves towards the fireplace while Nora pushes the settee forward and prises out the chairs, placing one at each end of the table and effectively blocking the entrance into the kitchen.

'It's a bit of a squeeze,' she says, with much more aplomb than Janet could have mustered in similar circumstances, and surveys the table, checking everything off a mental list. 'Would you like to sit down? Oh, I forgot a knife . . .' Janet stands so that the furniture can be eased once more to allow Nora access to the kitchen. 'Sorry it's so small.'

'Nora, please don't apologise. It's just so wonderful to see you settled and managing on your own. It's amazing what you've done.'

Janet is rewarded with a beaming smile. 'It's three years since I left Hillinghurst. I've been so lucky.'

'And you've worked hard. You deserve it, Nora. Every bit.'

Nora pours the tea and hands Janet the plate of scones, gently pushing the jam and cream in her direction.

'Mmm – my favourites,' says Janet. 'Did you bake them?'

'Yes, I did. I always liked to bake scones when . . .' She looks down into her lap, then lifts her chin and manages to look straight at Janet. 'My dad used to say my scones were heavenly.' She blushes.

'I sometimes get nervous when I'm cooking for company, worrying if cakes and Yorkshire puddings will rise,' Janet says.

'Do you?' Nora says incredulously, as though it had never occurred to her that Janet might ever be nervous, or maybe even that she ever cooks. Then she gives a little laugh. 'That makes me feel better.' Something tugs at Janet's skirt and she looks down, startled. A small, furry face peers up at her. 'Oh,' she exclaims in delight. 'Who's this?'

'Oh, sorry. I hope he didn't damage anything,' Nora bends down and picks up the black and white kitten. 'His name's Tuppence. I got him from the RSPCA. Isn't he lovely?'

'He is.' Janet reaches across to scratch the kitten behind his ear.

'I'd really love a dog, but I'm not allowed to have one here. I had a dog when I was a little girl. In fact, he was old but still with us when I . . .' She seems to falter, but recovers herself, though a trace of the old sadness shadows her face. 'He was very old . . .'

'Nora, I imagine it's still hard sometimes?' Janet probes gently.

'No, it's fine. I'm fine, thank you.' She smiles brightly, though it doesn't quite reach her eyes. They sink into a companionable silence. 'Oh, I have something else to tell you,' says Nora with a big smile, trying to persuade the kitten to get off her lap. 'Get down now, Tuppence.' She brushes some crumbs off her skirt. 'It's exciting.' She brings her hands together as if in prayer, then takes a deep breath. 'I've joined a choir,' she announces, with all the excitement of a little girl on Christmas morning.'

Now it's Janet's turn to beam. 'A choir?'

Nora glows. 'Yes. My singing lessons have been going well and Susan suggested that I might like to meet some of her other singers, and they invited me to have a cup of tea with them. They're all in the choir and they asked if I'd like to join.' The words come in a hurry and then she pauses, eyes wide with wonder. 'I could hardly believe it, but I went to just see what it was like and it's lovely. Everyone's so kind. So, I've been going for a month now.'

'That's wonderful, Nora,' Janet says, sharing Nora's delight. 'I'm thrilled for you. What fun!'

'Yes, it is.' Then her smile fades. 'I'm a bit worried though,' she says.

'Oh, why?'

'Well, Susan says that someone pays for my lessons – some charity. They want to be anonymous, so I can't even thank them.'

'I don't think that matters,' Janet says, looking away to hide her smile. 'I'm sure they would be so happy that their money's being well spent and enjoyed. I wouldn't worry about it.'

'Do you think so?'

'I do. They obviously just want you to enjoy your singing.'

'Well, I think it's wonderful of someone to do that and I really wish I could thank them.'

'Maybe you could give Susan permission to tell them how you're getting on every now and then.'

'Oh – that's a good idea! I will.'

Janet smiles then needs to look away. Her eyes alight on the ballerina and she points to it. 'Your ballerina is beautiful,' she says.

'It's musical,' and Nora reaches for it, turns the key and hands the pirouetting dancer to Janet. 'I've had it since I was a girl,' she says. 'My parents gave it to me for my fifteenth birthday.'

'How lovely.'

'I didn't have her for a long time – I wasn't allowed – but then I got her ...' and her voice trails off and she looks a little fretful.

She looks down at her hands for a moment, then gathers herself and lifts her chin and smiles. 'I have more news, too,' she says, as she takes the music box and replaces it on the chest. 'I joined the library,' she says, regaining her enthusiasm. 'I can get four books each week if I want to, but usually I only need two or three. The lady there is so nice. She asked if I'd like to go a couple of afternoons a week and tidy the books and look after the children's corner.'

Admiration floods through Janet once more. 'Really? Nora, that's great.'

'Yes, it is. It's like having a job – even though I won't get paid. I've never had a job, except at the hospital. Then it wasn't a real job. Being among all the books is so exciting. Look what I got this week,' she enthuses, picking up the three books from the chest and handing them to Janet.

'Oh, I love this book,' Janet says, fingering *A Story Like the Wind*. 'Isn't Laurens van der Post wonderful? I read it a long, long time ago. There's a sequel—'

'*A Far-off Place*?' Nora breaks in eagerly.

'Yes – that's it. I loved them both.'

'They're going to get it for me. Isn't that amazing?'

Janet smiles. 'Yes, it is.'

Nora looks down and picks up Tuppence again, hugging him to her cheek. Then she pauses and puts him down on the carpet, smoothing down her skirt and fiddling with the sugar bowl. 'Janet, I went to look at Fenshaw and my old home. My parents passed away some years ago but I just had a look at the house. I wish I'd been to see them earlier. I could have, if I'd asked. There are things I could have said that can't be said directly to them now … But I've said them out loud anyway, and, you never know, maybe they could still hear them.'

Janet pauses and dabs her lips with the handkerchief serviette. 'You're very wise, Nora. I think they probably heard you.' And in that moment, she too decides to say what needs to be said to her parents before it's too late.

'And how was it? Being there, I mean.'

'I thought I'd feel sad, or … something, at least. But I didn't feel anything, really. I knew nothing of their lives for the last fifty years.' She sighs. 'My father told Robert that Angela had died, years before I knew myself what had happened to my daughter. That was the final betrayal, really, I think. I felt dreadful that I had caused my mother to lose her daughter as I lost mine. But hers was alive. She could have found me, and didn't. I know I would have spent all my life trying to find Angela. But maybe there were things I couldn't know. I did my grieving years ago, so I'm all right, really.'

She smooths out her skirt and looks back at Janet. 'I'm sorry. You look sad. I didn't mean to upset you.'

'You haven't,' Janet says quickly. 'You just reminded me of something I need to do.'

Nora reaches across and takes Janet's plate and serves her another scone. 'I'm still sorry that I caused the break-up of my family and that each of us lost the life we could have had. It doesn't feel right that, in the end, I'm the one who survived and am happy.'

'Are you happy, then, Nora?'

'Sometimes I feel very happy. Sometimes I don't know. But I'm grateful to be free and have some life. And now there's the choir . . . and Tuppence, of course.'

Janet smiles. 'I'm so glad. You made it, Nora.'

After Janet has left following fond goodbyes, Nora stands in her little kitchen looking out at the view, her hands in the warm washing-up water, reviewing the day and feeling satisfied.

Before Janet arrived, Nora promised herself that she would keep the visit completely positive, and she's happy that she managed not to tell Janet about how at night thoughts still arise unbidden, creeping and cruel, arousing her from sleep, then perching somewhere in her consciousness, from where they taunt and harass. Night after night, she sits in the ECT queue listening to the protestations of those who've been taken first, then watching as they're wheeled out groaning, all the while dreading her own turn and that awful feeling that the top of her head has been sawn off. Or she scrubs the floor, knees sore, back aching, waiting for the mocking laughter, then the boots that march over the newly scrubbed area and the voice that screams at her to do it again. Or she's sprawled face-down on the floor with someone's foot on her back, while she quashes the humili-ation, compresses the rage, and fights down the urge to scream – just breathing and praying that she can hold on until the moment when she can cry into her pillow, biting her hand to stifle sound that might attract attention.

Many nights, she moans and squirms, clutching her pillow and burying her face, childishly hoping that hiding will make the bad memories go away so that she can find an island of peace in the sea of confusion. Sometimes she's tempted to fantasise like she used to that she's with her family, happy, and with Robert standing beside her, but though she used to be able to stretch out this fantasy for an hour or more, during which she'd hug herself and smile, in the end it would collapse like a burst balloon, leaving her desolate and lonelier than ever. Now it's just too hard to reach, and to trick herself into believing. Sometimes she muses that Dr Mason may have been right when he suggested it might be better if she considered her family dead.

But then she thinks of Joe and Gladys and Peggy and how glad she is that they were in her life. And, of course, Angela. Even though she died, Nora carried her and gave her life, and she will always have that.

Such memories over years had braided themselves together like a silken noose: soft and caressing even as it tightened around her throat – until one day she realised that she had the power to remove it and be free.

So now, here in her little flat, she's finding new ways to lift herself. She runs through a litany of wild flowers that she's seen; imagines shrews and field mice scampering, and the odd mole, finding itself strangely above ground, doing its hilarious scuttle on short stubby legs, curiously placed at each corner of its flat, rectangular body, as it looks for cover.

Then, at last, morning approaches, the world wakes up and it's not so bad. She fills her kettle and lights the little gas stove, sets out her cup, sniffs yesterday's milk and gives thanks that she's survived another night of 'freedom'.

Her enemy is unaccounted time. Everything is planned so that there are no treacherous caverns in which fear can linger, waiting to grab her and drag her to the depths where she could drown. If necessary, she goes to her lists in her notebook – diversions, distractions, time fillers, suicide avoiders. *Choose something. Anything. Go for a walk. Have a bath. Do a crossword.*

But sometimes, no matter what she does, anxiety rises and nausea spreads. Panic will be next unless she does something. Years ago, this would have led to her cutting herself, feeling the physical pain, watching the blood flow and then the relief as the emotional pain drained out with it. But that is no longer an option. She sees Janet's fingers on her wrist and hears her voice. *'No, Nora, this is now behaviour of the past.'*

And, even when the loneliness curls its cold tendrils around her feet and climbs up her legs, she can do something – scrub the already clean floor, wash the already sparkling windows, sweep the already pristine rugs, scour again the two-ring job she refers to as her cooker. And she survives.

And now she has Tuppence. He is her new responsibility. Something to live for.

Chapter Twenty-Three

Though Janet loves to drive, the train feels the better option for this journey. It also gives her a definite timetable – some structure – that may well be useful. She sets off at six when dawn is just breaking and, as the train ploughs through miles of fields still with their bales of hay or straw from the recent harvest, she tries to remember what this journey used to be like all those years ago. But, in the end, not much seems to have changed. England is England.

A memory wafts into her mind. She is about sixteen, sitting in the village hall at a meeting that her mother is chairing. Everyone stands as the lady at the front strikes a couple of chords on the old, somewhat out-of-tune piano. In unison, there is a mass intake of breath and, lungs expanded to their full extent, all the women sing.

> *And did those feet in ancient time, walk upon England's mountains green?*
> *And was the holy Lamb of God on England's pleasant pastures seen?*
> *And did the countenance divine, shine forth upon our clouded hills?*
> *And was Jerusalem builded here among these dark satanic mills?*

Yes, England is England from mountains green, to pleasant pastures, to clouded hills, to dark satanic mills and, as she approaches her destination, she wonders if the people will also still be the same or may have changed over the years since she saw them.

The phone call wasn't easy, but at least her mother said that her father said she would be welcome if she wanted to come. That's what he always said when he fell out with anyone, then he'd add, *'They'll need me before I need them.'*

What Janet had been unable, or unwilling, to acknowledge all these years was that she might need them. But maybe Ian was right, all the difficulties they had as a couple may well have started here, and now she needs help to put it right.

The woman who opens the door looks little like she remembers her mother looking, and yet, those eyes are her own and the worried, puckered brow is the same.

'Hello, Mum,' Janet says and her mother tries to smile and steps back, holding the door open. Janet steps through the door and leans forward to kiss her mother's cheek. 'Long time.'

'Yes. I'm sorry, Janet. So sorry.' And she's in Janet's arms and the years melt away.

'You've come then,' her father says from across the room, pushing himself up with his hands on the arms of the chair. 'How have you been?' And he struggles across the space between them and holds out his hands, which Janet takes in her own. As easy as that.

'Ian's not with you?'

'No, I thought I'd come on my own,' Janet says, trying to hide her shock at his frailty. No longer the proud strong father she knew. His white hair, the thick glasses, the shaking hands.

'He's always welcome if he wants to come.'

'I'll tell him.'

'Come and sit down. Edie, are you making a cup of tea?'

'I made an apple pie and some scones,' her mother says. 'I'll just put the kettle on.' She dabs at her eyes as she leaves.

Janet's eyes wander around the room. Little seems to have changed. Her school photographs are in their same cluster. The clay mallard ducks are still flying across the sitting-room wall, and the clock she bought them for their twentieth wedding anniversary is still ticking on the mantelpiece. Their wedding photograph is still on the sideboard: her mother wears a long white dress and a veil secured with a garland of orange blossom, a bouquet held in two hands; her father stands proudly smiling beside her, with his handsome unscarred face and unscarred mind. The man in this photograph never returned from the war. What he brought with him was a damaged brain, a ravaged mind and a wounded soul. Now she understands, and can be at peace with it. Her father stokes the fire and picks up his pipe, and all that Janet thought she would say, all that she rehearsed on the train, falls away. All is forgiven, dissolved somewhere in a twenty-year gap. What she has held all these years was just a memory. Nora has taught her how to forgive and let go.

Her mother arrives, pushing the same squeaky trolley with its two orange plastic tiers, one bearing the tray of tea and the cake and knife, and the other the plates and scones and paper serviettes. Janet stands and, as though she did it just yesterday, places a piece of cake on a plate and hands it to her father, then pours him a cup of tea and adds two spoonfuls of sugar. She catches her mother's smile and feels the love, gratitude and relief in equal parts contained within it.

Back on the train Janet composes a letter to Ian, though she's still unsure as to whether she will send it or not.

Chapter Twenty-Four

1991

Janet sits opposite Nora, regarding her with a worried frown. In the last year, Nora has flourished and their sessions, while often dealing with quite serious issues, are nevertheless filled with easy, meaningful communication. However, today things are different. So far, their appointment has been filled with stilted, half-finished sentences, strained silences and, more importantly, Nora seems to have regressed to the time when she would rather hide away than speak. There are only minutes of this session left and then there'll be no possibility of seeing each other for the next three weeks.

'Nora, I know something's troubling you and, as always, you don't have to tell me what it is if you don't want to, but I'd hate to think that you'd leave still feeling worried when we may have been able to resolve whatever's going on.'

Still there's silence. She looks up at the clock on her office wall – only eight minutes to go. Hardly time to process anything now, even if Nora did decide to speak.

'Well, we're just about at the end of our time for today, Nora. So, let's wind down. What are your plans for the next week or two?'

'I haven't any really. I'll be at the library and I have an appointment with Audrey.'

'And you're singing on Thursday?' Nora seems to fall into herself. 'Nora, is something amiss with your singing?'

'No.'

'Are you sure?'

'Yes.' But sadness stalks across her face like a shadow.

'Nora, we still have a little time if you want to talk,' Janet offers.

'I'm OK, really.'

'All right.' Helpless to do anything else, Janet knows she needs to shift the pace now if the session is going to end well. 'Same train as usual today?'

'Yes.'

'Right. So, we'll see each other in three weeks.' She stands and gives Nora her usual hug and opens the door, but after only a couple of steps, Nora pauses. Janet hasn't seen this behaviour since before Nora was discharged, and her heartbeat quickens.

'I'm sorry, Janet,' she says.

'For what?'

'I'm not really OK.'

'I know,' says Janet, closing the door softly.

Nora looks up and meets Janet's eyes, something she's refused to do throughout the session. She takes a deep breath. 'The choir is going to Berlin to sing.'

'Wow. But that's wonderful,' Janet cries.

'I can't go.'

'Oh . . . I see.' Janet frowns. 'Come, let's sit for a minute and you can tell me all about it.'

Nora returns to her seat. 'I haven't got a passport.'

'Ah . . .' Janet's mind starts to race. 'Well, maybe we can get you one. When are they going?'

'In early October.'

'Well, that should give us plenty of time, I think.'

'But that's not all,' and Nora keeps her head down. 'They're all wearing a kind of uniform.'

'A uniform?'

'A black skirt and a cream blouse.'

'Right . . .' Now she gets it. 'And they'll be flying out?'

'I don't know, but I think so.'

Janet thinks for just a moment. 'Nora, there's a fund for just this kind of thing. It would pay for your uniform and your ticket and maybe even to get some clothes to go in and have your hair done or whatever you want.'

Nora's eyes widen, incredulous. 'Really?'

Janet can't quite meet her eye. 'Really,' she echoes.

Nora's mouth gapes open and Janet can almost hear the questions formulating themselves.

'I'll tell you what. Leave it with me and I'll have a chat with them and see what we can do.'

'But—'

'No buts. Just give me a few days.' Her heart melts at the relief and gratitude that's written on Nora's face. 'Now you'd better get off for your train. I'll let you know what happens, or else I'll chat with Audrey and she'll let you know.'

The door closes and Janet rests back on her chair. She thinks for a moment and swivels round and dials Audrey's number. 'Hi. How are you? . . . Good. Me too. Audrey, I just had a session with Nora. She's doing well, but something's come up. The choir she's singing with is going to Berlin in October and she really wants to go, but hasn't got a passport, or the clothes she needs. Funds are available, but she'll need some help, I think . . . Oh, that's great. I have someone else just now, but I'll come back to you – or you can give me a call when you're ready . . . Oh, it's just a small fund that gives grants for exactly this kind of thing . . . Yes, will do. Thanks, Audrey. Perfect.'

Janet replaces the receiver and smiles. She can't think of a happier way to spend her money.

Bright and beautiful sunny Sunday mornings like this would usually lift Janet's spirits. But not today. She feels lonely and restless and, as she catches sight of two pigeons mating in the cherry tree, she vaguely wonders how long it is since she made love.

She has a backlog of dictation to catch up on and she determines that, on this, her third attempt, she'll get all the correspondence completed. She sighs and moves a hand towards them, but . . .

Maybe a shower, first.

An hour later finds her in her old red anorak and jeans at the Sunday market, carrying her purse, keys and a guilty conscience.

So much for good intentions. The weather's mood seems to be as fickle as her own, and it starts to pour with rain. Her hair quickly becomes plastered to her face and neck as the cold rain makes its way down her previously warm back. Really, she should just go home. The gaudy colours, Indian fabrics, crystal jewellery, antique boxes of loose buttons and knick-knacks that usually thrill her have lost their charm. No – correction. It's she who has lost hers. She hasn't even been able to think of a single quip, retort or playful greeting for any of the stallholders, or get into the good-humoured banter she usually enjoys. She'd have been better off doing the dictation– at least she wouldn't have the guilty conscience, then. *Come on, Janet,* she chides herself. *Get your act together!*

She sighs and moves to a stall of silk scarves, waistcoats, flowing tops and palazzo pants, seemingly in every possible colour, but keeps her head down and hopes she won't be seen by anyone. She fingers a piece of silk adorned with flamingos and exotic plants in a stunning mix of blues and green. Then, too late. The beautiful, round Indian stallholder sees her.

'Like mine,' she says, pointing to her brilliant sari of orange and flame, whipping the blue-green off the rack and billowing it out into its rich fullness. 'Or you can make bedspread.' She smiles.

Janet backs away with a weak, apologetic smile, but then hears an excited cry. 'Dr Humphreys? Is that you?'

She groans inwardly. *No . . . Of all the days . . .* But she turns around and tries to smile. 'Clara!' One of her young outpatients stands sporting a beautiful multicoloured umbrella, perfectly dry, perfectly coiffed in a glorious green waterproof ensemble, looking gorgeous. Meanwhile Janet, imagining the wet anorak, jeans, rat-tails hair and makeup-free face, wonders how she could still be recognisable as Dr Humphreys. She wishes a crater would appear in the pavement and swallow her whole.

Clara's face blanches with alarm. 'Are you OK, Dr Humphreys?'

'Apart from being cold and drenched, do you mean?' she grimaces wryly.

Clara smiles. 'My mother's just over there. She'd love to meet you,' and she cranes her neck over the crowd and waves to a stout middle-aged woman looking at ornaments encrusted with crystals.

Oh, please let me disappear, Janet thinks, but it's too late. Clara's mother is advancing through the crowd, vigorously bulldozing everyone in her way.

'Dr Humphreys! Dr Humphreys! We've heard so much about you.'

Janet squirms, but manages to summon a wan smile.

'My husband's somewhere around,' Clara's mother says, and she raises an arm and beckons wildly. 'Andrew – come and meet someone.'

He arrives and the conversation proceeds without much input from Janet, who feels as though she's drowning. She is peering around, desperate for escape, when the shape of a familiar head and shoulders not six feet away catches her attention. Thankfully, he is facing in the other direction. He is casting his gaze over a piece of jewellery, and fingering it with that hand she knows so well. She knows how it moves, how it holds a cup, how she felt when it used to touch her.

Her heart somersaults, as it always did. She can almost smell him, hear that lilting Irish accent, see the hazel of his eyes, the strong forehead with its brows almost meeting above the bridge of his nose, threatening to overwhelm the rest of his face as it tapers down to an angled chin that bears a cleft deep enough to make it impossible to shave there. That mouth. Oh, that mouth . . .

Her own mouth is suddenly a desert and she feels unable to articulate a single word. The world has become silent. She has to get out of here.

She lifts her wrist and looks blindly at her watch. 'I'm so sorry,' she mumbles to Clara and her parents. 'I didn't realise the time. I have an appointment. So lovely to meet you.' And she gives Clara a quick hug and inches sideways through the throng of Sunday shoppers, tears streaming down her face.

Chapter Twenty-Five

East Sussex is at its best in late August, Janet thinks. The trees are already changing into their autumn yellows and rusts, with the occasional stunning red sweet buckeye and acer. Distracted by the beauty around her, Janet almost misses the sign for Folgarth House. She turns left between stone pillars, then up the gravel drive with its sentinels of lavender and heather, immaculate lawns, busy herbaceous borders and well-tended rose gardens. She can almost see the little girls of the past in flouncy skirts and petticoats, their ringlets bouncing under lacy caps, laughing and chasing each other, interrupting the adults in their games of croquet.

She steers round the stone fountain with dolphin and maiden in eternal embrace, then pulls up into a parking space in front of the beautiful country house, now converted into luxury apartments. She gets out of the car, walks up to the door and rings the bell for one of the first-floor flats.

An old man in an Argyle jumper and fading tweed trousers opens the door and smiles. His white hair drapes over his forehead and he brushes it back with his hand and peers through his glasses. 'Dr Humphreys?'

Janet smiles, and warmth creeps across her chest. 'Dr Stilworth?'

His once beautiful face, still with its wide, generous mouth and intelligent eyes, lights up. 'Do come in. I'm so glad you managed to find me. Forgive me if I go ahead. I hate it when I'm in a new place and don't know where I'm going.'

Janet smiles and follows his limping gait, noting the slope of his shoulders and the delicate hand that reaches for the wall now and then to steady himself. He leads her into a generous living room with windows overlooking the front lawns and the magnif-icent woodland beyond. A climbing rose taps at the frame of the open window and offers the gift of its perfume. There are wool-len throws over the settee and chairs and a book lies open on the coffee table alongside a silver tray set for two. Bookshelves line the wall, surrounding a fireplace that is fitted with a modern gas fire and topped by old sepia photographs. Janet thinks how lovely it must be to live here.

'Nora speaks very highly of you,' she says when they're comfortably settled with cups of tea and shortbread biscuits. She notes the tender look that lit up his face when she mentioned Nora's name, and warms to him even more.

'That's very kind,' he says, taking a sip of his tea. 'So, tell me about you, Dr Humphreys. Why did you come to see me?'

'Well, as I mentioned on the phone, I've been working with Nora, and she's doing so well that I'd love to share her progress with you, since you were so important to her survival all those years. And it would be great if you could maybe fill in a couple of gaps for me – with regards to diagnosis, mainly.'

Dr Stilworth looks intrigued. 'Of course. What would you like to know?'

'Well, I noted that – at one time – Nora was diagnosed with schizophrenia . . .'

'Yes,' he says, frowning. 'Although I doubt that diagnosis would be given nowadays. There was certainly a time when she was psychotic, though.'

'Indeed. But I wondered if she might have slipped into a temporary psychotic state to escape an intolerably painful and stressful reality. What do you think?'

'Yes, could be.'

'She does have complex PTSD too and, of course, that can mimic so many other psychiatric conditions.'

'We didn't even know of such things in those days, I'm afraid, though we started to look at the results of battle stress in soldiers after the war. I have to say that I despised many of the approaches that we tried in those days – but we had to try something . . .'

He meets her eyes, and Janet is struck by the sadness and regret they hold. 'Dr Stilworth, you were a guiding light and a point of reference to which Nora could always return. No amount of treatment can replace that.'

'That's very kind of you, Dr Humphreys. But I sometimes look at what we could have done better . . .' He looks down at his tea, his hands trembling, and for the first time it occurs to her just how old he is now and how stressful her visit might be to him.

He shakes his head and meets her eyes once more. 'I'm ashamed now of what was thought to be good treatment then. It sounds lame to say it's all we knew, but sadly that's a fact.'

'I'm sure I'll look back in the future and say the same, but we can only give what we have to give.' She pauses, wondering if she's asking too much of him, but she presses on. 'You'd be so proud of her, Dr Stilworth. She's been living independently in a flat of her own for almost two years now, and for another couple of years before that was in a group home. She still has flash-backs occasionally and there are things that she can't or doesn't want to remember, but she's brilliant.'

'She was a very courageous young woman who had a hard time,' he says. 'Well, that's an understatement, of course. And none of them had it easy. The philosophy was that psychiatric patients were like badly behaved children and needed strong discipline and control. Sadly, of course, any situation where one person is placed in a position of control over another often attracts those whose aim is not to help or heal, but to dominate. Someone like that with a good brain and power can do a great deal of damage to the vulnerable in their care, and it can take a while for them to be detected and even longer to be deposed.' He sighs. 'Nora was pretty, bright and from a somewhat privileged background. She was also stoical and hardly ever complained. She was, therefore, a perfect target. Then, of course, there was such a rigid hierarchy that rendered those who might have helped impotent.'

He pauses and takes a sip of his tea, then he shifts his gaze and holds her eyes intensely. 'I'm not proud of my part. For some years I lived uneasily with a moral dilemma of leaving in protest or staying and appearing to condone. I stayed because I thought that, though I couldn't do much, I could do something. And I wondered, if I left, who would come after me and how it could possibly be even worse. That seems like an egotistical viewpoint now, but it's what kept me there.' He gives a weak, apologetic smile, then once again looks a little lost within his memories.

Janet controls an urge to reach out and touch him and somehow let him know she understands. Silence seems a wiser choice.

After a few minutes, he pulls himself out of his reverie. 'So sorry. Is there anything else I can help with?'

'Yes . . .' Janet hesitates. 'I thought long and hard about coming to see you. And also about the fact that I wouldn't tell Nora that I'm here.'

'Why?'

'I didn't know how you'd feel about it.' He puts his head to one side and his white hair falls gently over his brow. Once again, he unconsciously brushes it back with his pale, veined hand. 'As I said, Nora lives alone and works a few hours a week helping out in the local library. She loves the children's corner and, once a week, she reads them stories. She also sings in a choir, and that's why I'm here. She's going with them to Berlin, where they are to give a concert in a cathedral.'

Dr Stilworth's eyes light up and he shakes his head in gentle wonderment. 'How splendid! How absolutely splendid.'

'Yes, it is. She's so excited, and I really want this to be special for her. She so deserves this.' Janet takes a breath. 'I would love to go, but I just can't. I've been called to give a psychiatric opinion in court for another patient that week and it's just impossible for me to get to Berlin, and . . .' She pauses. 'Well, I wondered if you would like to . . . I know she'd be thrilled, and it would also allow you to see the fruits of your labour . . .' The words tumble out and, when she's finally finished, she watches in breathless silence as he sits back and just stares, saying nothing, though his eyes become moist.

'I would be honoured,' he says at last, in a low, shaky voice. 'Truly honoured. I don't travel much these days, but I'll make sure I'm there.'

Janet reaches across and covers his hand with hers. 'I know she'll be so excited to see you. Thank you so much.'

'That is absolutely my pleasure. You've brought me great gifts today.'

Janet beams. 'It's a joy to meet you. Thank you for giving me your time.'

'You're more than welcome, Dr Humphreys.'

'Janet,' she corrects.

'Tom,' he says, and they share a smile.

After chatting for a while, Janet glances at her watch and is amazed by how late it is. 'Oh dear, I need to get going. I'll send you all the details about Berlin. I'm not going to tell Nora that I was here; I want it to be a surprise when she sees you there.' Janet pauses. 'I want to thank you, Tom. You kept her alive.' They shake hands and Janet starts to turn, then impulsively turns back and gently kisses his cheek. 'Maybe you'll let me know how it goes,' she says.

'Indeed, I will.'

She slides into her Clio and sits for a moment, not wanting to drive away yet. She feels tearfully moved to have met this man about whom Nora has spoken so much. But now, sadness creeps into her chest. It's time for her to sort out the rest of her own life. It's time.

Chapter Twenty-Six

Janet stands by the window of this favourite hotel on the coast, once a romantic haunt, her gaze drawn out towards the horizon. Last night, the drive here gave Janet amazing views of the storm that has now ceded to soft wisps of honey-pink, vaporous clouds, which drape themselves nonchalantly across the heavens like swathes of gossamer. Echoes of thunder have been replaced by birdsong. She wishes her own turbulence could be quieted so easily. Nowadays, she tries to be patient and trust that she will not be beached for ever in her melancholy.

But it wasn't always this way. This is a hard-won peace. She thinks back to those awful days years ago when she had to hide in embarrassment lest anyone should see her in the drab plumage of grief and depression, unable to be the extroverted, brightly feathered bird they still wanted her to be.

Those days passed, of course, and she has survived. She's here. Wiser, more balanced, more mature, with her sense of humour restored and her brain and heart working as she'd thought they never could again. Though the pain lingers, she's strong enough to withstand it now.

She needs to walk. She slips on anorak and boots and heads for the beach.

Watching the seagulls frolicking in the lacy edges of the water and leaving crazy footprints in the sand, she remembers Martin as a toddler, testing out the shock of the cold water and giggling at the bubbles breaking over his chubby feet. The three of them searching for shells, squealing with delight at hermit crabs that scampered sideways down the beach, Ian's hand holding hers and the occasional touch of lips or cheeks, indulgent smiles and knowing glances. Promises for later . . .

And now she needs to revisit the promises – not only those, but the vows they made. She's learned much during these years they've been apart and, though there's been minimal contact, she has no doubt that there's still love on both sides. Could it be rekindled? Do they have to have lost everything for ever?

She pulls up her hood against the sand-carrying wind that tangles her hair and scratches her face, and tries to ride the wave of her sadness and grief, rather than pushing it away. Though there has been damage and interruption to both their lives, she has come to realise that it doesn't have to be irreparable.

A beautiful shell catches her eye – pale apricot and bright orange. It will be less vibrant when it dries. She feels it somehow represents her – originally vivid, vital, colourful, now faded and dry. She pops the shell in her pocket, where it nestles against the stones she has already collected. She'll wash and arrange them when she gets home.

Impulsively, she takes off her boots and socks, turns up her jogging bottoms and tiptoes into the water. It's cold and fizzy and her feet sink into the sand as each wave recedes; little pebbles, caught up in the current, wedge themselves between her toes. She remembers standing like this with her mother, both of them giggling as their feet disappeared under the sand. Her mother desperately trying to protect the picnic sandwiches from the wind; the two of them running about to catch every scrap of paper, making a game out of collecting the litter.

She stops and looks out to sea. And suddenly, it's time to go. Something feels resolved. She wants to be back in her own home. She wants to write in her journal and tease out her thoughts and make decisions. She stands for a moment. *It is as it is, Janet – but you have the power to change it.*

She turns and walks back barefoot, stopping to put on her boots only when she reaches the road.

*   *   *

Janet turns the key and enters her once-vibrant flat with its tiled hallway and paintings that she and Ian collected with such joy. Not for the first time, she wonders why he didn't take any of these. Perhaps because he knew how much she loves them. But they haven't given her much joy since he left. She places her keys on the dresser and glances at herself in the mirror. The woman who stares back looks sad and old; suddenly she gazes at her with loving concern, as though at last she understands. The anger is gone. It's been gone for a while. And now she's wiser.

Janet turns away, wanders to the kitchen and turns the kettle on, deep in thought. The faded photograph on the fridge door of her and Ian on their three-day honeymoon confronts her. Ian insisted they had those precious days together, despite the circumstances and their lack of money – he was still in university at that time. She eases it from under its little magnet and brings it to the light. She stares at their happy faces as they pose for the stranger Ian asked to capture the moment. They look in love. Of course, they were. Ian was right – he didn't *have* to marry her. He always loved her. It was all her unresolved insecurities, going all the way back to her childhood, that stood between them. Tears course down her cheeks and she switches off the kettle.

She walks into her bedroom and sits down on the bed, the photograph still in her hand, her eyes on the phone beside her. Slowly, her hand moves towards it, then withdraws as though it might burn her. She forces herself to pick up the receiver.

She dials the number with a shaky hand and begs her voice not to tremble.

'Ian. It's me.'

Chapter Twenty-Seven

Nora alights from the train at Marylebone and waits at the taxi rank, lifting her hand to her newly cut hair – and wonders what Janet will think about her wearing some lipstick. She's so excited, she feels like a teenager going on her first date.

These last weeks have been a whirl of activity. The ladies of the choir took her shopping, and she's now the proud owner of a long black skirt, a cream polyester blouse, two pairs of black tights and a pair of black leather shoes with a little heel, all of which she tries on every night before going to bed, then carefully replaces in her 'Berlin box'. She also has two new skirts – one pleated and maroon (the colour reminds her of Mrs Lampeter's best hat!), and one flared and forest green (when she was sixteen, she had a dress this exact colour and everyone said she looked nice in it). She's also bought two new tops to match and a navy cardigan with gold buttons, a navy-blue dress for the evening and a green woollen coat. And what's more, they didn't come from Oxfam, but from Marks and Spencer. She does, however, have a new handbag that was sitting just waiting for her in the charity shop window, of which she's very proud. It's real leather, as she keeps telling herself while she strokes its softness.

Flights are booked, and for the last week she's had almost daily meetings with Audrey to go through the schedule. In the evenings, alone in her little flat, except for Tuppence sitting on her lap, she thinks about how all of this has happened, and sometimes fears it will all turn out to have been just a joke, or a mistake, or a dream, and she braces herself to be brave and not complain if it turns out to be so, but to remember all the fun she's already had by just thinking about it.

Yesterday, Alice, the lady who stands next to her in the choir, took Nora to the hair salon in her car and collected her again so that, even if it had rained, her hair wouldn't be spoiled.

Today, she's dying to tell Janet about all that's happened. 'Nora!' Janet's eyes crinkle in greeting, and Nora thrills at her genuine pleasure.

'Turn around and let me look at you,' she says, and Nora promptly poses so that Janet can see the back of her hair. 'Oh, you look beautiful!' Nora smiles and blushes deep red. 'And lipstick! Oh, my.' Janet chuckles, enjoying the transformation.

'Can I show you my passport? It just came this morning.'

She watches with pleasure as Janet looks at it closely. 'I wish I had a photograph of you a few years ago to compare,' Janet says. 'You look ten years younger now. I'm so happy for you, Nora.'

Janet hands back the passport and Nora places it carefully in her handbag, then produces train tickets, flight tickets, details of her hotel and a photograph of the red-brick cathedral in which they'll be singing. She talks about each member of the choir in detail, while Janet seems to revel in her delight. 'And Mrs Thorpe – she's my neighbour just across the landing – is going to look after Tuppence,' Nora finishes breathlessly.

'So, Nora, have you got everything you need now?' Janet fusses. 'A suitcase or a travel bag?'

'Yes, thank you,' Nora says shyly.

'Are you sure? Is it big enough?'

Nora's brow creases in thought. 'I think so. It was big enough for all my shopping.'

'Which shopping?' Janet queries

'*My* shopping.'

Janet hesitates. 'Your clothes shopping?'

'No. My other shopping.'

All at once, Janet understands and her heart melts. 'Nora, do you mean your grocery shopping?'

'Yes.'

Bless her. 'Nora,' Janet says gently. 'Do you mean a bag from the supermarket?'

'Yes, I lent my brown case to someone else and they never gave it back. But I'm sure the bag I've got will be big enough.'

Janet pauses, her mind whirring, and she knows she needs to tread carefully. 'Nora. I'd like to give you a bag of mine if that's OK. It'll just be a bit easier and stop your new clothes getting crumpled.'

'It'll be all right, honestly.'

'Well, it might be,' she says, 'but will you let me give you another one, just in case? If you don't want to use it, that's fine, and you can keep it or give it back to me next time we see each other. Will that be all right?'

Nora treats Janet to that new smile with its hint of pale pink lipstick. 'Yes. Thank you, Janet. That would be lovely. I'll take good care of it – and I promise to give it back.'

Janet promises to pop down on Saturday morning and leave the bag with Ellen. 'I'm sure you're going to have a great time, Nora. I want you to really enjoy it.'

'I'm sure I will, though I'm a bit scared.'

'I'm not surprised. It's a huge thing. Did you ever go abroad before?'

'Never.'

They chat about Berlin – the sights, the shops, Janet's favourite places, and the itinerary.

'I've got a new navy dress for the reception on the first evening,' Nora says proudly.

'Nora, do you have any jewellery?'

'Only my brown beads.'

'Would it be all right if I put something in the bag that you can wear that night and for the concert? And you can give it back to me when you come home.'

Nora cups both hands over her mouth and her eyes fill with tears. 'I would love that,' she says.

Tears well in Janet's eyes, too. 'No problem. Now, are you sure there's nothing else that you need?'

'No. I have everything. Janet, I can't say thank you enough . . .'

'It's going to be wonderful. I'm so sad I can't be there. I'll be sure to make it to your next concert.' She holds out her arms. 'Now, come and give me a hug and then off for your taxi.'

Chapter Twenty-Eight

Nora can't believe she's here in this magnificent red-brick Gothic church in Berlin. She's staggered by its beauty – the delicate ornaments, the sturdy pillars, the intricate decoration all wrought in brickwork, the tall tower, the belfry. The walls rising out of the paved floor leading to silent dark galleries that overhang the precept, and everywhere, the eternal presence of the legacy of music and singing spiralling upwards, lifting the energy directly to the face of God.

Nora looks down from the transept and out across hundreds of eager faces and suddenly questions her vision. Could that really be Joe? Certainly, there's a man who looks very like him in a wheelchair in the aisle. But it can't be. She blinks and looks away then back to him. He breaks into a broad smile and raises his hand just a little to wave, then quickly brings it back to his lap with a little apology tugging at his mouth. He appears to be wearing a suit – something she's never seen before – and his usually unruly hair is slicked down and combed to one side. She remembers so much of their long time together, of the friendship that rose like a flower out of the desert of Hillinghurst, and her heart fills with warmth for him and with gratitude that he helped to save her. But how did he get here?

She feels surprisingly calm. This is where she needs to be today, and everything is fine. Only one thing is missing – Janet – though Nora understands that she would be here if she could.

She checks the bow at her neck and runs her hand over Janet's pearls, just as her friend Alice comes alongside.

'Nervous?'

'I'm OK,' she manages. 'I just can't believe it. I'm so grateful.'

And Alice squeezes Nora's fingers and then lets go. Together they simply survey the scene before them. 'It is rather grand, isn't it?' Alice says. 'I haven't been to Berlin before.'

'Neither have I, but Janet was telling me about it. If we have time tomorrow morning, I want to go to the Island of Museums and see the Ishtar Gate. Shall we go together?'

'That would be great, if we have time. It sounds like you could be quite the tour guide, Nora.'

'Janet also told me about Café BilderBuch, where we could have lunch and where sometimes there's someone playing the piano.' Alice puts her arm around Nora's shoulders. Nora remembers how she was just a couple of years ago, much of the time hardly daring to go out of the house, worried about whether she'd remember her way around the small town in which she lives. And now here she is, offering to take charge of their free time in a foreign country! She sends a thought of gratitude to Janet and wishes again that she was here. She looks up at the high arch with its intricate carving, the choir stalls polished with such love and dedication over so many years that the burnished wood fairly glows in the flickering light of the candles in their brass holders.

And now, it's time. Nora is in the front row. A signal ripples around the group and the silence descends, every eye focused on the conductor, Herr Schimmer, in black tie and tails. His hands, held out in front of him, hold each and every one of them as securely as if he were touching them individually. He nods to his choristers then turns to face the audience.

'*Guten Abend, meine Freunde,*' he begins. 'Welcome to our international evening for peace. We have with us today three choirs as well as our own church choir and I know that you are going to enjoy our music. So, let's not waste time. We begin our programme tonight by welcoming our friends from England. First is the Puccini, then the Fauré and lastly, "Ave Maria".'

As the first notes of the organ flood the cathedral, Nora's

heart opens, and as Herr Schimmer signals with an elegant hand, she begins to sing. She is transported with a joy she remembers from her early adolescence – that amazing feeling of transcendence as she allows her voice free rein. It's almost as though it is a separate entity, that the music is flowing through her without effort and she is but an observer, a listener to her own music.

The final chords of the Fauré ascend heavenwards. There's a moment of hush and then the audience erupts into an applause that reverberates throughout the cathedral.

When it finally dies away, Herr Schimmer gives Nora a little smile, and a twitch of his fingers beckons her forward. She advances a little, her memory swinging back to when she was just seventeen and choirs were assembled to mark the occasion of the election of Pope Pius XII. It was a glorious event made all the more special by the fact that it was Nora's first time as the soloist. She can still hardly believe that she's here, having the opportunity to do it again. She takes a breath and lifts into the music, her voice strong and clear.

Ave Maria, gratia plena, Dominus tecum.
Benedicta tu in mulieribus . . .

And she's soaring. Nothing exists now but the music. She's home. She's whole. She's fully Nora in this moment.

Finally, the rapturous applause subsides. Herr Schimmer smiles at her, his admiration and respect radiant on his face. Nora bows to another crescendo of applause. This is beyond any dream she could ever have conceived. She's here. She's alive and her heart swells with gratitude and joy. *I did it! Janet, I did it!*

She gazes down at Joe who is clapping furiously, his cheeks glistening, and she smiles for him alone. This evening will last her until she dies.

The final chords are still ringing in Nora's ears as she walks towards Joe. He reaches out his hand, drawing her towards him until finally they touch and she bends to give him a hug – something she's wanted to do for many years but had never dared.

'I can't believe you're here,' she whispers.

'Wouldn't have missed it for the world.'

Then a vaguely familiar figure stands up from its seat on the pew beside Joe and looks into her eyes. 'Nora . . . '

'Dr Stilworth!' She's immobilised, incredulous, for what seems like a long moment, and then smiles and places both her hands in those he has stretched out towards her.

'Nora, you were wonderful,' he says. 'Inspiring, truly inspiring.' They both just stand looking at each other, beaming. What else is there to do? They are beyond words.

'Thank you, Dr Stilworth,' she says. 'Thank you for taking care of me.'

'I wish I could have done it better,' he says, the light in his eyes dimming slightly.

'No. You did it,' she says. 'Dr Stilworth, you saved me.'

And he smiles a completely different smile to the ones she remembers from all those years ago. 'I hope you're proud of yourself – that you can sing like that and in front of all these people.'

'Dr Stilworth accompanied me on the plane,' Joe says, his face shining. 'Janet and Audrey put us in touch.'

'I wish Janet could be here now,' she says. 'This feels like all my family.'

Dr Stilworth slips an arm around her shoulders and gives them a little squeeze. 'Yes, we're all your family.'

Chapter Twenty-Nine

Standing in the courtyard of Lincoln's Inn Fields, Nora looks up at the imposing building, feeling a bit dazed. Even though she read in the newspaper two months ago that Robert had died, having been fighting cancer for some years, the telephone call had been a shock. Thankfully, a stroke had taken him in the end, before the cancer had the opportunity to claim his beautiful mind.

At the funeral, she'd stood in the back of the church with Audrey by her side as they carried him in, with the card that Janet had sent clutched in her hand for comfort. Nora had known no one there, nor did anyone know her. She assumed that the elegant man standing by the coffin crying silent tears was his partner.

And now she's here, at this place she'd never heard of until a few days ago. She takes a deep breath and enters.

'Good afternoon, Miss Jennings.' The thin and balding man with gentle, sympathetic eyes smiles down at her, offering his hand. 'I'm sorry to meet you like this.'

Nora lowers herself into the proffered leather chair and stares at the envelope on the desk in front of her, her name written upon it in a hand that she remembers from long ago.

'This letter is for you, Miss Jennings. Would you like some privacy?'

She nods. 'That would be kind, thank you.' She can't seem to look away from the envelope and her hand moves towards it almost unconsciously.

'Would you like a cup of tea? Or coffee?'

She withdraws her hand. 'Er, no . . . No, thank you,' she says, not looking away from the letter.

'Some water, perhaps?'

She finally looks up. 'No, thank you.'

He nods and bows out of the room, closing the door quietly behind him. Nora grabs the letter, holds it to her face as though she could feel him through the ink. She slides her finger under the gummed flap. She smells it, but there's nothing of Robert. Just the smell of the cream vellum and something else vaguely familiar. Violets? Surely not.

She unfolds the vellum and there, within its creases, is a lace-edged handkerchief embroidered with the letter N. She lifts the handkerchief to her face, closes her eyes and sniffs at the trace of the scent she always used to wear. Tears threaten as it transports her back fifty years. She inhales again and holds her breath, then turns her attention to the letter.

My dearest Nora,

The enclosed may mean little to you, but it has been of great import in my life ever since our evening together when I asked you for something to keep. You gave me your handkerchief. Some men carried a lock of hair, an amulet or talisman into battle. My tunic pocket contained a memory of you. It did me well. It made life bearable and meant that I never abandoned hope of returning, despite the fact that I abandoned so much else, including my self-respect, my self-image and you. That small piece of linen has continued to be the source of comfort it always was. It was placed by my bed when I was unconscious in Stoke Mandeville and has been with me ever since. By the time you read this, I will no longer be needing it.

Nora, I've regretted so many times that the only time that I came to see you – that first Christmas morning – I left without doing so. There was a misunderstanding that, I'm ashamed to say, allowed me to escape. Later, I made myself believe that it was best not to upset you, but probably, at the heart of it, was guilt and shame, and cowardice. The latter is something for which I cannot forgive myself and will carry with me to the end now.

It's too late to say all the unsaid things, or to redeem the sins both of omission and commission, but I want to say that I'm deeply sorry and ashamed of my failings and for the misery I caused you and the suffering that you had to endure alone.

You see, even then, I already had feelings for boys, but thought they were just childhood fantasies, since I always loved you. But in the weeks following that one perfect evening, I knew that my homosexual urges were still strong and would in the end destroy us. I was filled with confusion and I avoided you, while I tried to sort out my mind. I left it too late, for then came the dreadful news of what had happened to you and I froze. I told everyone that I was called up to the forces, but that wasn't true. I volunteered in order to get away and have time to think. I wrote to you many times, but didn't send the letters. But one was in my battledress pocket when I was taken to hospital. I asked for it to be sent to you; I hope you received it.

Money can never make up for what you've lost, but maybe it will make things more comfortable for you in your latter years. What you choose to do with it will be up to you.

Tears spring to Nora's eyes and she clutches the paper so tightly that it crumples. She rummages for her handkerchief and then reads on.

But there's something else that I must now tell you. I'm sorry that this may be very shocking for you. It was for me when I learned about it. I went to see your father the day I found out about your incarceration and told him that I was the father of your child and that we should be married. He then shared with me the horrible truth about the nature of our relationship.

When my father became very sick with testicular cancer and both he and my mother knew he wouldn't live long, they discussed my mother's yearning for a child. He was rendered sterile by his illness. They agreed that they would approach your father to see if he would be willing to provide semen that my mother would have a chance to fulfil her desire. This all sounds so horrendous now and one wonders what on earth they were thinking. I've spent long hours over the years wrestling with it. The only conclusion I've drawn is that it would have been such a shameful thing to even consider artificial insemination as a Catholic in those days, and they therefore wanted to keep it in the family – in every way, it seems. Obviously, he agreed, though I don't know whether your mother did – or even whether she knew about it in the first place. But it makes sense of why your father always called me 'my son' and why we had such a special bond in the early years, though we became somewhat estranged after the war when I found out what had happened to you. You see, Nora, I am your half-brother.

Nora almost lets the letter fall as she tries to absorb this new, shocking information. Her mind races back to the night after which everything changed. She's back on the stairs in her night-gown, her hand clutching the rail of the staircase, her mother screaming, 'I'll never forgive you.' *Oh God!* She feels herself blanch and wishes she'd accepted the offer of water. Nora holds her chest and tries to staunch the wound that reopens yet again. She closes her eyes, squeezing the lids together to prevent the flood that could so easily swamp her. *'Robert . . .'*

She stares out of the window, counting her breaths as Janet has taught her to do in moments of stress. 'I'm all right. It's all right,' she whispers. 'I can survive.'

Eventually she turns her attention back to the letter and reads the last paragraphs.

It would have been considered dreadful for us to be cousins and to have a sexual relationship, but this . . . Now you have the right to know, though I am heart-sore to tell you. Neither of us knew, and we cannot do anything about it now, but, again, I apologise from the depth of my heart. I wish I could say this to you face to face.

My time is now limited. The dreaded prostate cancer that takes out so many of us men has got me too. Though my life took me on a totally different path than either you or I may have expected, as did yours, my love for you has remained always. I hope that does not raise anger in you now, as I know it could.

My lifestyle has been, let's say, alternative, and less traumatic than yours, but has not precluded love and sorrow, guilt and shame. These last years have been the most calm and peaceful, as I found love and companionship with my beloved partner, George. I hope to find more peace when I finally seal this envelope, though I'm truly sorry if it brings you less. Please, if you can, forgive me, Nora. I'm sorry that I hurt you by things I did and did not do.

When I finally make my exit, I want you to have most of what I have. George will have my share of our home and its contents, but he is a man of independent means and needs nothing more financially. He knows about you and that I love you as always. I know it may appal you, but I love you both and always will.

When you receive this I will be elsewhere – drifting in the breeze, playing in the waves and rock pools as we used to do. I'll be rustling the leaves and smelling the flowers and I'll be waiting for you. So, till the next lifetime . . .

Yours, always, in love
Robert

Nora traces the words with her fingers, lingers over his name, then reads it all again, finally retracing the *'Yours, always, in love'*.

She folds the pages and, with fumbling fingers, places them back in the envelope with her handkerchief.

She sits quietly. The clock ticks away, until finally she gathers her bag and the letter and stands steady and firm. She needs to go home.

Back at her flat, feeling somewhat shaken, Nora still clutches the letter as though she'll never let it go. There's only one person she wants to talk to now. One person she wants to share it with. She dials the number she has to use in emergencies only.

'Janet?'

'Yes, Nora. Are you OK?' Janet says, concerned.

'Could I have an appointment, please?' Nora is pleased her voice sounds so calm.

'Of course,' Janet says, though there's a hint of confusion in her voice. 'Did you go to the meeting this morning?'

'Yes.'

'Do you need to talk now?'

'No, thank you. Not till I see you.'

Nora can hear Janet flicking through her diary. 'How about tomorrow afternoon?'

'Yes, please. What time?'

At three thirty precisely, Nora walks into Janet's office, looking young and radiant in a summer dress, a bunch of summer flowers in her hand. Janet stares in surprise. From the phone call, she was expecting a very different Nora.

'I brought you these,' Nora says, smiling broadly at Janet, who offers the now customary hug.

Janet takes the flowers, buries her face in them and sniffs appreciatively. 'Thank you, Nora, they're gorgeous,' she says. She places them on her desk and indicates that Nora should sit down. 'What happened?' she asks, settling into her own chair.

'There was a letter from Robert.'

'And?'

Nora pauses. 'It was with his will . . .' She hesitates, clearly struggling to find the words. Finally, she meets Janet's eyes. 'Janet, he left me nearly all his money.'

Before the session, Janet had determined not to show any emotion, no matter what Nora said, but now she gasps, her hands flying to her mouth.

Nora's face slips into a rather mischievous grin. 'It's a great deal of money.'

Janet sits back in her chair, feeling her shoulders fall. 'Wow!' she breathes. 'That's . . . well, that's . . . incredible.'

'It is. I'm going to buy a little house and have a dog. And a piano.'

Janet chuckles through the tears that prick at her eyes. 'That's wonderful, Nora. Just wonderful.'

'I think I'll have a bungalow by the sea. I always wanted to live by the sea. I'm sure Robert would like that.'

Janet leans forward, enthralled by yet another new insight into the woman she's known intimately so many years. 'Yes, I'm sure he would.'

Nora lowers her eyes, then lifts them shyly. 'Janet, there's something else.' She opens her handbag and produces Robert's letter. 'It would be hard for me to tell you, so I'd like you to read his letter. Sorry. It's quite long.'

Janet holds Nora's eyes questioningly for a moment, then takes the precious letter and starts to read, back-tracking occasionally to make sure she's understood fully. There it all is – the answers to all Janet's questions about this ill-fated love story that has defined Nora's whole life. As she reads about the awful secret that Robert kept for the rest of his life, her breath catches and she raises her hand to her face and her eyes to Nora, but Nora's are resolutely focused out of the window. What a tangled mess.

As Janet folds the letter, they meet each other's eyes.

'When I showed you the photo of him from the paper, you said we looked like brother and sister . . .' Nora shrugs. Then something akin to defiance flits across her face. 'He loved me, Janet. Right to the end, he loved me.'

'Yes.'

'I just wanted you to know, that's all.'

'I'm deeply honoured.'

Nora smiles. 'You and me both,' she says.

Chapter Thirty

1994

The kitchen clock says five past seven. Janet butters her toast, careful not to get any grease on her fitted white shirt and smartest navy skirt. On the radio, Terry Wogan is wittering on – something about socks lost in washing machines and spoons left in washing-up bowls. She chuckles at the absurdity of his morning chatter.

Suddenly arms encircle her from behind and Ian nuzzles his favourite place at the nape of her neck. 'Busy day?'

She leans into him then turns to kiss him briefly, and hands him a plate of toast. 'As always,' she says, reaching for the teapot and carrying it to the table. 'You?'

'Same.'

They sit in comfortable silence, each with a sheet of the morning paper, as they breakfast in the way that couples secure in each other's love and content in each other's presence do. Janet peers at him over the top of the paper, taking in all that she loves about him, and once again feels a swell of gratitude that they finally found each other again. He feels her eyes on him and looks up, smiling.

Ten minutes later she's in her suit jacket and bends to kiss the top of his head. 'Got to be off. See you tonight.'

'I'll be right behind you,' he says. 'Any idea what time you'll finish?'

'Around six, I imagine. I'll ring if I get held up.'

'OK.'

Celine Dion soothes her through the morning traffic. She thinks of Ian and his quiet, sweet ways and wonders how she ever doubted that he loved her. She smiles as she touches the silver bracelet he bought her that first weekend they went away after they got back together – how long is it – three years ago now? Then she shifts her focus to the day ahead. Busy as always. The morning passes in a blur and the next time she glances at the clock, Janet is astounded to find that it's lunchtime. If she deals with the rest of the patient notes quickly, she'll have time for a quick snack. She usually has a midday appointment but, oddly, found there was nothing in her diary today – which is fortunate given how behind she is. She picks up her pen to get going when her secretary Melanie pops her head around the door.

'Janet – you have an appointment in the patients' common room.'

'Are you sure? There's nothing in my diary.'

'Yes, you definitely have a meeting downstairs.'

'A meeting? I don't remember organising any meeting.' Janet is baffled.

'Janet – you're going to be late,' Melanie says, fussing like a mother.

'All right, all right. I'm going. Do I have an agenda or anything? I'm not prepared for a meeting.'

'Janet, just go.'

She stands up grumpily and heads down the stairs, muttering to herself all the while. She opens the door to the common room and stops in her tracks, and gasps.

In her long black skirt and the silky cream blouse with the bow at its neck and ties trailing, Nora stands, smiling – a broad, deep smile, with none of the timidity that used to constrain it. She moves towards Janet, taking command of the whole room, delight, laced with amusement, playing in her eyes.

'I came to sing for you.'

Janet can't speak. She takes in the shining eyes, the gently styled hair, the hint of blusher and the pale pink lipstick. She hasn't seen Nora since she moved to the coast, though she has photographs of the bungalow with its flowery garden and the little scruff that Nora rescued from the RSPCA.

'For me?'

'A concert for one,' she says with a steady voice that oozes self-confidence. She reaches out and hugs Janet, who is feeling strangely shy and wrong-footed by this unexpected, undreamed-of gift.

'Where would you like to sit?' Nora says, coming to her rescue.

'Nora, you look beautiful,' Janet finally manages, trying to hold back the flood of emotion that threatens to sweep her away. 'Just beautiful.'

There was a time when Nora could not have accepted a compliment and would have shied away, but today her smile widens even further. 'Thank you,' she says.

Janet decides on the sofa, and settles into its ample softness with its chintz tea roses all around her. Nora turns to Susan, who is seated at the piano. She nods, then takes her position slightly to the fore.

Glowing, Nora looks directly at her much-loved Janet, and clasps her hands at her waist. She makes no introduction, but is breathing and obviously pacing herself as Susan caresses the notes of the prelude. And then she closes her eyes as she inhales slowly and steadily. Strong and clear and with perfect pitch, she begins.

I can't cover up my feelings, in the name of love,
or play it safe, for a while that was easy,
and if living for myself, is what I'm guilty of,
go on and sentence me, I'll still be free.
It's my turn, to see what I can see, I hope you'll understand,
this time's just for me ...

As the song ends, Nora gives a slight bow, her eyes twinkling – the little girl peeping out from time gone by. She tilts her head to one side, smiling into Janet's tear-soaked face, then turns briefly to Susan. Janet stares at her, awestruck – this woman who courageously fought and won a victory over captivity, loss and abuse. Janet can hardly breathe.

Flashes of Nora, as she was, attempt to parade across Janet's mind, but they find no purchase, for she's engrossed. The swell of Nora's chest, the movement of her lips, the clarity of her diction, the sparkling richness of her voice, the beauty of her – these hold Janet mesmerised as tears brim again in her eyes. Nora smiles mid-note, her eyes filled with love and something else – compassion! It is she who is offering compassion to Janet. Compassion and gratitude in equal parts.

As the cadence settles and the sound of Nora's voice retreats, Janet brings her hands together as though offering a prayer, and bows her head so that her lips settle on her fingertips. Applause feels inappropriate, but she lifts her eyes and taps her fingers together as she smiles at Nora, and nods. She dares not speak. Everything is understood between them.

Nora gives a slight bow, a small smile playing on her lips.

'Now, I want to sing you one of my favourites,' she says simply. Her stance shifts a little, she lifts her head proudly, and appears quite changed. She rests one hand on top of the piano and is now half turned away, treating Janet to a different angle of her face and indeed to a whole new face of Nora. But when her first notes are due, she turns at the last moment and faces Janet as she begins. And Janet is lost. Lost in years of memories of this beautiful woman's recovery and the honour of having walked with her.

Janet can see the girl who laughed and enjoyed performing for her family and others. And at the end of the song there's a pause and then Nora laughs, bending forward in a kind of bow, yielding to the joy of the moment.

And then, the laughter is gone and Nora straightens and nods once again to Susan, then brings her eyes back to Janet and takes a deep breath, her hands clasped in front of her.

Ave Maria, gratia plena, Dominus tecum.
Benedicta tu in mulieribus . . .

Clear and clean, Nora's voice is totally in her command, delivering, seemingly without effort, this prayer; this pledge of gratitude. Nora is home in herself at last. She has won. And as Janet listens and watches, and knows that her work here is complete, she rejoices. This is what it's all about. This is the goal. This is the reward. They hold each other's eyes. No longer doctor and patient, but just two women, equals.

Nora bows and offers her hands to the pianist, who now steps out to stand beside her and smiles knowingly at Janet. They bow in unison.

Janet rises, tears streaming down her face, yet smiling as broadly as she's able. 'Nora, I don't know what to say. This was so beautiful. Thank you. Thank you. I can't tell you what this means to me.'

Again, Nora bows, and moves forward with both hands outstretched. 'We did it, Janet. We did it.'

Acknowledgements

So many people have helped me on my journey that it's impossible to mention each of them individually. However, first of all, I'd like to thank my beloved Les who has been the wind beneath my wings for over sixty years and whose love and support I always cherish. Then my beautiful daughter, Lesda, who has encouraged, supported, listened, cried and laughed with me over Nora's story, as well as typing, formatting, sorting out my technical issues and helping me hone my computer skills. Thank you, Angel. And the beautiful Tilly who has supplied me with enough playfulness, hugs, amusement and laughter to leaven any sombre moment.

Thank you to my wonderful friend and soul sister, Claire Gilman, who read the first draft and encouraged me to submit it. At Hodder, Rowena Web, who was my non-fiction editor in the 1990s, read it and promptly sent it on to fiction where Thorne Ryan took over as my editor and has worked unceasingly to help me fashion a raw manuscript into the book you find here. Thank you, Thorne – you've been amazing – and thanks also to the copy editor, Penny Isaac, the proofreader, Sharona Selby, and the whole Hodder team.

The Arvon Foundation has also been an inspiring presence over many years, and I'd like to thank the tutors and fellow writers and others who have been part of my journey while writing the novel and also adapting it to a screenplay. What amazing people I have met through Arvon – I thank all of you for being in my life and I love the way we cheer each other on.

My other soul sister, Annie Lionnet, has been a beautiful presence in my life for more years than either of us might care to remember and has been a championing voice throughout. Thank you, Annie. Scott Hunt is one of the kindest, funniest people I know and an amazing psychiatric nurse and an old friend. Thank you, Scott, for always being only an arm's length away. I'd also like to thank Silvio Andrade, Emma Craig, Margaret Martin and Tara Hawes who have held the fort for me while I've been busy writing, and Melanie Blanksby, who is also a supportive voice in my ear. Then there is my dear friend, Linda Miller, who I just love. Thank you for always being there, Linda. And Lisa in Texas. So many friends, students, patients and colleagues – too many to mention individually – have graced my life over the years and over continents. Each one has taught me much on the journey to all of us becoming better versions of ourselves. One of my mentors from the dim and distant past was Dr Robin Farqueharson, an amazing psychiatrist, a wonderful, caring man and an inspiring teacher who showed me what a scientific art psychiatry could be and modelled a deep respect for patients that I have tried to emulate. Thank you, Robin. I have never forgotten.

To all who have accompanied me on my journey in whatever capacity – I thank you for all you taught me, for all we shared, for however brief a moment. And most of all, thank you, Nora. What an amazing woman you were. Thank you for entrusting your story to me and nagging me to tell it. This is for you.